FOREVER WEREWOLF

MICHELE HAUF

HARLEQUIN®
entertain, enrich, inspire™

Recycling programs
for this product may
not exist in your area.

ISBN-13: 978-0-373-88555-8

FOREVER WEREWOLF & MOON KISSED

Copyright © 2012 by Harlequin Books S.A.

The publisher acknowledges the copyright holder
of the individual works as follows:

FOREVER WEREWOLF
Copyright © 2012 by Michele Hauf

MOON KISSED
Copyright © 2010 by Michele Hauf

www.Harlequin.com

Printed in U.S.A.

CONTENTS

Dear Reader,

I'm thrilled to present this double volume of were-wolf romances to you. In *Forever Werewolf* you'll meet my newest werewolf hero, Trystan Hawkes, who has a complicated family history, and must learn to embrace that before he can truly love another. And then *Moon Kissed* features the first werewolf hero I ever wrote about, Severo, and man, do I adore that guy. I'm so happy you get the opportunity to read about him now if you missed the first time it was released. I hope he'll steal your heart as quickly as he did mine.

Now, I write my stories in a world I call Beautiful Creatures. Sometimes characters show up in other books, and other times children of a previous hero and heroine couple might have their own story. If you are interested in learning more about my world, do stop by Club Scarlet online at clubscarlet.michelehauf.com. I've also begun making "boards" on Pinterest for each of my books. There I pin pictures of the people who inspired my heroes and heroines, places, things and homes that are also featured in the books. Find me as toastfaery. It's fun!

Michele

When Lexi shrugged, the most amazing thing happened.

It struck Tryst so hard, he slapped a hand to his chest to slow down his suddenly rapid heartbeats.

"What?" she asked.

"You know what's even more amazing than your skills on the slopes?" He pointed to her face. "That gorgeous smile. Lexi, I just gotta say, right now I so want to kiss you. But I feel like I have to ask your permission, or risk a sharp left hook to my jaw."

That chased away her smile. "Right. Well. I'll see you tomorrow, Hawkes."

Lexi marched off. Even in the snow boots, she managed a sexy hip-shifting sashay. Tryst whistled lowly.

His inner wolf howled, and then, Tryst let it escape, carrying out a long vocal song that declared his interest in Lexi and placed a challenge to any who would protest.

**Also available from
Michele Hauf**

HQN Books
Her Vampire Husband
Seducing the Vampire
A Vampire for Christmas
"Monsters Don't Do Christmas"

Harlequin Nocturne
*From the Dark #3
Familiar Stranger #21
*Kiss Me Deadly #24
*His Forgotten Forever #44
Winter Kissed #52
"A Kiss of Frost"
*The Devil to Pay #55
+The Highwayman #68
+Moon Kissed #72
**Angel Slayer #90
**Fallen #109
The Werewolf's Wife #133
Vacation with a Vampire #139
"Stay"
Forever Werewolf #145

**Bewitching the Dark
+Wicked Games
**Of Angels and Demons*

LUNA Books
Seraphim
Gossamyr
Rhiana

MICHELE HAUF

has been writing romance, action-adventure and fantasy stories for more than twenty years. Her first published novel was *Dark Rapture*. France, musketeers, vampires and faeries populate her stories. And if she followed the adage "write what you know," all her stories would have snow in them. Fortunately, she steps beyond her comfort zone and writes about countries she has never visited and of creatures she has never seen.

Michele can also be found on Facebook and Twitter and at michelehauf.com. You can also write to Michele at P.O. Box 23, Anoka, MN 55303.

FOREVER WEREWOLF

Chapter 1

The stretch limo rounded a plowed country road that had segued from asphalt to gravel about three leagues south. The area was remote, perfect for a pack to live in relative privacy, though there was a village not far to the west. The village catered to mortals with a taste for quality skiing and secret liaisons in cozy cottage hideaways.

The gravel road was lined in frost-coated trees. The sky was white, the road packed with white snow. The proverbial winter wonderland.

A remarkable castle rose from the snow-blanketed valley and into Trystan Hawkes's backseat view. His father, Rhys Hawkes, had told him the fifteenth-century castle Wulfsiege was something to see. He had understated the remarkable structure.

Set in the Hautes-Alpes region of southeastern France, the multiturreted castle, forged from pale limestone, was surrounded by waves of pine forest, and mountains capped with pristine powder. The almost-white stone blended the castle against the landscape in an eerie effect that must have been a sudden shock to marauders from the past as they marched upon the fortressed structure.

A literal wall of snow, sheered off by a plow, fenced the left side of the road as they approached, as if a glacier, pushed just far enough, had decided to stop and rest for centuries. Pale winter sun glinted on the wall of snow and flashed as if across steel.

Trystan ached to ski or snowboard the gorgeous powder. His wolf pined to lope along the forest's edge under the moonlight on four legs instead of two.

"Should have brought along the board," he said to the driver, who pulled the limo to a stop at a massive iron gate coated with more of the hoarfrost and flashed his credentials to the gatekeeper. "Man, I'd love to shred that stuff."

"The Alpine pack hosts the games every other year," the driver said in a cheerful voice. "Edmonton Connor is the principal. Wolves from dozens of packs across the world show for the competition."

"Competition," Tryst muttered, feeling a blood-deep competitive streak flash through his veins. "Winter games, as in skiing and snowmobiling?"

"And snowboarding and two- and four-legged races. It's quite the spectacle. This isn't the year though. Next year."

Tryst gave a disappointed whistle. "I will most definitely be back."

"It's quite calm here today. One would never guess just yesterday the area experienced a fierce snowstorm.

Covered an icy layer of December snow with a foot of the fluffy stuff. Pretty."

Pretty, Tryst thought, but also dangerous. Mother Nature may be capable of producing stunners like the view he'd admired while driving up, but she could also be a bitch in areas like this set between mountains and valleys. Sudden storms could trap recreational skiers without warning.

"We've arrived, Monsieur Hawkes. Shall I wait?"

Tryst tore his gaze from the immense limestone front of the castle, where purple banners depicting a wolf rampant whipped in the wind, and dug in his pocket for his wallet. Then he remembered this was a limo the pack had sent to pick him up from the nearby village, and not a cab. Before that, he'd cabbed it from the airport to the village. The flight from the Charles de Gaulle in Paris had been rough. He hated flying, unless it was unimpeded through the air on a snowboard over extreme white powder.

"Must partake of the pow while I'm here," he muttered.

He lived for physical competition, and winter games were his sport of choice. Skimming down fresh powder, icy snowflakes misting his face, his body in complete control of the board—heaven. He couldn't believe there were actually games for his breed. Outstanding! Too bad he'd come here during a year when the games were not featured.

"I'd say drive on," he said to the driver. "I have to hand the package directly to the receiver, and it may take a while. Heck, I hope to have a look around while I'm here."

And learn more about the pack, was what he didn't say. Pack life intrigued him. He'd not grown up as part

of a pack, and the allure of a tightly knit group of werewolves living together as family was irresistible to his
wondering heart.

"Enjoy the weather, *monsieur*."

Tryst stepped out of the limo and tugged the small
titanium case, handcuffed to his wrist, along with him.
"Thanks, man," he said. "Be careful on that hairpin turn
going out. That was a doozy in this long car."

The driver nodded and drove off.

The wind blew Tryst's scatter of hair across his face.
Brushing it away, he trudged over the packed, icy snow
that glossed the courtyard before the massive castle,
eager to see the inside of this fascinating place.

"Wulfsiege." He loved the name. It conjured images
of medieval werewolf warriors defending their homes
and family against ancient marauders.

His father had been born in the eighteenth century,
but he'd never regaled Tryst with tales of his past. Tryst
figured his dad hadn't seen armored combat, though the
man had certainly experienced defiance and struggle
thanks to his mixed heritage of werewolf and vampire.

He paused, inhaling a breath of courage. Yes, it was
required. For the haunting taunts of *outsider* lived in his
brain. A slur used too often against him when he was
younger and even, on occasion, now. Could he do this?

"Of course I can," he whispered. But a defensive
clench of his fist was unavoidable. He never let down
his guard.

A weird rumble, almost like thunder, alerted him.
He cast a glance to the strange white sky that looked
solid, as if he could take a bite out of it. "Couldn't be.
Not in February."

Instinct prickled the hairs along his arms under the
layers of sweater and ski coat Tryst wore. He cast a

glance along the sharp wall of snow not five hundred yards from the castle grounds. Tryst tilted his head, wondering what he was looking for and sensing he should see it. But he did not, so he brushed it off as nerves. Never before had he entered a pack compound— or castle—and he wasn't certain how they'd accept this outsider.

Once through the doors, the castle opened to a vast space that resembled more a streamlined airport lobby than a medieval stronghold. While the interior limestone walls had been retained, the three-story space was all glass, steel railings, and an escalator even glided up to the second level. Not very sporting for a werewolf to take an escalator, he mused.

Tryst exhaled. So far, so good.

To his left, a wall of windows looked over an open-air stadium that featured bleacher seating set up against the castle exterior, and looked out over a snowy field marked with flags and a judges' stand. A person didn't need a seat in the open-air stadium to get a good view of the action; they could stand and look out the window.

Damn, he wished this had been the competition year.

A pair of males wandered near the glass wall, heading toward the hallway that led north and he knew by their familiar scent they were wolves. They lifted their heads, sensing him, and eyed him curiously.

Here it comes.

Tryst gave a friendly wave but lowered his eyes. His father had told him a little about pack hierarchy, and it wasn't wise for an unaligned wolf to hold eye contact with a pack wolf unless he wanted to eat his own teeth for breakfast. Hell, Tryst hadn't needed a coaching session to know that one was truth. Some things he just needed to learn through experience, and he had a wealth of experience under his belt.

The wolves approached him, bruisers with wide shoulders and hands clenched in fists. Heads lifted as they looked him over, their sweaters stretched across ample delts and biceps. While Tryst was tall and broad, and had a tendency to always be the largest man in the room, he judged the two to be close in size to him.

He offered his hand to shake but they stared at it. "Trystan Hawkes," he said. "With a special delivery for the principal."

They exchanged looks and one asked, "What pack are you with?"

"Paris," Tryst answered easily. He didn't say *pack* because he wasn't going to lie. He waited to see how long it would take before they figured out he was not official.

"Paris pussies," one of them muttered, and smirked.

"Wait here," the other said. "We'll get Rick."

They strode off, keeping a keen eye over their shoulders as they did so.

The adrenaline racing through Tryst's body crashed and he exhaled, his tight muscles relaxing. He'd passed that test.

"All werewolves here," he muttered after the wolves must have decided he wasn't a threat, and assumed their path north. He'd never been around many of his kind in any particular instance.

Admittedly, he'd led a sheltered life. Growing up in Paris, and homeschooled by one of his father's good friends, Tryst hadn't begun to associate with other werewolves until his teen years when he'd go out at night in search of them. Learning the ways of packs had been an eye-opener, sometimes an eye bruiser. Though he had never been part of a pack, he was considered an omega wolf, like it or not. And most pack wolves did not like him because he was the son of a half-breed vampire/werewolf. *Son of a longtooth* was his least favorite slang term used against him. *Outsider,* being the most bruising and mentally damaging. But he'd stood his ground against the pack wolves and had managed to gain their friendship, if not a leery trust. From a few, at the least.

The lure of pack life stirred his wanting heart now. It wasn't that he'd not felt loved growing up—he had—but what he really wanted was to fit in, to be with his own breed and to know that kind of family. He'd missed something by growing up with vampires.

"*Monsieur?* Can I help you?"

As a suited young man who smelled like wolf, but who looked like *GQ,* approached him, Tryst explained, "I'm the courier from Hawkes Associates to see Principal Connor." His gaze darted quickly from the man's narrow shoulders to his polished leather shoes. "Are you Rick?"

"Yes." The man checked the iPad he held nestled against his forearm and then nodded. "That's Lexi's arrangement. Wait here. I'll get someone who can help you."

"No problem." Tryst saluted the man, who hurried off. "Real tight operation they've got around here." And not as imposing as he'd expected.

He started toward the north hall, the chain from his wrist to his case shushing across the titanium shell. He sensed a cafeteria close by for he smelled roasted meat. The crackers and peanuts on the airplane hadn't done much for his aggressive hunger. Hell, he was a big man; he needed fuel. All the time.

"Hawkes Associates?" a woman called after him.

Tryst swung around and sighted in a gorgeous, petite bit of darkness and light. Heeled white leather boots that rode to her thighs clicked on the stone floor as she strode purposefully toward him. A long white winter coat, pristine as fresh powder, swayed out about her knees. Her slicked-back black hair contrasted sharply with the coat, and the black, wraparound sunglasses flashed blue chromic lenses. She worked the winter Matrix look nicely.

Stopping before him, she hooked a white-gloved hand at her hip, which revealed she wore all white leather clothing underneath. The pose also exposed the white grip of a pistol she sported at her hip, but Tryst immediately knew it was a flare gun because he always packed one on any skiing venture.

Interesting. Matrix chick was sexy and deadly, in a safety kind of way. He nodded appreciatively. And a wolf, to boot? He could smell her wild pheromones enhanced with a burst of citrus, and his wolf howled inside at the prospect of standing so close to a gorgeous female of his breed.

Female wolves were not so rare in Europe as they were in America, but their packs and families protected them as if gold, and were very choosy about whom they were allowed to interact with and marry. Or so Tryst's dad had told him. He'd met a female wolf in a nightclub once, and indeed, members of her pack had carefully watched her every move. He hadn't been able to say more than "Hey, baby" when a bruiser had forced him to the opposite side of the dance floor where the vampires lurked. He'd challenged the guy to a fight, as his pride had demanded, and had limped for days after. Still, he'd counted himself a winner simply for surviving the beating.

It surprised Tryst this woman was out in the forefront and with no apparent male to guard her. He looked around. No guards posted in secret nooks, not even security cameras tucked at the ceiling or in corners.

"Trystan Hawkes," he offered, holding out his hand.

She shook it, firmly. The brief contact, though shielded by her leather glove, sent a scurry of excitement through his system. He was touching a female werewolf and no one was stopping him. A triumphant howl blossomed in his gut, and it was only with great restraint that he kept it silenced.

He wished he could see her eyes beyond the blue lenses, but the mystery heightened her appeal. Her mouth, prettily natural and not painted with bright lipstick, smiled softly, and Trystan imagined kissing those lush lips—

"You're here to see Principal Connor?"

"Er..." He snapped out of the fantasy. He shouldn't even go there in his mind, because if he so much as looked at a pack female the wrong way he suspected he'd never get out of castle Wulfsiege alive. "Yes, I've a package for your pack leader from Hawkes Associates." He tapped the case. "I've been instructed to hand it directly to him."

"Of course. I wouldn't have it any other way." She appeared to assess him from snowcapped boot toes, up his white-and-gray snow camo pants and over his Gore-Tex jacket to his shoulder-length hair, which he never remembered to comb. And no, it was not red, it was auburn.

Tryst winked, just in case her eyes were on his.

She gave him a "really" tilt of her head, and he felt the admonishment, but that didn't erase the smile he could not stop.

"Wait here," she instructed. "I'll check with the principal."

"No problem. I didn't catch your name?"

"No, you didn't." She turned and marched off in a precise line that took her around the steel railing that curved along the castle wall, and out of Tryst's sight.

"No, you didn't," he mocked. "Tough chick. But sexy. And a wolf. Whew!"

The howl still clambered for release and his smile went full-on goofy. Tryst shrugged his hands back through his hair. He figured every wolf in the castle had to have his sights set on Miss No You Didn't. But had they spoken to her as he just had?

Didn't think so. He was so ahead of the game.

On the other hand, a gorgeous chick like her was probably already mated to the strongest, most alpha wolf in the pack. He shouldn't get his hopes up. But the fantasy was always a kick. And hell, look up *glutton for punishment* in the dictionary and his face would be featured.

A sudden unnatural roar lifted the hair all over his body.

Tryst swung around and saw the massive cloud of billowing snow just before it broke through the glass wall that overlooked the stadium. The entire castle shook. Male shouts punctuated the calamity.

Tryst lost his balance but managed to stay upright. The roar, as from a beast unearthed after long centuries of hibernation, engulfed the area—and then it suddenly grew deathly quiet as if a damper had been clamped over all.

Or a heavy wall of snow.

With glass and snow scattering across the tiled floor, Tryst turned to find the lobby doors through which he had entered had gone dark. The window that had once looked over the stadium area was also dark and filled in with a wall of snow.

"Avalanche," he muttered, and started toward the hallway down which the female werewolf had left. She had walked right by the window.

Werewolves ran by him, shouting for help. A few were bleeding. The structure of the castle seemed intact as Tryst let his eyes scurry up and down the limestone walls, and he guessed the walls must be three or more feet thick if built so many centuries ago. He hoped so.

He sighted the female wolf in the long white coat and called out to her, but she was running toward him, shouting orders into an intercom device she held to her mouth.

"You all right?" he called as she ran past him.

She nodded. "Get away from this wall! It could collapse inward."

"Right." He turned and ran along beside her. "We need to go outside and see where the snow moved and what areas it covered. How many outside do you think?"

"Too many," she said. "A group of at least a dozen was out skiing." She ran off ahead of him.

Trystan stopped in the lobby, standing near the shattered glass and snow. The wall hushed in an icy cold wave of air that crept up the back of his neck like a deadly poison. Fresh snowfall over hardpack last night, and then today a group had gone out skiing? That had been asking for disaster.

He didn't think the snow blocking the window would move in any farther. But having been in the vicinity during a few avalanches, he knew there was always danger of aftershocks and even another avalanche. The people inside the castle needed to be moved to safety, which could be the other side of the castle. He didn't know the layout.

The female wolf raced by him again, telling whoever was on the other end of the walkie-talkie to start gathering the castle's inhabitants and move them. She had a plan, so Tryst would leave that to her.

But if anyone had been outside, they could be trapped under heavy snow. A rescue team had to be formed. He'd worked on a team once to bring up a mortal couple who'd been trapped eight feet under snow, and so he knew what to do. He needed a few strong men. And they had to move quickly. No one lasted for more than a few hours under snow, and in fact, most mortals could withstand no more than half an hour unless they had a pocket of air and their lungs hadn't been crushed.

Werewolves had an innate ability to heal, and could withstand a lot. He figured if any wolves had been buried they had maybe four to six hours before death.

Alexis Connor marched through the Wulfsiege lobby, her boots crushing broken glass, and her mind racing in twenty different directions. They'd experienced avalanches before, but never one that had hit directly on Wulfsiege grounds or that had caused such damage as she now assessed.

The north window had been busted out, and she couldn't be sure if the surrounding wall was stable. The medieval castle walls were thick, but she had felt the walls and floors shake, as if an earthquake had occurred. She had to find Liam, he was the only pack member she knew who might be able to make an assessment on the structure thanks to his past, which involved a stint as a construction foreman.

She'd rallied two wolves to move everyone they

could find in the castle to the south rooms and the keep, which was the sturdiest place she could imagine, with nine-foot-thick limestone walls and which had originally been built to keep out enemy invaders.

Today, the snow had proved a malicious invader.

She briefly wondered if her sister, Lana, had made it to safety, and then knew she must be with her fiancé, Sven. Surely, the Nordic Warrior, as some in the pack called the blond bruiser, would protect her. Lexi wanted to look for her, but more urgent was ensuring her father's safety. She hadn't gotten to his room to let him know the courier had arrived before the avalanche struck. The principal's room was in the south tower, and he was the first she'd radioed when the avalanche had struck. He hadn't responded, but he was ill, so he could have slept through it all. She hoped for that. Father didn't need another thing stressing him out and pushing him closer to the unstable edge he trod.

Liam raced past her with a bleeding wolf in arm. The Irish werewolf was broad and stout, quiet yet constant. "He was just outside the doors and was slammed up against the glass when it hit," he explained to her. "His body must have been crushed but he's breathing."

"Natalie and Reese are setting up triage in the keep. Take him there. Have you been able to get outside? Do we know who was outside?"

Liam shook his head. "Where's Vince?"

Vincent Rapel was pack scion and had assumed control over the pack during the principal's sickness. Vince was a dutiful, capable wolf who would seek her immediately at any sign of trouble, because he understood Lexi's standing in the pack. She may be a female, but she was truly the second in command under her father's reign. She handled the security for the castle, and nothing happened here without her knowledge. Chatelaine was her unofficial title, which she liked much better than the official one she had been born with—princess.

"I hope Vince is all right," she said under her breath as she observed the scatter of wolves heading toward the safe sections of the castle.

A sound on the roof alerted her, and she nodded, confirming what she knew but hadn't come to mind until now. "The roof access. The best way to get a good look at the damage."

Racing toward the escalator, which was stalled because the avalanche must have taken out the electricity, she took the unmoving stairs two at a time yet paused before pulling open the roof access door. It was on the wall hit by the snow. It could be unstable. Yet it was far from the shattered glass window.

She gave it a pull. It opened freely, and she was not hit with snow. Rushing up the stairs, the brisk winter air smacked her in the face and she tugged up the coat hood over her head. The sun shone too brightly for the disaster that had just occurred, which reminded her how deadly Mistress Winter could be beyond her deceptive cloak of glittering white snow.

A crew loitered at the edge of the roof, shovels in hand, and one held a long thin stick. A ski pole? The snow wall had pushed all the way up to the roof. As Lexi approached the men, she saw that the entire courtyard at the front of the castle, where visitors and pack members arrived and departed, had been covered over with snow. Probably ten to twelve feet deep, she decided, and it had pushed all the way up to the doors of the storage shed, where they kept the snowplow and pack vehicles.

Two men were carefully making their way down the snow mountains formed up against the castle walls.

"What's the situation?" she asked anyone who would answer, noting that Vince was not standing in the crew. "Who is that?"

"Said his name was Trystan Hawkes," one of the men offered. "He's the one that suggested we go down with shovels and sticks to start looking for men. Just jumped right in and took charge. Said time is of the essence."

Lexi lifted her chin, not sure how to take that. She liked a man who took charge and, especially in a situation like this, they needed someone to take command. But did he know what he was doing? He could be risking his life by stepping on unstable ground.

"Said he helped rescue a couple after an avalanche in Germany," another said. "The guy knows what he's doing. Where's Vince?"

"I think he was with the skiers this morning," the other man replied.

Lexi's heart dropped. If the scion was trapped in the snow, they had only hours to get to him before the unforgiving snow crushed his lungs. While werewolves could withstand much, they were not immortal, and his death would prove slow and suffering.

She cast a glance at the man with wavy red hair who appeared to be sniffing as he walked. Even if a man were buried deeply, the werewolf's senses should be able to track him. He towered over the pack members. A natural leader who stood out among the average. He calmly delivered instructions to the men. That command appealed to her inner need for order, and touched a curious part of her that lifted her chin and kept her eyes pinned to the bold newcomer.

"Trystan Hawkes," she whispered against her gloved hands as she clasped them to her mouth to keep her face warm. "What have you brought to Wulfsiege?"

Chapter 2

Wind whipped icy crystals up about the site where Trystan had sensed a heartbeat under the hard-packed snow surface. He'd stowed the titanium case in a cubby near the cafeteria on the way outside. Now he instructed the three men digging to be cautious: a live body was beneath the snow. They didn't want to cause further injury with a misplaced shovel. But, as well, they had to act quickly.

None of the pack members had been wearing transceivers, as skiers often did, so the search proved difficult. They had been digging for over an hour and the sun was falling toward the horizon. Tryst left the diggers to continue the search for more live bodies. Using a makeshift probe, a ski pole he'd broken off the basket to poke through the snow where he sensed life, he directed another team of shovelers.

"Here. He's closer to the surface. Can you sense the heartbeat?"

The first rescuer to arrive nodded and knelt to the ground, listening. "Can't be more than a foot under. I can hear him breathing."

Thank the gods, werewolves had supersensitive noses and hearing.

Tryst rushed over to another trio who dug where the snow was perhaps only five feet high, near to the front of the storage shed. The ski team must have been heading in for the day, or else the avalanche had carried them this far, which seemed unreal but not out of the realm of possibility.

"Another?" he asked.

"Yes, here's his hand."

Tryst bent and clasped the hand sticking out of the snow. The cool fingers clasped back, strongly. Good energy there. "Hurry," he instructed. "He's going to be okay."

Shouts from the first dig site brought him around to assist as they pulled a limp body from the snow. Tryst bent to listen at the wolf's chest but didn't hear a heartbeat. He grabbed his wrist, but the man did not react and his hand fell limply across Tryst's leg.

"Hell, it's Vince," one of the wolves who had been digging said. He knelt beside Tryst and bowed his head. "Pack scion."

Not good, Trystan knew. If the principal was ill, then the scion was the next in line to take charge. This news would shake the Alpine pack to its core.

"Bring him inside. Carefully," he said. "There may yet be life in him. Get him to——" He didn't know if there was a medical team on site. "Bring him to the female wolf. What's her name? The one walking around like she's running the place?"

"Alexis?" The man who had knelt next to Tryst smirked at him. "She likes to think she's in charge. But yes, she'll know what to do with Vince." The wolf stood and ordered the men to place the scion's body on a stretcher. "I'm Liam. Just Liam. No last name." He offered his hand to help Tryst stand. He had a good, firm clasp and friendly eyes, and he actually met Tryst's stare straight on because he was the same height. "What's your name?"

"Trystan Hawkes. I had just arrived at Wulfsiege with a delivery to the principal when the avalanche roared in through the castle wall. I'm here to help for as long as you need me."

"We can definitely use another man, especially one who has had experience with avalanche rescues before."

"No problem. I'm going to find the female and make sure they've got triage set up."

"Before you go, one thing you should know about Alexis."

"What's that?"

"She's the principal's daughter. One of two Connor daughters. Alexis is a cool number. Watch you don't get on her bad side."

"Thanks. I think I'll be too busy for that to happen."

On the other hand, if he clashed with the gorgeous Alexis again, he'd welcome the experience. A bad side? Let it be naughty bad....

By midnight the men who had been digging nonstop since the avalanche had occurred before noon, were called in for the night. They'd found six men. Five had been alive, all with brutal injuries, yet, Natalie, the witch doctor on staff who had lived with the pack for decades, had diagnosed they would heal. The sixth, the scion, was dead; no methods of revival had proved successful.

According to Lexi's count, that left six still missing. She doubted any could still be alive, yet Trystan Hawkes insisted, with blind determination, they continue the search.

"You never know what we wolves can withstand," he said as he accepted a change of gloves and boots from Lexi's assistant, Rick, because his were soaked.

He walked up to her and met her with his bright blue stare that seemed so out of place in this dire time. His gaze sparkled with an innate sort of well-being she couldn't understand. When had a man ever truly looked at her in such a nonthreatening manner? She had to look up at him because he was so tall. Imposing, in a strangely gentle manner.

"If a pocket of air is trapped near the victim's face, he may stand a chance of survival," he explained. "You've got six men still missing, and I'm not stopping until we've found them, dead or alive. No man should be left out there as his final resting place."

"Why?" She had to ask. The wolf was not aligned with the Alpine pack. He should care little for a few strangers.

"Why?" He frowned, yet that expression did not dilute the radiance glowing from his eyes. "How would you like it if you were the one trapped and someone asked me why?"

She nodded, taking his curt response as the admonishment it had been. Lexi was accustomed to male dominance, but this time it didn't rankle her as much as it usually did, because he was only trying to help. And his devotion to the rescue touched the hard, cold place in her heart that she often wished could grow warm.

"At least eat a bit before you go out again. We've prepared sandwiches and there are sports drinks just around the corner on a table outside the cafeteria. Don't be stupid, Hawkes. You need the energy."

"I can manage a few minutes." He headed toward the food, his heavy boots clomping with his lanky strides. Shaped differently than the pack wolves, he was longer, leaner, but no less muscled.

Lexi watched as he tilted back a sports drink in one swallow, then grabbed another and sucked that down as quickly. Accepting a turkey sandwich stuffed with veggies, and thanking the women manning the food table, he ate it as he marched out the lobby door and back into the brisk winter night.

Outside, the winds whipped relentlessly, nearing thirty miles an hour. Here in the valley, where one would think they'd be protected, it was as if the winds scooped down to scour the land. Lexi knew the weather had to be brutal, yet Trystan Hawkes's determination glowed like a bright aura only a psychic could see.

The other wolves helping the rescue efforts were all as determined, but seeing this stranger step into the role without question or ties to the pack intrigued her. What kind of man would do such a thing? Sacrifice for others he didn't even know? Exemplary—

"Who's the tall redhead with the freckles? He certainly stands out from the pack like a bright red warning beacon."

Lexi turned to find her sister, Alana, looking fresh as ever with perfect makeup and blond hair swept into a smooth, tight bun. She never went anywhere without bright red lipstick. Or the five-inch stilettos. Lana Connor was a Tiffany kind of girl stuck in bargain-basement hell. Apparently she had not been volunteering in the keep with the wounded, but then Lexi would have been knocked over had Lana even asked after the well-being of the survivors.

"I don't know who he is," Lexi offered. "But he just may be the most honorable wolf I've ever met."

"Is that so?"

She sensed her sister's eligible bachelor radar go up. Lana might be engaged to Sven Skarson, but that didn't keep her from flirting with every wolf who risked his life by returning the heartless flirtation. She was beautiful, spoiled, and could have any man at whom she batted an eyelash. It was a game, Lexi sensed, a defense mechanism of sorts. Because she knew she was safe, Lana played with social and pack boundaries. Lexi was her sister's opposite—she put up a cold front, knowing she was safe from any of the pack's amorous attention.

Lana was the pretty one; Lexi was the smart one. She'd grown to accept the distinction between them, and for some reason, Lexi had never cared about Lana's random flirtations.

Until now.

"He's not your type," Lexi said quickly. "He's a hard worker, and is more concerned with helping others than himself."

Leaving that verbal slap hanging, Lexi marched off toward the south wing to look in on her father.

"I almost forgot!" a man shouted down the hallway as she neared him.

Trystan Hawkes had a way of putting himself near to her, not touching yet just a little too close, challenging her own personal boundaries. He huffed from running and carried a titanium suitcase that she had remembered seeing when he'd first come into Wulfsiege.

"I came here for a reason, and I think what I have with me may be timely. I'm supposed to hand this directly to the principal. Your father?"

"Principal Connor is my father. But I can take that for you."

"No, I, uh…can't."

"Monsieur Hawkes, with the events that have occurred, protocol has changed—"

"Sorry. I have specific orders to put it in only your father's hands. Instructions stipulated by your father to mine according to the contract he signed with Hawkes Associates when assigning us as security advisors for his stored items. Please, can you take me there quickly? I need to get back outside."

It wasn't a breach of protocol, but it could be dangerous for her ailing father to have visitors. Still, if her father had requested whatever was inside that case—something he had chosen to store at Hawkes Associates and not here at Wulfsiege, so it must be valuable—then she would not question.

As well, she didn't mind spending a few more minutes with Hawkes. She wanted to observe him, figure out what made the handsome wolf tick.

"Come with me."

The principal's private quarters were set in the south tower of the castle, as far from the damage as one could get. Lexi thanked the nature gods for that small blessing.

Though the principal's room was located in the tower, the space was massive, but Tryst couldn't move his thoughts from the urgency of the rescue to do more than flash a look around the room, not really taking in details. There were still wolves outside. It had been over eight hours since the avalanche hit. They were likely dead, but if the slightest chance existed any could be alive, he had to find them.

Alexis, still dressed in white leather and still sporting the sunglasses inside—though the conference room she led him into was lit with low light—gestured he approach the man seated in a leather chair at the end of a long table. It was an easy chair, and the leg rest was up. A plaid blanket covered him to the chest.

Tryst laid the titanium case on the table and said, "Sorry to be in such a hurry, Principal Connor. My father sends the elixir inside this case with his blessings and wishes you a speedy recovery."

The elder wolf stared at him with mouth agape. Salt-and-pepper hair curled about a narrow face with loose skin that indicated he must have lost weight and perhaps was normally much more fit. His heavy-lidded eyes made him appear old and weak, yet they stared at Tryst, stunned.

It was then Tryst realized his lack of protocol. He should bow or kneel, or—something—before a pack leader. His father's instructions rang loudly in his thoughts. He should have waited to first be spoken to.

No time.

"Forgive me. I apologize for the protocol I am stepping on and of which I probably made a huge mess. But I have to leave. The avalanche. There are still many from your pack missing."

Principal Connor didn't say a word, merely lowered his tired eyes to the titanium case.

With that, Tryst did bow and backed from the room. He looked to Alexis, who also gaped at him with her soft pink mouth parted, and then knowing he hadn't the time or the fortitude to make political amends, he turned and raced down the spiraling tower stairs.

"What the hell was that disaster?" Edmonton Connor rasped at his daughter.

Lexi should have explained protocol to the man on the way up to the tower, but she had blindly expected him to behave. Or to have a rudimentary grasp on pack procedures. He'd shown such courage and leadership so far. Was he not a member of a pack? Had he never approached a principal before?

"He's heading the rescue team, Father. Please accept my apologies for his rudeness. If I had known…" She sighed. She'd been running on full throttle since the disaster, hadn't eaten, and right now was feeling as tired as her father looked. "Trystan Hawkes has helped our men bring up six who were buried under the snow. And he seems determined to find the remaining six."

"I see." Her father looked aside and smoothed his palm caressingly over the titanium case. "I suppose I can overlook it this time. Knowing his father, Rhys Hawkes, I should have expected the insubordinate behavior. He didn't bring up his son in a pack."

"He's an omega?"

The principal nodded. "Where is Vincent?"

Lexi sucked in a breath. This was the part of chatelaine duties she did not enjoy. Reporting to her father was easy. She'd been doing it all her life, ever since her dreams of growing up like Lana had been smashed at puberty. But she never liked delivering bad news to her father, which had to be done on occasion, and most especially now, when he was not well. Stressful news could make him weaker, but neither would she dream to hide the truth from her father.

"Vincent Rapel didn't make it. Natalie and Reese looked him over and suspect all his bones were crushed. She also concluded he died instantly as a rib bone appeared to have pierced his heart."

"The witch doctor?" He named Natalie that because she was a real witch who had been taken in by the pack decades earlier. She'd been nurse to Lexi and Lana when they were little, and Lexi had great respect for her, though she knew her father often conflicted with the woman's "spiritual" ways. "She suspects? She concluded? We need a real medical doctor here, Alexis. Immediately. If there are wounded, they'll need more than herb-craft and moon voodoo."

"Father, don't worry yourself, please. Reese is working alongside Natalie, and you know he has medical training."

"Veterinary training." He grunted and slammed his shoulders into the easy chair. "We are not dogs. Why I allowed Natalie to recruit him is beyond my ken. Call Paris. There's a few practicing werewolves in the city. Check with Rhys Hawkes, he'll have their contact information."

"I will. You should be in bed resting. How are you feeling?"

"The same. Weak. Like my blood is sinking to my feet. I'm so light-headed. But this." He slapped the case. "I've had this for ages. This may be my last hope."

She had no idea what was inside the case but would learn soon enough. "Do you want me to call Natalie here to help you with it?"

He sighed, his drawn face saggy. "Yes, she is my only option at the moment. And Alexis?"

"Yes, Father?"

"I'll have to elect a new scion since I'm not doing so well."

"Don't talk like that. Whatever Monsieur Hawkes sent along in that case will help you recover, I'm sure of it."

"You don't even know what it is. Nor do you have any idea who Rhys Hawkes and his son Trystan are."

That statement took her back for a moment. What did it matter if the man had helped only since arriving?

"Trystan seems trustworthy and a man to have around when the chips are down. He's focused. He impresses me."

"Yes, well." Edmonton sighed and gestured she help him to stand. "Be wary, Lexi. He is not from this pack."

"I will."

Lexi walked her father into the attached bedroom suite and helped him onto a bed topped with a plush goose-down coverlet.

Her father was a young wolf, only a century old, and had been the picture of health two weeks ago. But he'd begun to decline, slowly yet steadily, and three days ago he'd taken to his bed. The witch doctor hadn't a clue, but Natalie kept divining her father's blood, with no results.

Edmonton wouldn't let her cast a healing spell upon him, because he didn't believe in witchcraft.

Another reason Edmonton's mistrust of Natalie ran deep was due to the affair he'd had with her twenty years earlier, after Lexi and Lana's mother had died. Edmonton Connor was a rogue of the first water, and never apologized for it. Lexi understood he needed connection, love and, yes, to answer the physical cravings all werewolves felt. But the past few years, as far as she knew, he'd not taken any woman under arm or even to his bed. Instead, wanderlust had brightened Edmonton

Connor's eyes, but he tamped down the urge to travel because he had a pack to look after.

Now he'd been reduced to a feeble man who looked as old as he should be were he mortal. And for no apparent reason. Werewolves did not suffer mortal ailments. He'd not been physically injured. How to understand his failing health?

"I'll contact Monsieur Hawkes and ask for a recommendation on someone who practices on our breed," she said, and kissed her father's cheek. "I'll have him flown here as quickly as possible to look over the casualties in the keep and then I'm going to assign him to your bedside. I love you, Father."

She took the case and left, blowing him a kiss as she closed the door behind her. She'd bring this to Natalie. She trusted the witch any day.

Chapter 3

The day had been long, and Lexi startled awake from her sitting position by the arched door opening into the keep. Her room had not been damaged, yet she hadn't made it back there after overseeing the disaster and establishing triage in the keep. Now she stretched her legs out before her and arched her back. She hadn't removed her long coat and she was warm. Too warm, almost stifling here in the windowless room that may have, in centuries past, often housed the entire castle inhabitants as they waited out the enemy.

Rubbing her eyes beneath the sunglasses—she never took them off—felt great. Checking her watch revealed it was three in the morning. Most of the keep was quiet, save a few who sat near the cots with wet towels and worried looks as they tended the wounded.

She stood, stretched again, and decided she could

manage a few hours of sleep in her own bed, and a shower. Her kingdom for a shower.

She did have a small kingdom, actually. Well, Lana was the one who insisted on exploiting the princess title. Lexi thought it was ostentatious. Daughters of werewolf principals were referred to as princess—their sons were princes—but that didn't make them royalty or heirs to a nonexistent castle and crown. But they did live in a castle and, despite the lacking crown, Lana certainly liked to play up the privileged princess routine. It worked well for her. Entitlement had always been her mien.

Lexi would rather choke on a watermelon than play soft, pink and delicate. If she didn't have a hand and nose to the action, she wouldn't know how to function. It was a natural compulsion to show her father how much she was willing to help. It was hard enough to get his attention, what with Lana's pandering. Her sister could win a new Porsche with a bat of her lashes, and she had two in the shed to prove the power of that expert move. Lexi owned a battered old Range Rover. It got her where she needed to go, and that included flooded roads, muddy ditches and icy drives.

Wandering through the darkened halls of the castle, Lexi tugged off her coat and pushed the sunglasses up onto her head. It always took a few seconds for her eyes to adjust and color her surroundings a little brighter than when wearing the glasses, even despite the darkness inside the castle. Her breed had excellent night vision.

Her exhaustion felt as if she were dragging lead pipes for legs, and her shoulders ached. A cup of chamomile tea after her shower would relax her into a restful slumber.

Suddenly she stumbled and, before falling, caught herself with a balance of her hands. Turning swiftly, she saw she'd tripped over a man's legs. He sat sprawled on the floor across from the lobby doors that had been blocked off with wood boards. Bitter cold air whisked through the hallway about her shoulders and she shuffled her coat back on and tapped down her glasses before kneeling to shake the man's shoulders.

"Monsieur Hawkes?"

He mumbled something but didn't open his eyes. His coat lay over his legs, and melted snow from his heavy pack boots puddled around his feet and legs.

"What are you doing here?"

"No place to sleep. Tired. Still missing…one man."

It had been a good eighteen hours since the avalanche had struck. And this wolf had been working steadily to rescue the missing men. Only one left? He must have fallen asleep standing or, apparently, sat down and nodded off. Even wolves eventually got exhausted and couldn't go without sleep.

She tugged his arm, provoking him to a grudging stand. "Come with me. We've a few open rooms."

He twisted toward the boarded doors, which swung her around ungracefully as he looped an arm over her shoulder and stumbled a few steps as if a drunken man. "Have to find last one."

Walking and talking in his sleep, this guy. "You can resume the search after you've rested. Is there a backup team out now?"

"Yes, three men volunteered. They've had rest. But I should help. Can't let them down." With a shake of his head, as if to chase off the exhaustion, he suddenly set back his shoulders and assumed a modicum of alertness. The move stretched him a head taller than she. He blinked a few times in the cool darkness. "Princess Connor. Sorry, I didn't know it was you."

"It's Lexi," she said, and tugged him toward the south wing. "And you're not going anywhere but to bed."

"Best offer I've had in a long time."

She rolled her eyes. She had walked right into that one. For lack of practice in defense of horny males, surely. She couldn't remember when a man had last flirted with her.

"We've a guest room that you can use. Shower, have something to eat, and sleep. I'll make sure the night shift doesn't stop until you rise to replace them. I want to thank you for your hard work. You certainly went above and beyond the call of duty for our pack."

"It's nothing anyone else wouldn't have done."

Actually, she believed it was a lot, and anyone else would have thought twice before jumping into the fray such as Hawkes had.

"Sorry about how rudely I treated your dad. I wasn't thinking. My dad grilled me on the correct protocol before I traveled here, but my mind was elsewhere. I haven't had experience with a pack before."

"Don't let it bother you. Father is already over it, I'm sure."

"Did the elixir help?"

"Not sure. Our doctor administered a dose not long after you saw him. If you pray, Monsieur Hawkes, please pray for my father."

"I do pray to the universe, and I will put in a good word for your father."

She unlocked the guest room door with a slash of her control card, which worked on all doors in the castle, and strode inside the dark bedroom lit by a ray of pale moonshine. Nearing fullness. Perhaps three more days? She'd lost track of the monthly cycle since her father had become ill. While normally instinctual about the moon phases, she was too discombobulated by the day's events to summon clear thought.

Hawkes trudged inside, his boots forming small lakes in his wake. He pulled off his sweater and tossed it aside without care. The wolf slapped a palm to his bare abdomen and rubbed it, looking about the room with a long yawn.

He had a fine form. Not so bulky as the wolves in the pack, but certainly one of the biggest. Trystan was long, lean and hard with muscle that ridged his chest and stomach. Was it solid to the touch? Would her cool fingers warm against his pale skin?

Lexi stopped the divergent thoughts when she realized her tongue traced her upper lip. She forced herself to look away from the appealing sight. The wolf was still sleepwalking. He didn't realize he was posing and flexing with every stretch he made. Couldn't.

"Why are you wearing sunglasses?" he asked.

"I always wear them. The light hurts my eyes," she said, offering the classic lie.

"It's dark in here." He sat on the end of the bed, dressed with the thick goose-down coverlets Lexi loved to snuggle into, and lay back, stretching out his arms above the spray of wild, red hair that he wore as if a defiant flag.

She strolled into the bathroom and turned on the light. "The shower stream is fierce. For reasons beyond my knowledge we have excellent water pressure here in the boondocks. You'll love it. There should be fresh towels and linens in the closet. I'll see about finding you some clean clothes and have the maid drop them off."

The werewolf didn't answer so Lexi peeked inside the bathroom closet to be sure there was soap and towels. Everything looked presentable. She liked to run a tight ship, and was pleased the maid kept up the extra rooms. It was the least they could offer to the man who had selflessly aided their pack today.

Crossing the room, soft snores lured her to the bedside. Arms stretched above his head and feet still on the floor, the fascinating wolf had fallen asleep.

She leaned over him, inspecting his rising and falling chest. Her fingers played in the air but inches from his skin, unwilling and—wisely—not touching. He was a fine piece of work. A few freckles spotted his shoulders and along the side of his muscle-strapped torso. She started mapping them out, tapping the air with a finger and wondering if she could form the constellation Orion....

"What are you looking at, Princess?"

Startled upright, she took an abrupt step away from the bed. "It's not Princess, it's just Lexi. And I was..." Taking mental inventory of his steely abs and connecting the tantalizing dots. "Good night, Monsieur Hawkes."

"It's not *monsieur*, it's just Trystan. Friends call me Tryst," he said on a sleepy rasp. "And you'll always be a princess to me, Lexi." He yawned and turned his head to the side. "So pretty" came out on a murmur.

Lexi paused in the doorway and pressed her forehead to the door frame. He'd called her pretty. She had no earthly idea what to do with that compliment.

Trystan woke to the smell of bacon and maple syrup. Aware someone was in the room with him, he rolled over on the bed and realized he was wrapped like a burrito in the bedspread. Hell, he always conked out like a log after a hard day's work and often fell asleep wherever he could manage. How'd he actually make it to a bed?

The image of a pretty werewolf with dark hair and mysterious sunglasses came to mind.

"Lexi," he whispered. She'd made an offer to share the bed with him if he recalled correctly. Probably not a correct recall, and instead a dream. Heh.

"Hello?" He rolled out of the burrito wrap and sat up, shrugging fingers through his tangle of hair and shaking off the hangover of coming instantly upright and awake.

"Breakfast and a set of clothes for you, *monsieur*." An elderly woman in casual dark slacks and sweater stood at the door. Must be the maid. He didn't get the sense that she was wolf, though. "Principal Connor wishes to see you in an hour."

"Thanks. Where's his room again?"

"Down the hall at the end of the south wing. Take the stairs up to the tower." She left, closing the door quietly.

The door wasn't even closed before Tryst stood over the tray of breakfast, lured by his nose and the savory scent of heaven. He gobbled down a few slices of bacon and tilted back the first cup of coffee without taking a breath. The pancakes followed in huge bites. Man, he was starving. And they certainly knew how to feed a hungry wolf here. Six pancakes, eggs, bacon and sausage, camp fries, and granola with yogurt.

"I could get used to this."

Living in Paris, in his bachelor pad that overlooked the Eiffel Tower, he normally didn't cook for himself. Most nights he ate out, and kept a collection of take-out menus on his iPhone. And if on a date, that meant he couldn't consume a huge meal, as usual, because he didn't want to freak out his date by revealing his monstrous appetite. It took a lot to keep a grown wolf full.

Mortal women ate so little and gave him condemning looks to see him gobble up his food. It was as if food of any sort disgusted them, and how could he possibly eat it?

He usually dated mortal women, but he'd yet to fall in love. And though he suspected the cards wouldn't deal him love anytime soon, he was hopeful. Raising a family and starting his own pack was tops on his wish list.

He missed that he'd not been raised in a pack. While his father was half werewolf, he didn't shift to werewolf form too often, because that side of him was vicious and violent. His werewolf was actually ruled by his vampire brain, and the vampire inside Rhys Hawkes was always pissed at the wolf for denying it the blood it desired.

So Rhys remained in vampire form most often because then his kinder, gentler werewolf mind ruled, and though Tryst had adjusted easily to his father's mood swings—he'd grown up knowing nothing else—he quickly realized if he was going to learn what real, full-blooded werewolves were like, he'd have to find a few wolf friends. Which hadn't been easy.

Unaligned wolves were not often welcomed to chum around with packs. But Tryst had managed to secure one close friend, an ice demon named Axel Fergusson, who had taught him things his father could have never thought to talk about. Axel knew about werewolves because he had once been one himself—actually, still was—before being cursed by Himself because he'd dated Bloody Mary, the chick who was known to be Himself's girlfriend, so Axel had had it coming, Tryst figured.

Axel had been his lifeline. Especially when it came to dating advice. Never approach a pack female unless you have a death wish. Even if she gives you a wink. But if she's alone, then go for it, and enjoy the ride while you could, which was never long. Pack females tended to surf the Parisian nightclubs for unaligned wolves as a vacation from their usual pack males. But they were never serious, just looking for some fun away from home. The different. The outsiders.

Ugh. Tryst hated that term.

Pouring his third cup of coffee, Tryst cautioned himself to slow down and enjoy the meal while he could. There was still another man missing, and if the crew that had worked through the early-morning hours had not found him, Tryst had work to do.

The maid had said the principal wanted to see him? Hmm, yes, he should go and apologize for his brisk treatment of him yesterday. At the very least, he should have bowed before the elder wolf. Rhys would not be happy to learn about his faux pas.

Tryst finished the last sausage link and stood back from the clean plate. A shower and a quick shave were in order. He had a long day ahead of him. Fingers crossed, that day would involve meeting up with the pretty princess who had been staring at his half-naked body last night.

"She wants me," he said. "Score!"

He tossed an imaginary basketball and landed the trick hoop shot because he was so good, and yes, the woman wanted him.

Now he just had to sniff out any competition from the males in the pack, and then approach the target with confidence yet caution.

Alexis knocked on the guest room door. It was seven in the morning, which wasn't early by any means, but she didn't hear a sound on the other side of the door. Was the wolf still sleeping? He deserved the rest. The night team had not found the remaining man, so she entirely expected Hawkes would be out poking about in the snow as soon as the sun blinked across his eyelids. He'd bring up a dead man, surely, but his dedication heartened her.

She was fascinated by those with an ability to fit into any scenario or surrounding effortlessly, such as Hawkes had seemed to do here at Wulfsiege. Herself, she was never quite sure how to become a part of something even as innocuous as a conversation. It wasn't shyness, but a touch of introversion. Okay, a lot of introversion. Her sister had gotten their father's extroverted gene. And the pretty gene. And the popularity gene.

"Get over it," she muttered with a roll of her eyes. Why was she feeling so sorry for herself suddenly? "This is not you."

It was exhaustion—that was all she could summon as an excuse.

Lexi beat a fist on the door, and it swung inside on the third pound, almost hitting the grinning werewolf in the face. Wet hair dripped onto his shoulders and spilled in tears down his bare, buff chest. She found herself following the trail of water down, down over rigid abs, and through a thatch of red hair to the tight wrap of a white towel hugging his square, utterly graspable hips.

Trystan Hawkes stretched an arm along the door and winked at her. "You look as happy to see me as I am to see you, Princess. What's up?"

At the double-edged question, she hastily averted her eyes from the mysterious folds of the towel. Good thing she wore dark glasses. "My father will see you now."

"Not like this he won't. Come inside. Let me pull on some clothes. The maid brought me something to wear."

"I'll wait out here."

"In the hallway? That's so security thug, which is not you. Seriously, come in and sit down. I'll dress in the bathroom. Wouldn't want to flash daddy's little princess."

"I am not daddy's princess," she said, finding she'd already followed him into the room. Lexi turned to face the door. Had she closed that? "Alana is."

"Yeah?" he called from the bathroom. The door was open and steam misted out. "Is that your sister? Think I saw her during the chaos last night."

"Yes, she's…" Pretty, and attracted all the wolves' eyes. "Yes."

"Then you must be daddy's secret weapon."

"I am…" What had he meant by that?

Stepping closer to the bathroom door, she drew in the spicy aroma from what she knew was the guest soap. Cloves and leather were her favorite scent. So manly, so… Hell, what was she doing? She didn't have time for romancing a fantasy.

Turning her back to the door, she crossed her arms and hiked out a heel. She wore gray today, from boot to neck. It was easier to go monochromatic, because when she started to mix colors bad things happened and people stared. Attribute that to her eyes, she figured. And enough about that.

"Yep, he put the sister out as bait," Tryst called from the bathroom, "and keeps the smart one close by his side. Head of security, right?"

"Castle chatelaine is my official title."

"What's a chatelaine? Oh, wait, I think I heard a song about that once. 'Miss Chatelaine…'" he sang.

She smiled at his rendition of the k.d. lang song, which she happened to like. "The chatelaine oversees all the domestic business in the castle, such as the kitchen, and preparing and ordering food for meals. Stocks. Events and parties. I keep track of the accountant and lawyers. As well, I oversee security."

"So you do it all—yikes."

Trystan walked right into her. Lexi abruptly stood straight. She'd been leaning a little too far into the bathroom doorway. Just soaking up the scent she admired. Yes, that was it.

She adjusted her sunglasses, which he'd nudged north when her forehead had bumped his chest. As her hand had pushed away from his abs she felt the rock-hard ridges and her fingers curled, wanting to touch a little longer. He burned her softly. How long could she hold her skin against his heat without igniting?

"What are you looking for, Lexi?"

"I, er…" Indeed, what had her fingers wanted to grasp, as if a lifeline she desperately needed? She crossed the room swiftly and grabbed the door handle. "You ready?"

He shook out his hair. Bending, he fluffed it a bit before the mirror, which managed to tousle it more messily. But he seemed happy with it, because he nodded at the mirror and winked.

The man and his winks! It wasn't a flirtatious move. It was more of a tic. Or some kind of code for arrogant overcompensation?

Lexi tucked her head down to smirk, and noticed a streak of water darkened the front of her gray slacks. She'd gotten too close. What was that about? Keeping her personal boundaries—about five feet of distance from others at all times—had become like breathing to her, and to all in the castle. Everyone knew to walk a wide circle around her. When had those boundaries become so…permeable?

"You're all about blending in, aren't you?" the wolf asked as he pulled a soft blue sweater over his head and tugged it to cover the abs she wanted to lose a few hours observing. The sweater, perhaps a size too small, conformed to his structure, making him appear even more naked. And the blue really captured his blue eyes and made them dazzle even more. "Dressing in one color so you don't stand out. Though wearing sunglasses inside is pushing it."

"My, aren't you Mr. Blackwell? Coming from a man who wears camo pants and a blazing blue sweater. Who taught you to dress?"

"It's what the maid brought me. Though I do like this sweater." He slapped his abs and gave them a rub. "It's soft. Is this cashmere?"

Lexi bit her lip to keep from saying it wasn't soft at all but incredibly hard. Her mouth curled, but not up. He was just too…much. Too there. Too in her face. Too… gregarious. Powerful. Honorable to a fault. Yes, appealing in a way she'd never thought a man could appeal. Or was it that she'd never taken a moment to consider a man's charm?

"Let's go." She opened the door and marched down the hallway, expecting him to follow, and hopefully not like the gushy, bouncy puppy he had a tendency to emulate.

The werewolf princess wanted him. She hadn't been able to keep her eyes off him, and she had almost snuck into the bathroom while he'd been changing. How much did that rock?

The woman was not as cold as she led others to believe.

He suspected she wasn't aware of her sensual side, something he was very tapped into, according to his former lovers. The Princess of Cool hid behind the pressed, exact clothing, those mirrored sunglasses and an icy demeanor. He bet she never wore jewels like the sister he'd gotten a glimpse of last night. Too flashy, that blonde chick. And spike heels in a castle surrounded by snow? So wrong. Lexi Connor sparkled without unnecessary adornment.

Like right now, she moved as if carried by a graceful yet urgent wind. Her strides were sure but quiet, as they took a curving hallway that spiraled into the narrow south tower.

"This is like some kind of old castle," Tryst commented. "So authentic."

"Built in the fifteenth century by a former financial minster to King Charles II."

"And surrounded by perfect powder for skiing. I love this place. It's tight! You live here all your life?"

"Yes, I was born here."

"So what's up with your father? My dad didn't tell me a lot. He was in too much of a hurry to send me on my way here after getting the call from the pack's witch. What's that about?"

"Natalie is our doctor and she's a witch."

"Cool. A real witch doctor."

"I've had a medical doctor summoned from Paris to help with the wounded and assess my father's condition. He should arrive this afternoon if the helicopter can land."

She paused before a double door fashioned from rich, varnished oak and studded with metal nail heads much like a medieval castle door. "The principal is...under the weather. Natalie isn't sure what it is, but his health is declining."

She looked aside and Tryst sensed her unease talking about it. Must be hard for her, virtually running the castle, and having a sick father to worry about. And now the avalanche? The woman exuded strength and endurance, yet she appeared to be losing some steam.

"And I'll warn you not to press him about his health. Keep your conversation strictly business, or I'll see that you're removed from the castle."

"Good luck with that. A guy can't even walk through the front door, let alone be *removed*. But I suspect we'll get the snow dug away from the storage shed today so we can use the snowplow. I need to get outside to help find that last man. How long is this going to take?"

"I have no idea. I'm as surprised as you my father wants to see you again after you were so quick with him last night."

"I intend to apologize to him for that, Princess."

"My name is—"

"I know." He pressed a hand to the door above her shoulder. "Alexis, the cool, calm beauty who won't show anyone her eyes because that kind of connection would be too intimate."

She gaped.

"Guess I hit that one right on the nail, eh?" he said. "But I prefer Lexi, the smart, cautious chick who is going to break down sooner rather than later and give me a big warm smile."

Her gaping mouth shut and her brows curved downward. About as opposite a smile as she could manage.

He wouldn't stop working on her. He knew a smile lived somewhere behind those blue mirrored lenses.

"Take me to your leader," he said with only a modicum of seriousness.

With a perceived roll of her eyes, she pressed a digital combination on the door lock and walked inside the room, announcing her arrival as she did so, "Father, I've brought Monsieur Hawkes to see you."

They passed through the meeting room. The long, polished conference table stretched ten feet before the two-story windows on the far side. A few leather couches sat near the entrance, and a massive fieldstone fireplace occupied the entire wall to Tryst's left. A video conferencing system sat in the middle of the table.

Medieval castle meets hi-tech office. He liked it.

Lexi had disappeared through a side door, which she had left open, but Tryst hung back. Nerves made him shake loose fists near his thighs. He never got nervous. Fear had been beaten out of him in his teenage years. But the place intimidated him. He stood within the inner sanctum of a pack principle—and only last night he may have offended him.

He'd always wondered what it would be like to live within a pack. To live under their rules and society. To have a leader to look up to, and to follow a specific hierarchy that placed each and every wolf in rank.

Growing up with his mother and father, he'd not had anything resembling a pack. They'd treated Trystan as if he were a werewolf from birth, because Rhys had said he just knew. A child born with mixed heritage never really knew what he would become until puberty. Trystan had always related to his father's gentle werewolf side anyway. Yet heaven forbid, he should ever reveal his paternity. Pack Alpine would make mincemeat out of him.

Worse yet, if they knew his mother was a bloodborn

vampire, he'd never get out of this castle in one piece. Sure, wolves and vamps worldwide stood on reasonably peaceable terms, but they'd never seen eye to eye. Make that eye to fang. Tryst had learned to be leery around vamp-hating wolves. Hell, he may have a bit of prejudice toward longtooths themselves, but that was changing after meeting his half brother, Vaillant, last year. Vaillant was a blood-born vampire, as well.

Strange family ties.

"Enter."

At the monotone invitation, Tryst assumed a more menial posture of slightly bowed head and lax shoulders as he entered Principal Connor's private quarters.

The massive bedroom boasted a four-poster bed clothed in dark browns and blacks. The walls and floors were stone, and medieval-looking tapestry rugs had been scattered here and there. An enormous HD television hung on one wall between a moose head and what appeared to be a boar head sporting massive tusks. Tryst was not keen on killing wildlife, and he kept a cringe to himself.

Over by the windowed wall, Tryst saw the man seated on the overwide windowsill. Sunlight beamed across his figure so he couldn't make out an expression or posture, and a plaid blanket had been spread over his lap.

Now his good judgment snapped to the fore, and, as his father had directed him, Tryst went down on one knee and bowed his head, offering a respectful greeting. "Principal Connor, it's a pleasure to meet you. Again. Thank you for your hospitality. Please accept my apologies for being so brisk with you last night. I was more worried about finding the men lost in the snow than protocol."

"He doesn't seem so unruly, Alexis." The principal directed the words at his daughter, and then to Tryst he said, "I forgive you only because my daughter has told me of your relentless quest to help find my pack members. Have they all been accounted for?"

Tryst looked to Lexi, who he expected would have the tally.

"Still one missing," she offered. "Sandra. Liam believes she was running out on the track right before the avalanche."

"A female," the principal said with cheerless calm. "And so young. I had just approved her engagement to Vincent. That is unfortunate."

Tryst felt the old wolf's grief. Losing a female—hell, anyone—was a tragedy. And she'd obviously been ready to start a new life with marriage to the scion, probably eager to have kids, and build the pack. Both would be counted as a great loss.

He shouldn't be here. He could be doing more good outside than on his knees.

"Come, have a seat over here," the principal said to Trystan. "The sun is high and bright this morning. I love the rare winter sun."

Casting Lexi a raised brow—had the principal earlier referred to him as unruly?—Tryst accepted the invitation and sat across from the principal on the easy chair covered in what may have been pony hide. The rough hide felt nasty under his palms, so he fisted his hands on his thighs.

The principal was not old, and should not appear old, for wolves lived a good three centuries, aging slowly and gracefully, as was Rhys. He looked a little pale, though his smile felt warm and Tryst's apprehensions sluiced away.

"As much as I would love the chat, Principal Connor, I feel compelled to head outside and join the search. But if you'd allow me my curiosity, can I ask what it was I delivered to you last night?"

"Your father didn't tell you?"

"The mission to bring it here was so urgent, he slapped the case in my hands and sent me off. I know only it was an elixir of some sort."

"Alexis."

The principal's daughter stepped in and took the case from the table by the bed, gently setting it on her father's lap.

The principal held up a vial of violet liquid in the beam of winter sunlight. "Wolfsbane."

"Wolfsbane?" Tryst shoved backward and his boots scraped across the stone floor loudly. He ignored Lexi's reprimanding glance. "Can I ask why you requested something from Hawkes Associates that could bring your death, Principal Connor?"

The elder wolf tilted the vial in observation. "I've had this stored with Hawkes Associates since the turn of the twentieth century. You just returned it to me. A gift from a warlock who warned me someday what could cause me harm may also bring me good. Wolfsbane can bring a werewolf death or, if administered in the proper dose, give life. Or so one can hope."

He handed the vial to his daughter, who took it in her gloved hand and went to place it on the bedroom vanity.

"You have a need for either?" Tryst questioned.

"You're very bold, boy. Always a detriment to those wolves not raised in a pack."

"Forgive me. I'm trying. Pack life fascinates me, but there is much I have to learn."

"It isn't your fault you were denied the pack experience. I know your father well." Edmonton tilted his head in that same assessing manner Lexi had when they'd first met. Tryst had been weighed and measured far too many times to even flinch. "You hold a dangerous secret, boy."

Tryst averted his eyes from Lexi's curiosity. Would she ever take off those sunglasses? He didn't know if she knew the secret her father claimed to know, but he preferred she did not. He noted her fists tightened near her thighs. Of course her father would warn her against him.

Damn. So much for winning the werewolf princess. If his heritage were revealed to her, he was as good as mud beneath her kick-ass boots.

"Well, whatever it is you intend to use it for—" he gestured toward the vial of wolfsbane, diverting the conversation "—I hope you get the desired results."

Tryst offered his hand to Edmonton, though from what his father had told him, he shouldn't expect the gesture to be reciprocated. But the old man leaned forward, extending his hand. The handshake started Tryst's heart beating a little faster. He felt as though he'd been bestowed a great honor.

"Thank you, Principal Connor. I'll report to my father that you've received the package."

"Do tell him thank you from me, will you?"

"I will. Uh, would it be okay with you if I remain at Wulfsiege to finish the rescue operation and help your pack dig out? I've nowhere else I need to be, and I do enjoy the hard work. Besides, right now, the only way out is on foot."

The principal cast a discerning gaze over Trystan. He suspected that he didn't quite measure up to the principal's standards, the old man knowing what he did about

Trystan's lineage. It mattered little. And then it did, because he felt the princess's regard so close behind him.

"You have my permission to stay until we're dug out," the principal offered.

Tryst nodded and backed from the room, swinging around as he entered the conference room. He had a long day ahead of him.

"I must see to finding a replacement for the scion quickly." Edmonton tapped the vial of wolfsbane his daughter had returned to him. "Who knows how much longer I have." He sat back and closed his eyes to the warm sun beaming across his face. The first dose had done something. He hoped. He did feel stronger, able to sit up without wanting to curl forward and close his eyes to the compelling yet often painful sleep. "Where is Sven?"

"Toddling after Lana, most likely."

"He's not helping with the rescue team?"

He heard his daughter's smirk, and knew she had no respect for the alpha wolf who was engaged to his other daughter. He liked Sven. Called the Nordic Warrior for the reason he'd arrived at Wulfsiege a year ago after his pack had been annihilated by vampires, yet he had fought them boldly and still wore a scar along his torso. The young wolf was commanding, and quick to sniff out danger, though Edmonton did tend to turn an eye away from the man's lack of work ethic. If he could delegate, he'd make a fine leader.

"Don't tell me you would consider Sven for scion," Alexis dared to say.

"Watch your tongue, girl."

He didn't like it when she was aggressive toward him. Toward others it worked well and kept them at the distance she preferred, but around him, he insisted she be more docile.

"And who would you recommend?" he asked.

"Liam."

"His mother was an American."

"And you only trust Europeans? Oh, Father."

"Don't *oh, Father* me, Alexis. You've developed a decidedly acid tongue of late. I cannot endure your rebellion when I am so weak. When's the doctor due to arrive?"

"In a few hours. Do you want to wait for the next dose until after he arrives?"

"No. I'll have you call in Natalie so we can administer another injection. I actually feel better after the first dose. I think it may be working."

"I will," she said, standing and tipping down her sunglasses to look over the rims at him. "You sure you're feeling well this morning?"

"As well as a man who suffers a mysteriously debilitating ailment can feel."

She snatched the vial and then gave him a hug. He didn't squeeze back. Affection tended to spoil a welltrained child. Alana was proof of that. He couldn't lose Lexi. Not yet.

"Lexi?"

"Yes, Father?"

"Be careful around Trystan Hawkes."

"I am always careful around everyone, you know that. But Hawkes is not a threat to anyone."

"He's also not a full-blooded wolf."

"What?"

His daughter's gasp hurt his heart—and revealed her heart. Already she'd stepped across the invisible line she kept drawn around herself and had taken to the Hawkes man. He couldn't allow her to fall into a ridiculous fantasy.

"His father, Rhys Hawkes, is a half-breed. Half wolf, half vampire. And his mother is full vampire."

He waited for her reaction, but she swallowed and merely nodded, stunned at the announcement.

"I thought you should know. He's dangerous."

To her heart, and to his.

After excusing herself from her father's bedside, Lexi closed the door behind her and wandered down the tower stairs, her fingers tracing the cold stone walls for support. The man she was fascinated by was a half-breed? His mother a vampire?

Her heart beating rapidly, she jammed a shoulder to the wall and shook her head.

Here she'd been close to hope that the new guy was just interesting enough to intrigue her. She'd already begun to trust him. And she'd been gazing at him like some kind of lovesick dove. But he had vampire blood running through his veins. Not potential mate material. Not for the pack princess.

At least that is what common sense boldly said. While her heart, well, it whispered something too soft for her to interpret right now.

"Once again, you get the wrong end of the stick," she muttered.

With a sigh, she lifted her chin and marched down the hallway. Work would keep her mind away from her stupid mistake.

Chapter 4

They pulled up the female's body to a rousing round of cheers. Her fingers twitched, and that was enough for everyone to believe she was alive and had a chance at survival.

Tryst carefully handed her off to the team who would take her inside the keep for medical care. Earlier, a helicopter had brought in a doctor, one of very few who treated wolves as a specialty, because he was a werewolf himself.

Forgoing the offer of a beer from Liam, who had dug alongside him through the morning hours, Trystan wandered off from the pack who whooped and high-fived. It was a time for celebration. All missing pack members had been accounted for. Some had passed, but he knew they would be remembered and mourned as heartily as they cheered the living.

Trystan never missed a reason to celebrate, but it

didn't feel right to join in this time. This was not his pack. Not his family. And though they encouraged him to participate, he thanked them and wandered off around the side of the castle where the avalanche had knocked out the glass wall. What had once been an outdoor stadium was now a sloping heap of snow.

Poking the ski pole here and there, he verified the tight snowpack and that it was okay to tread. Not that he'd fall far, or do much damage if the snow layers did shift. And really? It would be sweet to jump from the castle roof on a snowboard and shred this slope.

He shouldn't think of capitalizing on the drifts after such a dire event, but his adventurous eyes were always keen for an excellent slope.

The weak sun hid behind white clouds and evening fast approached, with a noticeable drop in temperature. Tryst's breath fogged before him. The avalanche had cleared the decorative frost from surrounding trees, yet in a wide circle where disaster had not struck, the world was still coated with white. Weird. And humbling.

He was hungry and tired, but most of all he wanted a few moments to sit quietly and close his eyes, to reconnect with the universe and ground himself in the now. It was the best way to boost his physical and mental energy.

Stuffing his gloves in a pocket, he shook his head to scatter the snow and ice that had frozen in his hair as he'd worked up a sweat. His clothing was damp from exertion, and as soon as he sat down it would begin to freeze, but he'd ignore that because right now he welcomed the silence.

Hiking down the side of the hill formed against the castle wall, he landed on the walkway to the stadium seating, which was now all under snow. The walkway hugged the back of the castle and led to a stepped area graduated to walk out across a vast courtyard. A single yard light glowed over the courtyard.

Someone was seated on the upper step, elbows back and propped behind her. He guessed female, because of the slender line of the long gray coat. A fur-lined hood crowned her head, concealing the side of her face, but he knew it was the Connor princess. The bad one, as Liam had intimated.

Naughty bad?

Tryst's heart raced. He blew out a breath that fogged before his face. Yet suddenly his bravado fell. What did she know about him? Edmonton Connor had likely told her about his mixed-race heritage. Which meant Tryst had to play her carefully because he didn't want to lose her respect.

Sitting down next to her, about two feet away, he scanned the horizon over the treetops. "We found the female. Was Sandra her name?"

"Yes. Rick just texted me that she is alive. That's a miracle."

"She'd been crushed against a stone bench, and had managed to work her way beneath it as the snow moved over her, so had the space beneath for air. So lucky. I think every bone in her body is broken, but she'll heal. Women are so strong."

"You say that as if it's a fact that's been proved to you."

"It has been."

He bowed his head, images of his mother coming to mind. Tall, dark, yet regal in the most macabre manner, his mother, Viviane LaMourette. The *touched one,* as some would whisper behind her back.

But he wasn't about to divulge how it had been to

grow up with an insane vampire mother who would have bitten him on more than one occasion had his father not been vigilant in keeping him safe. He would have given his mother blood, but it wouldn't have rescued her from the wicked melancholy that relentlessly haunted her soul.

"It's going to be a gorgeous night," he offered. "In a few days the moon will be full and bright. I've always loved the moon for its bold white light. I bet its shine makes you look like a snow princess."

She tilted back her head, and the hood shrugged down onto her shoulders to reveal glossy black hair, unpinned and falling straight about her narrow face. A pert nose, soft pink mouth, and porcelain skin competed against those harsh, ever-present sunglasses.

"Do you ever take those sunglasses off?"

"No."

Too quick, that answer. Protective. And practiced. "It's cool. You've got the whole *Matrix* thing going on."

"Matrix?"

Tryst twisted to face her. "The greatest movie ever made? You're kidding me, right?"

"I don't see many movies. I'm too busy. And if I have free time, I'd rather read."

"Seriously? That is so wrong."

"Reading is good for a person. You learn things from books," she said mockingly.

"I know, but reading is so…static. I'm the type of guy who has to be moving all the time."

"Watching a movie for two hours doesn't sound very active."

"I agree with you there, but still, it wins hands down over books any day."

She lifted her chin, but didn't go so far as to sniff

in disapproval. Yet Tryst felt her disdain for what she guessed must be his lacking education. Ah, well, he couldn't win them all. The invitation to attend Oxford had been offered, but the idea of sitting in a mortal institution had been received with laughter from both him and his father.

"You don't do anything fun, do you?" he goaded.

"Why do you care?"

"Why shouldn't I?" he offered. "Fun is a necessity of life. And life, well, life is energy. The world responds to the energy you put out."

"It that so? Sounds kind of New Agey to me."

"To each his own."

He sensed she couldn't be that much of a stick-in-the-mud. A pretty woman like her must do things that made her happy. Otherwise, she wouldn't be so beautiful. Tryst believed the way a person led their life was reflected upon their face. It was an unavoidable result of karma. And energy. He'd once fretted over the freckles covering his skin until his mother had said something about them being giggle marks. Every time he'd laughed as a baby a new freckle had appeared. It had changed how he viewed opposition and challenges. Mom did have her good moments, and he cherished them like diamonds.

"You don't like me very much, do you?" he asked.

Again, the assessing head tilt. Tryst felt her gaze upon him, even though he couldn't see it, and he liked her curious regard even if it wasn't necessarily friendly. He loved when a woman looked him over and then decided to touch. Would she touch? Nah, she was one cool chick.

Didn't mean he couldn't play with her.

"Go for it, Lexi. I don't bite."

"What?"

"You were giving me the eye. I know."

She scoffed. "You are conceited."

"Yeah, but I'm also a threat to you in a way I can't figure out. And that freaks you and surprises me." He leaned closer and placed a hand next to her elbow on the step. Brushing his nose aside her silken hair, he smelled the faintest citrus sweetness. "You're freaked, admit it."

"Back off, Hawkes."

He sat straight, propping his elbows on his knees and looking over the grounds before them. A wiser unaligned wolf wouldn't risk sitting so close. Curiosity always trumped his wisdom. And who could refuse a challenge?

"Fine. I get it. You're the princess. You get to be the choosy one. You always this defensive toward men?"

"Yes."

That honest answer was refreshing, and also tossed a wrench into this challenge. Straightforward kind of chick, this princess. He'd never met one like her, and everything about her made him want to learn more, to delve beneath her monotone exterior and discover the brightness within aching for release. Lexi Connor harbored a bold and vibrant color inside her, and he would find it.

"My father told me..." she started.

Spine straightening, Tryst immediately sensed what she couldn't quite say. Hell, the principal had told her about his mixed blood. Of course, if the man wanted to protect his daughter from a nonpack wolf he would use whatever weapon he had at hand.

"What did he tell you? About me?"

He wasn't about to make it easy for her. For anyone. So he had a chip on his shoulder about his heritage.

Anyone wanted to make a big deal about it? He knew how to throw a punch. He had a missing molar, too, because he could also take a punch.

Lexi sighed and smoothed a gloved finger along the seam of her leather pants. "He warned me to stay away from you because…"

"Because why? Because I'm a strong male who knows how to take care of a woman? Because I don't mind getting my hands dirty to help another pack? Because I respect your father?" Feeling his ire, he flexed a fist.

"Because you're a half-breed."

Tryst pulled up his chin and released his fists. The principal had gotten his information messed up. "I'm full wolf," he said, cautioning the growl on his tone.

"How is that possible? Your father is half wolf, half vampire, and your mother—"

"Is a vampiress. But I don't have any vampire in me, trust me on that one."

"Sounds impossible."

"Yeah?" He couldn't punch his way out of this one. Damn. "And are you offended by the idea I might have a touch of vampire blood running through my veins?"

"I—"

"You pack wolves are all alike." He stood and kicked the toe of his boot against the stone step to shake off the packed snow, and to avert his growing anger. "You're all so tightly knit and exclusive. New guy comes along and you feel threatened."

"I didn't say that I'm threatened by you. Nor did I say—"

"Yeah, whatever."

He stomped up the steps, knowing if he didn't leave her now he'd only give her a real growl. And he would never do that to a pack leader's daughter. Any woman, for that matter.

Wow. She'd just strummed his chords and what an awful tune.

"I'm going to find something to eat, then get back to work shoveling out your pretty little castle, Miss Princess Trueblood."

So maybe he didn't have as good a handle on this challenge as he'd thought.

"Arrogant idiot," Lexi muttered after the angry wolf who stomped inside. "The vampire thing definitely rubs him the wrong way."

And rightly so, she figured. Vamps and wolves had been at odds for centuries. They honored an ineffable ceasefire at the moment, but there weren't a lot of wolves who would embrace a vampire as friend. Her father was friends with Trystan's father, Rhys Hawkes, but it was more a political relationship than an embraceable acceptance.

For good reason. Wolves didn't go near vamps because if bitten by a vampire the wolf would develop an insatiable bloodlust, and werewolves did not drink blood or feed on humans. Ever. It was an abominable practice. And vampires avoided wolves because they knew the wolf was stronger and could beat the crap out of them with one fist tied behind their backs.

So a young werewolf who had been born of a vampiress and a half-breed couldn't possibly be full-blooded wolf. Why did he believe that?

Of course, if he hadn't a hunger for blood perhaps that led Trystan to such a belief. But the blood hunger could emerge anytime. Lexi knew well that, genetically, things didn't always go as nature had intended in a wolf's body.

Removing her sunglasses, she didn't wince at the bright yard light. Light didn't bother her eyes so much as she would have others believe. Perhaps she was lying to herself as much as Hawkes lied to himself about having vampire blood in him?

He thought she held his mixed blood against him? Nothing had changed since she'd witnessed his selfless heroics. Save, now she knew her father would be upset if she so much as looked at Trystan Hawkes.

But she couldn't stop looking at him. He was beautiful, in body, mind and spirit. The world responded to his energy? What a cool life philosophy. And he was working that relationship with the universe in his favor. He continued to fascinate her, and more so now that he denied a part of his heritage. Her father would be crushed to learn what she thought about the unaligned werewolf. And yet, she'd never felt so rebellious in all her years and it was a feeling she wanted to explore.

But Hawkes must now think she hated him. She didn't like it when people formed the wrong opinion about her. The man needed to be set straight regarding how she felt about him.

Before heading to her room, she veered toward the lobby to check on the operations out front. The helicopter that had delivered the doctor had been able to land a mile up the road and the doctor had walked to the castle, but he'd reported that crews working six leagues south were clearing away where another avalanche had hit the edge of a village, so it could be days before the road crews reached Wulfsiege.

Perfectly fine. The pack owned a snowplow, which was parked in the shed, and the last she'd heard, the shed had finally been dug out. Soon, the area could be cleared, and crews could start working on repairing the damage to the castle walls. Life could get back to normal.

As normal as it could be with the principal up in the tower, suffering from an unknown ailment.

Hearing shouts outside in the courtyard, Lexi rushed through the boarded aisle leading from the front doors that had been hastily put up to keep the snow from blocking the entrance. She saw two wolves going at it near the big gold Caterpillar snowplow. Sven was easily recognized by his hard, square jaw, pale Nordic coloring and alpha growls as he swung a punch at the other wolf, who she also recognized.

So the lone wolf was getting into a fight against a pack wolf? Not wise. But surprisingly, a close physical match to Sven, who was the biggest, most brutish wolf in the pack. She'd sensed Tryst's growing aggression sitting out back on the steps. Perhaps he'd sought a means to expel the anger she had aroused in him?

An overwhelming desire to watch the Hawkes wolf in action pushed her to the edge of the circle surrounding the fight. No one made a move to tear the fighters apart. All cheered on Sven, their Nordic Warrior.

"Why are they doing this?" she asked Liam, who stood beside her.

Arms crossed in defiance of the fight—Liam had a tendency to take a stand on unnecessary violence—he said, "The new wolf thought he could handle the plow better than Sven—and he probably can—but you know the Nord."

A few of them used *the Nord* in a less than complimentary manner toward the boisterous wolf.

Truth was, Sven was an arrogant asshole. But Lexi

would never tell her sister that. Though, there were days she suspected Lana was not so ignorant regarding her fiancé's less than valorous traits. Sven was just another doll for her collection that she'd play with, then tuck away when bored. When Father had suggested they get engaged a few months ago Lana had agreed because it had put a smile on the principal's face. But Lexi sensed her sister had already grown tired of the Nord. And there were days she wondered if she should intervene, suggest she consider their engagement more seriously, and really think about the ramifications of spending the rest of her life as the man's wife. What did they really know about him since he'd arrived here a year earlier claiming he was the only survivor of a vicious vampire attack?

"They're fighting over who gets to play with the big toy?" Lexi sighed and had to jump back when Trystan's body tumbled toward her and slid across the ice to a stop before her boots.

He looked up, spit aside blood and flashed her a red smile. "Hey, Princess."

"Let Sven drive the plow," she said.

"He's never operated the thing before. He'll blow out the hydraulics."

Yes, he probably would, but she'd prefer that to seeing Tryst get his face pummeled just to protect the pack's expensive equipment. Was the man really so concerned over the correct operation of the machine, or was this some kind of power play?

Knowing Sven, it was a power play. But she wasn't sure about Trystan. He couldn't know that Sven was one step below the deceased scion and currently held all the power in this pack.

Liam helped Trystan up, and the red-haired wolf

immediately dove toward Sven. Lexi couldn't watch. And then, she couldn't keep her eyes from the powerful muscles that flexed under the blue sweater wrapping Tryst's amazing form. Where Sven was bulky and brutal, Trystan was lean, solid and agile. He dodged the punches more easily than his opponent, yet he didn't pack the strength behind his hits as Sven did. Rangy, he masterfully danced away from punches, and even those he took directly, he took with a growl and a smirking call for more.

"Marvelous," she murmured, then bit her tongue, hoping no one had heard her. Watching Tryst move warmed parts of her body that should put a blush on any woman's face. Lexi's lashes fluttered behind the dark sunglasses.

Again Tryst's body went flying, to land in the arms of a pack wolf opposite where Lexi stood. The lone wolf's eyelids shuttered. Blood streamed from his mouth, yet that goofy grin was fixed, as if cemented there by blood.

Please stay down for the count, she found herself thinking. And then, *So I can tend your wounds.*

"Had enough, outsider?" Sven barked at his opponent. He flexed his arms, tearing the shirt from his back to reveal what four hours a day in the gym had enhanced. Impossibly huge, veiny muscles.

Lexi was not impressed. And even less so when Sven winked at her. What a brutal pig.

"Fine," Trystan answered. "Destroy your only means of getting Wulfsiege shoveled out." He pushed from the man who had caught him and again spit blood on the pounded snow. "This isn't my pack. I don't give a crap if you want to break the expensive equipment."

He stalked off toward the castle lobby, and Lexi

turned to follow, but not before asking Liam to give Sven instructions on how to operate the machine.

She tracked Trystan's angry march toward the guest room, and before he got to the door he called back, "What do you want, Princess?"

"I just…" She had been looking for him before she'd come upon him fighting. "I had wanted to say something to you."

He bled at the temple and on the shoulder, and his sweater had been torn to reveal where repeated pummels from Sven's iron fist had left his skin red. Her fingers twitched to touch him, to offer tender reassurance, but she knew the male wolf all too well, and cautioned her need to pamper when what the man wanted was to stomp and punch and break something.

"So?" he insisted angrily. "What did you want to say to the outsider with the mixed heritage who seems to offend you by merely standing in your air?"

Stiffening her spine, Lexi lifted her chin. "I wanted to tell you that there's not a thing about you that offends me. So take that and shove it up your pity party, wolf."

Striding off, she aimed for her room, the only place she felt she could breathe and let her anger simmer. She'd wanted to offer the wolf a kindness and he'd forced her to deliver it with a blow. That wasn't her.

Nor was the angry wolf really him, she suspected. All that aggression must really mess with his karmic energy. On the other hand, he'd kept bouncing back after every brutal punch, almost as if he'd felt he deserved the punishment.

She paused at a corner in the hallway and turned to find Trystan Hawkes standing before the guest room doorway, his gaze fixed on her. He'd watched her walk away.

Her fingers flexed around the stone corner, but her legs did not move. Why was it so hard to leave his regard? She could stand here forever as long as he never looked away.

Your father did warn you. You should heed that warning.

Indeed.

Lexi bowed her head and stepped around the corner, breaking the tantalizing connection with the Hawkes wolf.

Chapter 5

From the south window, Lexi spied movement out be-yond the far running track. Actually it was the half-pipe that they kept plowed for the pack to use for exercise. Since the games were held every other year, this year it wasn't groomed, but it was still in nice shape for the few wolves who liked to snowboard.

Who was out there now, so close to midnight?

She smiled when she realized it could only be one very interesting man with a penchant for taking charge and picking fights. "Hawkes."

She wanted to rush out there, and then at the same time, she wanted to hit something. It hadn't been his fault he'd snapped at her earlier. The man was tired, had just been beat on by the Nord, and well, she figured the guy must have a huge chip on his shoulder having grown up a half-breed.

"Give him a chance," she whispered, feeling the rebel yell inside her flick a defiant finger at her father.

Knowing it would be wiser to turn around and head for the shower, instead she grabbed her white fox fur coat, put on her sunglasses, jammed her feet into some snow pants and boots and headed outside.

Time to discover the forbidden, and to see if it was worth all the fuss.

The half-pipe was a good walk away, but the moon beamed across the snow, imbuing it with a Faeryland glitter. Though she refrained from thinking about faeries, because she didn't want to deal with their malice and mischief. One wrong thought could bring the vicious sidhe to this mortal realm. Natalie had warned her often enough when she was younger to never step inside a toadstool circle for she may never be allowed return from Faery.

The wind lifted sprinkles of snow across her face, blown up from the edge of the half-pipe where Trystan snowboarded. He must have found a board in the locker room.

Arriving at the end of the big U-shaped ditch carved into the icy snow, Lexi sat on the deck, hanging her legs over the edge to watch the wolf perform a midair flip with such ease she couldn't help but whisper, "Wow."

He moved down the pipe on his board, gliding from side to side, his body graceful and agile. Across the way from her he took the air, popping and performing a hand plant on the deck, and flipped over backward, his body straight, arms out as he twisted and expertly landed on the side of the iced pipe. The control he exhibited was seductive, his movements seamless and practiced. He flew through the air, hanging suspended for long breaths and then landing expertly. For a man his size and height, the grace he exhibited was surreal. And sensual.

Lexi propped her chin in her hand and lost herself in admiration.

Swooshing toward her, he came up and jumped out of the pipe with the ease of making a step. "You watching me, Princess?"

"Not much else to do this late at night. And I'm no Florence Nightingale. I prefer to stay out of the keep and let the others tend the injured. You're very good. Must have lots of practice."

"Winter sports are my favorite. An ice demon taught me how to shred the powder. Actually, he's a werewolf inhabited by an incorporeal ice demon. Great friend, but a little chilly once every so often." This time his wink did not bother her in the least. "The pipe needs grooming, but I can work with it."

"That backward flip was impressive."

"Just can't keep your eyes off me, can you?"

She looked aside, rolling her eyes.

"Just because you're wearing those sunglasses doesn't mean I don't know when you roll your eyes at me." He thrust the board toward her. "Show me your best."

"I don't need to prove myself to you."

"Ah, come on. I'm just chilling after a long day, trying to have some fun. Really needed it, especially after the little spat we had. I'm sorry. You were right and I was wrong."

She lifted a brow. Someone had taught this guy all the right moves. But the statement felt too practiced so she wasn't about to grant him the win yet.

"This is relaxing for you?"

"Hell yes. Winter sports are like breathing to me.

How better to truly connect with the universe than when you are soaring weightless and without a thought for anything but the now? I like to fly at the end of the day. Put out my energy into the world. Also, it takes the edge off the pain."

She noticed the bruise on his jaw and was surprised because it should have healed by now. But then Sven's fists were made of steel.

"Boys battling over their toys," she said.

"Yeah, well, I haven't heard the plow lately, have you? You think the big lug already broke it?"

"Sven may be stupid, but I don't think he'd purposely try to destroy something so valuable. And it is late."

"You know him better than I." He stabbed the end of the board into the snowpack near her thigh. "So show me what you got. Oh, wait, I forgot." He bent so his face was right before hers. "You're a girl."

"Taunting me with your macho misunderstanding will not get a reaction."

"So you're all that? You even know how to use the board?"

"Who do you think tests the pipe after it's been made?"

"Seriously? Sweet! A chick who can handle the board. That's tight. Now I really have to see what you've got. Come on, Lexi, don't you want to show me up?"

Yes, yes, and oh, yes.

She grabbed the board and sized up the binding buckles. A little larger than her custom-made board, but they were adjustable, so would work in a pinch.

Shrugging off her coat, she tossed it aside. "Time to cut you down to size, Hawkes."

The woman working the fur-rimmed boots and body-hugging white snow pants did not realize how sexy she was. Or maybe she did, and she just didn't have the wherewithal to flaunt it at him.

"Nah, she likes me," Tryst muttered. "She can't stay away from me." Why else would she walk all the way out here after he'd angrily stomped away from her earlier?

Admittedly, he'd never had a problem with conceit, and usually if he went after a woman, she reciprocated. Must be his charm. He got that from his dad. But he liked that Lexi was not easy. In fact, she was almost too cold. Almost. If her father had warned her against him, Tryst would say he was doing better than most right now.

Lexi took position at the top of the half-pipe, shook out her arms, tilted her head around on her neck, then dismounted from the deck and performed a few easy alley-oops a one-eighty turn as she glided up each side of the pipe.

"Warm up!" she called, as she stepped off on the deck to start again at the side opposite where he stood.

"Looking fine," he said, and she was. Most women hadn't the control right out of the gate like she did. Nice. Then again, it seemed she was always in control. Girl like that needed to let loose, be a little free. Show him her inner color.

A spray of snow misted his face as she glided near him, twisting at the deck and dropping down gracefully to follow through to the other side. She used her hips and shoulders to steer the board and her body. A hand plant at the opposite side of the pipe saw her placing her gloved palm on the snow edge and following through over backward to glide skillfully down the inner side. She'd mastered the pop and plant.

He'd mastered it, of course, but occasionally it

tripped him up and landed him on his face. A face-plant burned like a mother, but it was worth the road rash for the resultant thrill. Besides, the wound never lasted longer than a good pipe session.

She glided up on his side, dismounting and spraying snow over his boots with her stop. "How's that, hotshot?"

"How was that?" Tryst pumped his fist. "Lexi, that was sick. I can barely work that trick. You must practice every day."

She shrugged—and then the most amazing thing happened. It struck Tryst so hard he slapped a hand to his chest because he needed to slow down his sudden rapid heartbeats.

"What?" she said.

"You know what's even more amazing than your half-pipe skills? It's that." He pointed to her face. "That gorgeous smile. I knew you had it in you. I knew it!"

When he expected her to drop the smile, and maybe even punch him, she didn't, and instead she continued to smile. And when he offered his fist, she returned the gesture with an enthusiastic fist bump.

"Lexi, you are freaking me out."

"Why? Because I don't always have to wear the security jacket and be all business? You don't have the first clue about me, Trystan."

"Call me Tryst, please. All my friends do."

"Tryst." That made her smile even more.

He butted the toe of his boot against the snowboard she'd jammed into the snow and, feeling a well of eagerness bubble up inside him, he went with the moment, ignoring whether or not what he was about to say was right or wrong.

"Lexi, I just gotta say, right now? I so want to kiss

you. But I feel like I have to ask your permission, or risk a sharp left hook to my jaw."

That chased away her smile. Dislodging the board from the snowpack, she handed him the board and tugged on her coat. "Right. So I'll tell Jones he can cut the lights on the field when I get back inside. I'll see you tomorrow, Hawkes."

And she marched off, without looking back. Even in the fur-rimmed pack boots, she managed a sexy hip-shifting sashay. Tryst whistled lowly.

"I blew it," he muttered. "It was a fast move. Too fast. I should have held back." He grabbed the board and stabbed it into the snow. "No, that's the way I roll. If the werewolf princess doesn't like it, then I'll have to change her mind."

His inner wolf howled, and then Tryst let it escape, a long vocal song that declared his interest in the woman and placed a challenge to any who would protest.

Lexi paused in the doorway to her room, taking in Tryst's long and rangy howl. She'd heard that kind of howl before—when a pack male was hot for a female. Her neck heated and her lips parted. He was howling for her?

No, she must be reading it wrong. Maybe?

Stripping off her boots and coat, she wandered into the bathroom to turn on the water and run a tub. Her muscles felt luxuriously stretched after the quick run on the half-pipe. She didn't work out nearly as often as she should. Chatelaine duties were dull and didn't require much energy.

The world responds to the energy you put into it.

She loved that. Everything about him was so different from any man she had known. Refreshing, open. Alive.

Sitting on the edge of the tub, she held her fingers under the stream of water, and adjusted the temperature. A squirt of cinnamon-scented bubble bath perfumed the room.

"He felt like he'd needed permission to kiss me?" She shook her head and stood, finding her reflection in the mirror. "Who are you, Alexis Connor? What kind of woman requires a man to ask permission for a kiss? That's so wrong."

And it was all her fault. She put up a cold front when around any male. It was something she'd been doing since her teenage years. The truth was just too painful, and it always freaked out the guys.

"You can't risk it," she said to the mirror.

She usually avoided meeting her own eyes in her reflection, but tonight Lexi studied her irises. "I'd scare the crap out of him. Will I ever be kissed?"

Chapter 6

Lexi inspected the tray of food that sat on her father's bed beside his thigh. He'd picked at the roast beef and had eaten all the mashed potatoes—his favorite—but hadn't touched the broccoli.

"Father, you need to eat to keep up your strength."

Propped against two thick pillows, he redirected his gaze from out the window, where snowflakes fluttered through the sky, to her. The drowsy look had returned, his eyelids heavy. He'd actually looked as though he was improving earlier this morning when she'd checked in on him, but now she feared that might have been a false hope on her part.

She speared a hunk of broccoli with the fork. "Remember I used to call these trees when I was little?"

He allowed her to feed him the vegetable but then shook his head for no more. "That was how your mother got you to eat them. It thrilled you to eat a whole tree in one bite. Used to call peas boulders, and arrange them around the trees. Your meals were quite the theatrics, as I recall."

She set down the fork and nodded, not wanting to look into his tired eyes and see the truth. How could they not know what was wrong with him?

"Did the doctor from Paris examine you?"

"He did. This morning. Took some blood and scanned it with a fancy gauge and is now waiting for results."

"That's good. I'll have to talk to him. I know he's in the keep now."

"How are the wounded?"

"Recovering. You know our breed is sturdy. But crushed lungs and bones take longer to mend. A few more days and most should be ninety percent better."

A tap on the door came in two rapid knocks and then one slow one.

"Tell your sister to come in," Edmonton said on a raspy whisper.

Lexi went to the door and Lana glided through with tears in her eyes. Lexi moved in front of her so their father couldn't see her teary state. "What's wrong, Lana?"

"It's Sven. Oh, Daddy!" She nudged around Lexi and went to snuggle on the bed next to the principal. "He's such a brute."

"What did he do?" Lexi demanded, feeling her ire rise. "Did he hurt you?"

Lana gave her a blank look and a screw of her mouth. "No, silly. He would never hurt me." But she looked down and aside when she said that. Lexi suspected otherwise, and that perhaps her sister was deft at covering up bruises. "He broke the stupid machine."

"The snowplow?" Lexi shook her head. Tryst had been right. And she should have done something to stop Sven from exerting his machismo just because he could. "Are you sure?"

Lana nodded. "Liam said it would take days to repair. Sven just flipped him off and told him to get to work. I hate when he's so rude to the rest of the pack. Makes me dislike him, but I don't." She turned to their father. "Unless you think I should, Daddy?"

Edmonton closed his eyes and stroked his daughter's blond hair, and Lana rested her head against his shoulder. "I want whatever makes you happy, Lana dear. We men can be brutes at times. I'm sure Sven was upset over what he had done and inadvertently took it out on you and the others. He's been through a lot, what with losing his whole pack. Give him the benefit of the doubt."

Lexi paced to the window and crossed her arms over her chest, her back to the cuddly twosome. She'd grown used to her father's nickname for Lana. Lana dear. Lana dearest. Sweetie pie. He only called her Lexi or Alexis.

What are you doing? Get over yourself. You and Lana have very different relationships with your father. It doesn't matter. Right now, Father's health is paramount.

"He's not eating as much," she said over her shoulder to Lana. "Maybe you can get him to finish his meal."

Lana stared at the tray of food. "If he doesn't feel like eating, we shouldn't force him."

"I'm not dead, and I can hear you two talking about me as if I'm not here. I'm just not hungry right now."

"He's not hungry." Lana pushed the tray toward the end of the bed. "Get rid of this."

Lexi picked up the tray, but couldn't help wonder

what had suddenly got into her sister that she had put up such a protective front. On the other hand, anything to get Daddy on her side. "I'll leave you two alone. I'll talk to the doctor and make sure you get another injection of wolfsbane before you doze off to rest. I'll look in on you later, Father."

"You were right, outsider."

Tryst turned from walking away from the cafeteria, where he'd grabbed a shredded pork sandwich, to find Lexi had caught up with him. He hated that word. And coming from her it felt even more ugly.

"You're admitting I was right about something?" He took a big bite of the sandwich, and said while chewing, "This I've got to hear."

"Sven broke the snowplow."

"Hell."

"Liam is a mechanic. Actually, he's a carpenter, too. Jack-of-all-trades, that guy. He estimates a few days to fix it. It's not like we're in a hurry to go anywhere. We've got a doctor and all the injured wolves in the keep are improving."

"What about your father?"

"He's…hanging in there."

"The wolfsbane not working?"

"I'm not sure. It seemed to have an immediate effect, yet now he is getting worse again. I don't know what is wrong with him, nor does the doctor. He's waiting to hear back from Paris on blood tests. He has some kind of fancy scanner that sends the information directly to the lab."

"You're worried about him."

"Of course I am. He's my father. And we have no

scion. The pack needs a leader, especially now, during this disaster."

"What about Sven?"

"He is my father's choice."

"Good luck with that, pack Alpine."

The day they let Sven lead the pack was the day the castle took damage from mortars and enemy marauders. It could happen. It *would* happen with that idiot in charge.

"So with the plow not working, I guess I'm staying on a few more days." He stopped at the guest bedroom door and, sandwich demolished, crossed his arms over his chest, leaning against the wall. "You able to handle having my ugly face around here that long?"

She shrugged but said confidently, "It's not so ugly."

Tryst straightened and put down his arms. "I can't figure you out, Lexi. You like me but you don't. You're offended by me but you're not."

"We women are complicated. You don't know that?" She strolled away, casting a glance over her shoulder. Man, he wished he could see her eyes. "Not much to do this afternoon. Looks like a storm is rolling in. You up for some hot chocolate?"

Twisting his neck to catch the sexy werewolf princess's tilt of head, Tryst tripped over his feet catching up to her. "I'm up for anything with you."

"Sounds more interesting than a movie."

He didn't miss the teasing tone in her voice. All systems fired and ready for action, Tryst followed Lexi to her bedroom.

Finally, a crack in her icy surface.

Whatever she was doing by inviting the wolf into her bedroom, Lexi decided not to question and just follow her instincts. Said instincts purred like a lost kitten in the wolf's presence. She'd never felt so *unresisting* around a man before. Every word he spoke turned her head toward him. His movements caught her eye and now she lingered on a hand gesture and the hard corner of his hip as he paced around the room.

Tryst settled on the two-seater couch before the window that overlooked the distant half-pipe. He held a cup of hot cocoa with tiny marshmallows floating on the surface. Lexi kept a coffee/cocoa machine in her room. His hair, loose and wild, glinted with sunlight and his long, lanky legs bent slightly at the knee, stretched before him, his feet finding hold on the ottoman.

Lexi curled up her legs and settled onto the seat next to him, but fit her body as close to her side as possible without touching him. She may be less resistant to a man's attention but she was a little uncomfortable being near one who made her feel so at ease. A weird mix of nerves and relaxation. What the hell?

He hadn't taken a drink, instead following her every move as if he was trying to learn her. It didn't unnerve her. It made her feel special. Like she was the only one he cared to look at. That had never happened to her with a man before. All she'd ever dreamed to have was a man's attention. And for it to feel easy and natural, like when she observed Lana with men.

A systems check made her realize she did feel relaxed. Not on guard. Huh. So weird that this new wolf could insinuate himself into her life and she hadn't even flinched.

"Take off your glasses, Lexi," he said. "I want to see your eyes."

A sudden flinch twanged at her heart and her defenses flashed back up. "I told you the light bothers me." She sipped the hot cocoa as a means to put an end to that direction in the conversation.

Tryst followed in kind. He propped an ankle across one knee and shook his foot nervously as he looked about the room. "I didn't expect the frills," he said of the purple ruffled bed skirt and the white ruffled pillows on the beds. On the walls, decals of roses—her favorite flower—brought a touch of summer to her room in the stark winter.

"What did you expect? Steel and black leather?"

"Sounds kinda kinky to me." He waggled a brow and she couldn't help but smile. "Lexi, you have a gorgeous smile. You should use it more often. Wait, I get it. It is a distraction from your eyes, yes? Clever, very clever."

"The same way you use that cocky attitude to distract from the kind and caring wolf you are?"

He set the cup on the nearby table where she had set the flare gun on top of a stack of romance novels, and crossed his arms defensively across his chest. "Just stepping in when help is needed. Who wouldn't do that?"

"A lot of guys. I respect that about you, Trystan. It goes a long way in…"

"In making up for the fact I'm not what you want me to be? I am full-blooded wolf, Lexi. You have to believe me."

"Doesn't matter want I want, or even what you think I want—which is completely off base, by the way. You can never dream to know my mind. Hell, from day to day, I don't even have a good grasp on it."

Especially now that he had intruded upon her hard, cold heart. A heart that seemed to soften with every minute she spent near him.

"Would it be so wrong if you were not full-blooded?

With a vampire for a mother I have to believe you have great respect for that breed."

"Oh, I do. Don't get me wrong. I have nothing against a longtooth—well, you know. The vampires in my family are family. But I'm still wary around the ones I don't know. It's a social thing I learned after I started hanging out with my breed. But trust me, the vampire gene passed me over and went straight to my twin brother. He's a blood-born vampire."

"Wow." Hugging a knee up to her chest, she leaned forward over her cup of cocoa. "You've a twin who is vampire? How did that happen?"

"Born at the same time, but we had different fathers. Rhys is my dad, and Vaillant's dad, well—guy was an asshole, and he's gone now, so I won't speak poorly of the dead."

"Your mother and brother are vampires. Your father half vampire. You've more vampire blood in your family than werewolf."

"And you're skittish about that."

"I'm not, but why does it concern you so much?"

He shrugged. "Just want to know where I stand with you. You're a pretty woman. Hell, you're sexy, and gorgeous, and you shred on the half-pipe, and…I'm attracted to you. I'm surprised half the wolves in the pack aren't fighting over you, or that you've not already been claimed by one of them." He tilted back the rest of the hot chocolate, wiped a brown mustache from his upper lip, then asked, "Why is that?"

The question pushed against walls she didn't want to bring down, or even open the door a crack. She had invited him here. Would it be rude to ask him to leave so quickly?

"What's wrong with you, Lexi? I don't mean to pry,

but seriously? There's gotta be something that's keeping the guys away from you. And I highly doubt it's because you're the pack princess. That only makes you more valuable in the eyes of a pack wolf. I know that much despite never having grown up in a pack."

"Was your pack peopled by vampires? Or were you in a tribe?"

"You're changing the subject."

"I am. And for good reason. I don't feel comfortable enough with you to expose my secrets."

"So you have secrets?"

He leaned forward, clasping his hands between his knees. His hair spilled forward and she wanted to run her fingers through it because it looked so soft and the color was brown and red and copper and she'd like to feel it against her lips.

"Just one secret," she whispered, feeling her defenses slacken. "Can't we be allowed one?"

"Oh, sure. Everyone has secrets. I thought mine was safe from you, but I'm glad your father told you. What you see is what you get. But what you see is definitely a werewolf."

She'd like to believe that. She could believe that. She would.

"You see everything around here at face value," she said. "What I want to know is why haven't you eyes for Lana?"

"She's taken. And I don't do blondes. I like them dark, mysterious and, apparently, a little cold."

She ran a palm down her arm. Her skin wasn't cold—oh. He'd been talking about her demeanor. *Oh, Lexi, when did you become the ice princess?*

Long time ago, her conscience answered with a sigh. Too long to change now.

She was set in her ways. Driven toward accomplishment, and blind to life's pleasures, such as getting the things she desired. She wasn't worthy of a true werewolf's attentions, and she had accepted that. Perhaps Tryst's mixed blood was all she could ever hope for in a mate? If so, then it was time to venture into the forbidden and take that chance she'd always wondered about.

She hadn't realized Tryst had moved until she noticed him leaning over her. He ran his hand along her jaw and gently cupped her head as he leaned in. He was going to kiss her, and much as her brain screamed to push him away, because that's the kind of girl she was—she didn't let any man take what he wanted from her—Lexi ignored her strict common sense and let whatever was going to happen, happen.

As their mouths connected, his hair spilled forward to tickle her cheek. Softly, his lips touched hers, not demanding. He wasn't sure if she would allow it, so he was using caution. Perhaps testing the ice, to see if it was safe to tread?

Please do, she thought. *Break my ice. Fall into me.*

Lexi spread her hand around his back, her fingers crushing into the soft fleece shirt that had to be a loaner. She clutched, pulling him toward her, following instinct and resisting better judgment. Tryst deepened their kiss, opening her mouth with a lash of his tongue to her upper lip. He traced along her lower lip and he flicked it across her teeth, teasing her to do the same. Their tongues pressed, tip to tip, then glided along each other. He tasted like chocolate and smelled like snow. The heat of him warmed her from crown to toes as it spread little fire trickles through her blood.

Lexi opened her mouth wider and danced her tongue with his, drawing him into her, luring without realizing she was leading him. The wolf groaned deeply and clutched her head with both hands, standing over her, straddling her legs, his knees crushed against her thighs. She wanted to pull him down onto her, but the position excited. He above and in command, and she taking what he wanted to give her, arching upward to meet him because she wanted to do that—to surrender to his command. To be his—a werewolf's lover.

And what he commanded stirred her heartbeats to a rapid pace and ignited a desire she'd long wondered if it even existed. By the gods, it did exist, and this wolf sparked it to a flame.

He threaded his fingers through her hair, the scurry of his slightly fumbling touch shivering down her neck and lifting goose bumps on her skin. Her nipples tightened. Wanting, so desperately, she arched up toward him, her knees bending and her foot curling out to tuck behind his knee.

Just when she thought to draw him forward with a clever turn of her toes, she heard someone clear their throat.

Trystan stood abruptly, the loss of his mouth against hers drawing up a soft moan from Lexi. She swiped her fingers across her hot, moist lips and spied her sister standing in the doorway, hands on her hips and an admonishing shake of her head bringing Lexi down from the thrill of the moment like a crash on the half-pipe.

"Uh." Tryst looked at her with a wince, then, shrugging a hand through his hair, sheepishly stepped toward the door. "I was just leaving. Talk to you later, Lexi." And he vanished, leaving her to face the brunt of Lana's accusatory smirk all by herself.

"What do you want?" Lexi asked, glaring at her sister through her glasses, and thankful that no one could see her eyes through the blue mirrored lenses.

"I'm not sure." Lana sashayed in and inspected the empty cup sitting on Tryst's chair. "If I said I wanted a handsome, virile wolf to kiss me like that, I'm not sure the outsider would give it to me, or that I'd welcome his touch. He's not one of us. And yet, you've snagged yourself a wolf, sister. I'm surprised."

"And why is that?" she asked, trying to pull a nonchalant blankness over her face, when all she wanted to do was lie back and revel in the delicious sensations of pleasure that still coursed through her body. "He's just a…"

"A what?" Lana waited hopefully, pushing the painful screw in deeper with her forced sweetness. "A good kisser? Does Daddy know you were kissing a nonpack member?"

"Don't tell him, Lana. He's not doing well. The last thing I want to do is—"

"Break the old man's heart." Lana pouted. "You know it would kill Daddy if he knew his daughter was fooling around with an unaligned wolf."

Good thing Lana had no clue to Tryst's heritage. She'd use that against him in a flash by going straight to Sven.

"Though he is cute." Lana coyly twirled a strand of hair around her finger. "How'd you manage to snag his attention? You walk around like an old pouty puss all the time. And those stupid glasses. Does he know your secret?"

Lexi stood abruptly, bringing herself face-to-face with her sister's smirk. "Lana, I swear I will—"

"Will what? You going to beat me up if I tattle? Just like your boyfriend beat up my boyfriend?"

"He is not my—Tryst was just trying to make sure Sven didn't operate equipment he had no sense in using in the first place, and look what happened."

Lana sighed. "Sven may be stupid, but he means well."

"He upset you so much you went crying to Daddy."

"I needed a hug. Is anything wrong with that? Well, you wouldn't know what physical touch is like. Or would you? You two were getting closer and closer—"

"Not as close as I've seen you and Sven. Sometimes it looks like the two of you are doing tonsil surgery on one another."

Lana tossed her hair over a shoulder and gave Lexi her classic imperious lift of the nose. "He's a brute, I admit that, but he's going to be the scion."

"Did Father tell you that?"

"Not yet, but who else? Sven is the obvious choice. And then when Daddy dies…"

Lexi gripped her sister by the sleeve. "Don't you dare say that."

"Well. I can see snogging with the outsider did nothing to settle your bitchiness. Let go, that's silk. It'll wrinkle." Lexi dropped her sister's arm. "Be careful, Alexis. You've never been in love before. Hell, you've never had a real, lasting relationship with a man. You might jump too far, and then, well, falling for an omega wolf won't be good for the pack, you know that. They'll beat the crap out of him if they know he's touched you. And if any bits of him survive that beating, they'll sweep him up and toss him out to feed the winter hawks."

"That's disgusting, Lana, especially coming from you."

"I'm just trying to warn you. I care about you, Lexi. You know I do."

Lexi nodded. "And the way you show it is so touching."

Lana drew her gaze down Lexi as if she were made of rock, a look she'd mastered when she was eight, before turning and sashaying out, leaving the bedroom door open.

Plopping onto the couch, Lexi closed her eyes and blew out her breath. Lana was right. Dallying with an unaligned wolf would set off every male in the pack. Despite the fact none of them would touch her with a ten-foot pole, the notion that another wolf could have her would never jibe with their pack creed: to protect the family at all costs.

She glanced outside. In two nights the moon would be full. Traditionally, the night before and following the full moon were nights of intense sexual desire for the male wolf. He needed sex to sate himself or the werewolf would come out. The full moon was the eve reserved to let out the werewolf for a much-deserved run.

Lexi usually stayed in her locked room on those two nights, not that any of the males came near her, but a few made attempts now and then. If they hadn't an outlet, like a visit to a nearby town to find a woman, or a mortal female they could turn to, or even one of the seven females in the pack, then they'd take themselves away from the castle for a long night run.

The avalanche had packed them inside the castle like sardines with no means to travel away. How would the pack males sate themselves tomorrow night? And would a nonpack male like Trystan have the same intense desires?

Trystan was wandering toward his room when the male he knew as Liam nodded at him and said, "I've just come from the principal's quarters. He wants to speak to you."

"Okay." That was weird. Another chat? "How is he doing?"

"Not well. So don't stay any longer than he wishes you there. Got it?"

"Right, thanks. Er, I heard you were working on the snowplow. Need any help?"

"As a matter of fact, yes. You got any mechanical skills?"

"I rebuilt the engine of my Jeep last year."

"All right. Stop by when you get a chance."

Tryst nodded and headed down the hall to the south tower, running over all sorts of scenarios in his brain. He'd be admonished for fighting with Sven, even though he had taken the brunt of the blows, and had officially been marked the loser. He'd be castigated for not keeping the idiot wolf off equipment he had no right operating. Again, he had tried. Or he'd be sent away because he was not needed here. How to leave though? He could take off walking and be in town in a few hours. No problem, save for the bitter winds currently burnishing the icy snow crust to sandpaper. Would the principal be that cruel? No doubt, in his condition, he would do whatever was required to keep his pack safe, no matter how much Tryst had helped thus far.

Prepared to accept the expulsion with grace and thanks, Tryst knocked on the door and heard a weak "Enter."

He wandered inside and through the conference room into the principal's private quarters. It was dark, with only a night lamp on by the bed. The principal set down an electronic reading device and settled his head against the pillow. He looked thin and his eyes were shadowed, the skin beneath them swollen and dark.

Going down on one knee, Tryst bowed his head for a few moments then rose. "How are you feeling, Principal Connor?"

"Not well."

"The wolfsbane not working?"

"It is none of your concern."

"Sorry. Any friend of my father's I also count as a friend."

"Forgive me. I'm testy. You didn't deserve that." Connor gave an acknowledging nod. "You are aware your father and I are friends in the manner that we agree to disagree, but rarely will you find us sharing drinks."

"Of course." While Rhys Hawkes was open and kind to all breeds, Tryst understood that the principal probably used some friendships for a political means. "Liam said you wanted to speak to me?"

"I've heard you've been tagging along behind my daughter."

"Uh…"

He wouldn't exactly call it tagging along. More like worshipping, taking any chance that he could get to catch her smile. And the kiss. That incredible contact between two hungry mouths. Hot chocolate and sweet lips and wicked tongue. Did he have to mention that?

"Principal?"

"Alexis is beautiful. I can understand your interest in her. But she's not on your radar, boy. I know you're stuck with us for a while, and I do appreciate that you are willing to help us dig out."

"I'd be honored if you'll allow me to stay on and help."

"That pleases me. You're one of few who is sensible

and seems to have some practical yet useful skills. But tomorrow night precedes the full moon."

Tryst nodded, sensing where the man was headed.

"Most of the males avoid my daughter for reasons she prefers to keep to herself. You, apparently, have not learned that she is like wolfsbane to the male wolf."

"I don't understand."

"What I'm saying, outsider, is you'd best get yourself away from the castle tomorrow night, and stay away from my daughter if you don't want me to have Sven tear your head from your shoulders."

Now that had been clear as a bell. "Message received, Principal. I'll take a nice long walk tomorrow night."

"And the night following the full moon, if you are still around."

"Of course. Is that all, Principal?"

"Yes." The old wolf coughed and Tryst could see how painful his condition must be as the man's face clenched and he clutched his chest. "Don't make me regret my kindness toward you, Hawkes."

Tryst bowed again and backed from the room. "You can trust me, Principal Connor."

He closed the door behind him and immediately regretted his words. He'd just agreed not to touch Lexi. What the hell?

But only on the nights preceding and following the full moon, his conscience prodded. *You can touch her any other time.*

He doubted the principal would appreciate Tryst's interpretation of his stern request.

"Hell." He strode down the dark hallway, feeling he was navigating a minefield. One wrong step in castle Wulfsiege, and he'd lose his head.

Chapter 7

Six in the morning and the castle grounds were quiet. Tryst plodded across the packed snow before the castle courtyard where Sven had managed to plow a few rows before breaking the equipment he figured must have cost the pack a cool quarter million.

He was a pretty good judge of character, and he'd known at first punch that Sven was not the brightest bulb on the string; nor did the bruiser conceive that the world was connected and he was not the star. Karma was going to give that wolf's knickers a fierce twist someday.

He wandered through the open doorway of the shed and past a bunch of parked cars. A red Porsche caught his eyes, and he guessed it belonged to the blonde princess. He wondered which one Lexi drove. He pegged her for a Range Rover, but possibly that brown Jeep 4x4 back in the corner, too. In the center of the huge shed sat the plow, where a bright work light hung from one of the yellow side mirrors. A man lay under the machine. His suede leather work pants were dirty, and his scuffed boots had seen a lot of wear.

Liam was an exemplary man, Tryst knew without having spoken more than a few words to him. The wolf was quiet yet observant and, like Tryst, seemed to live to help others and do whatever he could to lessen burdens.

"What's the prognosis?" he asked, squatting near where Liam lay.

"It's going to take a couple days for sure. He blew out the hydraulics. I had to order a part, which should be delivered in two days if the roads are cleared. You're up early."

"It's nearly daybreak. I never miss a sunrise. So can you use some help?"

A torque wrench was handed out from under the machine, and Tryst snatched it. "Find the hex bolt where I'm pointing," Liam directed, "and give it a twist."

He did as he was told and, with concentrated effort, the two managed to remove the hydraulic mechanism and lay it out on a cardboard flat in the center of the dirt-floored shed. Moving the light over the work area, Tryst wiped a smear of grease down his stomach. He had stripped to his shirt and jeans in the process of removing the hydraulics. Good hard work always brought up a sweat.

"You and Sven friends?" he dared to ask as Liam squatted over the floor, tracking the parts on the printout he'd downloaded online.

"Sven is a tool," Liam offered, and then shrugged, "Yet he's in line to become scion, although you didn't hear me say that."

"Not a wise choice for someone who may eventually lead the pack," Tryst commented. "Especially if the principal is ailing, and could be thinking incoherently. Should he be allowed to choose a successor?"

Liam shrugged. "This is an unusual circumstance. We hadn't expected to lose Vincent when the principal was in such poor health. Wish I knew what was wrong with him, if only so his daughters could have peace of mind. They both keep a stiff upper lip, but this is tearing them apart."

Tryst had noticed that about Lexi, though he wasn't sure about the sister. The blonde he'd read as a spoiled brat, prancing around in high heels and perfect hair. But that didn't mean she couldn't be torn up inside over her father.

"I think you should be scion," he proposed. "You're the most levelheaded wolf on the premises."

Liam granted him a rare but sheepish smile. "Yeah, but I'm not banging the princess. Though, I hear you're trying to."

"Bang Lana? Hell no."

"I'm talking about Lexi, the tall, cool, dark one. You've been tagging around behind her like a puppy wagging its tail."

"I have not." Tryst kicked the snowplow tire. "Maybe." He paced the edge of the cardboard flat and shoved his hands over his hair. "All right, she is pretty, and smart, and—"

"And trouble."

"What is that about? Why is it all the males seem to walk a wide circle around her? She is the best-looking female in the castle."

"Besides her sister," Liam suggested. He appeared to give that statement some thought.

"And what's with the dark sunglasses? I've never seen her without them. Do you know what her problem is?"

"Yes, I do, and if she hasn't told you yet, I respect her too much to blabber it to you."

Tryst sat before the big tire and leaned back on his palms, kicking out his boots before him. "Hell, it must be bad."

"It ain't a bouquet of roses, that's for sure. But you do know it's not wise for an unaligned wolf to go sniffing around the principal's daughter?"

"So I've been told. Principal Connor had a harsh word with me last night. He wants me to stay away from Lexi tonight."

"Just tonight?"

"And the night following the full moon. But he didn't mention the other nights of the month, so…"

Liam dropped the schematic and his eyes met Tryst's. "Listen to the old man, and fill in all those other days on your calendar. Trust me on this one, Hawkes."

Tryst nodded but couldn't inwardly agree with the terse warning. If no other wolf would go near Lexi, why couldn't he go for it? What could possibly be so wrong with the woman?

"You don't know the ways of the pack," Liam said, selecting a part from the layout before him and motioning for Tryst to find the part on the schematic. "They will kick your ass if you get too close to one of their females."

"And will you be in that ass-kicking crew?" Tryst asked.

Liam cast him a discerning once-over but didn't answer. "One of the guys said you were from the Paris pack. There's no such pack. Unless it's the Levalois pack. Bunch of pussies."

"Yeah, well, I didn't exactly specify—"

"Have you ever been in a pack, Hawkes?"

"Nope. My father was a lone wolf, and raised me the same way." He winced to know he was lying by omission, not mentioning *why* his father had never been in a pack. Liam deserved his truth but there were just some things Tryst had to hold on to. "I've always admired the idea of a pack, and have dreamed of being a part of one."

"I couldn't imagine being an omega wolf. It's got to be lonely. Doesn't your nature scream for family? A big one? And a devoted female of your breed?"

"Of course it does. And trust me, my family may be small, but they are weirdly distant. My father and I are close, but my mother, she's…she has a mental condition, and she's not always at the top of her game."

"Sorry." Liam grabbed another part and the two bent over the layout to figure what the next move should be. "No brothers or sisters?"

"I have a half brother." A full-blood vampire. Another omission Tryst felt he had to make. "We only just met each other about a year ago, because he was taken by faeries after we were born, so we're slowly getting to know one another."

Liam whistled. "Taken by faeries? Bet that's an interesting story."

"He's cool. He's a good man and has a gorgeous wife. I think we'll become close. Hell, we already are."

"I was an orphan pup," Liam said. "Edmonton took me in. Though when I was a teenager I used to wonder if maybe I was one of the principal's love children."

"As in more than one love child?"

Liam chuckled. "You haven't known Edmonton long.

The principal is a rogue. If it's truth, then I have at least a dozen half brothers and sisters in the pack. Although I've heard my father was an Irishman. So that's cool, too."

"Love children. Way to build a family."

"The principal's wife died when the princesses were young, and Edmonton was heartbroken. I don't think he could ever bring himself to make a commitment to a woman again, but that doesn't mean a man loses the need for companionship. Like I said, the man's a rogue, and usually is never without a fine female by his side. Only the past year he's been different. I think he wants to travel."

"Has he lived at Wulfsiege all his life?"

"Yes. As have we all. Though I did a stint in the village a few years ago. Expanding my horizons by working in a small auto shop, and doing carpentry jobs here and there, but I prefer living with wolves rather than mortals."

"So you got a girl, Liam?"

"Not in the pack. Right now the current squeeze is vacationing with her family in, of all places, Paris."

"Wolf?"

"Mortal. But she knows what I am, and I admire her for putting up with me. Takes a strong mortal woman to accept the werewolf, which she hasn't done yet, but I'm working on her."

"That's awesome."

"It serves as a means to an end."

"Means to an end sounds like the furthest thing from love."

"It gets me off when I need it most."

"I can understand that with the moon nearly full tonight. But what have you got against Paris?"

"Those pansy packs in Paris?"

"Hey now, I'm from Paris."

"They're citified. Couldn't drive a snowplow through a rainstorm without destroying the thing."

The two laughed and worked together to lift a heavy hydraulic column and position it on the cardboard work area.

"So what are you going to do tonight?" Tryst asked. "Since you don't have a woman at Wulfsiege, you don't hang around the castle, do you? I'm thinking of going for a long run."

"The males who do not have females here at the castle head out for a run as a pack. You want to join us?"

Tryst's mouth fell open. "Seriously? You would let me join you? The pack? I'd be honored."

"Meet up with us on the west side of the castle before midnight. We leave our clothes in an outbuilding designed as a post for before and after midnight runs."

"Thanks, man. I'll see you then."

Around two, Lexi strode the hallway before the destroyed glass wall that a couple wolves were currently boarding up, after having shoveled away the snow butting up against the outer wall. She'd located a construction crew that could come in a week and, anticipating the plow would be fixed and the area would be cleared so visitors could get in, had scheduled the work to be done.

"Lunch still available?"

She swung around to find Tryst walking toward her, his coat tied low about his hips and his face smeared with streaks of black grease. Yet through it all, his smile beamed and those big blue eyes radiated warmth. He looked like something she would like to slowly indulge in, as if he were a rich dessert.

Remembering the wolves not far away working on the window, she assumed her in-charge mode, setting back her shoulders and clasping the iPad with the open schedule app to her chest. "How's the plow coming along?"

"Great." He put an arm around her shoulder, intending to walk her toward the keep, but with a shrug from her, he dropped the arm. "Sorry. Was that too forward?"

"It is around other wolves."

"Right. Your father did warn me."

"He did? Then you should heed that warning." She hated saying that. She wanted him to ignore the warning and kiss her again—what her father or the pack thought of it be damned.

He shoved his hands in the pockets of his work leathers. "Do you want me to stay away from you?"

"I, uh—"

"Thought so. Have you eaten? Will you have lunch with me?"

Despite knowing that a warning from her father should be taken extremely seriously, Lexi could not resist the man's sexy wink. And really, he did need to clean up a bit, and she did have a washroom. "Let's go to my room, and we'll have lunch sent in."

"Sounds great, but let's make it quick. I promised Liam I'd bring back lunch for him."

Once inside her room, Tryst closed the door behind them and pushed her against the wall. He paused before diving in for a kiss, his eyes tracking her face, moving over the sunglasses and along the frame of her hair. He was waiting for something, and she instinctually sensed what it was.

She nodded, giving him the permission he sought. Without a word, he pinned her wrists to the wall and kissed her as if only she could feed his hunger. He was not aggressive, and he was. He didn't demand, yet he did. He took from her, but also gave. She threaded her fingers up through the ends of his hair, tugging, holding him against her, silently demanding in return.

When she ignored her brain and allowed her body to lead the way, she got everything she wanted. And more.

"Sorry if I offended you last night."

"I've already told you." She kissed his mouth quickly, then deeply, tickling across his tongue with hers in a fast tease. "Nothing you do offends me. Not even this." With a fingertip, she traced a smear of grease striping his jaw.

"Then tell me," he said, leaning his hips against hers and allowing her to feel his erection melding against her belly. So hard. So…long. *Oh, Lexi, control your purring desire to touch that.* "What is it that makes all the males in the pack walk a wide circle around you?"

Buzz kill. Like that, Lexi's desire plunged.

Pushing out of his embrace, she paced toward the floor-to-ceiling windows that overlooked the east courtyard. Apprehension tightened her shoulders and she clasped her arms before her stomach. The loss of his heat against her mouth teased up regret.

He had every right to know why the pack males avoided her. But the explanation wasn't easy. She didn't know where to start. One advantage to growing up in Wulfsiege was that everyone else had simply always known so she hadn't had to explain to them.

She respected Tryst, and she didn't want him to stop respecting her. Could she tell him? How to start?

"Lexi, I really like you. I sort of feel like we're two of a kind, standing on the edge, not really in the group.

I can't imagine there's anything about you that would make me do a one-eighty. Though, I should tell you, I'll be one-eightying tonight. Your father specifically told me to stay the hell away from you during the pre-moon."

She nodded, assuming Father would have said as much to Tryst, who wasn't dialed in to the pack ways but who must also experience the incredible sexual compulsion the males felt the days before and after the full moon. "That's honorable of you."

"Yeah, but it's going to be tough. I'll be thinking of you the whole time."

"You will?" She turned, and found it was hard to resist the urge to rush into his big strong arms. Nonjudgmental arms. He deserved to know her truth. Slowly, she approached Trystan. "I've been thinking of you a lot, too." Of him standing over her, commanding her body to rise up to meet his in a dance of passion. "When you kiss me…"

He broached the distance and swept her into a firm and demanding kiss that took away her breath and stole her sighs. It was as if he marked her with an indelible brand, and she wanted it to be visible, so she could show others that, yes, she belonged to someone.

"When I kiss you?" he prompted.

"It's like no other kiss I've had," she said, trying to sort out her feelings as she spoke them. "So intense. Like…"

"Like I don't think I'll ever find another woman who makes me feel the way you do when we come together, Lexi. Our breaths combine, our mouths touch. Our hearts beat for one another."

"Yes, like that. And I want others to know about it. To know that you've kissed me."

"That probably wouldn't be too smart right now."

"I know. They'd rip you apart if they knew you'd even touched me. Oh, Tryst." She extended her arms and stepped as far from him as she could without letting go of him. "I don't want to lie to you."

His frown creased the grease smudge on his cheek.

"Not really a lie, just lie by omission, which is almost as bad. I don't want you to think poorly of me."

"Lexi, I would never. If there's something about you that you need to talk about I am the guy you can tell it to. Me, the dude with the half-breed dad and vampire mother. Do you think it gets much worse than that?" He held out his hand, palm up, not threatening but waiting for her move. "You can trust me, Lexi."

"I think I can. And I know if it doesn't go well, at least I was honest with you."

"If it doesn't— Lexi?"

He held such confusion and gentleness in his eyes that she wanted to make it right between them. To not hide anything. And if he could not accept her at face value, then so be it.

With a decisive nod, she bowed her head, and pulled off her sunglasses, folding them carefully in her hands. Unable to meet the eyes of the one man she most wanted to please, she waited, wondering how exactly to go about this.

Too late to back out now. You've already taken off your glasses. You are *going about this.*

She closed her eyes. *Don't cry. You can trust him.*

The touch of Tryst's finger under her chin tilted up her face. Eyes closed and heartbeats thundering, Lexi fought the urge to flee, to hide away from the best thing she'd found because she didn't want to lose that best so quickly.

The stroke of his thumb along her lips urged her to

open her mouth. He traced her lower lip softly, so tenderly she wanted to moan at the aching sweetness of it. But her heart pounded with fear even as he smoothed over her cheek and dusted a fingertip along her lashes. Butterflies set free in her stomach, fluttering up and about her desperate heart, twining it with invisible and squeezing ribbons. Tryst's breath across her mouth softened her fears and…she opened her eyes and looked into his.

"Holy shit!" Tryst jumped back.

Lexi bit down hard on her lip, cursing her stupidity.

Chapter 8

"Your eyes…" He grasped the air between them and bent to study her eyes.

It was so hard not to close them again, but she'd done it. For good or for ill, Lexi had exposed her biggest secret.

"They're shifted," he said.

Yes, gold, the color all wolves' eyes turned after they had shifted to wolf or werewolf form—but never when in were, or human, form as she had been—forever.

"Is it the moon?" he asked. "Have you already started to shift for tonight? Do you want me to leave? Hell, Lexi?"

"It's nothing to do with the moon. Unfortunately." She rubbed her palms together, drawing in a breath of fortitude. "This is what I am, Tryst. This is my dark secret. My eyes have been this way since puberty. They are the only thing on me that has ever shifted."

He cocked his head into a querying tilt. "I don't understand?"

"I can't shift. I have never shifted to wolf or werewolf form. I never will."

"Wow. Really? That's gotta—" He frowned.

"Yep, it sucks," she finished for him, having thought the same thousands of times over the years.

"I didn't mean to say, well, I didn't say that." He slid a palm down her shoulder, his eyes never leaving hers. "So your eyes…"

"At puberty, when all wolves come into their first shift, my eyes changed from blue to gold, and then… nothing. No fur. No tail. Not even a howl. I don't know what is wrong with me, Tryst, and my father has had all the best doctors examine me. I'm…broken."

"No, you're not broken. You're just…not."

And he pulled her into a hug that surprised her because she had expected him to push her away and retreat as had all other males in the pack. They were frightened of her oddness, afraid she wasn't normal. Not right. Broken.

She was broken. If she couldn't shift, she could never become fully werewolf. And when wolves mated to procreate it was always in werewolf form.

"I can't shift," she said, "which means I'll never be able to conceive. Not the most appealing attribute in a mate to any male wolf with an ounce of pride and a paternal desire."

"Don't say that, Lexi. Any man would be proud to call you his. You're gorgeous. You're smart. You can kick my ass on the half-pipe any day."

She smiled at his way of trying to diminish the pain. She appreciated it, but she also wasn't stupid. Once her truth sank in, Tryst would walk that same wide circle around her as did all the rest of the pack.

"And you're not broken." He hugged her again and this time she almost slipped into believing that he genuinely cared. She wanted to buy into that belief. "You're just not finished yet. Right?"

"I will never be complete. But I've accepted it. I know I'll never marry and have children like Lana will, but there are things I can do to help the pack and make Wulfsiege the best place to raise a family."

"It'll happen," he encouraged. "The shift. It has to."

Because if it did not, she would die a lonely old wolf.

A knock on the door alerted them that lunch had arrived. Lexi put on her sunglasses and answered the door, bringing the tray inside to set near the bedside. When she turned around from the table, Tryst stood right there, in her space, forcing her to see him as she'd just forced him to see her truths. He pulled off her sunglasses and kissed each of her eyelids. Softly, lingering. She'd never known a man could be so gentle, and a sigh drifted from her lips.

"You're beautiful," he said, and kissed her mouth. "And you're perfect the way you are. Never believe anything else."

"You're too kind, but I've learned a thing or two about you. You're kind to everyone. You can't not help out, or provide assistance or an encouraging word. Your parents certainly raised you right."

"I do give them both a lot of credit. Even my mother. She taught me to respect all breeds and people with disabilities and those who don't look like us. It's a big, beautiful world, Lexi. We make it what it is with every word, every step, and every breath we take. I want to keep it beautiful."

"You're doing an excellent job of it. But like you said about putting your energy out into the world? Life is energy. The werewolf is your life. It is my life. But my werewolf energy just isn't working."

He kissed her forehead. Wrapped in his arms, she surrendered to the luxury of his embrace. Nothing mattered right now. It couldn't. She wanted to take in his energy. Maybe he could provide the life energy she lacked?

It was a strange notion. But she clung to the idea that her involvement with Tryst would only improve her life, perhaps help her overlook all that she was lacking.

"You go and take Liam some lunch. I had them bring extra sandwiches. I'm kind of tired. Think I'll just eat by myself and relax a bit, if you don't mind."

He nodded and, without another word, headed out with lunch in hand.

Lexi pressed her palms to the closed door, listening to Tryst's retreating footsteps. He'd left without argument, without begging to share a few more minutes with her. As teardrops spilled from her gold eyes, she fell to her knees cursing, for not the first time, her broken body and heart.

Tryst trekked to the end of the hallway and made a fast right turn, stopped, and pressed his back to the wall, head falling back and eyes closing as he exhaled deeply. The bag of sandwiches dangled from his hand.

She'd never shifted. Lexi was stuck in a weird kind of partial shift.

He could kick himself right now for his initial re-action, but he'd been freaked. Her eyes had been gold, like a shiny coin. They were—hell, *eerie*. And yes, he'd played it wrong.

Maybe. He'd recovered and given her a hug, but he suspected the damage had been done. He should have taken a deep breath before reacting.

"I'm an asshole," he muttered. "But she's still gorgeous. Still the same smart, sexy woman."

Her energy was stuck, stalled somehow. But if she couldn't shift, she'd never be able to have children, to give some male wolf a family. Like him.

"Don't think like that," he argued with his conscience.

But it was difficult not to. All his life he'd dreamed of family, of living within a pack and creating home and hearth with his own children. Four or five kids sounded about right to him. A mini pack.

And now? He'd met a woman who put him head over heels like a flip on the half-pipe. And even though all the cards were stacked against him, because he was not a pack wolf, he still had chosen to pursue the princess. The outsider had dared to stake a claim.

But now? Would his efforts be worth the final result, which promised no family? Could he sacrifice that dream for a girl he'd known less than a week? How did he know he'd never run into another like her? Someone who made his heart stop, his words fumble, someone who brought his cocky attitude down to a simmer. She'd hooked him with one perfect unabashed smile.

And he wanted to stay hooked.

"I have to. She needs me. And I need her."

Whatever the future offered him, he'd take it and make it his own.

Lana carried the dinner tray Sven had picked up in the cafeteria for her father. She'd been sharing suppers with her father for years. It was their time together to talk about how the day had gone. She appreciated that Sven ran to get the food for her because she didn't like the smell in the cafeteria. Cooking meat offended her. She had always taken ridicule for not eating meat, but it seemed cannibalistic to her on a level she didn't want to explore.

"Give your father my regards," Sven said, stroking her hair behind her ear and kissing her on the lobe.

She hated that. The kiss always echoed like a smack in her ear and he was slobbery. But his kindness overwhelmed the discomfort. He did have a kind bone in his body; Lexi was wrong about him.

Liam strolled toward them, hands in his pockets, his head held high. He was one of very few in the pack who did not look down when around Sven. Good for him. He smelled liked grease or fuel, and she remembered he was working on the broken plow. She was so conflicted about her feelings for Sven. It was difficult deciding how to feel.

"Liam." Sven reached out and tagged the wolf as he made to walk past them. "I want to know I have your support, man."

"For what?" While he maintained a level head and looked Sven in the eye, Lana had noted Liam never looked directly at her. And yet, with a glance over her shoulder, she often caught him looking at her only after she'd passed him by. It was a little creepy. Did he always watch her when she wasn't looking?

"I need you to support me to become principal of the pack," Sven said, as if the wolf were an idiot not to know what he was talking about.

"Principal? Our leader isn't dead, Sven."

"But he's ailing. We need leadership. You know we do. Now."

"I agree with that. No one expected Vince would be lost in the avalanche, but…"

Lana felt Liam's regard as if a warm touch at her cheek. She looked aside, hoping Sven didn't notice.

"But nothing. We've got to take charge before the principal dies and leaves the pack in chaos. I will ask you to be my scion, Liam."

She caught Liam's wince. Had he no desire to hold a position of authority? He was a quiet man who never did get involved in a fight or scuffle, but Lana thought he would make an excellent scion. Fair but firm. As well, he'd balance Sven's aggressive style of leadership with a cool head.

"I'd prefer to stand back and see what happens to Principal Connor."

Sven stomped before Liam, blocking his retreating steps with a hard shoulder to Liam's shoulder. The two wolves engaged in a stare down, from which Lana felt waves of tension radiating outwardly. "If you're not with me now, Liam, I can't bring you along as my second. You're either in or you're out."

Lana hoped the look she gave Liam was viewed as pleading, but he didn't even blink away from Sven's stare. And she wanted the quiet wolf to agree, for the reason that they needed a level head in leadership alongside her fiancé, but Liam shook his head and stepped back.

"Can't do it. Sorry."

He strode off. Sven's anger tightened the air and Lana felt the hair on her neck prickle.

"I should get this to Daddy." She rushed away. It was never wise to remain near Sven when his anger stung the air.

Chapter 9

The moon sat high and bright in the starless gray sky. Lexi pressed her fingers to the window, the cold fogging around her fingers as she gazed out across the grounds. The pack males had loped off toward the forest moments earlier, and bringing up the tail end of the group had been a gorgeous red-furred wolf.

She'd never known what it felt like to race across the snow on four legs, paws beating the ground, senses on ultrahigh. Lana had often boasted over the freedom of it, but also complained how nasty shifting could be when she returned home because when she shifted back to were form her hair was mussed and it left her skin dirty and in need of moisturizer.

Lexi thought it would be nice to come back to were shape feeling her muscles stretched and brushing off the dirt. To finally know her full potential as the werewolf she had been born. Why her body had gotten stuck in a partial shift—eyes only—she would never know. The doctors suspected she would never shift. Broken, she. And no satisfying match for any wolf who wished to raise a brood within the pack.

She couldn't imagine what it must feel like to crave the shift, or to crave the sex that could keep the werewolf at bay on this night. Her body repulsed those cravings.

Yet, deep inside, somewhere, she hungered for *him*. For another kiss. Another tender touch. Perhaps a claiming embrace. And her skin warmed and prickled to remember the scintillating allure of Tryst's skin against hers. Soft, their connection, then a little harder, warm and firm; it stirred her desire and she moaned with want.

Had his touch awakened something inside her? Tapped into her cold heart? Was it possible? Perhaps, but he could never reach the broken part of her that required fixing. No man could be capable of such a feat.

Watching until the red wolf disappeared around the copse of white beech, she then turned and slid down against the window, clutching her knees and burying her tears in muffled sniffles.

The pack raced over the snowy hillside, following Liam's lead. When in wolf form, the *were*—or human—mind was present but set back, not quite able to think in human thoughts yet capable of recognizing pack members by scent, and knowing things humans did yet unable to vocalize except with howls and yips.

Tryst surrendered to the animal within and took in scents of tree bark, snow and nearby animals as the world rushed under his paws. His claws dug into the snowpack, sending up whifs of snow in his wake. He dodged alongside one of the wolves and they raced, dashing at top speed, until slowing and coming to a stop at the peak of a hill surrounded by trees coated in white hoarfrost.

Moonlight glistened over the wolves' fur and puddled in the paw prints pocking the snow. Shades of white, gray and black painted the world, and everywhere the snow glittered, almost as if they trod faery grounds.

The males caroused, nipping playfully and dancing about one another. It did not become aggressive. Liam, tail held high, kept watch should any of the males snarl or defy another with a lowered head and revealing teeth. But, as well, this was a time of freedom, and none would be chastised for acting out as their nature demanded.

Liam put out the first howl, a long, high call to the night. The other wolves joined in, growing a chorus to the wild. Tryst added his voice, reveling in the shared camaraderie for the first time in his life. Jubilant, his wolf pounced through the powdery snow cover. This night he had found a home.

Near morning they returned to the outbuilding and the wolves shifted, coming to were form, their extremities stretching to human length, accompanied by groans and sighs as they left behind the freedom of the wild.

Tryst tugged up his jeans and nodded to Liam, who high-fived him.

"Thanks, man," Tryst said. "That was like nothing I've ever experienced."

"You could have it," Liam said, "if you joined the pack."

"The Alpine pack would admit a lone wolf?"

"You'd probably have to challenge a few of us to show your strength and intent, and someone would have to put in a good word with Principal Connor, but yes, I know you would be welcomed. All the men here tonight agree you are a good man."

"Wow." He didn't know what else to say to the generous offer.

Thoughts immediately shifted to his family in Paris. His mother, Viviane, was more sane than insane lately, and he never missed spending the weekend cooking outside on the patio with her and talking about her paintings. His father and he were close, and he often did jobs for Hawkes Associates, and would really miss that work, but he could do the same work at a distance, because the firm operated worldwide.

And then there was Vaillant, his vampire half brother. He was growing to like him, and they'd gone to nightclubs a few times together. Vail liked the faery clubs, which kind of freaked out Tryst, because his brother was a recovering dust addict—one reason he felt he had to keep a sort of protective eye on his older-by-two-minutes brother.

"You thinking about it?" Liam asked.

Tryst nodded. "Lots to consider."

"Just tell me when you're ready, and I'll talk to the principal. And try to avoid any more scuffles with Sven for now. You want to appeal to the principal, not beat up his choice for scion."

"Got it. Though, I think the guy has an innate GPS that navigates his fist to my face."

"Yeah, well, he's got it in his head he wants to become principal, so I'm not sure what he's up to, or of what he's capable. Lay low, in any case."

"Will do."

Tryst lingered in the building, pulling on his sweater

and boots while the other wolves filed out, heading back to their beds to sleep off the long and exhilarating run.

He couldn't help but wonder what Lexi would think of the idea of him joining the pack. Would she approve, or would having him around all the time offend her?

She'd said nothing about him offending her, and he'd taken that as an open invitation to get closer to her. Close to the one woman who attracted him as no other before her.

The one woman who could never satisfy his desire to start a family because she could not shift.

How crazy was it that she had never shifted? She'd never known the freedom of racing across the earth, or the power of shifting into half were, half wolf form as werewolf and really coming into her own life energy.

She couldn't know what she was missing. It must drive her insane with wondering and endless hope.

But Tryst knew one thing: he could be happy with a woman like her. Up to this point, he'd accepted that he'd probably have to marry a mortal, because female wolves were not jumping all over him, a lone wolf.

But to snag a mate who was werewolf? It would rock.

It might also drive him nuts if Lexi could never know the immense pleasure of mating while in werewolf shape. He'd done it once with a female wolf. While in were form he generally did not recall what his werewolf had done or experienced, but the remembrance of mating had stayed with him as a feeling rather than visual memory. Out of this world, insanely satisfying sex. Like nothing he could ever describe, but like everything he wanted again, and again and again.

"Lexi," he muttered. "What am I going to do about this mark you've scored into my heart?"

Was he falling in love with her? He'd been in love a

time or two with mortals, but this felt different. Stronger. Deeper. Compelling. Almost as if he was in the exact place he should be right now, and he shouldn't go anywhere else. Ever. Not without Lexi by his side.

Tryst wanted to go immediately to Lexi's room, but a crazy notion instead veered him toward the south tower where he asked permission to see the principal. As he waited outside the door, he smoothed back the hair from his face. He should have taken a look in the mirror, made himself more presentable. As Liam had said, if he wanted to be considered for the pack he should present a good front.

He hadn't made a decision about that yet. But he wouldn't ignore the proposition.

"Five minutes," the assistant told Tryst, and stepped aside to allow him entrance.

He could hear Principal Connor's raspy breathing as he entered the room. The man was lying in bed. He rushed forward, but as he got to the end of the bed, he remembered protocol, bent to one knee and bowed his head. "Principal Connor, thank you for seeing me. I'm worried about you. Is there anything I can do? Perhaps I can contact my father for you?"

The principal smirked and gestured for Tryst to walk around to the side of the bed. His head was supported by a thick pillow, his lips dry and his eyes bloodshot. Not looking as well as he had when he'd given him the terse warning yesterday. Tryst's heart went out to the man and his family. No one should have to suffer.

"My father knows the best doctors," Tryst tried, but the old wolf put up a hand to beg his silence.

"Thank you," Edmonton rasped, "for respecting my request. Last night."

"No problem. Your daughter is…" He shouldn't let

on that he admired her, but that would be lying. The old man must suspect he was interested in Lexi; otherwise, he would have never issued the warning. "I understand you love your daughter, Principal, but what I don't understand is your worry over her when you know she is unable to shift."

Edmonton choked and Tryst grabbed the water glass by the bed and helped him to drink. "Sorry. I shouldn't upset you."

"She told you?" the wolf rasped.

"Yes, she showed me her eyes."

"She must...have reason to reveal herself to you. You said...you would stay away from her."

"I am. I did last night. But I consider her a friend. And she is the castle chatelaine. We do run into one another."

"Be truthful with me, boy. What...does she mean to you?"

There it was. He couldn't lie to the pack leader. Doing so would put him in the same ranks as Sven. The Nord, indeed. And if it gave any reason for the principal to disapprove his future quest for pack admission, he couldn't regret the truth now. "I like Alexis, Principal Connor. I respect her. Admire her."

"Do you love her?"

Trystan shrugged. "It's been less than a week. I haven't known her that long."

"Tell me...boy."

The principal's anger was apparent in his sharp tone. Tryst did not want to risk upsetting him, thus pushing him into a weaker state. But he'd come here to make his truth known. He was no man to sneak about and try to pull one over on a person of such authority. His father would never allow him to use duplicity with friends.

"With due respect, Principal, I think I am falling in love with your daughter."

"That is enough." The principal coughed and gestured forcefully that Trystan step away.

He backed to the end of the bed and offered another respectful bow.

"I would never lie to you, Principal Connor. And I'm sorry if it offends you, but I don't think a guy can help who he falls in love with. I would never do anything to harm your daughter. And if joining the pack would change your opinion of me—"

"Leave her alone. Pack wolf or not, I'll not condone the two of you pairing up."

"But I'm determined to do this correctly. If the pack would have me—"

"We will not," the principal said with astonishing clarity. "No wolf with vampiric lineage…is worthy of my daughter, broken as she may be. You serve me no honor by ignoring my request to stay away from her."

"I did. Last night I went out with the other pack members. It was an honor to be invited along with them."

"Liam can be too kind. Know that I appreciate your help here at Wulfsiege, but I'll see that you are removed from the premises if you so much as look at Alexis again."

Hell, this was not going well. He didn't want to get kicked off the property, and he certainly wasn't improving his chances to be considered as pack material.

"I respect your wishes, Principal Connor, and will honor them. But unless Lexi is also in agreement, I can't promise she will do the same."

"You let me deal with my daughter, boy. Leave now."

Tryst nodded and left the tower room. That had not gone well at all. But he didn't regret standing before the pack leader and declaring his truths. If only there was a way to make the principal understand how much he cared for Lexi. It was apparent no other males in the pack had an interest in her. Shouldn't the principal want to see his daughter paired with another wolf?

Sure, but not one with vampires in his family.

"Damned vampire blood."

Smacking a fist into his palm as he charged around the corner in the hallway, Tryst ran right into the blonde princess. She collided with his chest. Standing a bit taller than Lexi due to the high heels, her hands roamed over his abs and she cooed, tilting up her blue eyes and licking her red lips.

"I found a big, strong one."

"Take your hands off me, Alana."

"Why? You afraid I'm too much woman for you? You prefer them broken, like my sister?"

"Your sister is not broken." He grabbed her wrist and she squealed sweetly. Her theatrics turned him off and toyed with the anger that simmered just beneath the surface. "Don't do that, someone will hear you."

"You worried Sven will beat you up again?"

"What's that about Sven beating on someone?" came a gruff voice from around the corner.

Tryst's heart dropped to his gut. The man had mastered perfect timing, to Tryst's detriment. He wasn't able to extricate himself from Alana's clinging, groping fingers before her fiancé saw them in what must look like an embrace.

"This is not what you think it is. She was touching me." He pushed the tiny blonde away from him, a bit too roughly, and she landed in Sven's arms with a distressed cry. Great little actress, she was.

"You are going to die, outsider!"

Yes, yes, he should have seen that one coming. Great. The day was going swimmingly, and all he'd done was shift to were form after a good long run and take a stroll through the castle.

"Now, Sven." Alana turned in her man's arms and gave him an Emmy-winning pout. "You were going to have breakfast with me and Daddy. Can you wait to kill him after that?"

The brutish wolf growled and his jaws ground together sharply. His biceps flexed madly. He was already strangling Tryst in his mind.

Tryst lifted his head, defying the wolf with a direct stare. He could do the biceps flex, but that would just be childish. He wanted to say, *Bring it,* but on the other hand, Liam's words to avoid Sven rang loudly.

"Of course, sweetie. Two hours," he said to Tryst. "In the keep."

"The keep is filled with the wounded," Tryst said.

"It's filled with my family. I want them to see me tear you apart, outsider. If you are late, you will be branded a coward and tossed from the castle like yesterday's trash."

"Got it," Tryst muttered as the twosome pushed past him, and headed toward the tower room. "Peachy."

Well, he did like a good fight, and Sven was the strongest wolf in the castle. If he was going down, best he do so under the Nordic Warrior's hand. On the other hand, he wasn't about to do any such thing as go down. He had begun to feel accepted, a part of this pack, and he liked that feeling. And he wasn't willing to give it up because of one idiot wolf.

Chapter 10

Lexi entered the keep, startled to discover a fight was going on in the corner opposite where the infirm were being cared for, though the few injured still occupying cots were sitting and had improved greatly. She marched over to the circle of wolves surrounding the fight and found Lana eagerly cheering on the two wolves who had stripped to jeans and boots and who were beating on each other with furious fists.

Tryst and Sven again?

"What's going on?"

"They're fighting over me," Lana cooed with a flutter of her lashes at Lexi. "Isn't it sweet? Sven caught Trystan with his hands all over me, and now he's going to rip the outsider's head off."

Lexi gaped, but upon seeing her sister's triumphant grin, she thought better than to assume that Tryst actually had been touching her. If her suspicions were correct, it had probably been Lana's hands on Tryst, not the other way around.

But then again, she *had* recently revealed her shifted gold eyes to him. Had he been so disgusted he'd decided to make a play for the prettier sister?

No, Lexi, you're smarter than that. And she knew Lana, Mistress of Inappropriate Flirtation, had mastered the art of doing anything for attention.

"Sven's an idiot," she said. Hands on hips, she stepped to the edge of the circle to observe the fight. "And Trystan can take him any day."

Seemingly offended her sister hadn't cried over the notion that Tryst might have been manhandling her, Lana tilted her a pouty lip and marched off.

"This is not going to go well should he want to join the pack," Liam said to Lexi as he leaned in. "I told him to fight a few wolves, but that he should avoid your father's choice for scion."

"Tryst wants to join the pack?" He hadn't mentioned that to her.

And where had he been all morning? She'd thought he might come in to say hello to her, but nothing. She really had scared him away. Hindsight shoved an awful knife into her side.

"I put the idea in his head," Liam offered. "He's a good man. Ouch." He winced as Sven's fist connected to Tryst's side right over the kidney. "That one is going to hurt for days. But he's holding his own."

Tryst stumbled toward Lexi, blood dripping from his mouth. A goofy smile slashed through the blood, and he grimaced when he leaned forward, obviously taxing the bruised kidney.

"I didn't touch her," he managed to mumble before Sven tugged him back to the battle by the nape of his neck.

"I know that," Lexi said, more to herself than anything.

Tryst would never betray her that way. He was too honorable. He wanted her, and she wanted him. Yet this fight was only going to wrench them further apart if her father got wind of it.

"You can't tell my father," she said to Liam. "He'll make Tryst leave today."

Liam gave her a look that seemed to cut through the dark glasses she wore and burrowed right to her heart. "I will do that for you, Princess Conner, but I can't promise Sven won't tell him. Or, for that matter, your sister."

"I'll take care of Lana." She just needed to twist Princess Troublemaker's arm a bit. "I can't watch this anymore. Bring Tryst to my room after he's beat what little sense Sven has out of him, will you? I'm sure he'll be in need of medical attention. Again."

Liam nodded, but she sensed the stalwart wolf was going against his better judgment. The wolf was the strongest, and wisest in the pack and she respected him and his means of honoring her father with hard work and utter devotion. She also suspected he had a secret crush on Lana. If only Lana would notice him, then perhaps the pack could be rid of the tic known as Sven once and for all.

Marching away from the fight wasn't difficult. She didn't need to see Tryst get pummeled. She just wanted to hold him and make the hurt stop, but not before she gave Lana a piece of her mind.

Lexi found Lana in her room, throwing pillows across the floor and stomping on them. Anger subsiding at the sight of her sister's silly tantrum, Lexi propped a shoulder against the door frame and waited out the storm. Had she ever acted that way? Maybe once or twice when she'd been twelve. Why had Lana not grown up? Is that what being spoiled meant?

Lana's moods had never bothered Lexi, yet she was seeing the same sister through a different light lately. Probably through Sven-tainted glasses, and that was the ugliest view she'd ever had of her sister. That man. Whatever he touched he destroyed.

They had needed a mother growing up. Lexi's throat tightened to think it, but it was true. Being raised by Natalie hadn't been the same. The witch had been more an astute governess than someone she and her sister could run to and put their arms around when they had needed a hug, or even a good cry.

Why her father had never remarried was beyond her. He certainly had taken lovers following their mother's death. Lexi had actually liked a few and had hopes for them becoming their mother. Yet she figured Edmonton would never replace his one true love, and while that warmed her heart, she truly wanted her father to be happy.

Blond hair swinging, Lana flashed a gaping moue at her. "How long have you been standing there?"

"Long enough to wonder what's up with you, sis?"

"What do you mean? Can't a girl throw some pillows around to get rid of her frustrations?"

She blew the hair from her face and assumed a modicum of calm, plopping onto the end of her unmade bed. When a pouty lip formed and it started to quiver, Lexi rushed to sit by her sister's side and hug her.

"Talk to me, Lana. It's something with Sven, isn't it?"

"He was just defending my honor against that stupid Trystan."

Lexi could read between the lines of her sister's frustration and jealousy. "He wasn't manhandling you, was he?"

Teardrops splattered Lana's pink silk lap, and she shook her head and sniffled what Lexi guessed were not fake tears. "No. He bumped into me as he turned the corner—which was very rude—but a complete accident. And then Sven saw, and well, I let him form his own conclusions. You know I like it when a man sticks up for me. Makes me feel special."

"Lana, you are special. And you don't need Sven to beat the crap out of a guy to prove it."

"Still, it's like he's willing to give blood to show me how much he loves me."

"And take blood by beating on an innocent man. What's so noble about that? That's not love, Lana. Are you and Sven all right?"

"What do you mean?"

"I worry about you sometimes, and I wonder. Like maybe you agreed to marry Sven only because you knew it would please our father. But maybe what you really want is something else. A something else you don't even have a name for."

Like the something else Lexi craved—shifting.

Lana huffed and shook her head. "There is nothing else, Lexi. We're both stuck here at Wulfsiege, destined to raise a brood—well, maybe not you, because you can't—but you know we'll be saddled with this big stupid castle forever. And the idea of giving birth abhors me. I'll lose my figure. And remember the time Frances gave birth in the keep and we watched? It looked so painful. I can't do it, Lexi, I can't."

"They have drugs for labor, you know. And Frances has always been overly dramatic. Besides, saddled with this stupid castle and pack? It doesn't have to be that way if you don't want it to be."

"Now you're just trying to make me feel better. You know the truth, Lexi. We are literal prisoners of our family blood."

Indeed. They were pack females. It wasn't like they could gather their belongings and load up their Louis Vuittons—or in Lexi's case, a large duffel—and move to a city. They couldn't enjoy the single life, dating other wolves—or even other breeds—without risking their very lives should the pack come after them.

"At least you've been given a chance at something different," Lana added. "He's cute and hot and so nice. Too bad Daddy won't approve of the match. But you're smart. Fool around with him whenever you can, Lexi. You have to take advantage of the sex while he's here. Because you know as soon as the castle gets dug out, he's gone. If Sven doesn't kill him first."

"Sven has some serious anger issues."

"Tell me about it. I think it's because he never really had a father, with him dying when he was just a baby. He's told me so much about his life before he came here. It wasn't pleasant. But it made him strong. That's how he was the only survivor of his pack when the vampires attacked."

Now she was getting closer to what she really wanted to hear from Lana. The intimate details between her and Sven.

"Has he ever hit you, Lana?"

Her sister shook her head but didn't answer. Lexi's suspicions rose. He could have hit Lana, and probably in a place where no one would notice a bruise.

"I'm serious, Lana, if he's hurt you—"

"No one would care," she started quickly. "Because that's the way they are, our alpha wolves. They're big and brutal and they're expected to be rough and tough. Not prissy like poor Rick. He'll never win a female."

"I suspect Rick is not interested in a female."

"Really? Oh, gods, I'm surprised Sven hasn't beaten the crap out of him yet. I know Sven looks at the bruises he puts on others as some kind of merit badge. Well, it's how it was when he was growing up in his former pack."

Not knowing what else to say, Lexi tucked her head aside her sister's neck. The two sniffled. It had been a while since they'd sat together in silence. But the silence didn't last long.

A huffing, bleeding wolf stomped into Lana's bedroom and his growl prompted Lexi to her feet to stand protectively before her cringing sister.

"Get out of here, Alexis," Sven hissed. "Your sister needs to wash this blood off my hands. I want that outsider gone from Wulfsiege!"

"He wasn't touching Lana," Lexi tried, and it took all her courage not to cringe as Sven leaned over her, growling and showing his bloodied teeth. He smelled rank. "Tryst had just bumped into her in the hallway as they turned the corner at the same time."

"Sounds like touching to me. Did you hear me? I said to get out!"

Lexi glanced at Lana, whose eyes were wet with tears, but her sister nodded that she should leave. Walking away was one of the most difficult things she had ever done, but when she got to the threshold, Lexi put a palm to the door frame and, drawing up a breath of courage, said, "If you hurt my sister, if you so much as push her, I will come after you, Sven."

Her body was slammed against the door frame, and an arm wrenched behind her back. Lexi winced as the brute weight of the wolf pressed her hard against the pink-painted wall. His breath reeked of blood.

"Tough words coming from a mistake."

She closed her eyes, tasting her blood trickle over her tongue. Mistake is what Sven called her. A broken mistake of a wolf.

"I'm warning you," he continued. "If you don't get rid of Hawkes before the full moon tonight, I will rip his head off and put it on a spike outside your bedroom window."

He shoved her out into the hallway and slammed the door behind her. Lexi stumbled forward, slowly coming straight and fighting the urge to cry or turn and beat against the door.

She completely believed he would do as he said if Tryst did not leave Wulfsiege tonight.

Tryst came to with a groan that built in his aching ribs and shuddered out over his burning flesh. Every part of him hurt.

No, that wasn't right. He couldn't feel his lips, so technically they didn't hurt.

"Stupid wolf," he said about Sven, but also about himself. On the other hand, he hadn't backed down from the challenge, and never would. It wasn't a death wish, just the only way he'd ever learned to stick up for himself. Fists proved to others he was a man, and a wolf worthy of any command he could take.

"You're still alive. That counts for something."

Before he could respond to the sexy female voice above him, water spilled over his head and down his shoulders.

"What the hell?" He groped for hold and his hands slid down the side of—a bathtub?

Tryst sat upright in the freestanding old-fashioned bathtub. He still wore jeans, but someone had placed him here without his knowing or consent. Lexi poured another pitcher of warm water over him.

"What are you doing?".

"Cleaning you up. You're bleeding like a skinned cat, and you need to soak those bruised muscles to promote faster healing. If you slip out of your jeans, I'll run the tub."

"Slip out of my— Why don't you leave me to do that? Hell, woman, take charge much?"

"Fine." She set the pitcher on a table and wandered out, calling back, "Take a bath. Soak a while. But don't linger. The full moon is out tonight. You don't want to hang around the castle, especially knowing Sven's werewolf likes to stalk the halls."

"Sven's werewolf stalks the halls during the full moon?" Tryst slapped a palm over his wet chest. "That wolf is insane."

And he had better keep a keen eye out in front of, as well as behind, him tonight. But to meet Sven when both were in werewolf form? The Nord had better keep a keen eye, as well.

Against Liam's warning, Lexi had asked the wolf to bring Tryst to her room after finding him sprawled on the floor in the guest bedroom. He'd survived the pummeling, but no sense in allowing him to bleed all over the floor and creating a big, messy job for the maid.

Lexi left him alone in her bathroom for an hour. Meanwhile, she paced her bedroom, counting off all the reasons she should tell Tryst to leave the castle tonight and never return. Sven would kill him—that's all she could come up with on her list for his departure. Because the reasons-to-stay list kept intruding.

The outsider wolf provided much-needed help around the castle. He'd helped rescue many. He kept an eye out for stupidity, like Sven. He was friendly and most of the pack males liked him. He wasn't horrible on the eye. He was a fantastic kisser. His body against hers would feel so good...

Lexi paused before the window. The sky was growing darker, the moon climbing in the sky. A few more hours and wolves across the world would shift to werewolf shape.

Except her.

And all she could think about was getting some skin-on-skin time with Trystan Hawkes.

She glanced at the bathroom door, wondered if he might have fallen asleep and decided she'd better check on him. He was wounded, and he could have taken a blow to the head. Didn't concussions require constant supervision?

"Tryst?"

She snuck into the bathroom, which was lit by a chandelier hung over the tub.

He watched her enter. She was aware of his heavy-lidded regard, but didn't comment as she walked around to the opposite side of the tub, in essence allowing him a longer look. Taking off her glasses, she set them on the vanity. No longer did she have anything to hide from him. Whether for good or for bad, she was what she was. If she offended him, he was good at hiding his alarm.

"How are you feeling?"

He groaned. "Like Sven ran over me with the snowplow. But I got a few good punches in and my head is still attached to my neck, so I guess I came out okay. Your father is going to kill me, though."

"I've taken measures to insure he doesn't learn about the fight."

"Really?" He settled back in the tub, his wet hair trailing along the white porcelain rim and his feet poking out the water at the opposite end. "Why would you do that?"

"Because I want you to stay at Wulfsiege. Liam said he put the idea of joining the pack into your head?"

She leaned against the tiled wall, which was five feet from the tub, but didn't dare move closer. If she did, she might want to peer more closely into the milky depths of the tub. He'd used the bath salts and his jeans lay crumpled on the floor, so he'd taken her suggestion of getting naked.

"Joining a pack is something I've dreamed of," he said, taking off the towel he'd had over his chin to reveal the deep purple bruise there.

"Oh, Tryst, does that hurt?"

"Course it does. But it'll be gone by morning. Shifting to werewolf takes away all wounds."

"Really? I guess I didn't realize that."

"I suppose not. What's it like, not having ever shifted, and yet watching your family and others all around you do so?"

"Makes me feel not right. Like I'm the girl standing on the sidelines, unpicked, after everyone else has been chosen."

"I wish I could make it better for you."

"You do make it better without knowing it. Just accepting me means a lot. Do you…accept me?"

"Hell yes. To be totally honest, your eyes still kind of freak me. They're just so gold."

"I know. It freaks me still when I look in the mirror. I try not to look at them too often."

"On the other hand, they're pretty cool. I've never seen my own eyes when shifted. Must be what they look like, eh?"

She nodded. His honesty was refreshing. And much needed. She also felt he wasn't trying to make her feel better by embroidering the truth with false kindness.

"Come over here." He extended a hand dripping with water. "I think a kiss might help bring the feeling back to my lips."

"They have no feeling? The bottom one does look swollen. Oh, Trystan." She leaned in and kissed him lightly, and he winced. "I don't want to hurt you."

"You never could. I'm tough. But apparently Sven is just as tough, though we called the match a draw. He didn't like that very much." He stroked a wet fingertip across her lip. "God, I want you, Lexi. I want you nestled beside me so I can feel your skin on mine. Your lips on mine."

She kissed him again and this time didn't pull away when he groaned painfully.

"That hurts so good," he moaned, and slid a hand along her back. "You had me brought here to your room?"

"Of course. It was either that or the keep, lying on a cot for everyone to look upon the poor, outsider wolf."

"Who never backs down from a fight."

"Yes, even when it involves my sister."

"She touched me. I rounded the corner and walked right into her. Wasn't even thinking because I'd just come from your dad's and he'd told me never to go near you again. So my mind wasn't on what had happened."

"I know. Lana is fickle like that. She likes to do things that'll result in having Sven prove his love to her. But I don't think that's real love. Feels so manipulative. You went to talk to Father again?"

"Yes, I told him I have an interest in you. I can't lie to him."

"And he told you to keep your hands off me."

"Exactly."

He stroked her hair and tapped her lips. She dashed out her tongue to lick his finger and tasted the cinnamon oil mixed into the bath salts.

"You're doing things to me, Lexi. I don't think the water is deep enough to hide it, either."

She laughed and then really wanted a look at what he was trying to hide under his hand. An erection? Mmm, it had been a while since she'd had a lover. A few mortals in the nearest town served her needs on occasion, but she'd never called any of them boyfriend. And to have a werewolf lover? It had never happened.

"Tonight you have to leave Wulfsiege to stay off Sven's radar."

"And your father's radar."

"Right. But come back in the morning to help Liam. And then, tomorrow night," she said, getting an idea and running with it, "don't run with the pack. Go to the village three leagues east of here. There's a little inn called the Green Fox set at the edge."

He tilted his head at her. "What are you suggesting, Princess?"

She ran her tongue along his finger and to his palm, where she made it pointed and traced down his wrist.

"You need sex on the night following the full moon to keep your werewolf satisfied."

"That I do. Especially since I didn't have sex last night."

"Exactly. And I need you. I mean, seriously, I really need you, Tryst."

"But I promised your father."

"And I'd never ask you to go against your word. But…who means more to you? My father, or me?"

"You, without question."

"So lay low tomorrow with Liam, then meet me. But only if you're serious about us."

"Us." A smile curved his swollen lip. "Hell, it'll be worth getting tossed out of Wulfsiege on my ass just to have one night with you. Can we make love?"

"That's what I had in mind."

"And I do love your mind. I'll see you then."

"It's a date. Now I'm going to leave you to get dressed, because if I see you naked, I might not let you leave, and that won't be good for your werewolf."

"Lexi?"

"Yes?"

"Promise me whatever happens tomorrow night, you'll keep your eyes wide open about us. I want you to give me a chance."

"I could say the same thing. No matter what happens, we'll not judge or make expectations."

"Deal."

She winked and left him alone before her desires forced her to jump into the tub and give him the skin-on-skin contact he'd asked for.

Chapter 11

"You going to be all right tonight, Father?"

Lexi removed the food tray from her father's bed. The curtains were pulled to hide the full moon, which usually glowed through the window. Didn't matter, the werewolf's urge to shift would come at midnight no matter if the moon was high and bright or hidden behind clouds.

"Why wouldn't I be?"

"I worry...." She stopped herself from saying her father's shift tonight might further weaken him. A werewolf only gained strength during the shift, and any wounds should heal.

She hadn't thought of that. Maybe the shift would actually do him good? The doctor still hadn't reported on the blood test.

"I know what you're thinking." Edmonton Connor sat on the edge of his bed, legs over the side. A maid had helped him dress today, and the sweater hung loose on his shoulders. He'd become even frailer, and it tore out Lexi's heart. "I look forward to the shift. If it happens. It might do me some good. I'm not feeling the usual pull tonight, though. You know what it's like—sorry."

No, she didn't know what that pull felt like, but she could guess it was instinctual and innate.

His eyes glittered with tears as they connected in the dim darkness. For the first time, she couldn't read her father's heart. Did he fear? Did he suspect death was near? Or was his courage merely shadowed by his illness?

"Would you like me to stay close tonight?" she asked.

He bowed his head and nodded. "Yes."

Lexi's heart fell. He was worried. As much as she was.

"Stop in later, will you? Maybe bring a deck of cards to keep your old man occupied."

"I can do that. I'll see you in a bit, Father."

She carried the tray out into the hallway but left the door open an inch. She'd take the uneaten meal to the cafeteria and then return to her father's room, where she'd sit in the conference room, giving him the privacy he required should he shift, and if not, she'd resurrect her rummy skills.

Passing her sister's room, she heard a groan, and was about to pass it off as the shift, when she realized it was yet early in the evening. Tray propped on an arm, she knocked on her sister's door. "Lana?"

"Lexi? Oh, come in. Please, hurry."

She entered to find her sister balled on the floor at the end of the pink ruffled bed. Blond hair was tangled about her head. She looked pale, and perspiration sheened her forehead.

Setting the tray aside, Lexi rushed to her sister. "Did he hurt you?"

Lana shook her head vehemently. "Stomach hurts. So bad. And I'm dizzy."

"Let me help you into bed. You're cool and shivering."

The symptoms seemed flulike. Lexi had read enough fitness and lifestyle magazines to recognize them. But those were mortal symptoms. Werewolves never fell to a mortal illness. Her breed was rarely sick, due to their excellent immune systems.

Lana slipped between the sheets, and Lexi scrambled into the bathroom to soak a towel in cool water and wring it out. If Sven had hurt her, she couldn't imagine it would manifest in such a manner. Unless she had internal injuries? Laying the cloth over her sister's forehead, she smoothed the long hair from her face and lingered on her cheek, which felt clammy.

"I think it was something I ate," Lana whispered. "Could have been some bad garlic in the potatoes."

That was a possibility. Though, Lexi had eaten the roasted pheasant served tonight, seasoned with a creamy garlic sauce, and it had tasted fine to her. She hadn't noticed feeling bad after, either.

"Did you eat only potatoes?"

Lana closed her eyes and shivered. "Brought Daddy his meal, and he didn't eat it. You know I love mashed potatoes, much as I'm sure they go straight to my hips."

Lexi glanced to the tray of unfinished food. The potatoes were gone. Compelled, she sniffed at the food. Beyond the copious garlic, it had an off smell, but that could be because it had been sitting for a few hours. Lana always expected the maid to clean up after her.

"Oh, I'm going to be sick!"

Lexi helped her sister into the bathroom, and while tending her, couldn't stop wondering if something had been in the mashed potatoes to cause such a violent reaction in her sister.

Poison? Struck by that horrible thought, she clutched her throat. Had someone been poisoning her father?

Tryst had left his clothing in the outbuilding and shifted to four-legged wolf shape an hour ago. He wanted time to run and put distance between himself and castle Wulfsiege. He'd been told there was a valley to the east where the pack went during the full moon, leagues away from people.

It wasn't so much people he worried about. His werewolf would not harm a human being, only freak them out and forever haunt their nightmares. It was his unfamiliarity with the area that troubled him. He didn't trust he wouldn't stalk right onto a highway, in full werewolf glory, and cause a crash. He had no desire to star in an impromptu horror movie.

His paws tracked the snow in an exhilarating race east, toward the moon. An instinctual part of him liked to chase that big glowing ball of light, knowing it was a part of him, and tried desperately to touch it, to hold it, maybe take a big meaty bite out of it.

When the inexplicable call to the ultimate shift tingled in his bones, he dodged toward the edge of the forest and as he did so, his back legs stretched and lengthened, bringing him tall and vertical onto two legs. Arms lengthened and bones liquefied and reshaped. His head grew larger and his maw stretched, taking in the night scents as a form of radar. The werewolf climbed up from the wolf and howled to the moon, grasping the cold air with deadly talons. This night belonged to him.

Sniffing, he scented a wild thing, not far away, its heartbeats thundering. Food. Deftly tracking the snow-pack, the werewolf sighted its prey and lunged.

Lexi snuck into the cafeteria, filing down the aisle behind the stainless steel serving counter and the wall that featured the hot-plate units where the food was kept warm during meals. All was clean and shiny in the dim moonlight that shone through the windows. She hadn't wanted to turn on a light and alert someone. The cooks would be out, preparing for the shift, as would the rest of the castle inhabitants, save Natalie and a few maids who were also witches.

She trailed a finger along the clean steel counter and eyed the refrigerator. Inspection found the inside stocked with plucked chickens and half a side of pork. Another fridge next to it contained fruits and vegetables that were shipped in weekly, along with sauces and condiments.

Not really sure what she was looking for but sensing she'd know it if she stumbled upon it, she eyed the spice carousel and turned the steel fixture slowly, touching the brushed steel container of each one, capped with a clear glass cover so the contents were revealed. None of the spices were labeled, but she assumed the cook knew them well.

Could any be used to poison a werewolf? Unlikely, if they were all innocuous cooking spices. But who could know?

Natalie would. The witch used herbs for all sorts of potions, concoctions and spells. Lexi had no idea how she got the healing results she did from her spells; nor was she aware of Natalie's full capabilities of the craft.

She was a witch of the Light and had taken a vow to harm none. Yet could she be behind her father's illness?

Lexi shook her head. It was unthinkable. Natalie may not be wolf, but she was a trusted family friend. Her affair with Father had been decades ago, when Lexi had been a toddler. The witch did not harbor bad feelings about it, and had once told Lexi she knew she and Edmonton would not make a good match exactly because of his mistrust for her craft.

She set aside that suspicion. Daring to tug open the drawer next to the knife butler, she eyed the collection of recipes and notes. Nothing there that read: *Use this to poison the principal.*

What was poison to a werewolf?

"Wolfsbane," she whispered, which is why she was surprised it had been utilized—successfully—as an antidote. But what was it counteracting? She hadn't the knowledge to make a guess.

A shadow traced across the window beside the drawer, causing Lexi to startle. The shape of a werewolf passed before the windows at the opposite side of the cafeteria. Out and about? Or keeping an eye on her?

She watched for a long time, and listened. An exterior door was just outside the cafeteria. No one entered, and a werewolf could not be so stealthy and quiet that she wouldn't hear something.

And then the door slammed inside the cafeteria, and in stalked a pale-furred werewolf.

"Sven." Lexi dropped the notes she'd been holding and backed toward the wall. Heartbeat galloping in her throat, she put up a defensive hand.

The werewolf leaped over the counter and landed on all fours in front of her. He smelled feral and growled deep from his chest. Coming upright to his full, imposing height, his steps slapped the tiles. His fur glinted with melting snow.

"You don't want to do this, Sven," she said lowly and with as much firmness as she could muster. "You want to be principal of pack Alpine? Don't fuck with the current principal's daughter. Got that? Do you understand me?"

The wolf snarled, showing her his teeth. He rushed her, slamming her body against the brick wall. The knives on the counter clattered and one of them slid off to the floor, barely missing the werewolf's foot.

Gauging how quickly she could grab a knife in defense, Lexi's arm flinched. Sven slapped a paw on the counter near the knife display.

Lifting her chin, she tried to look the werewolf in the eye, to not show him her fear, even as her heart pounded for freedom. He would hurt her. She had no doubt about that.

"Just leave me alone," she said. "You have Lana."

The werewolf dragged a talon across her collarbone. An icy burn sliced her skin. Where was Tryst?

You sent him away.

She was on her own. And she'd never felt more alone in her life.

Sven's furred maw brushed the side of her cheek. Could he hear her frantic heartbeats? Smell her fear? Of course he could.

He stepped back, lifting his chest, and let out a howl that she recognized as warning. Instinctively, Lexi cowered, sinking against the wall and bowing her head. If she could show him her compliance, he might leave her alone.

It worked. The werewolf turned and raced from the cafeteria.

And Lexi gripped her stomach to keep from getting sick.

Morning pried open his eyelids, and Tryst woke in the shed outside Wulfsiege. The doors were open and, shivering, he cursed his were body for having less resistance to the cold than when in wolf form.

He glanced about the hazy shed. Liam was inside bent over the snowplow, the socket wrench clicking studiously.

Tryst noted the clothing tossed over his bare legs. He dressed, thinking he'd love a shower but not sure he wanted to risk going inside the castle today. Lexi had been adamant he lie low.

"You have a good night?" a voice called from somewhere beneath the snowplow.

"Amazing. I love this country. It's the perfect place to let the werewolf roam."

"How's Paris looking to you about now?"

Tryst smirked and wandered, barefoot, around behind the plow. "We live outside the city on one hundred acres of land, but I've never experienced such gorgeous countryside on a run before. Really makes a man want to stay. What do you need, Liam?"

"Hand me the socket tray. I need a bigger size."

Tryst found the tray of sockets and handed it under the plow to Liam. "I'm going to hang in here all day, if it's okay with you."

"Yeah, that's probably best. I hear there's rumblings about the principal's sickness this morning."

"Such as? How is he?"

"Not sure how he's faring. But the word is that he

might have been poisoned. Supposedly Lana ate some of his food and she was sick all night. Couldn't shift."

"Wow. Who'da thought ol' Sven could be so vindictive."

Liam rolled out on the crawler and looked up at Tryst, the socket wrench clutched over his stomach. "I was thinking the exact same thing."

"What is that wolf's story, anyway?"

Liam shrugged. "He came to Wulfsiege a year ago. Charmed the principal with his tales of derring-do and successful escape from a vampire attack on his pack."

"Vampires attacking a pack? They don't do stuff like that anymore."

"Or so the city slicker believes."

"They do?" Tryst realized he knew little about the vast and complex world of his breed and how they related to the other paranormal breeds. In the mid-twentieth century vampires had hunted wolves with traps and put a bounty on their heads, but he'd thought that horrible practice long over. Truly, he had led a sheltered life. "You say something to Lexi about your suspicion of Sven?"

"Not yet. You going to see her later?"

Knowing it wouldn't be wise to reveal their plans for a liaison tonight, Tryst heeled the plow tire.

"I'll take that as a yes," Liam said. "Let's keep this to ourselves for now. We don't want to raise a stink if our suspicions about Sven are not true. Let me check into a few things first."

"Deal."

Lexi traced a finger along the fading pink line Sven's talon had drawn across her collarbone. Almost healed. She was glad she'd told Tryst to stay away today. She didn't want him to know how close she'd come to being one of Sven's chew toys. Tryst would go after the wolf, for sure.

She wasn't certain he'd come out the winner, though. Though matched in strength and size, Sven was maniacal. Unfortunately, crazy always trumped reason.

Eyeing the makeup she'd scattered along the bathroom vanity, she separated out the various pots of eye shadow, wondering which color would most distract from gold. Or would any color on her lids simply draw more attention to her eyes? She wore makeup so rarely this would prove a challenge just getting it to look right on her face. Maybe the brown?

She sighed, and shoved the lot to the side, leaning over and catching her head against her forearm. "What am I doing?"

She was trying to have some fun, and have a romantic liaison. To get some werewolf sex for herself, from a man who was genuinely into her, that was what she was doing. Something she had every right to claim for herself.

But the pack wouldn't see it that way.

Would tonight's meeting with Tryst seal his doom?

"You're being dramatic, Lexi." Like Lana. She smiled at that.

Chapter 12

After a leisurely stroll down the iced-over gravel road, Tryst found the Green Fox inn at the edge of a quaint little village and stomped his boots against the mail post before walking inside. He hadn't shifted because arriving at the inn in wolf shape, then shifting to naked were shape, would not have gone over well with the innkeepers. He was just about to ask after Lexi's room, when he decided he wasn't sure if she would have given them her real name.

The woman behind the counter, who looked like everyone's idea of what a grandmother with rosy apple cheeks and silver hair rinse should be, grinned and shook her head, saying in French that she knew what room he was looking for: the private cottage out back. She directed him outside, patting him on the rear as he left the main inn.

Thinking how much he loved feisty old grannies,

Trystan rubbed his ass, made way around the side of the Tudor-era building and found a path that wove through the pine woods. Lanterns lit the flagstone path, swept clean of snow and puddled with water around the glowing lights. A fox darted into the woods, dispersing a spatter of hoarfrost, obviously sensing Tryst's wolf nature. He knew his werewolf had had a fine meal last night, but was thankful he couldn't remember such gorge-fests. What he and his werewolf chose to eat—and *how* they ate it—remained conflicting tastes, that was for sure.

He had arrived at the threshold, ready to knock, when the door opened to reveal a gorgeous woman in a long, slinky red nightgown that hugged her subtle curves and revealed the high mounds of her breasts.

Tryst blew out a breath, taking her in. Luscious black hair dusted about her shoulders and arms, framing her narrow face and calling attention to her red lips. No lipstick on them, all natural and so red. Suddenly he loved the color red. And gold. Her eyes glittered, and they didn't seem so odd to him anymore.

Liam had said she had a bad side. Hallelujah for the naughty, bad side of Lexi Connor.

When he just stood there, struck by her beauty, Lexi grabbed his hand and tugged him inside. The single-room cottage was lit with candles in the windows and near the high tester bed. A bottle of wine decanted in an ice bucket and two goblets reflected firelight from the hearth.

"Wow. All this for us? Just what are your plans, Miss Chatelaine?"

"I'm going to seduce you," she said, sliding a hand up his shirt and tugging open the top two buttons. "You okay with that? Or is this too forward?" Her sexy pout abandoned, she wrinkled her mouth into a frown. "Hell, it's too forward. I don't know what I was thinking—"

"No, not. Just. Right." He wasn't forming multisyllabic words because she'd stolen the breath from him, and he wanted to take it all in. The candles. The wine. Her. Red. "You. Pretty."

"I think the cat has your tongue, wolf. What's become of the big strong outsider?"

"He's been dazzled senseless," he offered. And suddenly the word he hated most felt softer and less cruel. "You're so beautiful, Lexi. What did I ever do to deserve you?"

"You've always been yourself, true and brave, from the beginning. Nothing is sexier to me than an honest man."

Bracketing his hands at her hips he held her back to look at her. Sleek black hair spilled down to her breasts, and slid over the red silk. Beneath the silk her nipples were hard and her fingers glided there to touch them, testing him with the subtle tease. His icy princess had certainly thawed.

"What's wrong?" she whispered. "You're not saying anything."

"Because everything is right."

He leaned in and imprinted a kiss between the twin curves of her breasts. Smelled like cinnamon there. He nipped her soft breast. Lexi tilted back her head and sucked in a breath.

"Look at me," he whispered.

She gifted him the odd gold gaze that should have warned him off, but instead it only made him draw her closer and slide his hands up along her silk-covered back. If no other wolf would have her, then good for him. She was his. Let no man take her away from him—or risk death.

Tryst wanted to ask after her father but cautioned himself against breaking the mood. She'd tell him if there was trouble, and hell, she couldn't be in such a playful mood if the principal was in dire straits.

"Wine?" she asked.

"Sure. But only if you let me drink it from your mouth."

Making a noise of satisfaction, she poured wine into a goblet. Dipping a finger into the glass, she sucked the liquid slowly from her skin. Tryst swallowed. All systems alert, and he was heading for some serious shred, full speed ahead.

Lexi sipped the wine and stepped up to him, holding the goblet stem between her fingers. From her kiss, he tasted the wine and drank deeply of her, taking her moans into his breath. He couldn't hold her tight enough. He wanted to mold her against his form and learn her curves and lines as they fit to his.

"So good," he whispered. "Mine."

She took another drink and set down the goblet. He dove in for another taste and wine spilled out of her mouth and onto his chin. She licked the trail, following it down his neck where the tease of her tongue tightened his muscles and shot electric tingles throughout his system.

Tonight was the night he needed to have sex until he was sated to keep the werewolf at bay. He could let out his werewolf, but it wouldn't be fair to Lexi. That was something he generally saved until after he'd gotten to know the woman well. And could she ever have sex with him when he was wolfed out and not feel lacking? He wouldn't do that to her.

Hell, he was getting ahead of himself. A gorgeous woman insisted on tasting every inch of his flesh— she had found his nipple, bringing it to a hard pebble.

"Lexi, you make my body shiver."

"That's a good thing. Take off your shirt. I want to lick every inch of your crazy hard muscles."

"Sounds… Oh, yeah…"

"You have so many muscles. This might take me a while."

"Take your time."

Buttons popped from their stitches as Lexi tore away the shirt from his chest and tugged it down and off his arms. He'd never liked that shirt, anyway. Her tongue wandered along his shoulder and dipped to the crease between his arm and chest. The slick of her tongue hit an erogenous spot on him. Crazy, good. Relentless in tasting him, the sweep of her hair over his skin and the spicy cinnamon scent made him crazy for more of her.

"Your werewolf have a good run last night?" she asked.

"Uh-huh. Still wants out tonight."

"Then I'll have to do something about that for you. You need to be sated, yes?"

He murmured a satisfied noise, finding words un-available as he slid the thin red straps from her shoul-ders and down her arms. The gown followed, over her small breasts and her hips to land at his feet. She arched against his body, pressing her chest beneath his, for he towered over her. But a perfect fit, nonetheless.

"I've never been with another wolf," she said.

"Really? Wow." Knowing that really made him want her.

Lifting her, he set her on the bed and crawled over

her luxurious length, taking her breast into his mouth because he couldn't stand not tasting Lexi Connor's sweet, cinnamon skin.

Candlelight flickered in Trystan's hair, gleaming like gold, ruby and copper. A treasure that belonged to her. Lexi swept his hair across her face and moaned from her core as his attentions to her breasts brought her body to a jittering hum of desire, want and urgency.

He could bring her to orgasm by licking her nipples, she sensed that, and her body hummed in response to his devouring her. She wanted to go slowly, to learn him and explore all of him, but the newness and erotic connection of their skin did not preach patience, and all she wanted was to soar alongside this gorgeous man.

"You're perfect," he whispered, his kisses trailing down her belly. The mantra felt real and she forgot that she was broken. "Made for me. Want you badly."

"You have me, Tryst. I'm yours."

"Lexi, your skin… How can a girl be so soft? And yet so, so strong."

Never before had such sweet nothings been whispered to her. Everything he did drew her into him, his wild, rough manliness, his intense contact, his sweet tender words. Could a woman orgasm from words alone?

His fingers played over her mons, toying with her dark curls, and he followed with his mouth, tasting, touching, teasing at her skin, her thigh, along the crease where her leg joined her torso, and down, deeper, to the very center of her. Her body had begun to shiver in anticipation of his next move.

"You afraid?" he asked softly. "You're shaking. Lexi,

it's all good." He kissed her thigh and gave her hip a playful bite. "You want me to stop?"

"No!" She laughed because her nerves had gotten the better of her, and since when had cold, hard Lexi Conner been so nervous around a man? Hell, she had been the one to initiate this scandalous night of debauchery. "It's all better than good. You just make my body shiver, Tryst. I like everything you're doing."

"How 'bout this?" He lashed his tongue along her folds and then delved deeper, tasting her slowly.

She gripped his hair and spread her legs wide to receive his attentions. "Oh, yes."

Conversation was no longer necessary. As long as he kept doing what he was doing... Lexi tilted her face against the pillow and cried out at the gorgeous pleasure that circled her belly and mons and played a crazy beat at her pinnacle.

She'd found him. The man who could please her without regard for her broken bits. And if it never went beyond a wild affair she could be satisfied at having experienced the ecstasy of being kissed, touched and tongued by Trystan Hawkes. A werewolf.

Grasping the bedspread, her heel slipped as her leg muscles went from tense and tight to lax, and then back again. The universe waited to explode at the tip of Tryst's tongue. He was almost...there...

"Lexi, come for me. You're so close. I can feel it."

The subtle, slippery pressure of his finger at her nub set her free. Shoulders digging into the spread, she cried out as orgasm swept her into bliss. This one was strong, quaking in her core and radiating out through her extremities. The shiver turned to a blissful wave. She released her voice because all the goodness exploded out of her and into the universe.

He crawled alongside her, still wearing his jeans, and spread a hand over her panting stomach. "I've never seen a more gorgeous thing. When you come it's amazing."

She smirked and blew out a breath. "Loud, I know."

"Yeah, but wow. That's a lot of energy to come out of such a small woman."

She laughed and buried her face in his winter-sweet hair. "You said the world responds to the energy we put out?"

"Threefold. Life is coming at you with all it's got, Lexi. Take it all in and shred the wave."

"You're the only man who has ever been able to control me like that."

"Don't tell me…"

She nodded. "Never had an orgasm with a man before."

"That's just wrong. Lexi, seriously?"

"It's all right. I know how to take care of myself. But I like it better when you do it."

"And never with a wolf before?"

She shook her head. "The pack has never been interested in broken ol' me. Oh, Tryst, that was good." Twisting her body, she pressed her hot, sex-heated skin to his. "But those jeans have to come off."

"Not sure it's possible. My hard-on is making them too tight."

She slid a hand over the zipper and marveled at the bulge that strained beneath the fabric. "Hurry, I wouldn't want you to injure yourself. I need to see you, to hold you. Tryst, I want to suck you."

He shoved down his jeans and a mighty erection sprang up against his stomach. Trystan kicked off his pants and crawled on top of her, crouched like a lion over his prey. Lexi grabbed his thick cock and the expression on his face made her smile.

"My turn to control you," she said, and pushed his shoulder. He took direction and landed on his back, allowing her to crouch over his body. "We're going to blast the universe with our energy tonight."

"Hallelujah!"

She kissed his neck and over the hair that spread across his shoulder. "I love your red hair. It's so sexy."

"It's auburn, never red, sweetie."

Smirking at his semantics, she moved down to his chest, where fine auburn hairs danced about his nipples. She loved the tickle against her nose. Squeezing the tiny nipple elicited a wince from him.

"Hurt?"

"So good, Princess, so good."

Hand wrapping about the man's main control, Lexi moved kisses slowly down his chest, kneeling near his shoulder. He kissed her leg and slid a hand between her legs where she was slick and so ready. His stomach was dotted with freckles and she followed the line of auburn hair down to the fierce, bold shaft that stood upright, demanding attention. Reaching the swollen head of his penis, she licked the mighty, smooth curve of him. His fingers clutched her leg.

She dragged her tongue down his length, loving the salty, masculine taste of his most manly and powerful muscle. It was wide, thick, and she wasn't sure if he could fit inside her. But she was willing to try because riding him was all she wanted to do.

He parted her legs and she felt the hot lash of his tongue trying to reach her moistness. "Straddle me," he said. "And suck me."

Now that was a command she wanted to fulfill. She

moved a leg to straddle his head and he pulled her hips down to satisfy his hungers while she moved his length in and out of her mouth, sucking, licking, drawing up his moans, the slow, steady rhythm of his hips asking without demanding.

Wrapping her hand about the base of his cock, she worked him up and down while keeping the head of him in her mouth. She was close to another orgasm just from the few lashes of his tongue between her legs, and she could sense him nearing the edge, as well. His shaft grew steely hard and so hot. Beneath her fingertips the vein that stretched the length of him had swollen. His hips shook and the hands clutching her hips dug in hard.

It was all too much, and everything she wanted. As the orgasm twisted in her core, Lexi lifted her head and cried out as her lover mastered her yet again. Trystan reached climax at the same time, his cock held firmly against her chest as he came between her breasts, spilling heavily.

He picked her up and tossed her back against the pillows, a rough move that made her feel controlled in the best way possible. Dragging a corner of the sheet across her chest, he wiped her skin clean, then traced her lower lip and showed her the glisten that had come from him. "Love that you did that for me, Lexi. But we're just getting started." With an eager grin that revealed his gorgeous white teeth, he spread her legs and fit his hardness, which hadn't softened from climax, against her folds. "I need to be inside you, feeling your wet heat. Please, Lexi."

"Yes." She reached down and guided him forward, pulling his hips toward her as he entered her and invaded her roughly. He swore and gasped and clenched his jaws as they fit together tightly.

Pistoning inside her, he gripped the back of her neck and brought her up to his chest. She clung to his arms, but couldn't wrap her fingers about his massive biceps. They were tight and tense, hot with strength as he mastered her, claimed her, filled her. Their bodies slid, skin against silken wet skin, in a harmony of wildness.

Hard to imagine she'd known him for such a short amount of time. Even harder to imagine not spending the rest of her life with him, inside him, surrounding him, possessing and claiming him. And in turn, giving herself away to his mastery. And loving every moment of it all.

Wrapped in a tight clutch, they came together, Tryst's muscles hard and shuddering against Lexi's hot skin. Eyes closed she drew in the wild, masculine scent of him, the pungent tang of cinnamon heating the air and the smoky flame from the nearby candle. It was a perfume she would never forget: the scent of their bonding—for as much as they two could bond, considering werewolves should both be in werewolf form to officially bond.

If this was as good as they could ever have it, she could die a happy werewolf.

Tryst grabbed the wine bottle and sucked down half of it in a few swallows. He offered the bottle to her, and, sitting up, Lexi took a more ladylike swig.

"Wine, candlelight and my favorite woman," he said. "This night is the best."

"I can't believe that." Then she silently cursed herself for even saying that. She shouldn't put down what they'd just shared, but seriously? She couldn't be his best.

"The best," he reiterated. "And only going to get better. Once more?" he whispered, his fingers toying with her achy wetness.

Lexi smiled with her entire body, twisting on the bed to open herself to anything and everything he had in mind. The male wolf needed to be sated on this night following the full moon, and she was no wolf to deny him.

"I like it when you do that," she cooed. He slid his fingers inside her, his thumb remaining against her swollen center. "Mmm, like that. Harder, lover. Mark me."

He buried his face against her neck and bit her softly, kissing, biting, nuzzling, sucking and tasting. All while his fingers found a new sweet spot within her that she hadn't been aware of. She tucked her head against his and kissed the crown of his head. He was hers. If only for tonight.

"Come for me, lover," he whispered at her ear. "Show me you love what I do to you."

The orgasm took away her breath, and Lexi's cry of joy suddenly segued into a wolfish howl. It startled her and Trystan. He jerked away from her, studying her eyes, and as he opened his mouth to say something, her body lunged forward.

Something was not right. Her hips felt as if they'd just…shifted. And her lungs squeezed inside her chest, but it wasn't so much painful as…opening.

She grabbed Tryst's arm and he yelped because she'd clamped down too tightly.

"Lexi?"

"I don't know," she gasped. Her spine moved. Actually *moved*. "What's happening?"

Chapter 13

Her body transformed before his very eyes. His gorgeous princess was actually shifting to werewolf form. She said it had never happened before. So how could it now?

Had sex done it for her? Released her from whatever stasis her body had been in since puberty? Couldn't have. She'd had sex before.

Tryst brushed the hair from his face and swung his legs over the side of the bed, but didn't approach as Lexi's body changed and her spine lengthened and sleek black fur grew from the pores on her arms, shoulders and legs. Her maw lengthened and teeth jutted in brilliant white daggers.

She must be freaking. Or maybe she was joyous? He was thrilled for her, but a little worried she wouldn't take it well because they'd been having sex, and usually when a couple of wolves did so they either wolfed out before or after but never during the act.

Wow, he must have some kind of miracle power in his cock. Or his fingers, because he'd been getting her off with slick strokes when she began to shift.

When finally a gorgeous werewolf stood in the center of the cottage, claws gleaming and head tilting to take in her surroundings, Tryst decided to sit back and let her explore, take her own time and move where she wanted to. He didn't fear her werewolf. At least, he didn't think he should fear it.

On the other hand, this shape was new to her. There was no telling how she would react. How would her werewolf see him, an apparent man in were form? She should know him by scent if not appearance. He hoped.

Without a glance toward him, Lexi's werewolf let out a long, triumphant howl. Then she darted toward the door and kicked it open, running out into the night.

"Not good. You can't run through the village, Lexi. Shit!"

Tryst tugged up his jeans and, grabbing a blanket from the bed, took off after her, bare feet slipping on the icy steps. Spying her tracks, and relieved they led around back and toward the woods, he raced through the snow.

The werewolf was fast, and had much better traction on the slippery snow than Tryst did running barefoot. He must have tracked her through the forest for a half a league before coming upon a clearing that opened before an iced stream. A frozen falls gleamed with reflections of moonlight. Snow, ice and hoarfrost covered over all, gifting the space with an enchanted glimmer that felt sacred to him as he entered the quiet cove.

And there, standing before a huge, flat rock was

Lexi, naked, now in were shape, huffing, her bare back to him. Moonlight crowned her tresses with a princess tiara of unfathomable light and surface darkness. Her skin, moistened with perspiration, glittered like snow. She lifted her head, sniffing the air. She'd sensed him.

Tryst stepped forward but did not want to crowd her because she could be out of sorts, or just plain stupefied by what had occurred. Turning, she spied him, and her expression looked panicked. Then she smiled, but the smile quickly dropped. A palm clutched at her belly. Her eyes pleaded with him. Panic, concern and confusion swept her face. And the smile returned. Genuine. So filled with joy.

"You did it," he said softly. "Lexi, you shifted."

She nodded positively and stretched out her arms to entreat him to her. He approached with the blanket and wrapped it about her shoulders, then kissed her forehead, her eyelids, her mouth. Nuzzling his body against her sweet, sexy heat, she felt twenty degrees warmer than he.

Here was home. Nothing felt more real than that right now.

"I shifted," she declared in a stunned whisper. "I really did it. I transformed to werewolf. Did you see?"

"I did happen to notice that. You are a gorgeous werewolf, Lexi. So beautiful. And look." He stroked a thumb over her rose-blushed cheek. "I knew I'd find your color. You absolutely glow, lover."

"Really? Do you think so? Tryst! I just ran through the forest in werewolf shape! That's the most amazing thing that's ever happened to me!"

She performed a jumping leap of a hug and wrapped her legs about his hips. Her joy spread through his bones as he spun her about at the edge of the iced stream beneath the wondrous moonlight.

"I need to do it again," she said, searching his eyes. "Shift to wolf this time. Do you think I can? I need to try. Oh, Tryst, can I try?"

"You can do whatever you want, lover. Your eyes."

"What? What about them?"

He touched the edge of her eyelid. "They're blue. Lexi, your eyes have shifted."

"That's the color they were before puberty. Oh, gods, it's really happened."

She kissed him deeply, clinging to his arms, his hips, becoming a part of him. Giving him home and trust and love and all the things he had dreamed to have. Were they all to be his? Now that she had shifted and found her color and— What was he thinking? This was her moment, not his.

Drawing back with a wicked smile on her face, she said, "You did this to me. It's all your fault. You, making love to me, made me shift!"

"Well, maybe." He wasn't going to take the credit. It could have been any number of things that had flipped the switch in her brain and body, allowing her to shift. But he had been the guy who'd made her come. It had been quite an orgasm, too. "Okay, I'll take some credit."

"No man has ever been able to do it before. It's you, I know it. We were meant for one another. Do you think? Oh, let's shift together. I need to try to shift again to know that it's real and not a fluke. Please?"

He cast a glance around the area, confirming it was about as safe from human eyes as possible. "Okay, but we return here so I can claim my clothes when we're done, and then back to the cottage for you."

"Yes!" She clapped gleefully and the blanket slipped to the ground.

Tryst pulled her against his body and ran his palm up her stomach to her breast. It was cool and firm and demanded a kiss. Dipping his head to her softness, he tasted her cool/hot sweetness, growling against her skin because she was so good, so right for him.

"Can we have sex as wolves?" she asked with a gleeful glint to her pretty blue eyes.

His erection tightened against his jeans. "Hell yes. Wolf sex, were sex, werewolf sex. Anything you want, lover."

"Then try to catch me if you can." She scampered over to the huge rock, a naked winter sprite, and turned to wink at him. "So I just think about shifting and that's how it works?"

He nodded, shrugging a hand through his hair. Man, he was proud of that woman. For years she had suffered the foul treatment of her fellow pack males, and had walked in her sister's shadow, yet she'd never let it bring her down, and had risen above it all as Wulfsiege's chatelaine. And now, for all her hard work, she had finally been rewarded.

He hoped it hadn't been a fluke.

Lexi closed her eyes tightly, which he knew wasn't necessary, but she'd get the hang of it—if the shift worked. He pressed crossed fingers to his lips and didn't have to wait long.

Lexi's body began to change, her bones shortening, and she crouched as her hair fell over her face while her hands and feet shifted to paws. It was a fast shift, one that most humans would barely notice. One minute they'd be looking at what they thought was a human, then within a blink, they'd see a wolf standing before them.

A dark-furred wolf with a sheen of silver fur tracing her belly and paws turned and looked at him. The wolf barked at Tryst—a challenge—then took off through the forest.

Back by the stream, Lexi came into were shape next to the blanket her lover had thoughtfully brought out for her. She wasn't cold by any means. Her skin was warm and her muscles were deliciously taxed. She'd never be cold again. She had shifted both to werewolf and wolf shape. And she'd had sex with Tryst while they'd been wolves, and could remember that she had wanted to be taken by the red-furred wolf and had submitted to him in the forest.

Wrapping her arms about her shoulders, she hugged herself out of joy and then released a squeal when Tryst appeared out of the forest, loping forward. She bent and held out her hand and the wolf wandered right up to her and licked her fingers and face. His fur was thick and so soft. She hugged him and let him lick her skin.

And then his arms wrapped about her and his licks became kisses that found her mouth. He shifted to were form and the two made love again on the blanket beside the frozen falls.

They wandered back to the cottage, elated, hand in hand, the blanket tugged about her torso. Lexi knew Tryst had to walk back to Wulfsiege, because if anyone saw her return in the car with him in the passenger's seat there'd be questions.

"I don't think I can tell anyone," she said as they sorted through the cottage, putting things in order in preparation to leave.

"They'll guess if you don't wear your sunglasses." He kissed her, then pulled her over to the small vanity stand beside the bathroom door. "Your eyes are blue, lover. Like the sky on a cloudless day."

She inspected her eyes and still couldn't believe it. After all this time. "This is the color they were before that first abbreviated shift. They're the color of my mother's eyes."

The enormity of what had occurred through the night hit her and tears spilled down her cheeks and slipped into an irrepressible smile.

"What's wrong? Don't cry, Lexi. It's going to be okay."

"I know it is. That's why I'm crying. I'm just so happy. And I know that it could have never happened if it hadn't been for you. Trystan, I love you."

"I love you, too. I really do. I think I loved you the moment you took off your glasses and showed me who you really are."

"We bonded out there by the stream. As wolves. I don't remember much of it after I shifted, but I know we had sex."

"That's the way it works. Might be weird if we had total recall of it, but I know it was awesome. We'll have to introduce our werewolves. That will be the ultimate bonding."

"Tryst, do you know what that means? I've shifted. I can have a baby, if I want to. It's just too incredible. It's kind of hard taking it all in."

"You'll be walking cloud nine for days, and I'll be looking up at you, cheering you on." He slid on his shirt but, when he tried to button it, found all the buttons were missing. They'd been torn off during their hasty lovemaking.

Shrugging the shirt up, Lexi pressed a kiss to his chest. "You're so good to me."

"I want everything good for you. And us. Lexi, what are we going to do?"

She nuzzled against his chest, freckled across the shoulders, and clung to the ends of his hair. She knew what he was thinking. Her father would never allow Tryst to have a relationship with her because of his mixed heritage. The principal was going to freak when he discovered she had shifted because of having sex with Tryst. Was there a way to keep that a secret forever? It didn't feel right to her, but until they could figure out how to handle this, she'd wear the sunglasses.

"Liam will have the plow fixed today," he said. "The courtyard will be serviceable by afternoon, and most of the snow will have been cleared away from the castle. There won't be any reason for me to stay after that. Though I would like to stay on until your father gets better, just to know for sure, and report his return to health to my father."

"What about staying for me?"

"Lexi, I want that more than anything, but can I do that? Will your father allow it?"

"Challenge Sven to become scion."

"Yeah?"

"I'm sorry. But Liam said you were considering joining the pack. If you really mean it, then prove it to me."

"I'd love to have a pack to call my own, but I'm torn between taking what I want and doing what is right for my family. My mother...I don't know how she would handle me moving so far away. I would travel every weekend and visit her, but still. I haven't told you about her condition. She's good most days."

"You said something about madness?"

He nodded. "She was buried alive for over two centuries by the guy who fathered my twin brother. A witch's spell kept her alive and aware inside a glass coffin deep under Paris."

"Oh, hell, that's horrible. She was aware of everything?"

He nodded. "For two centuries. Put in there in 1785. Rhys, my dad, just found her twenty-seven years ago. She was pregnant before she was buried, and she gave birth to me and my brother nine months after she was found. So you can imagine her mind is not in tip-top shape. But most days she's cool, so long as she drinks blood daily. She used to come after me when I was little. My father pulled me away from her fangs on more than a few occasions."

She touched his chin and silently offered her understanding. She couldn't imagine what it must have been like to have grown up with a mother like Viviane. Her mother had died when she was three, but she'd never missed her much because she hadn't known her well.

"Would you ever consider moving to Paris?" he asked.

"And kill my father more swiftly than the poison that is killing him now?"

He tilted her chin up and in his eyes a deep concern steadied them on her gaze. "Liam mentioned something to me about poison. I didn't want to bring it up earlier because you were, well, in a sexy mood."

She kissed him. "Yes, poison. It's a suspicion. His condition improved after an initial dose of the wolfsbane, and the next day it was like he'd been set back two steps. Like maybe someone increased the dose of poison that had been slowly killing him."

"That makes sense. I wonder how we can check. It must be in his food."

"But Lana has been bringing him his food…" Her heart stopped beating for a second. Lana? Could she… No. Never. Otherwise she would have never eaten the mashed potatoes and gotten sick herself.

But she was engaged to a wolf who had his sights set on scion—or even principal. "Sven?"

Tryst shook his head. "We need to test your father's food. Fast."

"Natalie can do it. She's a witch, but also our resident doctor and herbalist. Yes, now that you've said that, I think it could be true. Sven is a loose cannon. And he's been with the pack such a short time. I never have trusted him. I've got to get back. I don't know how I'll hide it."

"Hide what?"

She snuggled into his embrace and kissed him. "Us. My having shifted. I've never felt so good. I'm so excited about this. I want to jump and shout and tell everyone. It'll be a hard line to walk once back by my father's side."

"He'll get better. We'll make sure it happens."

"With you by my side, I think it can happen."

She kissed him quickly, and he stopped her from a hasty retreat with a long, lingering kiss that melted through her skin and made her bones liquid, as if she were shifting but so much sweeter.

"Whatever happens," he said, "don't forget that I love you. I would do anything for you, Lexi. And I will always do what I have to, to make things right for you. No matter what."

Chapter 14

Lexi tried for discretion, asking the chef if, at any moment, he had ever left the food alone while tending the meals. The old wolf, who wore a scar along his neck, and who had never been overly friendly, gave a gruff shrug of his rounded shoulders. "I'm too busy slaving over your meals to have a moment to myself. Why do you ask?"

"Uh…" How to ask straight out about the poison, without mentioning the actual word? "My sister was sick yesterday and she thinks it was something she ate."

The chef slammed a knife, blade down, on the butcher block, making Lexi jump. "You saying it was something I prepared that made her sick? I use the freshest and finest ingredients. My kitchen is spotless. I've never been accused of such a thing."

His voice rose and Lexi tried to tamp down his anger with a placating hand between them, while she felt, more than heard, the other wolf enter the cafeteria and Sven's voice boomed out, "What's wrong, Jacques?"

"The princess here says my food made her sister sick."

"I didn't say that, exactly." Lexi caught Sven's lifted chin. He eyed her narrowly, and she could read his thought process. He knew she suspected. His werewolf had found her in here just last night. But she had nowhere else to turn, no other option than to just lay it all out there and let the chips fall where they may. "Every time after father has eaten, he gets worse. Maybe it's poison?"

"You think so?" Sven's jaw worked, tightening the muscles in his neck. "And you think Lana was poisoned? She looked fine this morning."

"Did she go out with you last night on a run?"

Sven's shoulders stiffened. "What's it to you?"

"I think she stayed in her room because she still didn't feel well. Poison is the only option I can come up with to explain Father's illness."

"Yes, maybe." Sven rubbed his jaw, giving the impression he was thinking hard thoughts, but Lexi suspected differently. "Ever since that damned outsider came to Wulfsiege."

"No, Trystan did not arrive until—"

"That's it! It's the outsider!" Sven stomped out into the hallway and declared to the wolves walking by, "He's poisoned the principal!"

"Hell." Not the way she'd wanted this to go.

Despite her arguments that her father had been sick *before* Trystan Hawkes had arrived at Wulfsiege, half the pack, group-minded, followed Sven's orders to locate the outsider wolf. They'd dragged Tryst from the snowplow that Liam had pulled out into the courtyard, and into the dungeon—yes, a real dungeon lurked in the bowels of the castle—and chained him up in a cold, dark cell that hadn't been swept in centuries.

Lexi clung to Tryst's body, his arms stretched out to the side and wrists secured in manacles. They weren't silver manacles, but still, the iron hinges fit his wrists tightly. Despite her position as chatelaine, she had not the authority to go over any male's head and demand Tryst be released. Nor did she have a key to the manacles.

"I won't let them kill you," she said.

"Kill?"

"I don't think they'd do that." But with Sven heading the vanguard, she couldn't be sure.

"Just make sure you find who is really poisoning your father," he said. "We both know it's not me. That means the culprit is still out there and your father is not safe. My bets are on Sven. Have you spoken to the principal?"

"Not yet. I'm headed there next. But I don't want to leave you. I can't. Oh, Tryst."

"I'll be fine. If they keep me chained down here and don't get a mind to slice off my head, I'll just be bored."

She kissed him, lingering at his mouth because she wanted to take his breath into her and know him with every breath she inhaled. To somehow steal a part of him to keep forever.

"Don't do that. It'll only remind me of what I can't have."

She kissed his chest and smoothed her palm over his stretched abs. "I'll be back as soon as I can."

"I don't think that's a good idea. You might be seen

coming down here. You've got to sneak out of here, as it is. Lexi, be smart, for your father."

She nodded, but stepping away from him—chained for no reason—was the hardest thing she'd ever had to do. She hated Sven, and all the males in the pack. Finally she had found her birthright, and had become unbroken, and, as usual, the pack spoiled it all. Her sister was right: they were literal prisoners here at Wulfsiege, destined to live out their lives under the control of the pack males.

Tryst shifted his feet and the manacles clacked. Thankful they were not silver, she suddenly had a thought. "Silver?"

"What did you say?"

"Silver in his food? It's possible. If a very small amount were administered."

"You're thinking about your dad's meals? It would have to be microscopic. Lexi, if silver enters our bloodstream it would tear us apart."

"Unless the killer wanted to do it slowly, make it look like something else, such as poison. A minute amount of silver, if not completely pure, might not have such an immediate and catastrophic effect. I have to look into this. I love you!"

As she topped the final stair and stepped out into the hallway, Lexi walked right into Liam. He growled at her but stepped back, putting distance between them. Reaching for her sunglasses, she fumbled them out of her pocket and they dropped to the stone floor.

He quickly bent to swipe them up, and just as he was going to hand them to her, he said, "Look at me."

She shook her head, still looking aside.

"Princess," he said firmly. "I know he didn't do it."

"Then why didn't you stand up for him?" She looked

him directly in the eye and he gaped at the sight of her eyes. So let him look. She didn't care anymore. She wanted to shout to everyone that she belonged to Tryst and that he was the only wolf in the castle capable of making her whole.

"You've shifted?" he asked.

She nodded. "It was Tryst. He—"

He put up a palm to fend off further explanation and handed her the glasses. "Put these on. Now would not be the best time to let that secret slip."

"Be happy for me, please."

He nodded. "I am. Hawkes is a good man. I'll…do what I can to see he is treated justly. Not sure what that is, though."

"We both know Tryst is innocent. I suspect Sven is poisoning Father, but not with what we'd think of as poison. I asked in the cafeteria, but the chef was tight-lipped. And then Sven barged in and now Tryst is in chains. But Lana is the only one who has been bringing Father his meals."

"Have you talked to your sister?"

"Not yet. She would not be involved, Liam. She was sick last night after eating Father's meal. Do you think it could be silver?"

"Hell."

"Administered in minute doses to make it look like poison? Or something that had trace amounts of silver in it? No, Father would notice, yes? Silver should react more violently in our breed. Oh, I have to figure this out. For Father's sake and for Lana's. She's not safe with Sven. He could be using her to deflect suspicion away from him."

"Sven can make your sister do anything. Hell, if only I— No. The guy is no match for me."

"Don't say that, Liam. You're a match to any wolf in this pack. You could take Sven down easily."

"Yes, but you know I prefer nonviolence, Princess."

"I would never ask you to act against your morals. Let me talk to Lana and see if she'll tell me anything. Will the pack leave Tryst alone? I worry that Sven will go after him and kill him."

"I'll make sure that doesn't happen. We do not mete out justice with death, you know that."

"Thanks. I need to see my father before I find Natalie."

"Sven has put a guard at his door."

"I can be let in to see him."

"I'm not so sure. Be careful."

She put on her glasses and then squeezed his hand. "Thanks. I know who I want my father to name as the pack scion."

He smiled, but it was forced. "Right now we need to concern ourselves with getting to the bottom of your father's illness. He's the principal, and we must protect our own."

His horribly out-of-tune whistles echoed off the cold stone walls, so Tryst stopped about halfway through the Metallica tune. Just made the atmosphere creepier, anyway. But the silence wasn't helping, either. He couldn't hear anything above, or sense anything beyond the chilly frozen ground that hugged the thick castle walls. Not an insect skittered the lonely cell; nor did he sense anyone would bring him down a nice hot lunch.

He could break out of the chains with ease. Just needed to shift to werewolf and the iron manacles should pull free of the wall, but he decided against that. Until he was prepared to take on Sven and had real proof the wolf had actually poisoned Lexi's father, his raging against the pack would do no one any good and probably see him dead.

Silver? He couldn't imagine it could be administered in such small doses as to slowly kill a wolf, but he was no expert. He just knew he avoided the metal—all werewolves did—for fear of death.

"Wonder what Dad would think of me now?" he muttered.

His father would likely laugh at Tryst's situation, then urge him to break out of the chains and try to talk to the pack. Rhys always went for the talk before the talon. Not that he wouldn't defend his own with all his might, especially in werewolf form, which found his vampire mind controlling his thoughts and stirring him to a vicious aggression.

Tryst had inherited his father's common sense and innate desire to make all things right. Nothing wrong with that. But he still liked a good fight.

But it worried him that Lexi was up there, on her own, with no one to stand beside her for protection. In his aggressive state, Sven could do anything. And if he really *was* poisoning the principal, Tryst wouldn't put it past Sven to kill him and have it done with. If he had enough pack members on his side, they would support him.

Tryst wished he'd had a chance to talk to Liam. The wolf was Tryst's only ally, yet Tryst believed Liam was a pacifist. What a waste of that man's muscles.

He whistled a few more bars of the heavy-metal tune and wondered how long he could stand by and let the world fall down around him.

"Not long," he muttered, and gave the manacles a testing yank.

Chapter 15

Lexi spied Lana's perfect swish of hair and grabbed her sister by the arm, pulling her down the hallway and into her room. She pushed her sister against the wall.

"Whoa! Lexi, what's the deal? Don't be so rough. I still don't feel well."

"Well enough to hang on Sven, as I just saw you doing while he preached to the pack about how the evil outsider needs to die. Talk to me, Lana. You know the truth."

"You are acting wild and erratic, sister. It's a good thing they've got the outsider chained up. He's making you crazy."

"Trystan Hawkes has nothing whatsoever to do with my anger right now. Nor has he a thing to do with poisoning Father. You know well that Father was ailing long before Tryst even arrived at Wulfsiege. He brought an elixir with him from Rhys Hawkes that Father believed could heal him."

"That's not how Sven explains it."

"Sven is an arrogant asshole that you don't even love. Why do you allow him to influence you, Lana? You're so smart. Think for yourself."

Lana shoved roughly past Lexi and paced over to the window. "I do think for myself. I'm just not like you, so independent that you chase away any man who will look at you."

"Please, Lana, don't even start. You know why the pack wolves avoid me."

"Because you're broken." She spun, hands on hips, chin lifted triumphantly.

And in that moment, Lexi could no longer endure her sister's snide comments and demeaning treatment. Lana thought she was the cold one? Lana had mastered cold cruelty in spades. And Lexi put most of the blame on Sven.

With a frustrated sigh, Lexi took off her glasses and tossed them onto the nearby bed. "I'm not broken. It just took me a while to come around."

Her sister's eyes widened, her mouth fell open in a gape. "Your— Ohmygod. How did that happen? You've shifted?"

"I found my mate," Lexi said. "The one man who could make me whole."

"The outsider? Father will kill him!"

She gripped Lana's arm to keep her from running out and rushing for Sven. "You will not tell Father a thing while he's doing so poorly. Don't you even care that he's suffering and any stress will only make him worse?"

"You're the one who slept with the man who is poisoning our father!"

"He did not— Oh!" She yanked her sister's arm, hating herself for the angry reaction the moment she did it, but it startled Lana, who backed up against the wall, palms to it. "I'm so sorry."

Lana didn't say a word. Her look stabbed into Lexi's thawed heart with the tip of an icicle.

"Listen to me," Lexi said softly. "I love you, Lana. I hate seeing you bullied and controlled by Sven. He's… changed you. And I think he's involved you in something so heinous that you wouldn't believe it even if you knew the truth."

Lana shook her head, rubbing her arm. "It's not fair. You get the nice one. He's so damned kind! And helpful, and respectful. And look at who I'm saddled with."

It was the first time Lexi had heard her sister confess her true feelings for Sven. And about time.

"Listen, Lana, you were sick last night because you ate Father's food. You know that is truth. It had been poisoned, or tampered with in some way. And you know who's doing it."

She tilted her head down, avoiding Lexi's eyes.

"Lana. You suspect, don't you? I know he's involved you, but I don't think you realize it. Has Sven access to silver?"

Lana gasped. Her hands started to shake.

"Oh, sweetie, it's not your fault."

"But it could be. I don't know anything about it, Lexi, I swear it to you. But, I think you could be right. He's been so angry lately, and he really wants to be principal. I saw a vial of some silver liquid in his room the other day and asked him about it."

"What did he say?"

"He said it was real silver, and he keeps it as a reminder of what could kill him. I thought that was so twisted, but then, knowing all he's endured in the past, it made a weird kind of sense. You think he's been putting silver in Daddy's food?"

"I can't be positive. A few others suspect Sven. I want to talk to Natalie to see if she's aware of a means to deliver silver to slowly kill."

"Oh, my gods, Lexi!"

"We need to prove Sven's been poisoning Father, and if we can, he will be ousted from the pack. You don't love him, Lana. Just tell me that and I'll make sure justice is served against the real criminal."

Lana nodded, a simple confirmation. Lexi pulled her into a hug. "It's going to be okay."

"Daddy is going to die," she said on a sniffle. "And it's my fault. I brought him his food!"

"It's not your fault," Lexi rushed out. "In fact, you getting sick may have been the catalyst to helping him. We may have never suspected if that hadn't happened. But you need to help me now. We need to learn the truth about Sven."

"I don't know if I dare. He's rough, Lexi. He'll kill me if he suspects I'm going against him."

Unfortunately, Lexi believed Lana's fears. And she couldn't allow that to happen.

"Then you won't go against him. You'll just be the pretty, loving fiancée you've been to him. We can do this without you. I'll figure something out."

Lana pressed her palms to Lexi's cheeks and studied her eyes. "So you really shifted? Because of Tryst? How?"

"We were having sex and it just happened." Lexi took her sister's hand and nuzzled into the palm. "He's the man for me. I love him."

Her sister hugged her tightly. "I hope you get him."

* * *

Reese said Natalie had gone out into the forest. She collected tree sap and ground mushrooms, and all sorts of odd things to use in her healing concoctions. So Lexi headed to the south tower. The wolf standing outside her father's door put back his shoulders and lifted his chin as she approached.

"Step aside, Harris," she said, not slowing her pace. He was one of Sven's closest friends. "Where is Rick?"

The wolf, who had grown up alongside Lexi yet had always hung with the pack males, took a step to the left to block her entrance. "Sorry, Princess Alexis, I've been told no visitors. Only the doctor is allowed past this door."

"He's my father. I will see him."

He put both hands to her shoulders and squeezed in warning. It was apparent he wasn't going to physically take her down, but he was following his orders seriously.

"Harris."

"Alexis, please, I've been ordered."

"By whom?"

The door opened and Sven stepped out from the conference room. The Nord towered over Lexi and used that height to his advantage. "By me. I'm assuming Vincent's role as scion while your father is sick. He's not in his right mind to make important decisions now."

"Not in his right mind? I just saw him this morning. We had a conversation. He knew exactly what he was talking about. If he's gotten worse I must see him."

Sven's block was rougher than Harris's had been. He pushed Lexi against the wall and held her there with a hand beneath her neck. "I'm doing this for your own good. You're emotional, Princess. It's not good for your father to see you like this."

And if Sven had a hand in her father's illness then he wouldn't want anyone to get past him now. She couldn't allow this to happen.

Lexi kicked high, and managed a knee to the inside of Sven's thigh.

"Grab her," Sven growled, and Harris went for her legs.

Lexi kicked madly. She was able to ram an elbow into Sven's jaw before freeing herself and stepping away from both males. Supporting herself with her hands to the wall behind her, she huffed out frantic breaths. She'd never get past the door now. If only her father would use a cell phone, she could call him, but he preferred landlines, which the avalanche had taken out.

"You can't keep me from my father," she said. "I'm going to find the doctor."

"Doctor's in the room with him. You run along and check the wounded in the keep like a good little girl."

She flipped him off with a flick of her fingers beneath her chin, and marched away. Now, more than ever she needed to gather help for her father. But all she could do was imagine crushing Sven's head. A task she was incapable of accomplishing.

Anger tightening her fists, Lexi stomped through her bedroom and peeled away her shirt and kicked off her shoes. If Natalie were still out in the forest, she would find her and get to the bottom of this. Heading out the door, she trotted down the steps and through the courtyard. She was so angry right now she needed to release some of it before attempting a calm conversation with the herb-hunting witch.

With but a thought, her body began to shift. It was

so easy she laughed as her bones and muscles moved, and the laughter echoed across the snow cover and segued into an abrupt yip as her wolf voiced the remnants of her frustrated anger.

Dashing north, she headed toward the forest, along the fresh powder that had packed in on top of the snow moved during the avalanche. Every scent and sound was amplified, honed by her senses, to a fine symphony of the world.

Her paws took the slope with ease, and she tracked the forest edge for many leagues, not scenting the witch. Perhaps she'd missed her?

Suddenly the ground shifted. The wolf yelped as snow began to flow in waves beneath her feet, and she was toppled to her side, her four legs flailing and tail twisting in an attempt to right herself as she was moved along with the massive amounts of snow.

Chapter 16

Tryst strained against the manacles secured to the dungeon wall. He'd heard it. A dull, thudding *thump* that could only be another avalanche. His heart fell to his gut. Ears perked, he listened for noise, anything, calls from above that would assure him the castle inhabitants were safe, but his sensory abilities were muffled within the stone walls.

Damn it! He needed to be free. And right now, if the pack was dealing with another avalanche, they wouldn't have time to worry about him. Which was a good thing.

Dare he make an escape? It was the coward's way. Yet he'd been falsely accused and had every right to his freedom.

The door to the dungeon creaked open and footsteps shuffled hastily down the stairs. Liam clanked the keys against the manacle.

"Another avalanche?"

"Yes." Liam released Tryst's wrist. "Lana said she saw Lexi head out for a run."

"What?"

"She's missing. Possibly buried beneath the snow. So are some of the pack. I'm going to head the search for the men. You need to go after the princess."

"Where was she?"

"Lana says east of Wulfsiege, where the avalanche originated, on the same slope as the original occurred. Also, Sven is going off on how you're to blame for the weather, as well as poisoning the principal, so avoid him if you want a chance to help Lexi."

The last manacle fell away from his wrist and Tryst slapped Liam across the back. "You have a team to help you?"

"I do. And having watched you the first time I know what to do. I've got it under control."

"Is the principal safe?"

"Yes, though he is very weak. Go! If you don't find her I'll hold myself responsible for allowing that bastard Sven to chain you up in the first place."

"Thanks, man. I'll bring her back."

They raced up the stairs and Tryst headed for his room to pull on pack boots, snow pants and a coat. He grabbed a ski pole from a storage locker in the hallway and snapped off the basket. Racing out into the hallway, he headed toward Lexi's room, because he knew she would have gone out the back door.

He ran right into Sven.

The Nord drew back his arm, loading his fist and— Tryst dodged the fist and came up with a right hook beneath Sven's jaw. The idiot wolf's head jacked back on his neck, his eyes rolled backward, and he fell against the wall, crumbling into a heap. Out cold.

"That's just the beginning, asshole."

Tryst leaped over the wolf's prone body and raced through Lexi's room. The outer door was open. She must have been in some kind of mood to leave it that way.

The air hit his face like one of Sven's fists. The bitter cold must register below zero. He couldn't believe Lexi had gone out for a run, but then, elated with her new ability to shift, it had probably been just the thing to chase her mind from all the trouble lately.

Hell, where could she be? He studied the grounds outside her room and found many boot prints. It took a while to find the right kind of tracks, but he did locate wolf paw prints and scented her. He tracked after them in were form because he needed to stay this way so he wouldn't arrive at her side naked and without the proper tools to dig her out.

"Please don't let her be buried," he muttered, choking down his rising fear. "She has to be safe. I don't want to live without you, Lexi."

He knew the danger of something so unassuming as snow. A wall of it could level trees, move cars and crush buildings. And take lives.

He muttered prayers to God because his father had taught him there was a supreme being, and even though werewolves tended to not have an organized religion, they were spiritual and honored nature. Tryst believed in karma so he had to wonder what Lexi had done to bring this upon herself. What had *he* done?

By coming together had they pissed off the karma gods? Everything between them had seemed so right. Sure, no one in the pack wanted them to be together. Could that be it? The ignorance of others had brought this upon them?

No, it had to be something wider, more vile. The poisoning of Principal Connor had to be the reason for all the bad things that had been happening at Wulfsiege.

He added prayers for any other wolves who had been buried, and that Liam and his team would find them quickly.

Focusing, Tryst paused at the edge of the moved snow. It looked as if a spray of white, lumpy frosting had scattered across a smooth confection. He sniffed and closed his eyes, sensing a heartbeat nearby. A rabbit? No, a gray fox darted across the snow. Yet he still sensed the heartbeat, and knew it was familiar.

"Lexi?"

A moan swung him around. There, at the edge of the tree line, he saw the hand. The fingers wiggled.

Dodging for what he knew was his lover, Tryst began to dig and uncovered black hair and snow that was soaked with blood. "Oh, Lexi, no. Please be okay."

A broken branch lay against her side. She'd been stabbed, but where?

Slowly, and methodically, he uncovered her body, scraping away the icy snow, stopping halfway to take off his coat and lay it over her torso because she was naked. She must have shifted after the avalanche. When a wolf is wounded in werewolf or wolf form, it comes back to were form without volition.

"Princess, oh, my lover. Please, say something."

He brushed the snow from her cheeks and when he thought to lift her head, instead he leaned in and kissed her forehead. She could have broken bones, and if her neck had been hurt he risked causing further damage by moving her too much. Her skin was cold against his lips.

Blood pulsed from a wound at her shoulder and he

pressed his palm over it. Hot and oozing, the smell of it tickled his nose. The odor was so strong, and particular.

"Lexi!"

She couldn't be dead. He'd just found the woman with whom he wanted to spend the rest of his life. Karma wouldn't do that to him. It just could not.

Blood pulsed from the wound. He wasn't up on arteries and veins, but suspected something like that must have been damaged. The branch must have acted as a blade, cutting deep beneath her skin. He slapped his palm over the wound, remembering to put pressure on a wound, but he couldn't recall why or where he'd heard that.

Drops of blood spattered the air, and he swiped the hair from his face. Dashing out his tongue he tasted his lover's blood, sweet and hot on his tongue. He swallowed. What kind of thought had that been? Sweet blood? Awful to think such a thing at this moment.

Bending, he kissed her cold mouth, leaving his lips there, hoping to bring some warmth to her. He bracketed her face, pressing his warm palms over her cheeks. "Come back to me, Lexi. Don't leave me."

He breathed into her mouth, not attempting resuscitation—her breath came softly. She was alive and breathing. He kissed her face all over, slowly, methodically, determined to bring warmth to her skin, while he continued to apply pressure over the wound. Lying on top of her would warm her skin, so he did that, gently, stretching along her body until he rested the length of her.

Kisses to her jaw tasted blood and he swept his mouth down her neck and close to the wound, licking the hot blood.

Tasting it.

She belonged to him. His sweet broken princess had

become whole in his arms last night. Nothing could take her away from him now. He would stop the bleeding, he had to.

He pressed his lips to the wound. And something inside him moaned…with pleasure.

Chapter 17

Lexi came to with a moan, but her lungs felt crushed and all she could do was wince and murmur. She sat against a tree trunk. The sky was dark. Moonlight jeweled across the wickedly deceptive snow. Wrapped about her shoulders and torso, she found Tryst's coat. She didn't know it from sight but rather from his scent. She tugged the coat tightly to her naked body, realizing she didn't feel cold, only achy. Somewhere she smelled blood, and assumed it must be her own.

An avalanche had struck when she'd been in wolf form. She'd always known a wolf's body reverted when wounded, but was surprised it worked automatically.

She felt broken everywhere, but sensed of all her injuries, none was too severe. Her shoulder screamed with pain, yet that, too, didn't feel life threatening. Though to crane her neck aside, she saw that's where the blood scent came from.

Five feet away sat Tryst, back to her, his head down. A mound of snow had been piled beside her. He must have dug her up from the snow. Her rescuing knight. He would always be there for her. He couldn't have come into her life at a better time. Certainly, a trying time, but she would not survive it without him, she felt sure.

She cleared her throat and he whipped his head around.

"Lexi. You're awake. Thank the gods. You're going to be okay. The wound stopped bleeding. After…" He turned away from her.

She sensed something graver than her being slammed to the ground by a wall of snow was going on inside his brain. Why wouldn't he come to her?

He lifted his hands to reveal they were covered with blood. Her blood? Hell, she must have really been hurt. She wanted to beg him to come to her, but her throat burned and all she could do was gasp.

"I'm so sorry," he said. "I… This shouldn't have happened."

No man could prevent acts of nature. But Lexi knew, if possible, Tryst would have stood before the wall of snow and held out his arms if it would have kept her safe. It was her fault for going out on her own when she should have stayed in and tried harder to see her father. Sven's audacity had made her so angry.

Father. She needed to get to him. He wasn't safe if Sven had assumed control. And what about Natalie? If she had been anywhere in the area when the avalanche had struck, she could be buried, as well.

"Natalie?"

"What's that?"

"The witch. She may have been out here."

He shook his head. "I sense no other beating hearts, Lexi. Are you sure?"

She shook her head. She hadn't sensed her while out running, so she hoped the witch had already headed back to the castle before the disaster struck.

"Help me back," she managed. "To Wulfsiege."

Tryst crept across the snow to her side. It was no small exaggeration to say he was covered with her blood. It was all over his shirt and neck and smeared on his cheeks and hands. He held out his hands before her as if to offer an explanation for something she didn't have the strength to figure out.

"What is it?" she asked. "Hold me?"

He moved in but then shook his head. "Your blood."

"I'll be fine. I can feel the wound is already healing."

"It shouldn't have healed so quickly. Not without my…"

"Tryst, what is it?"

He bowed his head to the ground near her thigh and she felt his hair at her fingertips and clutched for it. Why wouldn't he touch her? She needed him to touch her.

He began to shake his head.

"Tryst, you're freaking me out. I'm wounded, but I'll heal."

"You will. You're strong. But the wound on your shoulder was deep. Had to have torn an artery." He looked up at her. Tears streaked through the blood on his cheeks. "It got in my mouth. Your blood."

"I can see that. You're coated with it. Use some snow to wash it off. I'm going to be okay, Tryst. Look. I can sit up. I think I can even walk on my own if you help me to stand."

"Lexi." His stare drilled into hers and she waited for him as if awaiting another wall of devastating snow. "It got in my mouth, and I *tasted* it." He looked aside. His Adam's apple bobbed with a swallow. A sigh fogged in the air before his face. "And I wanted more."

She opened her mouth but couldn't enunciate the words that banged against her tongue. *Vampire. His mother is a vampire. His father is half-breed.* Tryst thought he was full-blood werewolf? Impossible. She had never believed it, had thought he was fooling himself. Had his parents' lies deluded him?

"I drank your blood, Lexi. And I think my saliva closed your wound and made it heal faster. Just like a..."

"Tryst, it's okay—"

"It's not okay, Lexi. It will never be okay. I'm a fucking half-breed." He stood and kicked the snow with a pack boot, then let out a shout and beat the air with a fist. "Damn it! This wasn't supposed to happen."

Lexi swallowed. Now she saw the blood on his chin, staining his neck, as if it had poured from his mouth. A werewolf would never consider such a heinous act. Drink blood for survival, or worse, for pleasure? Sacrilege.

"But that doesn't matter right now." He gestured with a curt slash of both hands before him. A decisive move. "I have to get you back to Wulfsiege."

He started to lift her and she pressed her fingers to his lips. "It's okay, Trystan, I love you."

"We won't talk about this. Not now. Your safety is all that matters."

And he lifted her into his arms and began the treacherous march back to the castle without saying another word to her.

"Don't go to the keep. Just take me to my room," Lexi said as Tryst climbed the outside stairs up to the castle.

"You need medical attention. There are doctors in the keep."

"Bring Natalie to my room. Tryst, they'll see my eyes."

Hell. He'd forgotten about that. Another secret to keep. But the biggest secret of all had just been revealed. Something he'd never believed could happen to him. Never. He'd known from birth he was full-blooded werewolf. Rhys had made him believe that. His mother had often lamented his lacking vampiric tendencies. Had it all been carefully constructed lies?

He could still taste Lexi's blood in his mouth, and it was not an awful taste. And that thought slammed him like a wrecking ball to the gut.

Was he half vampire?

He couldn't be a damn longtooth. He was full-blooded werewolf.

Kind of shot that to hell by slurping up your lover's blood, eh?

Karma really was a bitch.

"Tryst, please."

He did not veer from his path to the keep. "You can tell them it was the avalanche. It did something and now you can shift. That's a great explanation. Like maybe it shifted the bones in your body and then the shift came naturally to you. Then you never have to tell them you were sleeping with me."

"But I don't care anymore. I want to tell the world I love you and that you're my lover and that you were the man who made me whole."

He winced. He hadn't done that. It had been a fluke. Had to be. If he was half vampire, no way could he entice an unshifted werewolf to fully shift. Just didn't make any sense.

He was an outsider. Always had been, always would be.

He stopped in the hallway that turned toward the keep, and she protested, shuffling out of his grip to stand. "I will always do what is right for you, Lexi."

"And setting me aside when I most need you to hold me is right?" She shook her head. "That was wrong to say. I'm sorry."

"You need a doctor to look at the wound and make sure it isn't infected. And I need to find Liam. Others were buried in the avalanche."

"Oh, hell, I didn't even think of that. Yes, you need to help them. You shouldn't worry about me."

He caught her head between his palms. "Don't apologize for asking me for what you want. I just—hell, I told you I drank your blood. Doesn't that blow your mind?"

She winced. "I don't want to think about it too much."

"Yeah? Well, I need to put some distance between us right now because the smell of the blood on your skin? It's driving me crazy. And the fact it's driving me crazy is so off-the-chart insane I don't know how to deal with it."

"Oh. Yes. I didn't think of that. Yes, help me to the keep. How will you know about…?"

The unspoken entreaty regarding his true nature. Werewolf and vampire? Was he like his father, one side controlled by the other? She wanted to know, to have answers, but knew that it had all happened so quickly Tryst couldn't even have the answers.

"I don't know anything," he said sharply. "But I do know I need to wash this blood off me right now."

They arrived at the keep and he delivered her to a cot and made sure the doctor they'd had flown in attended her immediately. Natalie was there, and Lexi called her to her side. Tryst refused triage, explaining it wasn't his blood, and quickly escaped the confining walls of the keep and snuck to his room without running head-on into Sven the Idiot.

Tearing away his shirt as he entered the room, he raced into the bathroom and splashed water over his chest and face to clean off Lexi's all-too-enticing blood. It spattered the vanity and mirror and he tried to wipe it away but only ended up making a mess. Shucking off his pants, he dropped the denim to the floor. The red covered his skin as if a mutant disease trying to soak into his pores. It looked and felt like the worst kind of horror movie he had seen.

After soaping up, he dug in the linen closet for a clean towel and managed to erase the evidence of his wicked encounter with something that was so beyond his realm of understanding, he could but stand in front of the mirror and stare at his skin, reddened from the rough scrubbing.

"Rhys," he whispered. He needed to call his father and ask him about this.

But even more, he needed to find Liam and insure the others had been found. And to do that without running into the one wolf who had a death wish aimed directly for his heart?

Watching the water run pink down the drain, Tryst punched a fist against the mirror. The glass cracked but did not shatter.

"What the hell are you?" he asked the distorted reflection. "Have you been a monster all your life?"

Curling his fingers against the mirror, he sought the answers from the silvered glass. Silver, the werewolf's bane. He wondered if Lexi had learned anything about the suspicious poisoning. So many thoughts polluting his brain and the one that rose to the surface was hideous, like a piece of refuse stained with muck.

He had never discriminated against any breed, and had always accepted his father and mother. But growing up believing he was wolf, and now to learn otherwise, was mind-blowing. And the stress was only going to increase the longer he went without answers.

He thought of Lexi and her inability to shift like the rest of her breed. It must be what she had felt all her life. And then to finally be given the power to transform last night? Her world had changed for the better.

And his had just fallen off a cliff.

Chapter 18

He had to put aside the fact his whole life had been a lie. Sorting out the rights from wrongs would have to wait. Right now, there could be wolves trapped out in the snow. Tryst dressed in the stained outerwear—he rubbed off Lexi's blood as best he could—and ran down the hallway and outside. He spied a team of four near the new snow cover opposite of the stadium. It hadn't come close to the castle this time, about a quarter of a mile off, and he raced across the snowpack.

Liam stood near three wolves digging frantically in the snow. Tryst spied the leg slowly being revealed. "How long has he been under?"

"Maybe an hour," Liam said. He stared off over the landscape that the avalanche had altered. "He's the only one. The rest are accounted for."

"Thank the gods for that."

Liam nodded. "I can get behind that thanks. How's Lexi? You did find her?"

"Battered and bruised, but she's going to recover. I took her to the keep." Tryst swallowed back his rising heart. Every pulse of it returned the taste of Lexi's blood to his tongue. He felt like the worst kind of outsider not telling Liam the whole truth. "I thought I'd lost her."

Liam slapped him across the back. "We're a tough breed. Where's Sven?"

"I don't know."

"We need to keep an eye on him. He's been hanging around Principal Connor's room."

Tryst turned his back to the men digging out the man under the snow and spoke softly. "Lexi seems to think her sister may know the truth. That she might be inadvertently involved in her father's sickness."

"Lana would never do such a thing."

"I know, man, but you also know Sven. He could be forcing her, or using her in ways she can't even imagine."

"I've got to put a stop to this."

Tryst put a hand on Liam's shoulder, surprised at the man's sudden anger. "Are you going to accuse him without proof?"

Liam shook his head. "No, that would be foolish. How can we obtain proof?"

"I think Lana is the key. We need someone to talk nice to her." Tryst eyed Liam's tight jaw. "Someone who cares about her, and has her best interests in mind."

Liam got the hint and, with a nod, silently conceded he would take the task in hand. He turned and bent to help the rescue team, while Tryst offered to run for a stretcher to carry the wolf inside.

He bounded through the castle halls, remembering

he'd seen a stretcher in the keep. That the avalanche had only claimed two victims this time—and both had survived—was something to be thankful for. Tryst realized he already held pack Alpine in close regard. He knew only a few pack wolves, yet he counted each and every one as family. If they hurt, he hurt.

Hoping to check quickly on Lexi while in the keep, he raced toward the inner stronghold. But when he heard the angry growl behind him, he knew he didn't want to take that trouble into the keep with him. Curving around, Tryst came up with his fists to meet the charging Sven.

"You are going out in a body bag," the wolf growled. "Today!"

"They're beating him again. Sven wants him dead. I can't stop him!"

"Tryst?"

Lana nodded frantically.

Lexi grabbed her sister's arm and stood, a little wobbly and light-headed, but she was on two feet and that was all that mattered. "I talked to Natalie. The wormwood was missing from her supplies. She said silver could be infused in it and delivered in small amounts. Go to Father," she said to her sister. "Tell him what you know about Sven and the silver."

"I can't."

"You have to! Lana, I will protect you from Sven."

"You can't! He's too strong. He's pummeling your man right now. And I'll be next if I tell Daddy anything."

Clinging to her sister's arm, Lexi forced her to meet her eyes. "Don't you want our father to live? By not telling him, you wield the killing blade as much as Sven. Lana, please."

Behind them, Lexi saw Liam enter the keep. He made eye contact with her.

"Liam, where's Tryst?"

"They've thrown him out. He's still alive. I wouldn't allow the pack to follow Sven's murderous commands. But I had to fight them back when they tried to go after him."

"Thank you, Liam."

"He can't be here, Princess. He's not right."

"You see?" Lana looked Liam up and down. "Even he wants Tryst out of here."

"Who told you he's not right, Liam?"

"Sven said he's half-breed—that his parents are vampires—and Hawkes didn't deny it. Is it true? Is he half-breed?"

She had known it would come to this. And with Tryst biting her earlier out in the snow, she knew he could no longer deny his wicked truths. The pack would never see beyond their ignorance to the good-hearted man Tryst was. And with good reason. Werewolves and vampires simply did not mix.

"It's something he just discovered hours ago. We don't have any answers right…" she faltered, her head feeling light "…now."

"Princess, you should be lying down," Liam said. "Let me help you back to a cot, and then I'll escort Princess Lana to her room."

"I don't need an escort anywhere."

Lexi pushed away Liam's arm as he tried to put it around her shoulder. "Do you really believe that between Sven and Tryst, Sven is the better man to keep in the pack?"

Liam shook his head. "If I were principal, Tryst would be my scion. I would not question his heritage. Well, I would, but I know he'd give me all the right answers. It is the man's honor that impresses me."

"Don't forget you said that. Lana." She hugged her sister more for support, because her legs still felt weak. "I want her to tell father about Sven. He has a supply of silver in his room and Natalie said it can be used with some herbs that were stolen from her. Lana needs to tell Father what she knows, but she needs some encouragement. A strong arm to lean on."

"I offer you all my support, Princess." He made a bow before Lana.

Lexi felt her sister squirm in her arms. She couldn't do this alone, but with Liam by her side it would be less frightening.

"Let me help you?" he entreated Lana.

Lana sighed. "I just need to think about this a bit. Can I do that, Lexi? Please?"

They didn't have time for Lana to think and back out because she feared Sven's wrath, but catching Liam's stern gaze, Lexi conceded. The big wolf, with an offer of his hand, led Lana out of the keep. Liam would convince her to talk. She hoped.

Tryst had been thrown out? He couldn't have gone far, and most likely he'd been beaten again. That man was a glutton for punishment. At the same time, she knew he kept taking those beatings because he didn't want to leave her.

Slapping a hand against the wall for support, she made her way down the hall toward the foyer. She approached a gang of bleeding yet triumphant wolves who were high-fiving each other while congratulating themselves on ousting the half-breed outsider.

She marched right up to Sven, who stretched tall and sneered at her. "What do you want, bitch?"

He certainly was going to fall hard, she thought.

"Take a look at this, guys." Sven gripped her jaw hard. "Her eyes have changed."

"She's shifted," one of the males said.

"It—it happened after the avalanche." She hated the lie, but it felt necessary now as her nape stiffened and her heartbeats increased.

She struggled from Sven's grip and backed away, sensing the testosterone humming in the air was not to her advantage. And she was still so weak. "Your days are numbered, Sven. And anyone who follows you should heed that warning."

She cast her gaze over all the men, who met hers with an aggressive lift of head or a derisive snort. She wasn't about to bow to any of them. Yet she smelled their power, their aching hunger. For her. She should walk away, calmly, without looking back....

"We tossed your vampire lover in the snow," Sven said. "I'm going to get the plow out and drive over the longtooth's body."

"He is not a— You go near him, and I will fight you to the death," she said, ignoring her instinctual need to flee.

The males grunted and eyed Sven.

"I look forward to tussling with you, little blue-eyed one. You might have more spunk than your sister."

"If you ever touch Alana again—"

"What? You're going to fight me to the death? Don't you know, you can only participate in a death match once, sweetie?"

The males chuckled.

"You are not worthy of this pack. And it will be known soon enough."

She turned and Sven caught her with an arm across her chest, easily wrangling her into his grasp. When another wolf grabbed her leg and the howls began, Lexi knew she had walked into the worst situation of her life.

Chapter 19

Their hands were all over her. Her muscles, weak and sore from being trapped in the avalanche earlier, had not the strength she needed to fight. Pushed to the floor, Lexi's arms were held back and her ankles secured by hands. Sven stood over her, his split lip bleeding as he cracked a wide, vicious grin.

And in that moment Lexi thought that if she could detour this horrid wolf's sights from her sister, then let him do his worst. At least Lana would be safe from him now.

"Say, please, blue eyes," Sven said on a growling rasp. "And I'll make you mine. We can lead the pack together. You're much stronger and smarter than your sister." He bent and clutched one of her breasts through her shirt. "Bet you like it rough, too."

She tried to kick, and shouted as loudly as she could. And then one of the hands at her ankle let go. And the other hand. She heard men shout, and one of them yipped in pain.

Sven's head was yanked back by his hair, his arms flailing out for balance. Behind him Lexi saw Tryst, his face bloodied from a beating. His snarl revealed long, sharp fangs that were not indicative of the werewolf.

The hands holding her arms suddenly transformed and talons cut through her skin. With a howl, Sven began to shift, and his henchmen joined ranks. Lexi used the distraction to scramble away along the wall.

"You all right?" Tryst managed, even as his body began to shift.

She nodded.

"I love you. Don't forget that. This is what I have to do."

He'd said that before: he'd always do what he must to make things right. No matter what. With six wolves shifting around him, Lexi feared for her lover's life, but she would not beg him to hold back the rage. Indeed, this was what he had to do.

Tryst's werewolf took over his were form, and turned to meet the brutal attack of five werewolves. Lexi couldn't watch. He would be torn to shreds this time, no doubt about it. Tryst had not gone up against any of the pack in their werewolf form—their most powerful shape. He may be strong, but against five?

He slashed an arm about, catching a charging wolf in his talons and brutally slamming him to the floor. Deep slashes cut through the fallen wolf's furred chest, but he did not stay down for long.

Two wolves jumped Tryst. Lexi noticed Sven stood back, observing. She hated him and wanted to kill him herself. The urge to shift came upon her.

"No," she gasped between tight jaws. Clenching her

fingers, she fought against the overwhelming compulsion. "Too dangerous." She had to let Tryst do this on his own.

A long and rangy wolf howl echoed down the hallway. One of the pack members stood back from Tryst, clutching his throat where the sinew had been torn and the artery shot out blood. The other wolves stepped back, suddenly fearful. They moved behind Sven, who maintained position yet did not approach Tryst.

Lexi's lover stood before the pack, arms flexed and talons bloody. His chest heaved. From his mouth dripped blood, his inordinately long fangs revealed. Not a werewolf or a vampire, Lexi thought. But something even more powerful, born of the two and forged into some sort of hybrid.

"That is enough!" Liam, the originator of the warning howl, rushed onto the scene, a length of chain in hand. Behind him he was flanked by a group of pack males, the ones Lexi knew went out with him for midnight runs. He took in Lexi on the floor, blood splattered over her legs and face, then cast his gaze over the offending wolves. "I've orders from the principal to take you under house arrest."

The werewolf Sven shifted to were form, laughing, as he assumed Liam had meant Tryst. His cohorts all shifted in kind, some fully naked while others wore shredded jeans and bits of shirt hanging from their shoulders.

Tryst remained as werewolf. Or vampire.

What was he? He looked werewolf, yet those fangs were not right. They were designed for piercing, not tearing, as were the wolf's canines.

"I'll help you with the chains," Sven said, stretching out a bloody hand toward Liam.

Liam stepped up to Sven, followed closely by the group of males who had not shifted. "My orders are to take you under arrest. Do you come peacefully or are we going to have to do this the hard way?"

"Me? Look at that monster!"

Tryst lifted his mighty head and clenched his talons.

"He's destroyed the peace here at Wulfsiege," Sven argued.

"You've had a hand in the destruction long before Hawkes ever set foot on this property." Liam handed one of the males behind him the end of the chain. "Looks like we're going to have to do this the hard way."

"You'll never take me." And, with that, Sven was running out the foyer door.

The wolves who had helped him attack Lexi now backed away and rushed off.

"Come on!" Liam led the chase after Sven.

Lexi pulled herself up against the wall and cautiously approached Tryst. He stood well over two heads higher than her, and his ginger-furred form was taut with muscle. The talon slashes across his chest had already begun to heal.

The werewolf reared from her hand and stepped back. "Tryst, it's all right."

He growled, and it was more warning than kind. Did he not want her to see him like this? Those...teeth?

"Sven is going to get what he deserves. You're safe now."

The wolf charged her, pressing her against the wall and pinning her in with a paw to either side of her head. He towered over her, his maw speckled with blood and those long fangs taunting her. He wanted her to look at him, to see his distorted truth. And in that moment,

Lexi's newly warm heart wasn't sure how to feel. To love him? To fear him? To pity him?

She felt each of those things at once.

Touching the fur under his jaw, she slicked her fingers through the blood that belonged to one of her pack members. A pack member who would have raped her had Tryst not come to her rescue.

And yet, what breed had her rescuing knight become? Would he crave her blood? Insist upon drinking it, which would, in return, give her a nasty craving for blood? She didn't want that. But she did want him. Yet how to make that happen baffled her.

"I don't know what to say," she finally offered.

With what looked like a confirming nod, he stepped back from her and ran off toward the south wing, where a back entrance opened and didn't slam shut behind him.

Lexi returned to her room, stripped off her clothes and got in the shower. She wanted to erase Sven's touch but made the shower quick because she had too many things with which to deal. She'd been mentally bruised by the near rape, but she had to stay strong—too many people needed her right now.

After cleaning up, and talking to Liam to insure Sven had been chained in the dungeon, Lexi joined Lana by their father's bedside. Lana gave her a questioning look when she sat down in the easy chair by the window, but Lexi was determined not to tell her about what had happened in the lobby. Lana knew Sven was mentally unstable; no sense in making it even worse.

Their father slept, so Lana had gone to talk to Natalie with Liam at her side. After Lana had confessed her belief Sven was poisoning him with silver, Natalie had known what to do. She couldn't fight silver poisoning with the wolfsbane as it had been delivered by Tryst, so had mixed a special blend of herbs into the wolfsbane she promised would bring improvement and fight the poison. Holly repelled evil, and Natalie had named that as a key ingredient.

"Where's Tryst?" Lana asked quietly.

"I don't know." It was the hardest thing to keep tears from her eyes as Lexi looked out the window and across the darkening grounds below. Snowflakes fell silently. All the energy put out earlier had subsided and it was as if the universe cried now. "I think he left Wulfsiege."

"You think? That means he didn't say goodbye to you?"

He had said goodbye. In a manner. He'd forced her to see him, the true monster he had become. A monster that had come upon him without warning.

Because of her blood.

Sitting on the windowsill, Lexi tugged up her legs and nestled her chin on her knees. Had she truly been the catalyst to releasing the hidden vampire within Trystan Hawkes? If so, she'd never forgive herself for that. But if not her, perhaps it would have been someone else. They would never know. And yet, he had released her trapped werewolf, and that was something she would be thankful for always.

"I love him," she said, and searched her sister's eyes. Blue. They were alike now.

And Lexi had never felt more different. So set aside from the pack and her family, all that she had established about her as safety and home. She wanted to break free, as had her werewolf. But she could not—did not want to—do it without Tryst by her side.

Lana joined her on the windowsill and pulled her into

an embrace. For Lana to offer encouragement meant their worlds had turned a one-eighty. She needed comfort as desperately as did Lexi.

"I'm sorry about Sven," Lexi managed.

"You shouldn't be. He's an asshole."

The two laughed a bit, then, embracing, allowed their laughter to become tears.

By morning, the sisters woke to their father's smiling face. Edmonton Connor reached out for his daughters and they joined him on the bed.

"How do you feel?" Lana brushed her father's hair from his cheek and gave him a kiss.

"Much better. The best I've felt in days. I do believe Natalie's wicked potion is working. Who would have thought the witch doctor would come up with an antidote before the licensed doctor?"

"Dr. LeTreq assisted Natalie," Lexi said. "They're working together to insure you get the best care."

"What's been going on around here?" Edmonton asked. "I thought I heard howls last night."

"Sven's been taken to the dungeon," Lexi provided. "He's been poisoning you with small doses of silver, Father."

He gave his daughters a pleading look.

Lana nodded. "It's true. I found the vial of silver in his room. Forgive me, Daddy, I didn't know."

He cradled her head against his chest, stroking her hair. "I'm just glad you figured things out. This past moon was the first I haven't shifted in decades. It was the worst feeling. I…now I know how you must feel, Alexis. I'm so sorry."

His pity felt wrong and misplaced. She couldn't not share her good news with him. Be damned that it had been because of an unaligned wolf. From this moment forward she would put out all her energy into the world, and hope it served others as well as it had served her.

Lifting her head, she looked into her father's eyes, and a smile was irrepressible. "I've shifted, Father. And I can't lie to you. It was Tryst. We made love, and the shift came upon me."

"Well. I really have missed a lot." Edmonton stared into her eyes, tilting his head in wonder. "My daughter has finally shifted. You feel…okay? Had no problems?"

"I've never felt so good in my life. I've shifted to both wolf and werewolf shapes since it happened. Please, don't be angry with me."

"Angry?"

"Because it happened with Tryst."

"Ah. Well." He sighed and clasped her hand, and pulled Lana in closer. "We've much to catch up on, we three. And much to discuss, it seems. But first, I'm a bit peckish this morning."

He'd accepted her confession with much more calm that she had expected.

"I'll go make you some eggs," Lexi offered. "And I should call Tryst's father," she suddenly said, and tugged out her cell phone.

"Why call Rhys Hawkes?"

"He needs to know you're getting better, and…" She wanted to tell him about Trystan's discovery that he was half vampire. Surely, he should know what his son was going through right now. "I'll be right back."

Tryst had snuck into Wulfsiege while the sun still hid behind the tree line. After shifting to were shape, he had no clothes, and he didn't like the idea of breaking into someone's house in the nearby village to steal clothes just because he wanted to avoid looking into *her* eyes again.

He couldn't do that to her, or himself. He had to see Lexi one last time.

He had no idea how to tell her goodbye. He didn't want to say goodbye. He wanted to say *Hello, I love you, stay by my side forever.* But he didn't belong at Wulfsiege as much as she didn't belong in Paris, living with a werewolf who didn't know what he was anymore.

Hell, he knew what he was. An outsider.

Sorting out this whole vampire thing was foremost. But where to begin? Shame curved his shoulders down. He'd become some kind of monster that was werewolf and yet he had craved the blood from Lexi's attackers last night and had eagerly ripped into one wolf's throat, drinking down his blood because it had tasted good. How sick was that?

Werewolves did not drink blood for survival. Tryst wasn't sure if he needed blood now, but he was offended to know he liked the taste of it. Hell, he was treading crazy to even think about liking the taste.

"Don't think about it," he muttered. "You know real crazy, and you're not it. Yet."

Thoughts of his mother shamed him even more. She hadn't asked for her madness. She was not crazy, but suffered from a brutal injustice that had injured her very sanity.

He hadn't been served an injustice but, rather, was being forced to face something that had always been part of him. Had it? Had vampirism flowed through his veins since birth? It made logical sense. His mother was vampire, and his father one by half. The default for his makeup should include a hunger for blood. Yet, he'd denied it all his life, and his parents had played into that denial.

A knock at the door lifted his head. It was her; he scented the cinnamon that lingered about her as if perfume. Too soon. He needed more time to work up a goodbye story. An *I love you so I need to hurt you by leaving* excuse.

"Tryst? Is that you in there?"

He mumbled, "Uh-huh."

"There's a visitor here to see you."

Visitor? Only one he could think of who might care to have a civil conversation with him was Liam, and that wolf would have knocked himself and come in.

The door opened and in walked Lexi. Dressed in dark gray, she exuded a still menace that disturbed him. She kept her eyes from fixing to his. Her dark hair spilled over her shoulders and she was not wearing her sunglasses. Never again would she have to hide.

So pretty. He'd bitten her. *Hurt* her.

And he could—hell, was that her heartbeat he heard? And what was that tempting smell. It wasn't— No. *Don't think it.*

She was followed into the room by Vaillant, his half brother.

"Bro," Vail said, giving him a mock two-fingered salute.

Right now, Tryst's heart ached to draw Lexi against him, but seeing his brother here—the last creature on this earth he'd expect to see at Wulfsiege—he wasn't sure what was up.

Lean and long, the vampire was dressed all in black. Platinum and ruby rings glinted on his fingers, and silver studs riveted along the sides of his pants. "Heard you were having a bit of trouble up here, so I thought I'd stop by."

Tryst looked to Lexi, who offered a sheepish shrug. "I don't want you to leave Wulfsiege, like I know you're planning. I was desperate, so I called the one person I thought you really needed to talk to right now. Well, I called your father, but your brother showed up instead. I'll be in my room."

She closed the door behind her, and before Tryst could rush after her, Vail whistled and said, "She's one hot number."

Tryst sat on the bed and blew out a sigh, too troubled by life to bother with shoving his brother for the rude comment about his woman. Because she wasn't his woman anymore. Couldn't be. Now that Lexi had become a shiftable werewolf, she could never love a half-breed. It made little sense if she wished to have a family—a normal family.

Normal. What a crock. He'd been a fool to believe he was a normal werewolf. Look at his family.

Vail strode about the room, touching the table lamp made from a hunk of carved oak and the plaid lampshade. He tilted his head back, inspecting the overhead light fixture. "Seriously? Is that made from some kind of animal horn?"

"Elk," Tryst said of the chandelier his brother looked over with disgust. A half-dozen antler racks had been tied together with wire to form the awful thing. "Can't believe you came all the way up here."

"Alexis was very convincing when she spoke to Rhys. And, the news that my werewolf brother is suddenly drinking blood was too intriguing to ignore."

"She told Rhys that? Hell." Tryst put back his head and shook it.

"So, is it true? You finally come over to the dark side and join me and your dad?"

"Hell, Vail, don't do this." Tryst jumped up and paced before the bed. His muscles yet ached from the beating he'd taken yesterday. For some reason, when he'd shifted to werewolf, he felt…stronger, and more powerful, yet even sorer this morning. "I've lived my whole life thinking I was a werewolf."

"And spent the past year beating on me because I'm a longtooth."

"Sorry." The first time he'd met his half brother, Tryst had shoved him against the wall and spit the cruel moniker at him. "We both know those punches were love taps."

"Uh-huh. Whatever you say, bro."

"We've the same mother. I love you, Vail. I have nothing against vampires. I just—"

"Don't want to be one yourself. I imagine it's quite the shocker. You've spent your childhood running away from mom when she came at you with fangs. Your dad's vampire is the nastiest thing this side of the Bay of Biscay. You've never been in a pack, and don't know how pack werewolves live. So, you're really sucking the red, red wine now? What happened?"

Rubbing the back of his neck, Tryst didn't want to get into this. And he did. Lexi had been wise to alert his family. He needed to talk, to figure this out. God, she was so good for him.

"I found Lexi buried in the snow after another avalanche hit. She was bleeding profusely. As I was digging her out, her blood got in my mouth, and the next thing I know…"

"Tastes damn good, doesn't it?" Vail's grin wasn't

creepy, but right now it was the last thing Tryst wanted to associate with drinking blood—a smile.

Tryst nodded, and wanted to tear out his duplicitous heart for that small agreement. "One thing I do know—werewolves aren't supposed to drink blood. It's unnatural."

"Uncle Rhys drinks blood."

"But he's different. He's like two breeds in one body that struggle against one another constantly."

"Thanks to the faeries. Damned faeries." Vail had a distinct relationship with the sidhe, and it could never be called good, or even amicable.

"I know I'm wolf," Tryst said. "I've never had that struggle like my father. Hell, I've been in plenty of fights that resulted in blood getting spattered about. I've never had the urge to drink blood until…her. It's like Lexi woke up the vampire inside me. Because, just now when she stood in the doorway? I heard her heart beat and I had this craving for— Hell. I can't do this, Vail. It's not natural. I hate that your breed has to depend on mortals for your survival. That you steal their life from them!"

Vail joined Tryst at his side and punched him in the biceps. Hard. "You're an asshole."

"And you're a longtooth," Tryst said, but he meant it in the teasing spirit the two had developed over the past year that they'd been getting to know each other.

Two days after their births, Vail had been taken from the cradle by a faery in payment for Rhys's blood debt. Rhys had made a deal with a faery centuries earlier to contain his werewolf's blood hunger, in exchange for his firstborn. Rhys and Viviane had not known at the time that Constantine de Salignac, a vicious vampire who had raped Viviane in the eighteenth century, had fathered Vail; they'd simply thought of him as their son, like Trystan. Viviane had actually been pregnant for over two centuries, her body in stasis while she'd been imprisoned in a glass coffin beneath Paris by Constantine in retaliation against his brother, Rhys. The story of Tryst and Vail's birth two centuries later was remarkable.

Vail had only returned to the mortal realm last year on a revenge quest against Constantine. Tryst had met him for the first time in his father's office at Hawkes Associates, and had instantly disliked him, not because he was a vampire, but because he had a cocky air about him.

In truth? At the time, Tryst had blamed Vail for making their mother insane. It was the first time in over two decades he'd been given a scapegoat, something tangible on which to blame his fears and troubled upbringing—the vampire. Which he knew now had not been Vail's fault, but at the time it had been a means for Tryst to take out his anger over the fact that his mother was insane.

Over the past year they'd mended wounds neither had even acknowledged, and now Tryst loved Vail as the brother he was.

That still didn't mean he approved the method vampires needed to survive.

"So what kind of trouble have you been raising down here in the frozen tundra?" Vail asked. "You know it's nearing spring in Paris. I didn't think snow was allowed to fall this time of year. Bet you got the snowboard out."

Tryst chucked softly. He'd tried to teach Vail to balance on a skateboard on the driveway of his father's home but that had ended disastrously. Vail preferred fast, expensive cars. One of these days the vampire should consider taking a driving lesson.

"I delivered a package to the pack principal, then all hell broke loose. Two avalanches in a week, and Lexi finally shifting for the first time, and now me going longtooth."

"Shifting for the first time? The woman who showed me to your room? That sounds interesting."

"Yes, she'd never shifted at puberty."

"I think Lyric would like her. You know Lyric is pregnant?"

Lyric was Vail's vampire wife. They'd married a month after Vail had returned to the mortal realm. They were good for one another.

"Congratulations, brother. Let's hope the kid doesn't look like you."

"Hey now, I'm a handsome guy."

"Yeah, but lose the black, man."

"It's my tribute to Johnny Cash. And I told you Faery was a wild riot of color. It'll take me a while to get over the memory. So about this first shift…? Are you and she getting it on? Because she is sexy as hell, and if you're not, then something more serious than a little vampirism is wrong with you, bro."

"We've…come together. She had never shifted until, well, until we had sex."

"Ah. So you were like the switch that turned her on. My little brother has it in spades!"

"You could say that." Tryst allowed a moment of pride to lift his shoulders, but he wasn't so cocky to believe it anymore. "Her father, the pack principal, won't let us be together."

"Why not? I thought he and Rhys were friends?"

"They have a mutual business friendship, but I don't

think Edmonton Connor has ever actually shaken hands with my half-breed father."

"Ah. I get it. Packs are pretty exclusive, or so I've heard."

"Principal Connor cannot conceive of allowing a nonpack wolf to hook up with his daughter. And my mixed heritage doesn't help, either. When he learns it's confirmed I have vampire in me? I'll be chained up in the dungeon again, which is why I'm heading out of here."

"They have an actual dungeon? You picked the strangest place for a vacation."

Tryst smirked at his brother's attempt to lighten the mood. It was helping. If the situation had been different and he were merely vacationing in the Alps, he'd drag Vail out to the slopes and teach him to shred.

"So take sexy Lexi back to Paris with you," Vail suggested. "Does she love you?"

"Yes. I don't know. Since I discovered my blood hunger, we haven't talked. She couldn't even look at me when she brought you in. I can't look at her. But I heard her heartbeats, Vail. Am I going to want to drink her blood? How often? If I bite her, she'll develop a blood hunger, too. I could never do that to her."

"Yeah, that's a bitch. You bite a werewolf, they develop a nasty blood hunger. But wait. You could cut her. That would work. I think. It's the saliva in your bite that introduces the vampire's taint. And I suspect you, being only part vamp, might only need blood about once a month, and maybe you've not a strong enough taint to actually give someone your hunger, but I'll have to look into that one for you."

"Damn." Tryst flopped back across the bed. "I don't want this."

"But you got it. So deal with it. Consider it a bonus gift."

"I've never been keen on gifts. I'd rather spend time with my family."

"Yes, yes, cry me a river. If you start pouting I'm going to have to kick your ass."

"I can beat you with both arms tied behind my back."

"I know, but I think you've lost your mojo, bro. Look at those bruises on your face. They should have healed by now."

"You haven't been witness to the beatings I've taken this week. Pack wolves do not like omega wolves. I'm just happy to be standing and have all my body parts still attached. Do you know when I shift now, I get these crazy long fangs, like yours, only longer like a wolf's?"

"Is Rhys like that when he shifts?"

"I don't recall. I've never seen his werewolf much. He keeps it under tight control."

"Because when his vampire mind rules it likes to make his werewolf drink blood." Vail shook his head. "I understand the hunger is not like it is for me with you guys. What Rhys feels is an abominable thing. But it should be different with you. Not so compelling, maybe?"

"You've been vampire all your life," Tryst said. "It's natural to you. I've just learned about this new side of me."

"It'll take some adjustment. And about that lost mojo? I know where you can get it back."

"Don't say Lexi."

"Lexi!" Vail clapped his hands together. He cast Tryst a glittering eye. "It's always the woman who can bring a man around. Trust me on that one."

"How do you think Lexi can save me from drinking blood?"

"Well, I didn't say she could do that. I think drinking blood is going to be part of your life from here on. But she can save you from yourself and all your self-doubt. Don't give up on her, man. Sounds like you did something amazing for her, being the one to bring on her first shift."

"It was beyond amazing. I was so proud of her."

Vail slapped Tryst's shoulder. "Trust yourself, and let her into your heart."

"Dude, you sound like a greeting card."

"Heh. Guess I've softened lately. Lyric is already starting to show. I can't wait until I can feel the baby kick. I'm going to teach it to play baseball and kick a football, and to drive."

"Do not let your child near or in the car when you are driving. Promise me that."

Vail winked. "Deal."

"You're starting your own family. That's so great. I hope I can have that someday."

"You will have it, and I bet it'll be with the sexy wolf with the bright blue eyes." He clapped his hands and gave the antler chandelier another leery glance. "So I don't think I'm going to hang around. You should have seen the welcome committee eyeing me up. Yikes. What a sorry bunch of bruisers they were."

"This pack is troubled, that's for sure."

A ruckus out in the hallway alerted both men, and Tryst rushed to open the door. A group of wolves were dragging another down the hall who struggled fiercely and whose body was midshift.

Liam caught Tryst's wondering gaze. "Sven escaped the shackles."

Vail leaned over Tryst's shoulder and whistled.

"He's shifting," Tryst said. "You'll never get him to the dungeon in time."

"I know that!" Liam and the others struggled. A few of the pack members also began to shift, but it was too late.

Sven's body transformed fully to werewolf. One muscled arm lashed out, taking a pack member across the face with his deadly talons. He howled, beat the wall with a paw, then took off down the hallway toward the lobby.

"Go after him!" Liam called, as they raced after the escaped wolf.

"Is this what life in a pack is like?" Vail whispered to Tryst.

"I'm not even sure anymore," he answered.

"Just to be safe, I'm going to get the hell out of Dodge. I walked here from the village. Think I'll walk back."

Tryst clamped a hand on his brother's shoulder. "That's not a good idea. With Sven's werewolf on the loose you don't want to risk running into him. I think you've just become a guest of Wulfsiege."

Liam shot the vampire a look that didn't say hello so much as *welcome to the loony bin*.

"How is the principal?" Tryst asked Liam.

"Lana told him everything, and Natalie has since concocted an antidote for the silver poisoning. So far, he's holding steady. Steady enough to issue orders against Sven. He's appointed me scion."

"Congrats, man."

Liam slapped palms with Tryst. "Wish the situation would have been better."

"You're the best man for the job. So what's the plan?"

"First we catch Sven. Then, well… Were you leaving?" Liam asked.

Tryst assumed he would no longer be welcome, and would accept the command if Liam wanted him to go. "That was my intention. Wulfsiege doesn't need my help anymore, and I'm sure you've heard about what happened with Lexi when I rescued her."

"No, I didn't. Something you need to tell me?"

Tryst felt Vail's hand on his shoulder, a reassuring force that he appreciated. He couldn't lie to Liam. "I may have vampire tendencies. I…drank Lexi's blood."

Liam nodded. "Sven's been telling everyone about your heritage. But I had no idea…"

"It was how I was able to fend off Sven and his goons last night. When I shift now, I become something with fangs. I'm sorry, man. I didn't see it coming. Something happened to me when I tasted Lexi's blood. It woke up a part of me I never dreamed could be in there."

"So, you're like your father?" Liam asked, eyeing Vail cautiously.

"I don't even know. But I promise you I won't harm any in the Alpine pack, because I will leave as soon as Sven is shackled."

"But I need you here," Liam said. "With Sven running rampant we've got to protect the females and the principal. There's no telling what that maniac will do. And him?"

"Uh, this is Vaillant, my brother. He's…vampire."

Vail stretched out a hand to shake, and Liam didn't even pause to shake it. "You lay low," Liam directed the vampire. "You don't give us any trouble, we won't give you trouble."

"Works for me."

"You can't possibly want me to stay now," Tryst said.

"Sounds like you've got a lot of issues to work out, but I have to believe you're still the same honorable man who would jump in to help a pack of which he's not even a member."

"I want the best for this pack. They've become like family to me."

"Then it's cool with me, man. You're good stuff. Now if we really mean something to you, then help me hold this pitiful pack together, will you? We've got Lana guarded in her room in case the Nord should return looking for her. Where's Lexi?"

"I think she went to her room. Hell. Sven attacked her last night." Tryst's heart dropped. In the rage he was in, there was no guessing what Sven would do. He took off down the hallway. "Keep Vail in the guest room!" he called back.

"Too late, brother." Vail ran alongside Tryst. "I'm on your side, remember? And I figure sticking close to you is safer than being a sitting duck alone, eh?"

"Her room is just ahead." Tryst charged through Lexi's open door and saw the broken window. He heard Lexi's scream and didn't give a second thought to what he did next.

"Vail, tell Liam I found Sven and he's got Lexi! I'm going after him," he called as his body shifted to werewolf shape. He had no voice in this form, but he didn't need it.

His werewolf was angry, and he wouldn't suffer Sven to live if he harmed one hair on his mate's head.

Chapter 20

Sven's werewolf clutched Lexi against his hard, sinuous body as he stalked down the steps. Her feet dragged as she struggled and tried to wiggle her arms free from his iron-band-like clasp. At the sound of another werewolf's howl, Sven whipped around and pressed the syringe she had seen him carrying to her neck. She felt it prick her skin, but sensed he had not injected her.

Tryst's werewolf bounded out and leaped for Sven, soaring over the steps that marched down to the courtyard and landing on the ground before them.

Sven's talons dug into her stomach. He howled warningly at the werewolf who approached with a vicious howl.

"Stay back," she pleaded to Tryst. "There's silver in the syringe."

She knew, in Tryst's werewolf mind, he could understand her words. But would his rage allow him to control his anger? For that matter, how long could Sven grasp caution without simply ramming the needle into her throat? Sure death pricked her flesh, but the werewolf had yet to inject her. With every step Tryst's werewolf took closer, Sven clenched her tighter. Talons pierced her side and at her hip. She noticed Tryst sniffed the air, scenting her blood. Hell, she did not need to deal with his vampire, as well.

Or maybe the vampire was just the thing Tryst needed to defeat a werewolf who was equal in strength to him.

"Please," she whispered. "Just drop me, Sven, and Tryst won't follow you."

With a snarl, Tryst revealed a row of wicked sharp teeth. He wasn't on the same page as Lexi, and she sensed Sven knew that. Not that it would matter. Sven had reached the edge, and he wanted to take out anyone he could if he was going to fall over that edge.

A woman screamed. At Lexi's bedroom door, Lana had run out. That perked Sven's ears. The needle pressed deeper.

"No, Lana," she managed, but her voice came out as a whisper. She didn't dare move her head for fear of the silver.

Sven howled, a claiming howl that cautioned her sister and stopped her from running out farther.

Tryst used the werewolf's distraction and pounced, landing Sven's shoulder. The connection loosened Sven's hold on her. Lexi stumbled free, scrambling across the packed snow to the bottom step. She looked about for the syringe loaded with deadly silver, but couldn't see the clear plastic and silver set against the blinding white snow.

Behind her the werewolves growled, and wicked, taloned paws smacked hard muscle and fur. Both were matched in strength in this form, and for every hit that Sven made to Tryst's body, Tryst returned with equal force and cruelty. He slammed Sven to the ground. The ice carried them down a slope, and they crashed against a tree trunk. A nest of birds fluttered out from the pine canopy.

Tryst swung his talons across Sven's chest, tearing open flesh and fur. It was hardly a killing blow. Lexi sensed he would not deliver a fatal blow, but wished he would. And then she did not. Her lover was an honorable man, who lived by and for his word. Murder was not part of Trystan Hawkes's arsenal, even should his life depend on it.

She shouted to Lana to go back inside and find Liam to bring out the chains. Lana nodded, and scrambled away.

Tryst yipped. His neck had opened up and blood spilled over his chest. With one great howl, he charged Sven, pushing the mighty Nordic beast to ground. Slapping a paw across his face, Tryst then jumped back and stalked before the fallen werewolf, waiting for his opponent to rise.

But he did not. Sven's body began to shudder, his limbs flailing and his heavy head pushing back into the bloody snow. Lexi didn't know what was wrong. The werewolf's pale-furred skin started to bubble. His arms jerked forward, pulling him into a sitting position, and she saw the syringe at the back of his neck. He'd landed on his own death. When Tryst had shoved him to the ground, the force of Sven's body meeting the syringe must have depressed the plunger.

The werewolf's howl twisted into an unnatural scream as his fingers began to split apart.

Lexi turned away as the first bits of the wolf flew across the snow.

Tryst shifted to were form. He stood, bloody hand held in front of him, his body curled forward, with his spine arched out, as if trying to get away from the blood scent yet at the same time compelled toward it.

Naked and bloodied, he knew none of the blood was actually his. He had pieces of Sven all over him. And his fingers were coated as his talons had shifted, leaving his skin red.

He smelled the life. It wasn't the same as Lexi's blood. Not appealing, yet not entirely disgusting, either.

"You don't need that vile man's blood. It will only taint you," Lexi said. "Come to me, Tryst."

He looked over the werewolf's remains. Had he done that? How?

When he met Lexi's gaze, it was as though the world fell away and only they remained. Hearts beating for one another, they spoke without words. He loved her, but he was confused by this new revelation in his very makeup. And she loved him. No matter what.

How could that be? After what he'd just done? He'd—had he killed a man?

"He fell on the syringe," Lexi offered. "It wasn't your fault."

"Hell." Tryst fell to his knees in the bloody snow. He felt Lexi's touch at the back of his neck and it was so gentle he closed his eyes and tilted his body to lean against hers.

"It's over," she said. "Let's go back inside."

Naked, slashed and bleeding from battle, Tryst nodded. He stood and she wrapped her arms about him and he fell into her embrace, taking what she wanted to give. Peace, comfort. A promise that, no matter what challenges faced them both, she was in it for the long ride.

As was he.

They trudged back into Lexi's room, where Vail waited with a long coat for Tryst.

"Some things I really shouldn't see," the vampire said as he spread the coat across Tryst's shoulders and stood back to let Lexi button it down just far enough to cover the important bits. "But you did take out that bastard with skill. Good going, bro."

"Murder is never good, Vail." Agitated, Tryst paced back and forth before the broken window. "I hate that I was forced to such an action."

Vail stopped him with a hand to his chest. The brothers faced each other down. "It wasn't murder. I saw the whole thing. He fell on the syringe he had intended to use on Lexi. You did a good thing, brother. And nothing but. She's alive only because of you."

Tryst nodded, accepting but knowing he could never forgive himself for being the catalyst that had ended another man's life. He'd never done so before. He must never do so again.

He pulled Lexi to him and she snuggled against his wounded body. "How is your father?"

"He's still very weak, but the doctor said he's improving. Natalie made an antidote to the silver."

"That's the best thing for the pack." He kissed her head. "I think I need to lie down. I took some deep talons to my back."

His world wobbled and went black.

* * *

Tryst woke to the vision of, not a gorgeous woman leaning over him, but Vail's black-lined eyes staring at him. The vampire wore some kind of black ointment around his eyes, saying it helped him to see faeries. Made him look like a rocker.

His brother winked and smacked Tryst's cheek. "You fainted, bro. Thought only girls did that. But then we saw the wounds on your back and I figure I'll give you that one."

Tryst winced and wriggled his shoulders. "I'll heal."

"I know you will. Your little wolf chick doctored you up and you're already looking fifty percent better. She's with her dad right now. Told me to stay and keep an eye on you. I can't seem to get away from this place."

"Wulfsiege kinda sucks you in, like it or not. You hungry?"

Vail shot him a castigating glare.

"Right. Sorry." Tryst sat up and winced at his aching…everything. "Thank the gods for the women-folk, they know how to take care of us."

"Oh, yeah."

"So you said Lyric is pregnant? What are you hoping for? Boy or girl?"

"Healthy in mind and spirit." Vail plopped onto the easy chair by the bed and put up his boots on the end of the bed near Tryst's bare feet.

Tryst wore a towel around his hips and was bandaged along his arm. "Did she get me onto the bed like this?"

"No, I had to help, and let me tell you, you owe me one for that. Like I said, some things a brother should not have to see. I can't imagine the shit you have to go through to insure you shift near available clothing."

"Heh. You're just jealous."

"Oh, yeah? If you need me to whip it out and compare—"

Tryst held up a hand. "Spare me. I'll take your word for it. Hell, I'm hungry."

"Lexi said something about bringing you sustenance. She's all about making you happy."

"I'm surprised she can even be around me after what happened."

"Watching a werewolf explode would turn anyone's gut."

"It's not that. Well hell, that was horrible. I have never seen the like before, and don't ever want to see it again, but we still haven't talked about my new   "

"Condition?"

"Yeah. I love her, Vail, but I don't want to take away her options. She's a gorgeous werewolf princess. She could have any man—any full-blooded wolf—as a mate. She shouldn't be stuck with something like me."

Vail screwed up his lips then exhaled. "You're not that different from Rhys. Every time you put yourself down you also put down your father. And I don't think you're the kind of guy to do something like that."

"I would never. I love my father. Hell, I just need time to take it all in. My life has changed."

"Ch'yeah, no kidding. So now that the big bad wolf is dead, you think it's okay for me to slip out of here?"

"You hate hanging around me that much?"

"No, chatting with my bro has been great. When it hasn't been harrowing. And when I haven't had to watch you get beaten or tortured. Or gotten to see the wolf explode. But I told Lyric it was a quick trip, and do you know how crabby women get during the first trimester? And she craves weird things like reptilian blood. Green Snake is a total mess around her lately. She gives him the eye. I've seen her do it."

"That snake creeps me out, but I'd hate to see it sacrificed. Bring her some flowers and have sex with her all night. That should distract her."

"I already do that. I've got to up my game."

"Diamonds?"

"She does like sparkly things. Like me," he said with a flick of his beringed fingers.

The door opened and Lexi entered with a serving tray. "Oh, I'm sorry. I would have knocked, but I thought you'd be out still."

"And I think that's my cue to leave. You're going to be fine, bro." Vail clasped hands with Tryst. "Only because she's looking after you." He kissed Lexi on both cheeks and bade the two of them au revoir. "See you back in Paris soon!"

"Thanks, Vail. Say hi to Mom for me, will you?"

"I'm seeing her tomorrow. She wants Lyric to come over so she can paint her portrait. Nice meeting you, Lexi."

"You, too," she said, and closed the door behind Vail. "So you're going home?" she asked, setting the tray over his lap as he settled back against the pillows. He didn't miss the tightness in her voice.

He patted the bed beside him but she didn't move to sit. Not that he shouldn't expect her reluctance. "I don't want to go anywhere without you, Lexi."

"My home is here at Wulfsiege, you know that."

"I know. And I'd never ask you to accept me now that things have changed drastically."

"What? Because you've learned you're half vampire doesn't change much with me."

"Lexi, you're lying to yourself."

"Don't tell me what I'm thinking. I know how I feel about you, Tryst. This…" she stroked her neck where the bite wound had faded "…doesn't change that." She smiled a little. "Despite the fact that you once told me you didn't bite."

He had said that. Hindsight was a bitch. "I'm going to start drinking blood because my body will demand it. I can't even wrap my head around that. How can you?"

"I have lived with a debilitating condition for years. I have an insider's look at being different. Being vampire may change your needs but it doesn't change you as a man. And I love the man you are, Tryst." She sat on the edge of the bed, facing him, and touched the back of his hand, tracing from one freckle to another.

Her touch was too soft, too perfect. He didn't deserve acceptance from her. The monster inside him didn't deserve it.

"It will change me. This strange new part of me is too fresh yet to even be clear what will come of it. You can't want what I can give you now."

"Are you trying to get rid of me?"

"No." He sighed, longing to pull her against him but not knowing how to do that now. What if he felt her heart beat against his chest? Would the scent of her blood push him over the edge? "I want you as my mate. I just don't want it to be something you agree to because you feel sorry for me."

"Please, Tryst, you've got quite the ego. Feel sorry for you? You just defeated the strongest wolf in the pack. You are healing rather rapidly because you are so strong, and you're the sexiest hunk of wolf I've ever laid eyes on. That's absolutely nothing that demands pity. Not even your weird mixed-blood family."

She smiled at that, and Tryst's face softened. "You're kind of weird, too, Princess."

"I know, but I'm probably a lot more interesting than if I were plain old normal. We can't all be perfect like Lana."

"Alana is far from perfect. Who would want perfection when weird and imperfect offers so many fascinating details?"

"You have a point. And Lana has been dealing with a lot. I shouldn't have said that about her. She needs strength right now. I know, as much as she and Sven were at odds, she'll take his death hard. I checked in with her, but she was resting so I didn't want to disturb her."

"I'm sorry. I shouldn't have taken justice into my hands like that. All I could focus on was you. You were in danger. I had to get you free."

"You didn't kill him, Tryst."

"I know that, but—"

"But nothing. Sven's death was the only way Wulfsiege will ever be safe. Had he succeeded in poisoning my father, pack Alpine would have grown monstrous under his direction. Now eat your supper, my big strong wolf. You need strength to mend those wounds."

She pulled the cover off the meal and the delicious scent of beef gravy and mashed potatoes curled up to Tryst's nose. He grabbed the fork but didn't dig in. "I'm not so sure about the potatoes."

"I watched the chef prepare them myself. And, I tested them. They've got parmesan and butter in them," she said with a teasing lift of voice.

"You tested my food? You really do love me." He dug in, devouring the creamy potatoes.

"That's my man. And when you're finished, there's dessert."

She got up to collect his torn clothing from the floor, and Tryst inspected the tray for the mentioned treat. "I don't see any."

"Is that so?" With a flick of her wrist, she unbuttoned her shirt and let it fall open to reveal the inner curves of her breasts.

"Almost finished," he said, shoveling in the food so he could get to the dessert.

Lexi turned on the shower to warm up the water. It had been a long day. One flick of Sven's hand could have seen her the bloody mess across the snow instead of the Nord. It was hard not to think about.

She wouldn't. There were still too many other things to worry about.

But knowing that her father was on the road to recovery, she could now finally take a breath and relax. And she needed it. She dropped her clothes into the hamper and left the bathroom door open, because she expected her man to come looking for a treat after he'd eaten.

Her man. Her werewolf.

It sounded too good, because she wasn't sure he was completely hers yet. She wanted Trystan Hawkes. Werewolf *or* vampire. Okay, to be honest, she would prickle if he were completely vampire. But a trace of vampiric tendency mixed in with the true werewolf he was? The vampire thing freaked her a little, but it was something she could accept. Yes, even knowing that it would go against pack rules. Her father would be horrified to know she was in love with a half-breed. Her heart hadn't given her any other option. She'd fallen for him.

She'd wait until he'd fully recovered to spring that

one on him. But she wasn't blind, she knew her father had his suspicions about her and Tryst; otherwise, he would have never warned the wolf away from her. And hell, she'd told him he had been the catalyst to her shift. She couldn't regret the truth.

And she knew Tryst wanted her. He loved her. But things had altered over the past few days. Much as she believed, in his heart, he hadn't changed his mind about her, she couldn't be sure how his emotions would react with this new vampire part of him.

And now that she could shift, that meant she could become pregnant. What kind of child would she have with a man who was werewolf *and* vampire? The notion disturbed her, but if that meant the child would be like Tryst, a werewolf who craved blood, then she had to accept that.

Could she accept that?

Was it the right choice to make, to abandon the pack and family simply because she was in love? Did love blind one's senses? Of course it did. That's why people got divorced after a few years, because the love eroded and they began to look at their mates in a new light. Or that was how she figured things like that went.

"You're getting ahead of yourself," she thought.

She wasn't sure about anything, but her heart screamed that, yes, what she had started with Tryst was right, and that together they would figure out how to walk toward the future.

She hoped he wished the same.

The water streamed over her skin and she let out an audible moan of pleasure. It seemed as though since Trystan had arrived at Wulfsiege nothing had gone slow or normal. To grasp but a moment of silence and pleasure now felt too good to be true.

Leaning forward under the shower stream, she tilted back her head. The water beat upon her breasts and down her stomach. She soaped up and just when she almost dropped the soap, it fell into a wide, strong hand that cupped it near her hip. Sneaky. She hadn't heard the stealthy wolf enter the bathroom.

Kisses bulleted down the back of her neck and across her shoulders. His hand slid up the soap to glide over her breasts and tightened nipples. Her body reacted with a sensory tickle all over.

"Have a good meal?" she asked.

"Not as good as dessert is going to be."

"You healing?"

"You tell me."

Lexi turned and he put up his palms on the shower walls to let her look over his back. She ran her hands along the wounds that had scarred into tight ridges of skin and would be completely gone by morning.

"All good?" he asked.

She slipped her hand around his hip and circled her fingers about his slick, heavy erection. "Mmm, all good."

Hugging up against his slippery body, she pressed her cheek to his back, her lashes blinking at the water streaming over their skin, and glided her coiled fingers up and down his shaft. With a groan of encouragement, her wolf kept his hands to the wall, allowing her free rein over his body. It didn't take long for her to bring him to climax. Tryst howled as he came, his voice bellowing against her body that limned his torso.

"You are a nut," she said. "Someone probably heard that."

"Then let them be jealous. I've got the sexiest female in the pack, and she's all mine."

"Are you finally starting to believe that? That I am yours?"

"For now." He turned and threaded his fingers through hers. So much unspoken. They would talk about it. Later. Now was for contact, connection and lovemaking.

He kissed her and lifted her so she could wrap her legs about his slick hips. "You don't have any of those sticky things on the floor of this shower. Let's get out."

He carried her out and set her on a towel strewn on the floor in front of the vanity. Lexi caught her palms against the vanity rim, and before she could turn, he grabbed her hips and his cock slid along her thigh. Tryst's hand lifted her chin and she twisted back to kiss him. He snuggled his slippery erection against her back.

"Put that inside me," she said to his reflection in the mirror. "Right now."

His hand slapped the counter beside hers while the other directed his bold length inside her. Lexi bent forward, taking him in fully. The thickness of him filled her and it was the best feeling. Owned, she, and happy for it.

"Hot." He plunged in and out quickly, but he did not ignore her needs, slipping a finger around her hip and down to slide over her clitoris. "You're so hot, Lexi. On fire."

She wiggled her bottom, and he gripped her hips tighter. "Right there," he said, and she had to agree. He'd found the exact spot that was making her gasp and bite her lip and…release.

And when he heard her powerful cry, Tryst rammed one last time, spilling inside her. Lexi thought about birth control. She wasn't using any, she'd never had a reason to because the pack males shunned her. And then she didn't care because she wanted to give her mate a child. Half werewolf or full-blooded wolf. It didn't matter to her. It really didn't.

And then she didn't worry at all, because she knew she could only get pregnant while in werewolf form. That was something they'd yet to explore, but if she had her way, it would happen soon.

When she felt Tryst skim a canine tooth along her neck, the sensation shocked sensual shivers down her arms and to her breasts, teasing her hard nipples. A bite a sensual experience? Possibly. But only from her lover.

Dare she risk developing a hideous blood hunger as a result of his bite? She hadn't from the first bite, so maybe his bite was not so potent? It made a weird kind of sense. On the other hand, what did she know? Or him, for that matter?

If you love him, you love all of him, and will take whatever comes along with that love fangs and all.

She spread her fingers back through his wet hair and tilted her head against his cheek. "If you want me, you can have me. I trust you. Whatever happens."

"Oh, gods, Lexi, I crave the taste of you. It's so strong." He clenched a fist against her stomach, obviously fighting the craving.

"Don't fight it. I give you permission."

He nodded. "I want you, but not with my teeth. Vail said if I don't use my teeth, the vampire taint shouldn't affect you. Won't give you that nasty craving for blood." He pulled open the vanity drawer and shuffled around inside, his cock still embedded deep within her. "This." He pulled out a straightedge razor that she used on her legs. "You willing to give this a try?"

She nodded and thrust up her wrist. "Do it here."

The blade's cut stung for but a moment, but as soon

as her lover's mouth sealed over the wound, Lexi again cried out. The one being bitten was supposed to experience a swoon, and this must be it. Dizzied by the sensation, she gasped and bit her lower lip. Her core tightened, her clit tingled. It was as if she could feel her blood moving through her veins, tickling her insides in the most sensual way.

While Tryst gently moved his cock back and forth inside her, he sucked out her blood, moaning and muttering how sweet she was. It felt…a little wrong, but mostly too good for her to ask him to stop.

Tryst thrust back his head and he shuddered in climax against her body, and then he twisted around, holding her firmly in his arms and settled to the floor as they both succumbed to a heady, loopy kind of blood bliss.

Chapter 21

Tryst rolled over in bed, snuggling against Lexi's warm cinnamon-scented body. They'd made love without words. Kissing, touching, joining, becoming. There wasn't a spot on Lexi's body he hadn't explored with his fingers, skin and tongue. He knew the shape of her lips when they were opened in ecstasy, and the heat of her pleasure when her skin rubbed against his. He knew that she mewled sweetly when he nuzzled his nose at the back of her knee, and that she really squirmed when he tongued the arch of her foot. She cried out boldly when she came, and he liked to think it was her wolf unleashed and proud.

The woman's color was so bright he could never drown in her because she'd always light his way.

He drew his nose along her neck and down her arm to her wrist, scenting a faint hint of blood from the cut. The smell sweetened the air, and stirred up a twinge of guilt. He'd hurt her to serve his own twisted desire for a taste of her sweetness.

She put a hand back to run through his hair, which sent shivers down his spine.

"Can you do this with me?" he asked. "I cut you, and I didn't even give thought that I was hurting you."

"I told you it was okay. Tryst, I know this is new to you, and I'm willing to go along for the ride. I thought about it, and I'm willing to learn right alongside you. Look what you've done for me. You've fixed a broken werewolf."

"Yeah." He rolled to his back, staring up at the ceiling in the darkness. "But now I'm broken."

She slid a hand down his abs, toying with the curls nestled around his cock. Her hair skimmed his chest, tightening his nipples. And he got another hard-on. So he was easy. Blame it on sexy Lexi.

"You're something even more," she whispered. "I think you're going to be so strong and powerful now, you won't even know what to do with yourself."

"You are so positive. Here I thought I was the positive one. Karma has really been screwing with me lately."

"How do you know your newly discovered vampirism isn't a gift from karma? A new kind of energy for you to share with the universe."

He tilted a look down at her bright eyes. "Never thought of it like that."

"Well start." She kissed his chest. "Because I cannot endure a man who feels sorry for himself."

"I would never do that."

"You've been treading pity lately, buddy."

She saw things in him before he even saw them—and

she was right. "Fine. I'll call it quits on the pity party. But there's still your father to face. We have to be truthful with him. I won't lie to the principal."

"I agree. I...told him we made love and that I shifted because of it."

"Oh, great. How'd he take that? Bet the man has had a silver bullet fashioned with my name etched on the casing."

"No, not that badly. He said we needed to talk when he got stronger. Let's give him a few more days."

"To carve my name in that bullet? Oh, Lexi."

"We can spend the time in bed."

"Mmm, I like that suggestion. Though, I should probably check with Liam, see if he needs help with anything today. And weren't you going to check on your sister?"

"Yes, I should do that." She kissed the head of his cock, which tightened at the blissful tease. "But she is a late sleeper. And you're still recovering from all the beatings you've taken lately, and those deep talon wounds."

"But—"

She squeezed her fingers about his shaft, silencing him much faster than a finger to his mouth would have. The woman did know exactly how to control him.

"And if you even think of leaving this bed, I'm going to have to wolf out on you and show you who's boss."

"Please?"

She nipped the head of his shaft playfully and sat up, stretching back her shoulders to lift high her pert, tight breasts. "We need to do that. Make love as werewolves. Let's do it tonight in the forest with the moonlight shining through the trees. Yes?"

"I can never think of a reason to deny you a thing, Princess."

"Good. Until then, I'm still not letting you out of bed."

Her lover's rhythm hypnotized her. He held her up against the wall, her legs wrapped about his hips, his hips pistoning his cock in and out. Eyes closed, Tryst had arrived at another realm. Teeth biting down on his lower lip, he'd give a little smile, then open his eyes and wink at her.

Lexi dragged her fingernails down his neck and over his chest, pinching both nipples so his satisfied smile switched to a wince of pain.

"For that," he muttered against her ear, and nipped the lobe, "you must be punished."

Setting her on the bed, he disengaged their intimate connection and turned her over with a flip of her hips. He swatted her across the derriere. Crawling over her, his strong, powerful arms curled up under her torso and clutched her up against his sweat-slick body. And then he pushed her forward, her palms catching on the bed, and spread her legs.

"Mmm, doggie style," she said. "Hardly a punishment."

He gave her another swat that stung hotly. "It is if you don't get to watch."

"Watch? Watch what?"

She tried to turn her head to look over her shoulder, but his hand gripped her neck, keeping her from doing so. She felt him slide his hard-on between her legs, so close to her folds, but not close enough to touch. Squiggling, she tried to direct him higher but realized this was her punishment. Tryst moaned as his hand moved up and down his shaft.

Lexi clutched the sheets and shifted her hips. Still no luck. She reached back, but he moved just out of her reach, so she instead slid her fingers into her sex and found her own rhythm.

Tryst's hand at her neck moved to grip her hair. He pulled, but not hard, cocking her head back. "You want it?" he growled.

She smiled at his command. "Yes."

"How badly?" The slick of his hand bumped her derriere, and she lifted her hips, trying to find him, to lure him into her. "Tell me you want me."

"Gods, please," she said, tucking her head forward and biting the sheet. "Come inside me, Tryst. Put your big, hard cock inside me. Show me I'm yours."

"Lexi, you are mine. All mine," he growled as he slid inside her with a bellowing moan. He reached around and slapped his hand over hers, keeping her fingers at her pinnacle and following her motions with his fingers. "Yes, like that. Show me how you like it."

His body shuddered against hers. He was so close. She loved when he took her hard and howled like the wild creature he was. Lexi gripped his fingers and slid them along her folds, drawing up her own shudders, and together they came.

His body fell upon hers, and his arms wrapped about her stomach, taking her with him as he rolled to his back and kissed her neck. Together, they fit their lax, exhausted bodies and fell into a well-deserved slumber.

Lexi pulled on a soft black pair of yoga pants and spied Tryst's torn plaid shirt on the chair where she'd tossed it earlier. Every fiber of her wanted to pull on that shirt, snuggle into his essence and rub him all over her, but she didn't. If someone saw her wearing his shirt, there'd be questions. Besides, she already had his essence all over and inside her.

She glanced at the man on her bed, the sheets strewn to reveal his soft penis draped over a hip, and his legs bent in an exhausted pose. He deserved a few winks of sleep after their afternoon of lovemaking.

And she needed to talk to her sister. And forage for food. Her belly rumbled for sustenance.

Tugging a gray fleece over her head, she flipped her hair over the collar and padded out of the room, barefoot and hoping she wasn't called to any major situation in the fifty feet it took to walk to Lana's room. Things had to get back to normal after all they'd been through.

"Please?" she whispered. "The pack needs normal."

Lana stood against the open door frame, a smile lifting her mouth, which relieved Lexi's fears her sister would be inconsolable.

"I was wondering when you'd venture out from your den of wild and crazy sex," Lana teased. She tugged Lexi inside and closed the door. "You two have been going at it all day."

"Oh, hell, could you hear us?"

"No. Well." Lana winced. "Sometimes. He has a very happy howl."

Lexi laughed and pulled her sister to sit on the edge of the bed with her. "That he does. But I shouldn't have been so selfish. How are you, Lana?"

"Seriously?" Her sister lifted her shoulders and her chin, displaying surprising lightness in the wake of what had happened. "I think I'm kind of happy. Is that wrong? Lexi, I'm being cruel, right?"

"Because you're glad an overbearing, cruel, lying bastard is out of your life? I think you're taking it exactly as you should be."

"But he is dead. And I did care a little about him."

"He would have corrupted the pack," Lexi offered. She squeezed her sister's hand. "You know that."

Lana nodded. "It's for the better. I don't blame Trystan, either. He did what had to be done."

"It wasn't his fault. Sven fell on the syringe loaded with the silver that he'd intended to use on me."

"Ohmygod. I didn't see that. Liam dragged me inside and wouldn't let me watch. Oh, Lexi, I'm so glad you're safe. Sven definitely got what he deserved."

"You are allowed to cry and grieve, Lana. I'd be worried if you didn't."

Lana nodded, swallowing, and Lexi knew she was, indeed, fighting tears. "I have cried. And I will cry more, I'm sure. I just need to digest it all. I think this will be good for me. A break from a man. I usually always have a boyfriend. Though, I do already feel lonely. That's so wrong, isn't it?"

"You'll never be alone, Lana. You have me and Father. And as soon as the dust settles, I know a handsome pack male will start sniffing around you."

"I don't think I like any of the males in this pack. They're all so brutal."

"There are some who are kind and quiet. You just need to open your eyes to that sort of man."

"I'm used to being ordered around."

"Give it time. You don't need to jump into anything. Hey, I was going to stop in the cafeteria. You hungry? Want me to bring you back something to eat?"

"No. I ate a few hours ago when everyone else did. When you were busy."

"I'm in love, Lana."

"I know, I can see it in your eyes. Your beautiful blue eyes. He's good for you. Don't let him go."

"Father will have the final say in whether or not we can continue our relationship."

Lana nodded. "He's doing even better today. He took a walk outside with me this morning."

"That's wonderful. I have to go see him, but I'm sort of avoiding it for the reasons you can imagine. Did he say anything to you about us?"

"Nope." Lana kissed her cheek. "Go. Refuel, and then make that man howl again. I think I'm going to listen to some music. Loud."

Lexi returned to the room at the same time Tryst opened the note Rick stopped off to deliver from the principal.

"What's that?" she asked.

"From your father. He wants to see me." Tryst pulled up his pants and searched for his boots.

"Don't go," Lexi said, setting down the supper tray. "The food is hot. Wait until the morning to talk to Father."

Until after they'd made love as werewolves, was the unspoken statement. It had been a promise, an act that would bond them as mates much like marriage bonded mortals. Tryst wanted that more than anything right now. But…

"I won't disregard a direct order from your father, especially not the pack leader."

"Are you afraid of him?"

"Yes. I mean, it's not fear, just a healthy respect. He

is the authority around here, Lexi, and I'd never disrespect that."

"Liar. You've been seeing me. That's exactly what Father doesn't want."

Tryst sighed. "I know, I know. But I can't stay away from you. And I did tell him I would keep my distance but that you were your own woman, and I couldn't keep you away from me. It's all your fault," he said with a trace of humor to his tone.

"What if he tells you to stay away from me?"

"That's what you're worried about, isn't it?" He pulled on a button-up plaid shirt that had been borrowed from some random wolf in the castle. It fit, but was tight across the shoulders. "I'll stand up to him and tell him I love you."

"No, you can't."

"Yes, I will."

"He'll say there's no way a half-breed could ever have his daughter. What will you say to that?"

Tryst sighed and shrugged. "I guess I'll have to wing it. I'll always do—"

"You'll always do what is right for me." She spread her arms about his waist and kissed him at the base of his neck. "Well hear this, wolf. What is right for me is you. Don't forget that."

"Permanently imprinted on my brain. Now, how do I look? Good enough for your dad?"

She played with his hair a bit then kissed him. "Good enough for me, and that's all that matters. Go, but if you're not back in an hour, I'll come looking for you."

"If I'm not back in an hour, you'd better check the dungeon first." He kissed her playfully, but his heart was already dreading the meeting. It wasn't going to go well. He knew that with every ounce of his being.

* * *

"You've fucked my daughter?"

Tryst made to reply, but Edmonton Conner had gotten his energy back, in spades.

"How dare you?"

Liam stood beside the oak desk, behind which the principal sat, looking over some paperwork. The old wolf looked as if he'd risen from the ashes. Once the poison had gotten out of his system, it had really sped up his recovery. He didn't look a day over forty now.

Tryst eyed Liam, and the new scion held a stoic pose, yet he thought he saw sympathy in the wolf's look. Tryst was grasping, though.

"I, uh…"

"Out with it." The pack leader stood and slammed a fist on the desk, startling Tryst only because he hadn't been prepared for such authority after having witnessed the man struggling in the throes of death.

"I have," he said, bowing his head in respect. "I've gone against your wishes. But I won't ask your forgiveness."

"And why is that? You, a half-breed lone wolf, do you place yourself so high above us all you think you are in no need of forgiveness?"

"No, Principal, not at all like that." He shrugged a hand through his hair, then splayed it out before him, finding only the truth on this tongue. "I love your daughter, Principal Connor. And she loves me."

Edmonton scoffed and walked around the side of the desk, slamming his arms across his chest. He strode to the window, where sunlight beamed across his curly mop of dark hair. Dark as Lexi's hair. She must have gotten that from him, Tryst thought wistfully. Perhaps their mother had been blonde, as was Lana. He would have liked to meet her, even if only on his way to being kicked out of the castle. Yet again.

"Principal—"

"Silence!" Edmonton barked. Pacing, he rattled a fist near his thigh, his jaw tight.

Tryst judged the man a worthy opponent to any wolf, even obviously still in recovery. His eyes held authority and dared Tryst to step over an invisible line.

A line he'd already shredded and tossed over his shoulder. Lexi had been right—he'd lied to her father, and now he must take the punishment.

"Liam?"

"Yes, Principal?"

"What you've told me about this wolf—this un-aligned, half-breed wolf who dares to taint my lineage—it is all true?"

Liam exhaled and nodded. "Yes."

Tryst's heart dropped. What the hell kind of report had Liam given the leader? He'd thought he and Liam had gotten along well, but was there more than one two-faced wolf in this pitiful pack?

No, he couldn't blame Liam for any observations he'd given to the principal. As scion he must have an eye out for protecting the pack.

"Well, then." Edmonton turned, sliding his hands into his sweater pockets. His jaw softened, and Tryst thought he saw a smirk tilt the corner of the old wolf's mouth. "I must say, Liam speaks very highly of you, Trystan Hawkes."

Tryst exchanged glances with Liam. The quiet wolf cracked a small smile.

"You've the makings of a fine scion," the principal continued, "and I'm of the mind to make you the Alpine pack scion."

Twisting his neck to check both men's expressions, Tryst determined from their unflinching expressions they were serious. He didn't know what to say, except, "But Liam is the new scion."

"Yes, and no." Edmonton chuckled and slapped Liam across the shoulder. "I have bigger plans for this man. First, I want to know your intentions toward my daughter, Hawkes. Do you mean to ask for her hand?"

"I uh…" He hadn't thought about that, but marriage wasn't so far off his radar.

"Come on, boy. You've been the catalyst to her first shift. You've more than taken your liberties with my daughter. And you dare to pause when I ask your intentions?"

"Sorry, sir, I haven't even decided if I will stay here. I thought the invitation to join the pack had been rescinded."

"Why should it be? You took out that bastard Sven."

"He fell on the syringe, Principal."

"Semantics. The blight is gone and I want to know your future plans."

"I don't want to go anywhere without Lexi. I love her. Of course I would marry her if she'd have me."

"Good. You'll accept the position of scion?"

"I… Yes?" he said, knowing his family back in Paris would be stunned, but also knowing, in his bones, this was where he needed to be right now. "Yes," he said more firmly. "I accept, Principal Conner. Thank you for the honor."

"Then I'll expect to hear good news from Alexis soon regarding her engagement?"

Tryst nodded. "As soon as I can get a ring, I'll ask her. You, uh…don't have a problem with me being, uh…"

"Half vampire?"

Tryst winced. "You don't know all of it."

"Liam gave me what little information he has. You've bitten Lexi?"

He lowered his head. "I have not bitten her, but I have tasted her blood. But I don't think it'll be like my father with me. I'm wolf, with vampiric tendencies. I have cravings, but I don't think the blood is a requirement to my survival. It'll be a learning process."

"Either way, it's quite a mess, eh?"

"I would never harm your daughter, Principal. I swear to you I will never give her the blood hunger. I won't bite her. Ever."

Edmonton stepped before Tryst and gave him a look that Tryst felt pierce his soul. "I will hold you to that."

The two of them shook hands and Edmonton slapped Tryst across the back, setting him off balance. Indeed, the old man had gotten back his strength.

"I've never seen my daughter happier. And she's now able to shift. Quite a miracle. You're the man to keep her so. Now as for you, Liam."

The principal paced between the two of them, finger to chin in thought. Liam drew back his shoulders, militarily alert, his chin lifted dutifully.

"You are aware I've been longing for a mate lately?"

"There was a rumor, Principal," Liam answered. "But I never subscribe to rumors."

"Yes, well, with my sickness I succumbed to a horrible melancholy. I have the desire to leave Wulfsiege. To go off adventuring," the principal said in a fantastical tone that gave Tryst a smile. "To put aside the worries and concerns of looking over the pack, and just…fall in love. To know if it's even possible after losing my one true love who gave me Alexis and Alana."

Tryst exchanged looks with Liam; both were incredulous.

"Now I am going to do so," Edmonton continued. "And in my stead, I name you, Liam, the new pack principal."

Liam's jaw dropped open.

"You are the best wolf for the job. The only wolf. The one man in the pack whom I have watched grow from a pup to a strong, powerful and reasonable wolf. There are days I consider you my son, you know that, Liam."

Liam bowed his head and nodded.

"You are humble yet brave. Wise yet open to all things." Edmonton turned to Tryst. "You've many of the same qualities as this fine man, but you've not been in a pack to know its ways. You will learn. And you will be a fine right-hand man to Liam." He turned back to the other wolf. "Will you accept, Liam?"

"I do," Liam answered proudly. "I will lead the pack in the manner you have, with swift justice, wisdom and strength."

Edmonton embraced Liam and the two exchanged a hearty man hug. "There's just one thing. No pack leader should be without a wife. You must marry immediately and get your new wife with child, and help grow the pack after the horrible losses we've incurred."

"Principal, I... There is no woman I feel so strongly for at the moment."

"Love will come," Edmonton said. "And, as luck would have it, I've already chosen your bride for you, as is my prerogative. Alana."

Tryst held back a chuckle at the sight of Liam's expression. He could tell the man was trying to hold back a full-on freak-out.

"But your daughter—" Liam started. "She doesn't even like me."

"But do you like her?"

"Well, of course, she is beautiful. Every time I pass her I cannot resist staring and I generally end up walking into a wall, but—"

"Then it is settled. True, Lana has been through much lately, what with that idiot, Sven. I initially liked the man, felt sorry for him, but he certainly pulled the wool over my eyes, eh? Lana needs a strong man to overcome her difficulties and make her happy. You are the man to do that, Liam. I welcome you into my family once again, but this time as my son-in-law."

He shook Liam's hand heartily, while Liam looked to Tryst with a lost, *help me* plea.

"We will celebrate tomorrow night!" Edmonton announced. "I will announce my plans to adventure, and then I will name Liam the new principal and we will present you and your fiancée. I'll let Alana know you've agreed to marry her," he added, as if an aside that should be taken care of before the party. "And Trystan, you'll stand beside Liam as scion. I couldn't be more pleased, gentlemen. You both make my heart happy."

Edmonton pulled the two into an embrace.

"So?" Lexi spun around from combing her hair before the vanity when Tryst wandered into her bathroom.

"It went…"

Her smile dropped at the sight of his frown. "Don't tell me Father kicked you out. I'll go with you. I don't want to be anywhere without you."

"Really?" He pulled her into a hug and kissed the crown of her head. She smelled sweet. She smelled like his. "You'd go back to Paris with me? Leave your only family? The closeness of the pack?"

"It would be hard leaving my family, but not the pack. Yes, I would leave with you in a heartbeat. I love you, Tryst."

His heart warmed to hold her. For the first time in his life, everything felt right, as if all the pieces had fallen into place. Finally, he knew the love and protection of a pack. A pack that was soon to become his own.

"I can't believe Father would kick you out—"

"Your father named me scion."

She would have stumbled out of his arms had he not deftly caught her.

"And he named Liam the new principal," he explained before she fainted. "Lexi? Stay with me, sweetie. That means I'm going to stay here. With you. For as long as you'll have me."

"Oh, my gods. Father is stepping down as principal? But of course, he's had such wanderlust of late. Oh, I'm so happy for him. And Liam. He's the only possible choice for leader. And you? My handsome lover, the new scion?"

"What do you think?" Tryst flexed a muscle then assumed a stoic yet commanding pose. "Scion material?"

"Oh, yes." She tugged him into the bedroom and pulled off his shirt. "Let's celebrate."

"Lover, I would love to, but—"

"Don't tell me you're going to be a workaholic and leave me alone in my room all day now that you've a title?"

"No. But I intend to do whatever is required of a scion, though I'm not entirely sure what that is yet. I have…an errand to run. Your father wants to party tomorrow night. Before that, I need to pick something up."

"Like what?"

"Top secret."

She crossed her arms and affected a pout. "It's getting late."

"It is, but I haven't forgotten our date out in the forest."

"Wolfed-out sex?"

He winked at her. "I'll meet you under the moon."

Chapter 22

Tryst tromped over the snowpack and through the forest, following his lover's gorgeous scent. He mapped the world by scent, and Lexi's was the only scent that made his skin warm and effected a smile before he even knew he was smiling.

He pulled off his shirt and loosened his jeans, thinking he should have left his clothes in the outbuilding, but he hadn't seen Lexi's in there, and thought it better if their clothes were kept close at hand.

After a good walk through the pines and ash spearing the land, he saw her standing in a clearing corralled by beech trees. What was it that Shakespeare's faeries said? "Ill met by moonlight?"

Tryst had to admit, when in werewolf form, none of his breed looked too sexy. They were hairy and distorted, a human's lengthened form with a wolf's head.

Mortals screamed at sight of them, and other paranormal breeds were never too thrilled to stare too long.

And yet, Lexi's werewolf was the sexist thing he had laid eyes on. Moonlight beamed over her form. Her sleek dark fur shimmered almost blue and her tail curled teasingly when her head turned and she spied him.

Tryst grew instantly hard. He stopped, kicking off his boots and shrugging down his jeans. His body began the shift before he'd even tugged off the pants, and he tumbled, ungracefully landing the snow in half-shifted form.

Lexi's werewolf howled in their version of wolf laughter and she took off through the trees.

Coming to his feet, Tryst's werewolf kicked aside the abandoned clothes and tracked after his female. Her scent glittered in the air and affixed itself to his fur, luring him on. Swiftly he tracked through the forest, deftly avoiding the trees and taking the snowpack in long, sure strides. He slapped a tree trunk, dragging his talons across it. A mark. This land was his domain now. He would hunt here. He would live and help rule the pack here.

And tonight, he would bond with his mate under the moonlight.

Hours later, Trystan leaned against the rough, cool trunk of a white beech. Steam wavered from his sex-hot skin, cooling him nicely. Lexi had wandered off for a nature call, and she walked back now, her hair swinging around her elbows and her sexy gait taking the snow in delicate steps. Her skin steamed as well, and she looked like a moonlight goddess, her pearly skin framed by the lush black hair.

He tugged her to him and twisted her hair about his hand, holding her against his chest. "You're mine now."

"Yes." She kissed him above the nipple. "Always. We did it. I did it," she said in excited tones. "I never thought I'd know what it was like to mate in werewolf form. Thank you, Trystan. For everything."

He didn't know what to say to that. Pride filled him. As well as a humble thankfulness. He caressed Lexi's head to his chest, her hair spilling like silk over his hand. His werewolf hadn't bitten her, and he suspected perhaps when in werewolf form he wouldn't experience the blood hunger. Only when in were shape. Fine with him. At least he wasn't like his father, where his vampire ruled his werewolf and forced him to carry out evil deeds.

With Lexi in his arms, he knew he could accept what he had become, and make it his life. A normal life. A perfect life, with his werewolf lover by his side.

The following night, Lexi left Tryst on his own to prepare for the celebration while she oversaw the event to be held in the keep. The cots had to be removed and the room decorated and chairs and tables put out. She'd assumed chatelaine mode, and he wasn't about to get in her way.

He'd managed to find some decent clothes while in town last night, and fussed in the bathroom with his hair, when he realized the party was going to start without him. Slapping a hand to the secret something he'd bought last night, he shoved it in a pants pocket and ran out the door, buttoning up his shirt as he took the hallway toward the keep.

He passed a group of very familiar faces along the way and stopped abruptly. Turning around, he put out his arms and received his mother in an embrace. "Mom? And Dad?" Vail stepped up beside Rhys and cast him a wink. "What are you guys doing here?"

"You made no mention of a party when you called last night," Rhys said. The half-breed wore his salt-and-pepper hair beyond his ears now, and he looked a little scruffy with the beard stubble. "You weren't going to invite us?"

"I didn't think you'd be allowed. How are you here?"

"Edmonton called and said it wouldn't be a party without your family at your side. How are you, son?"

"I'm good. Great! The best I've ever been."

"I'm glad to hear it. We've much to talk about, I'm sure."

"Yes. I need your wisdom, Dad. But later, when we can find a few minutes alone."

"We'll figure it out. Together." He slapped Tryst across the back and hugged him.

He kissed his mother's cheek and smoothed aside her rich black hair. Her blue eyes beamed brightly at him. She looked lucid, too, which was always a good thing. "My little Chucklebelly is all grown up and leading a pack," she said.

"I'm not the leader, Mom, just the second in command. And if you ever forget that silly name you called me as a kid, I'll be so happy."

"Chucklebelly, eh?" Vail said. "Hadn't heard that one before. Nice."

"If it crosses your lips one more time, you'll be bleeding," Tryst said.

"Boys, don't fight," Viviane said. The exotic beauty laid a hand tipped in wicked, long black fingernails over her chest. "It hurts my heart when you are cruel to one another."

"We're just teasing each other, Viviane," Vail said to the beautiful vampiress. He hadn't gotten comfortable with calling her mom or mother after only being in the mortal realm a year. "Trystan knows I love him."

"You do?" She inspected his eyes.

"Of course I do, Mom. Best vampire brother a werewolf could have."

She stroked his hair. "Your father tells me you've the blood hunger. I'm so sorry. You've always feared that from me. I'm better now. I ask your forgiveness for scaring you when you were a child."

"Mom, you've nothing to be forgiven for. And don't worry about me. I'll get it all figured out. I have two awesome parents to learn from, don't I? Now, let's forget all that stuff and go celebrate, yes?" He hooked an arm in hers and led his family into the keep. "I want you to meet Lexi."

"She is the werewolf that you love?"

"Yes, and I need to tell you a secret." The announcer was calling everyone to quiet, so Tryst whispered in his mother's ear the secret he was bursting to tell.

Edmonton Connor, dressed in a stylish gray suit with a crisp white shirt and diamond cuff links, explained his wanderlust to pack Alpine, who had gathered in celebration this evening. Most were aware of the elder wolf's desire to travel, and nodded in understanding. He had led the pack for over fifty years. A long time in any pack's history. Retirement was his due reward.

All cheered heartily as Liam was announced as the new pack leader. He would make an excellent leader for their close family, and would restore order after the mess created by Sven.

Lexi had been told before the party the announcement her father planned to make, naming Liam as leader, and as well, his new fiancée.

She gave her sister a hug, feeling her minute trembles, and whispered in her ear, "He is kind, and will love you," as Edmonton announced the engagement of Liam and Lana.

"I know that." Lana, holding her head bravely and forcing a smile, clasped hands with Liam and stood before all to renewed cheers.

In truth, Lexi figured her sister was one step away from being a basket case. She had just come out of a horrible relationship with Sven, and needed time to breathe, make sense of what had happened and to reorder her life. But Father wanted things to move swiftly, and couldn't leave the pack until he knew Liam had assumed control and that his daughters were protected. It made sense. Most packs would do the same. But she could sympathize with Lana's fears and heartbreak. On the other hand, Liam had been puppy-eyed over Lana for years, so Lexi knew he would treat her well. So long as Lana didn't wear him down, as was her manner, she expected the couple would thrive.

Tryst's hand slipped into hers, and he kissed her amidst the hooting and howls of celebration. A moment just for the two of them. The man's caring heart only seemed to grow wider.

Beside him, his mother, Viviane, peeked around Tryst's shoulder and gave Lexi a smile. She'd briefly been introduced to his family when they arrived half an hour earlier, and had to say she liked them. Even if they did look uncomfortable—vampires standing amid the pack. Tryst had gotten his blue eyes from Viviane, and his build and square jaw from his father, Rhys. The vampire, Vaillant, was an interesting character, and she looked forward to getting to know him better.

"It gives me great pleasure," Liam called out, "to announce the new scion our former principal has named—Trystan Hawkes."

Lexi kissed her lover again then gave him a shove to approach the front where Liam and Lana stood beside Edmonton. Her father gave him a hearty hug and gestured he shake hands with Liam. The two new leaders stood the same height, and were the same build, though Liam was a bit broader in the shoulders. Together they presented a powerful front, and Lexi's heart warmed as she imagined the pack would grow to something amazing under their command. It would become a fruitful and loving pack. And she looked forward to every moment from this day on.

Tryst called the room to silence and said, "I've an announcement of my own. Well, it's not really an announcement. It's something I need to do before all of you, before this new family that welcomes me with open arms, and with my family present who have loved me over the years. Yes, I'm sure you've all heard about my mixed heritage. I hope it doesn't offend, and promise I will work to prove myself to all of you."

"You already have!" shouted out from the crowd.

Lexi nodded and clapped along with the rest in agreement.

"So here it is." Tryst walked up to Lexi, and she couldn't interpret his broad grin. She figured he'd kiss her and declare before all that she was his—which he had better do. But when he dropped before her onto one knee and took her hand, tears loosened in her eyes and her heart stopped beating for a few seconds.

"Alexis Conner," Tryst said to her, "I love you. I

would love you if you never shifted again. I would love you if you shifted every hour just for the joy of it. And I love that you accept me for what I am, even though I'm still not sure myself." He tugged out something from his pocket and slid it onto her finger. The gold ring clasped a diamond that glittered madly. "Will you marry me, Lexi, and be my mate forever?"

Overwhelmed with happiness, she plunged into Tryst's arms. He swung her around, and she whispered in his ear, "Yes, forever."

"So what did she say?" Vail called out.

Tryst kissed Lexi then pumped a triumphant fist in the air. "Yes!"

Epilogue

Three months later...

Lexi stood before a floor-length mirror in her bedroom while her sister adjusted the veil pinned to her head with a simple diamond tiara.

"I don't know," she said, looking over the white lace dress that clung to her body and swept out at her knees like a mermaid's tail. It was a hand-me-down from Lana. "I think it's too fussy."

"This is the dress you helped me pick out," Lana said. "If you'd wanted your own dress you should have said something. Tryst is standing at the altar waiting for you. Everyone is waiting!"

Indeed, they'd set up a celebration tent out back, behind the castle. Actually, it had been set up a month earlier, for Lana and Liam's wedding. Snow had still been on the ground then, and Lana had looked like a winter queen in this very dress and veil.

Lexi thought she more resembled an escapee from a lace factory gone wild. She shook her head and tugged off the tiara, handing it to Lana. "Rip off the fluffy part of the skirt."

"What?"

"Please? I can't walk down the aisle looking like a white Popsicle coated with hoarfrost. It's spring, and the buttercups are in bloom. I want this to be simple."

Lana wielded a pair of scissors. "Hold on. I'll figure something out." She went at the skirt. "Did you see Daddy's suitcases are already packed?"

"He's wanted to go off adventuring for months now. No reason for him not to. I'll miss him."

"I hope he finds a woman and has a wild and crazy affair. He deserves that."

"He will. Don't worry. He's headed to Brazil. Land of bare bodies and endless nights." Lexi smoothed a palm over her belly and grimaced at her reflection, turning to the side. "Do I look fat?"

"You look pregnant," Lana said with a chuckle. "Lucky girl."

"It'll happen for you. Soon."

"We haven't had sex yet." She tugged the extra fabric from the bottom of Lexi's skirt and stood back to look over her sister.

"Lana, it's been a month. What's wrong?"

Lana shrugged. "He's nice and all, but I still need some time. And Liam understands that."

"He'll be a good father."

"Oh, I know he will. I just—I'm afraid, I guess. Afraid to give my heart away again. You know?"

Lexi pulled her sister into a hug. "Take all the time

you need. The marriage was a rush job. You have to let your heart catch up."

"Thanks for being such a great sister."

They both turned to the mirror and Lexi asked, "So how do I look?"

"Like the princess you were meant to be."

When prompted, Tryst repeated the words, "I do," loud and proud. He couldn't take his eyes from Lexi. Who'd have thought a woman could look so sexy in a frothy white lace dress and with that gorgeous little baby bump swelling across her middle? Lexi was the hottest, sexiest woman he'd laid eyes on, and she was all his.

The officiator directed them to kiss, and Tryst grabbed the stupid bouquet of white roses from Lexi's hand, tossed them over his shoulder into the audience, and swept his wife up into the kiss he'd been wanting to give her since seeing her walk down the aisle toward him.

Toward their future. Toward their life together.

Lexi gasped as he pulled back. "I love you," he said, and then he knelt before her and kissed her belly. Smoothing his hands over the firm bump, he said, "And I love you, too, little one. Can't wait to welcome you to this world."

* * * * *

To learn more about Vail, Rhys and Viviane, stop by clubscarlet.michelehauf.com for information on their stories.

MOON KISSED

For Lyda Morehouse because she rocks.

Chapter 1

The asphalt blurred under Bella's running shoes as she abandoned her casual evening jog for a lung-bruising sprint. In the tropical humidity this sweltering midsummer night, her chest, back and face dripped with sweat.

Aware of the frenzied breaths close in her wake, she forced herself to push through the pain of exertion.

Escape. Don't let them get you.

She wasn't familiar with this neighborhood, yet she knew it formed the line of demarcation where the suburbs met the industrial north side of the Twin Cities. Not the best jogging spot for a lone young woman, especially with the streetlights out of order. The only light came from the distant neon of a string of nightclubs that peeked between four-and five-story warehouses.

Taking a long stride and ignoring her burning hamstrings, she made the curb. Thank God, she hadn't slipped. They'd be on her. To rob her or bite her or—

What *were* they? They had teeth. Long teeth. They had snarled and flashed fangs.

When she'd taken off running, they'd given her a head start, laughing, as a group of men will do when they wish to frighten a woman. She'd prayed they would simply stand there, not pursue her. But that prayer hadn't been answered.

Close by, the *ta-thum, ta-thum* of a train rolling over the iron track matched the heavy labor of her heartbeats.

She'd never be able to outrun them. But maybe hide?

To her right, a dark warehouse beckoned. The three-story structure mastered the corner of the block. The double-wide door gaped, a black maw.

Bella dashed inside.

Too late, she realized her mistake. She'd trapped herself. The entire block was dark. Who would hear her scream?

Lungs heaving, she struggled to stay upright on her shaky legs.

Darkness nudged up against her shoulders, making it difficult to even make out the walls around her. The windows were like glass-toothed open mouths against the dark sky. Dark masses of bulky objects—stacked, like lumber—forced her to tread carefully.

Her running shoe crunched on a loose board and she wobbled. Arms groping through the air, she swung blindly to stave off a fall. But equilibrium abandoned her.

Before she could hit the concrete, strong hands caught her about the waist and tugged her into darkness.

A man holding her breathed heavily, as if from exertion, like her. Warm breath wafted over her face. He smelled strongly masculine. Earthy. He was not one of her fanged pursuers. Yet she couldn't immediately determine if he was exactly a safe harbor.

His strong arms clasped about her arms and across her back. He took a step, dragging her deeper into the darkness. A boarded-up window, six feet to her left, admitted thin shafts of spare moonlight.

A piece of rough wood tore across her shoulder and a sliver snagged her T-shirt. Bella struggled. "Let me go. Who are you?"

"I've saved you from those wild idiots outside. No thanks?"

"If you let me go."

His nose brushed across her forehead, as if taking in her scent. "I don't think so."

His intense actions now frightened her more than being chased. Arms tight about her body, he studied her, as she did him. Face a breath from hers. Aggressive stance. Shoulders squared and hips firmly placed. He was twice as wide as she and a head higher. All brawn and muscle. Bigger than the many male dance partners she'd performed with over the years.

The thick muscles in his arms pulsed against her shoulders, squeezing her uncomfortably. He chuckled through his nose and continued his sniffing trail over her face, drawing down near her ear.

Repulsed, Bella squirmed, seeking a means to break the binding hold. Just as she felt a scream rise, a palm smacked over her mouth. She twisted her head, but he pressed so hard, her lips flattened against her teeth.

"Shh, pretty one." Her captor's voice was soothing and deep. It sounded far too nice—too attractive—for a man who might harm her. "They're here, preening about the doorway. You want me to release you and see how you fare with three instead of one? I bet they'll take turns."

A reedy moan escaped her throat.

Strong yet cautioning fingers dug into her biceps. "Listen."

Tears burning in her eyes, Bella listened. The three men entered the building, slowly, cautiously, their light footsteps landing randomly on two-by-fours scattered on the floor.

They'd all been taller than her; most men did rise over her five-foot-four frame. Dressed in black and looking more than a little Goth, the lanky trio oozed menace.

The supple thickness of her captor's leather jacket crushed her breasts and belly as he pressed his torso against hers. His solid muscles hugged her everywhere. Trapping her. Threatening her with each slight move he made.

A flicker of prudence cautioned her to remain still. Make no noise. Yet Bella slowly moved her fingers over the rough wood behind her. Must be a stack of pallets. If she could find a nail to use as a weapon...

A thin ray of moonlight struck the corner of her captor's forehead, illuminating dark hair slicked back from his forehead and over his ears. There was a pale shimmer in the one eye she could make out. Dark brown, wild and surrounded by shadowed flesh.

Had she stumbled into the arms of a homeless man? But he didn't reek of alcohol or body odor.

Still, she couldn't budge, and the hand over her mouth hurt.

A tinny clatter ratcheted up her heartbeats. Someone nearby stepped across the debris.

They would hear her thundering heart, she feared.

The man who held her forcefully nudged his nose along her cheek. His hot tongue dashed out to lick up a tear that fell down her cheek.

Though she wanted to retch, to scream, to kick out and fight for her life, Bella could only swallow the horror and pray she did not make a noise that would bring the others upon her. Four attackers would be unthinkable.

She heard feet shuffle nearby, and then a pallet of boards fell, nearly deafening her. The crash of wood connecting with Sheetrock released the odor of chalk. Apparently her would-be attackers were throwing things about.

"Where the hell did she get to?"

"Cool your heels, dude. She's in here somewhere."

A whimper tickled Bella's throat. Clenched tighter by her captor, she winced. Now both his eyes were visible in the slash of light, warning, teasing in a darkly macabre way.

He wouldn't toss her out to the others, would he? She sought his eyes to find the answer to that worry, but he tilted his head to listen.

"Did she run out the other side? The whole place is wide-open. Check that exit, will you?"

A wide hand explored her body from her back and around to her chest, slowly, without sound. When he squeezed her breast, she bit away a scream. A swallow put back the bile rising in her throat. Now he pressed his hand so hard to her mouth, his finger lay across her teeth.

"So sweet," he whispered in the calmest, most dreadful tone. "Your fear arouses me."

Woozy darkness toyed with her brain. *Don't pass out.* She had to stay alert.

Or would it be better if she didn't know how this night might end? Her life hadn't flashed before her eyes yet, so did that mean there would be only torture and pain?

Come on, Bella, she coached inwardly. *Where's your usual cheery optimism? You are safe. Just remain in this man's arms.*

Nausea coiled in her gut. When her leg muscles gave out, her captor tilted a hip into her to press her against the stacked pallets.

"Hold on, sweet," he murmured. "They may be hungry for your blood, but they can't scent a skunk in a garden."

Hungry for her blood? Did that mean they were—

No. Things—*creatures*—like that didn't exist. They were a gang of wild, drunk men out to torment a woman.

The fingers at her breast found her nipple. It hardened at his touch. She was not aroused. It was the fear heightening her reaction to every touch, sound and smell.

A hard pinch snapped her thoughts to the moment.

"Stay with the program, sweet," he muttered. "They're at the other end of the warehouse. They'll give up soon, I'm sure."

She mumbled behind his hand, and he pressed hard but then relented. "Quiet. Or it's your funeral."

When he took his fingers from her mouth, it felt as if they were still there. She wriggled her lips and opened her aching jaw.

"Cosmopolitans, eh?"

Startled at his suggestion, she realized he must smell the drink on her breath. But how could he? She'd had one during an afternoon meeting with a potential client. That had been six hours earlier. Of course, she hadn't eaten since.

"Wh-what are they?" she managed.

He shoved her head against his chest, which effectively muffled her utterance.

"Vampires," he murmured. "And they're hungry."

She'd gotten that impression the moment the one had flashed his fangs at her. This was so wrong. She didn't believe in vampires.

"They've left."

She struggled, but he quickly clasped her wrists before her. "They'll circle the building and roam the area. You're not safe yet, sweet, so keep calm. You can do that, yes?"

She nodded, conceding silently. He seemed willing to keep her protected and unseen, but why? For his own evil intentions?

"Mmm, but can I?" He again sniffed at her hair. A dodge of his head placed his mouth at her jaw. He licked it.

"I'm going to be sick," she whispered, hoping it would dissuade him.

Footsteps slapping the pavement outside the window

alerted her. Her captor again pressed her head against his chest, smothering her breath against the warm, rough-woven sweater he wore beneath the jacket. He held her so fiercely, she thought he might break a bone. One of *her* bones.

"Here, pretty, pretty," came a voice from outside. A low whistle teased the evening air.

The sound pinched Bella's heart, like a stretched spring snapping to a coil.

He was right. They circled the building. How long would they prowl the area before giving up? Could she keep from crying out when in the arms of another man who meant her harm?

A low growl, which sounded more like satisfaction than warning, preceded the press of his leg against her hip. He had an erection. The utter and sickening wrongness rent Bella's soul.

"Let's head back," someone outside shouted. "We'll find another."

Bella's spine straightened, her hope lifting.

"Give them five minutes," the man said. "Then they'll be far enough off for you to run."

"You'll let me go?"

"Of course. You don't think I'd take you right here in this dump?"

"You…you…" He'd said he'd let her go. The deal had been made. She wouldn't argue beyond it.

"I have your scent in my nose, sweet. No matter how far you run, I'll find you."

"No, please. You've saved my life."

"I've merely prevented you from getting raped and

your neck torn to shreds. I suppose you do owe me, though."

And she could imagine what he'd desire as reward.

"You impress me, mortal." His grip on her loosened, but still his torso held her pinned against the pallets. "Other women would have pissed their pants in your situation. Are you so brave, or somehow beyond fear?"

She breathed through her nose, fighting her raging heartbeats. Her forehead dropped to his chest. So weak. Just…exhausted, and yes, beyond fear.

He'd called her *mortal*.

Bella curled her fingers into his sweater. "Are you like them?" she asked, not knowing where the question came from. Nervous energy. Macabre fascination.

"A vampire?" His chuckle vibrated against her forehead. "Human blood docs nothing for me."

That didn't exactly answer her question. Bella leaned back, her head lolling across the wood pallets. She pressed her hands to his chest as a means to keep from collapsing.

"They've gone far enough now. Their scent is weak."

"Y-you…" Stress softened her voice to a whisper. "You can smell their distance?"

"Yes. Your fear is subsiding. Next will come shock or collapse. You'd best be off before you find you cannot move at all."

"Thank you." Yet another strange utterance when what she really wanted to do was kick the bastard and scream at him.

He stepped away, but they were wedged between stacks of pallets, and that kept him close enough to touch. Moving right, she tested his promise to allow her to leave. And when she tried the ground with her foot to see if it would be sure, a hand grasped her wrist and pulled her to him.

He wasn't going to let her leave!

"I'll take my reward before you flee."

"But—"

He crushed his mouth to hers with a violent and urgent kiss. It hurt, and it wasn't kind. But her mouth was already numb.

He pulled her into an embrace that lifted her feet from the floor and clasped her body against his like a monster picking up a child and ripping off its head.

But he didn't harm her. Instead, he groaned with pleasure.

Suddenly setting her down and pushing her away, he twisted his head and shook it fiercely, like a dog shaking off rain. "Go!"

She didn't need to be told twice. Sliding her hands along the boards to guide her, Bella found the doorway where she had entered.

"Go north," she heard him say. "They went south."

North, then. And she took off running.

Shoulders pressed to the pallets behind him, and eyes closed, Severo listened. Each of her footsteps poked at his muscles, as if to prod awake something long dormant.

He required no prodding. At this moment, he was more awake and alive than he'd felt in decades.

He'd been strolling the neighborhood, assessing the abandoned real estate, when he'd picked up the vile scent of longtooths on the hunt. Their obnoxious odor had triggered his gag reflex. Yet he had sensed the female's scent and had ducked inside the warehouse.

If he could save one human from the clutches of a vampire, then it was a good day indeed.

But what he hadn't expected was the way she'd made him feel. Or that she'd make him feel at all.

He had walked this earth for many decades and had given up hope of ever finding a true mate. Human females were so fragile, delicate, and not worth more than a few nights of pleasure.

This one was different. She was emotionally strong.

Could she be the one? A woman he could finally make his own. His mate. Forever.

Chapter 2

Sunlight woke her. Bella sat up on the couch and blew aside a stray fern from her face. An oblique muscle on her side ached, forcing her horizontal again. She stared up through the luscious green fronds.

"I slept on the couch?"

Her body ached. Her hamstrings pulsed. Her shoulders and ribs felt bruised.

She touched her tender lips. Tears slipped down her cheeks.

Something had happened last night to turn her world on its side and roll it off a cliff. If she put aside the possibility of near rape, there was the evidence that those bastards who chased her were...

Vampires.

And the creep who'd held her in perilous safety had confirmed her suspicion as if he knew it were the truth.

And he'd called her mortal, which put into question his own status.

"Oh, Bella, you must have bumped your head. You're thinking like a crazy woman."

Storybook creatures were not supposed to exist. A woman was supposed to fear serial killers, rapists and crazed gunmen loosed in city malls. Not men who looked human yet wanted to suck your blood.

Her heart began to race as swiftly as it had last night. Bella pressed a palm over her chest. She still wore yesterday's clothes. On the cotton shirt she saw a smear where his hand on her breast had dirtied the fabric.

A repulsive shiver chilled her from neck to hips.

Scrambling from the couch, she tore the shirt over her head and made a beeline toward the bathroom. Shedding her jogging pants, running shoes, panties and sports bra, she hit the shower, crying.

"Shake it off, Bella. That was a new street you took last night. You were not thinking straight."

She always walked to and from the clubs at night and had never once felt unsafe. A northernmost suburb of Minneapolis, her town was considered upscale and safe. She lived on a main strip where neat townhomes and lofts segued into a neighborhood of trendy dance clubs and restaurants. The dance studio where she practiced three days a week was but four blocks away.

Every other night she jogged five miles, usually down the strip, then through the city park that boasted manicured jogging trails and plenty of streetlamps. Never had she been attacked. The occasional catcall from a passing car or leer from a drunk huddled up against a storefront was to be expected. Heck, Benny the drunk, who nightly posted himself at the corner of Spruce and Second streets, always got a wave and a greeting from her.

She'd thought to take Declan Street last night, knowing it traversed a vacant section of older warehouses. She liked to explore. Her intention had been to go no more than a block, but once those men leaped out at her, her brain had switched from curiosity to flight.

Unfortunately, she'd run *away* from the safety of the well-lit strip.

"You put yourself in a bad situation. You dealt with it. You're safe and they didn't hurt you. Now get over it."

Spitting out warm water, she turned her back to the stream and reached for a bottle of shampoo.

Time to resume good old reliable Belladonna Reynolds mode. She was smart, stable, and could always be counted on to be responsible. Her web design clients praised her creativity and precision. The dance studio was courting her to teach. Even when clubbing with friends, she was the one who quit drinking first, called cabs for everyone and made sure they got their car keys the next day.

Cosmopolitans.

He'd smelled the drink on her breath. Which was entirely possible. Bella hadn't eaten yesterday after that late business lunch. Not wise, because she had been straining during that last mile of running.

But to smell how far the vampires had fled? How could he possibly have known something like that?

Vampires.

Even thinking the word made her want to retch.

Clutching the warm brass showerhead, she tilted her head to catch the water on the crown of her scalp.

Why was she so willing to accept what a complete stranger had told her?

She saw the fangs. Long and white, slightly curved, like a deadly blade.

But nothing could be worse than that hard, stolen kiss. He'd violated her in the sense that she'd relied on him for safety, and then he'd stolen it with his gropes and aggressiveness.

Bastard.

I have your scent in my nose. I'll find you.

"Don't think about it, Bella," she told herself. "It was a bad night." Should she call the cops?

What could they do? She hadn't clearly seen any of the men's faces. Once they'd flashed fangs, her better senses had vanished.

And she'd seen only parts of her captor's face. Though she'd never forget his lecherous growl. He'd seemed more animal than the vampires.

"Quit thinking that word," she admonished and flicked off the shower.

Stepping out onto the bamboo floor mat, she toweled herself off.

Today was Saturday. Though her web design business allowed her to work from home, she followed her no-work-on-weekends rule. With nothing required of her today, she usually jogged on weekend afternoons at the park.

Nix that, she thought. Perhaps the video store down the block would offer some comedies to clear her thoughts.

The doorbell rang. Bella glanced to the LED clock on the toilet tank. It was noon?

She'd slept so late. Deservingly.

"Seth."

Her best friend had said he'd stop by with tickets for tonight's jam at the club. He DJ'd and they expected a sold-out house.

Tugging a white watered-silk robe around her body, Bella raced out to the door, dodging the overgrown bamboo plant at the end of the couch. Seth opened the door with his key first and entered.

"Oh, sorry, Bella. When you didn't answer, I got worried."

He swung the key ring around his forefinger a couple times and tucked it in his pocket. Seth was a recovering emo who still loved the fringy eyebrow-dusting bangs and slim, fitted clothing. Recently, he'd graduated to techno club music in protest of the dirgelike tunes he'd once embraced.

He leaned in to kiss her cheek. His lemony aftershave always made her smile.

"What's this? Did you fall and bump yourself? Your jaw looks bruised."

All the bravery she'd talked herself into during the shower slipped away now that she stood in the safety of Seth's arms. Bella burrowed her face against his shoulder and sobbed.

"Okay, something's wrong. Let's sit you down and— Bellybean, it's okay. I'm here. Talk to me."

"Oh, Seth, you'll never believe the horrible thing that happened to me last night."

"Hell, Bella. Do I need to call the police?"

He steered her toward the couch. His bright blue eyes studied her as he touched her jaw gently. They'd developed a friendship during ballroom dancing classes in middle school. That friendship had deepened in high school, after a medical-careers class in eleventh grade. Seth had been Bella's model for compassion.

"Are you all right?"

"Just a few bruises," she said, sniffling. "Physically, I'm fine. Mentally, well… I was chased by three men."

"What? Where? When?"

"Last night."

"Were you jogging?"

She winced at his admonishing tone. "Yes, but I took a new route."

"You know I hate you jogging at night to begin with, but you promised me you'd stick to the parks and well-lit avenues."

"I was bored with that route." Sucking in gasping breaths, she forced up calm and bent a knee to kneel on the couch by Seth. "I have to tell you this fast, because if I don't tell someone, I think I'll go crazy. But what I have to say is so crazy, you might think I've already achieved insanity."

"You can tell me anything, Bellybean. If someone hurt you—"

"They were vampires."

He closed his mouth. Seth's gaze searched her face. Not accusing or condemning, just listening.

"Three vampires," she said. "They flashed their fangs and chased me. Seth, I know it sounds strange, but the guy in the warehouse said they were vampires, too."

"The guy in the warehouse?"

"I ran into an abandoned warehouse to hide, but someone was already in there. He grabbed me. I thought he was going to hurt me, but he kept me quiet and hidden until the vampires gave up and left. He said he could smell them and I feel like he was some kind of creature, too, and— Seth, doesn't this freak you out?"

Head bowed and hands between his knees, he blew out a breath. "Not as much as you think it should. I'm freaked you were chased. The guy in the warehouse— he hurt you? Is that how you got this bruise?"

She clasped a hand over his when he touched her jaw. "He was holding his hand over my mouth so I wouldn't scream and alert the others."

"So he protected you. Huh." Seth put a fist to his mouth, thinking. "Did the guy protecting you have fangs?"

"Not that I saw. He said he hated vampires, that they smelled vile. He smelled things a lot. Seth, I just told you I was chased by vampires."

"I know, Bellybean. Don't worry. I've known vampires exist for a while now."

"What?" Surprised by that calm statement, Bella shot up on one foot, the other leg still bent on the couch. "You *know* about vampires?"

The chilling rush of blood leaving her head turned her flesh to goose bumps.

Seth shrugged. "I've been dating one for a couple weeks."

An openmouthed gape was all she could manage.

"Sit down, Bella. You've just discovered that mythical creatures exist, and not in a good way, either. Are you sure you're okay? None of them put their fangs to you, did they?"

She was still too stuck on the "I've been dating one" part to summon a response. Dragging her leg from the couch, Bella paced around behind the couch.

Seth was her BFF. They told each other everything. Shared good times and bad. He'd been the one to encourage her to begin dancing again. And he was always the first with a hug when she needed one.

He'd told her about a new girlfriend a few weeks ago over soup and sandwiches at Panera. Bella had been stunned how quickly he'd started calling this mystery woman his love. Seth never dated long-term and preferred to keep his dating schedule open for late-night pickups after a gig at the club.

And he'd neglected to mention this newest fling was a vampire.

"Whoever it was that grabbed you did good," he finally said. "If those vamps had gotten their hands on you they would have bitten you. I wonder if it was a were?"

"A were—as in werewolf? Seth, you're killing me here. First, you neglect to tell me your girlfriend is a vampire. And now you're so casual about the fact that creepy horror creatures actually exist. I don't know what to think."

"It's a lot to take in, but accept the fact that you have proof vamps do exist and move beyond it, Bella. That's what you do."

"Yes. Yes, I believe. I mean, how can a girl *not* believe when she's seen proof?"

He turned and propped his elbows on the couch.

"And yes, I do mean werewolf. If he was scenting the vampires like you said, it's my best guess. Those things are like bloodhounds times ten. They can pick out a peppermint Life Savers in a city the size of New York. Put them on the scent, and set them loose."

"Oh, my God." Again the nausea rose. Bella gripped the couch. "He said he had my scent in his nose, and that he'd find me again if he wanted."

"Shit, Bella, that's not good."

"No kidding. The last thing I need is a werewolf tracking me down to—"

Finish what he'd wanted to start last night in the warehouse?

Bella sank to her knees. Seth bounded over the back of the couch and lifted her so she sat on the back of it. He nudged between her legs, his hands to her hips and his head bowed to her forehead.

"Just lie low, Bella. It's going to be okay. Last night was a fluke. Don't ever go down that street again. And stick to jogging during the day, will you? Vamps don't do daylight."

"Oh, mercy." It was too incredible that the silver-screen stereotypes were true. "And crosses?"

"Kill vamps dead. But only if they've been baptized."

"Christ."

"That's about the point of it. Oh, and stakes work pretty well, too, but from what I understand, you've got to burst their heart or else they'll bounce right back at you. Werewolves, on the other hand, can do daylight. So maybe I don't want you going out for a run at all."

"Seth, I'm freaked that you know so much and are actually dating a vampire. How does that happen? *Why* does that happen? Are you her slave? Is she sucking your blood?"

She grabbed his shirt and tugged aside the wide lapel to reveal a purple-and-green bruise on the side of his neck. "Oh, no, you *are* a slave."

"I'm nothing of the sort." He tugged his shirt collar to make it stand upright. Seth was all about fashion and the right haircut. "She doesn't take very much, and besides, it feels good."

"Good? To have some creature bite into your flesh and suck out your blood? Oh, Seth."

Bending and putting her head between her knees felt right, but instead Bella wavered before her friend. She wanted to hug him, but at the same time she couldn't touch him. A vampire had bitten him. What did that make Seth?

"It's all cool, Bella. I'm in love."

Panic strummed her voice. "Because she has you under her control."

"Because she is the most perfect woman I have ever met. She makes me happy, and I make her happy. Now, I want to be sure you're safe tonight, so this ticket will go to someone else."

"No, I want to go to the show. I've written it on my calendar."

"Heaven forbid, Belladonna Reynolds wavers from her schedule," he mocked grandly.

"Seth! I'm not going to hide in the dark like a mushroom. I can deal with this. Maybe. After I've wrapped my head around it. Vampires? Really?"

"Yes, Bella, really."

"Right. Really." She tucked her forefinger in his

jeans pocket, where she suspected he kept the ticket. "I want a ticket, Seth. Please? It'll be good for me to dance the night away and not think about other stuff."

He shoved a hand in the pocket and produced a Day-Glo green ticket and relented before she could take it. "Promise you'll take a cab to and from?"

"Maybe."

"Bella."

"The club is down the street, less than a mile. The street is well lit, and there are always clubbers and cars out well past midnight, so it's not like I'll be alone."

"Bella, among those clubbers are vampires. They are out there. And so are werewolves and demons and faeries and all other sorts."

"Oh, just stop, Seth. I haven't gotten sick yet, but you keep talking like you're such an expert on all those woo-woo things and I may hurl. Button up your shirt. I can't believe you'd let someone do that to you."

"Don't worry." He tossed her a charming wink as he tugged at his lapels. "She's very careful. If she took too much, I'd die."

"What?"

"That's not going to happen. She may even give me immortality. But that's my choice."

"You're not helping my need to hurl."

"Right. So tonight?"

"Is *she* going to be there?"

"Maybe. You want me to introduce you?"

Come face-to-face with another vampire after last night's adventure? "No."

"I understand." He lifted her hand and kissed the

back of it. "So you should go shower again, and maybe once more before you go outside today."

"Why?"

"I'm thinking you can wash off whatever scent you were putting out last night. Or, I know, wear that sexy perfume you have, the one that smells like cloves."

"You think the werewolf will smell me from… anywhere?"

"Don't start to cry, Bellybean. I just think it would be a good precaution."

His hug felt great, yet at the moment Bella felt her arms would never be able to grasp the reassurance she needed. Everything in her world had changed. How could she return to the cheery, stress-free, well-ordered life she enjoyed?

"Wh-what do werewolves do to people, Seth? I mean, if vampires suck blood, what about…"

"I'm not sure. They wolf out when the moon is full, I know that, which makes them into hairy creatures. Or so I've been told. I think they're real sex freaks, too. But again, it's only hearsay."

"Sex freaks," Bella muttered mindlessly. "When's the next full moon?"

"Couple weeks. Look, should I try to find out more info? Maybe I'll ask around if anyone knows a wolf in the area, see what you're dealing with."

She nodded. "That sounds good. But maybe it would be better to drop it all. Maybe he didn't like what he smelled."

Not judging by how he had groped her last night. And that kiss, so hard, and yet wanting. If she hadn't been freaked out of her gourd, she might have found it alluring.

An alluring werewolf?

"I think I do need another shower," she added.

Seth kissed her on the forehead. He was in entirely too good a mood after everything they'd just discussed.

Bella wondered if being bitten by a vampire released endorphins into the man's bloodstream. He had been extremely happy of late, so much so that she had briefly wondered if he'd been doing drugs. Seth was so against drugs, she'd not dared ask him about her theory.

The truth was worse than drugs.

"Come up and bang on the glass when you get to the club," he called as he strolled toward the door. "Love you, Bellybean!"

She waved him off and headed toward the shower.

What kind of scent had the wolf picked up from her? She'd been a sweaty mess last night.

And really, did she believe Seth's guess? The man had been a *man*. He wasn't a werewolf. Wouldn't he have seemed wolflike to her? Although, he had a beard and lots of hair...

"No, he wasn't. Couldn't be," she said as she turned on the shower.

But if she could buy the vampire bit, that meant she had to get on board with the werewolves, too.

Chapter 3

The music pummeling the innards of club Silver leaked through the open back doors. Graffiti scrawled across the brick walls had gotten a recent freshening up, and the bold colors glowed in the night.

A small group who couldn't gain access danced in the lot behind the elite club. The bouncers kept watch but seemed to approve. It was this way every evening. The management was even considering serving drinks outside to the unchosen.

Severo paused at the front corner of the three-story brick building to watch the line out front as some were gifted admission and others slunk away, pouting, yet determined to return another day for another go at admittance. The back-lot dancers were too gauche for those who wished entry through the front.

Slipping a hand in the pocket of his brown leather jacket, he tried to catch a few words of the song, but the beat was about all he could discern. Didn't matter. He wasn't a fan of the erratic music the clubs played. Lynyrd Skynyrd was more his speed. But he did like the atmosphere. The noise and crush of bodies put him out of his thoughts and into a mindless place where nothing really mattered.

But until he entered the club, he was anything but mindless.

He strolled down the front avenue and noted the black stretch limo parked across the street. Vamps, no doubt. They scoured the clubs, but in a subtle send-out-the-troops manner that brought potentials back to the horde. The higher-ranking vampires couldn't be bothered to go inside and mingle with the lesser humans.

Nasty longtooths. Severo hated them all, save a select few with whom he had the opportunity to establish trusting relationships over the decades.

The August air stirred a frenzy of gasoline, heat-softened tarmac, spilled booze, cat piss and perfume. When so many odors combined, he could easily acclimate and move above them, so to speak. They faded into the background as murk, allowing distinctive scents to rise.

One scent in particular surfaced. It was familiar, rich and enticing. He'd gotten but a taste of it, and he wanted more.

The shivery little rabbit who had fled the vampires and run right into his arms. She had seeped into him on an intoxicating cocktail of fear, adrenaline and—though she would deny it—arousal. Sweet, she still lingered on his tongue and in the pores of his flesh.

Bowing his head and marching forward, Severo gained entrance to Silver with a mere nod to the bouncers.

Seth spun Jayne's latest diatribe against the tabloids; she was the current "it" girl on the techno-funk scene. The crowd bounced, shimmied and jumped on the stainless-steel dance floor beneath epileptic-fit-inducing strobe lights.

Bella pushed her way down the entrance ramp, hung with thick black velvet curtains, and weighed the chances of getting up to the DJ's box. The dance floor was body to body. Seth was in his groove, fists pumping and head bopping. But she did manage to catch his attention with a quick wave.

She needed this night to lose herself in the loud music and redirect her thoughts from other things. Things that had stabbed at her brain all afternoon. She was still shocked at Seth's confession. But tonight it was all good.

As soon as she sipped her first cosmopolitan.

The shortest route to refreshment was straight across the dance floor. Finding the beat seductive, Bella slinked her way into the crowd. Ballroom and flamenco might be her preferences, but she could shake it with the best of them.

She inched her red spangled skirt up at her thigh and shimmied before a sexy dancer. He matched her move with a suggestive shake of his shoulders. It was all in fun. And man, did his teeth sparkle.

Spinning, Bella insinuated herself between two

women. They bumped their hips to hers and that made Bella laugh. She raised her arms above her head and decided the drink could wait. Surrendering to the beat took her to a great place.

Masculine hands stretched down her arms, and she rotated her hips. Together she and Mr. White Teeth rocked in a wide circle. It was overtly sexual, but she didn't feel the threat level she had last night. Even the flutter of fingertips tracing the swinging hem of her short skirt didn't offend her.

She was in control here. No one was going to chase her or try to take advantage of her. Not unless she wished it. And she would never ask to be controlled. Control was hers. Her life didn't function without it. And tonight she intended to take it back.

No wonder Seth was always so naturally high. Music did something to people. It moved them beyond the norm and opened their hearts and minds, even their souls. It was why Bella had navigated her way back to dancing after a five-year absence.

The smell of alcohol, something fruity like green apples, reminded her that she did have a goal. Dancing her way through the crowd, Bella spied an empty space at the bar and slid onto the slick silver plastic seat.

She knew the bartender and smiled at him. He shot her an acknowledging wink and set about making her "usual."

This club served the best cosmopolitans, and no, Bella did not have *Sex and the City* dreams of landing Mr. Big and wearing designer shoes. She was happy with her job as a website designer. And while she liked sexy spike heels, she'd take a healthy relationship with a stable man over Manolos any day.

The bartender slid a shimmery pink drink into her grasp and shook his hand at the dollar bills she laid on the counter. "First one's free for you, Bella."

Cool. She'd take a free drink any day.

The cosmo was sweet with a bite of sour. Crossing her legs and twisting to watch the dancers, she shifted her shoulders to the rhythm.

Behind a Plexiglas barrier, Seth danced and pumped his fist to the tunes he delivered to the masses. He spiked his hair on the nights he DJ'd, and it went a long way in transforming his usual emo look.

Dating a vampire?

You're not going to think about it, Bella. Have another drink.

She was about to signal the bartender when he placed another pink drink before her. Pleased he was keeping an eye on her needs, Bella tossed him a wink. But when she dug in her purse for cash, a thickly veined, dark-haired hand slid a five-dollar bill onto the bar.

Heat prickled the back of Bella's neck.

A husky male voice whispered, "Told you I'd find you."

Chapter 4

He had found her. In seconds her heart reached Mach speed, and she choked on her drink. The bartender spun a look at her, and she gave him a silly smile and a shrug.

Though she didn't dare turn to look at the man, she recognized his familiar scent. That deep, earthy odor that was also sweet. What kind of kook had she become that now she was scenting out people like some kind of... *No, he can't be.*

The person next to her vacated her stool, much to Bella's dread. The man didn't slide onto it but inserted himself between the empty stool and her body. A strong, muscled thigh pulsed against her bare thigh. The spangles on her skirt pressed into her flesh.

"How did you find me?" she asserted.

"I followed you. From your home."

"From my—" He knew where she lived? "Please

leave, or I'll get a bouncer and tell him you were threatening me."

"You won't do that." He reached for her drink and sniffed it. "That's how you smelled last night. Vodka and cranberries. You women and your pretty pink drinks. But your scent is different today. Lots of perfume." He sniffed at the air before her. "Cloves. Did you think to hide your natural scent from me?"

"Yes. No." Bella grasped her throat, so aware of her low-cut neckline. He'd noticed, as well. "I'm not comfortable talking to you."

"Good. I like a woman who is honest. And I'd hate it if you were one of those who hung on any man who will give you the time of day."

She pressed her hand on the cocktail napkin and inched up the wet edge. She was supposed to be safe here.

Bella looked aside. Seth was so close. Was he keeping an eye on her? A trio of scantily clad women danced before the DJ's box. Seth's mind was probably not on his best friend.

"Look at me," prompted the man who was sort of her rescuer. "Let me look at you. I could only imagine how gorgeous you were last night in the darkness."

She glanced at him and found his warm brown eyes. They were dark yet softer than they'd been in the moonlight. Not threatening. Even attractive.

"Your eyes are bright," he said.

Bella shifted her glance away.

To look into the man's eyes felt like complying with a request. And she didn't want to give him that boon.

You're in control of your own life, remember?

"You're not shy." Even amid the din she heard his low voice perfectly, as if they stood in a column of air set apart from the crowd. "Talk to me."

Hold conversation with a man who frightened her? Never. But she had to know...

"So are you really a—"

"A what?"

Still unwilling to meet his gaze, she toyed with the stem of her goblet. "My friend told me about vampires and how they really exist. And then he guessed you might be a werewolf." She whispered the word, as if she were swearing in church.

"Very clever, your friend. Is he the one in the box that you waved to when you first came in?"

"Have you been watching me?"

"Yes." The bartender stopped before the man. "Budweiser," he ordered. "So, you've recovered from your jogging adventure, I see. Wearing sexy sequins and flirting with men out on the dance floor? One would think you weren't so much traumatized by being chased as perhaps aroused."

"Bug off, creep."

She slid off the stool to find an escape, and as luck would have it, a path parted on the dance floor. The beat picked up and the entire crowd bounced, raising their hands over their heads.

Bella turned. Through the sea of waving arms, she saw no sign of the man. Or werewolf. Or whatever he was. Had she imagined speaking to him?

No, she could still feel the intrusion of his thigh against hers. Hot, solid, powerful. He'd marked her with his heat.

"Don't be stupid, Bella," she told herself.

She shuffled her way through the dance floor, intent on reaching the hallway that led to the back door and her escape.

She reached the ladies' room door just as a tall man in a leather jacket stepped before her and clutched her forearm. She hadn't noticed his clothing before. Just his presence. How did she shake this guy?

"You're in danger if you remain here," he said.

"No kidding? I'm in danger from you. Let me go."

He released her arm and put up his hands as if to say "I'll back off."

But he didn't back off. And though Bella could not see over his shoulder, she knew escape was but a dash away.

A couple of dark-haired men brushed roughly by her, and she had to lunge closer to the man to not get her feet stepped on.

"Vampires," he said close by her ear. "They're tracking you again."

"You don't know that."

"What? That they're vamps? Or that they're following you? They've had their eyes on you since you sashayed through the front doorway. What did you do to piss off the vamps?"

"Nothing. I didn't know they existed until last night. Now would you back off?"

"If I leave now, you're vampire prey. You want that? Fine."

He stepped around her. He favored one leg with a slight hitch. Within a few strides, he blended into the darkness.

His menacing presence gone, Bella could breathe now. The air in her personal space cooled.

She eyed the back door. The two *alleged* vampires loomed before the doorway. Their eyes didn't glow. They didn't flash fangs. Besides the matching black business suits and slicked hair, they passed for average human men.

Over her shoulder and ten feet away, her self-assigned protector held his hand out to her.

Pressing a hand to her chest, Bella realized her heart was pounding. Yet it wasn't music pummeling her insides; it was fear. So much excitement in two days would surely put her over the edge. Could a person OD on adrenaline?

The men at the door crossed their arms before them, their gazes fixed on her.

What kind of horror movie had she stumbled into?

Now she had two choices: take her chances walking by two vampires or put her trust in a man she couldn't be sure wasn't as bad as the other two.

She remembered what Seth had said. *Vampires bite. Werewolves are sex freaks.*

Choosing the lesser of two evils, Bella stepped quickly and slapped her hand into her self-assigned protector's palm. He tugged her down the hallway. When they reached the main room, he pressed her against the stainless-steel wall.

"I am what your friend guesses. Does that frighten you?"

"Listen, buddy, the only thing that frightens me about you is your need to shove your hard-on against my thigh. Give it a break, will you? I just took your hand to get away from those vampires. Now I'll be on my way."

"You need me to walk you out of here. There are vamps outside, parked across the street. Do you want to take a chance they are interested in you?"

"What is going on? What did I do? Twenty-four hours ago, you…you *people* didn't exist. And then my best friend tells me he's dating some vampire chick, and isn't at all surprised when I tell him I've seen three of them. And you're a freaking wolf?"

"I am a man. I only wolf out during the full moon, and I'll thank you to call it correctly."

Again he did that strange sniffing thing before her face.

Now Bella was getting angry. "Stop it. You're acting like a wolf, so I'm going to call you one. I'll have you know I don't like dogs."

He flinched, as if attempting to hold off a snarl. What? He didn't like being called a dog? *Then take a hike, buddy.*

Softening his expression, he shook his head, admonishing. "Just know that between me and those long-tooths eyeing you up and down, I'm the one who won't feast on your blood."

"Yeah? What *do* you do? Shake me around like a chew toy? Oh, mercy, I can't do this anymore. I have to leave."

"Let me escort you. This way."

Again he held out his hand for her to accept. Bella stared at the offering. This was so wrong. Much as she liked horror movies, she preferred romance and comedy and happily-ever-after. And she never left noisy bars with strangers.

"I'll hail a cab," she said but took the man's hand.

He led her toward the front door. "If you want to wait for a cab, that's your choice. But I beg your trust to allow me to escort you home. It's not as though I don't know where you live."

At the reminder Bella's world began to swirl.

He squeezed her hand. "Don't faint on me, sweet. Come."

The rush of air as the door opened smacked her to reality. He tugged on her hand, and she merely followed, moving around the waiting line of hopefuls.

The street was busy with passing headlights. The werewolf tugged Bella close to the wall and they walked along it. He walked with a slight limp, as if he favored one leg. When they had reached the end of the block, not far from the end of the line of waiting hopefuls, the man slowed.

"So your friend is dating a vamp? Did he mention her name?"

"No," she answered. "I don't know anything. And for that matter, I don't have your name. If you're going to stalk me, it would be good to have a name to give the cops."

He smirked and drew her close, more as a means to allow others to pass by as they headed for the line. "Severo," he said. "And you are Bella."

"What? Are you psychic, too?"

"I heard the bartender use it. See the limo?"

A shiny black stretch was parked five car lengths

down from the club entrance. Dark windows did not reveal passengers.

"Vamps," he said. "And if my guess is correct, it's Elvira."

"You are so kidding me. Not the mistress of the dark?"

His smirk didn't touch mirth. "Her name is Evie, but I call her Elvira because she fits the cliché to a T. If she's the one your friend is dating, you may as well write his eulogy now. I wonder..."

"His eulogy?"

Again he shoved her against the wall.

"I'm getting so sick of you pushing me around." But as before, she was unable to wriggle free from his powerful grip.

Their noses touched when he leaned in. "How close are you and your friend?"

"Me and Seth?" Talk about intense eyes. They were deep brown but alive with wonder as he held her gaze. Not so much menacing as...attractive. "We've been friends for a long time. We're best buds."

"Any reason for Elvira to believe you two have been getting it on?"

"No! Seth is like a brother to me."

"Do you two hug and hold hands?"

"Why?"

"I think you may have pissed off the wrong vampiress. My wager says those vamps after you last night were sent by Elvira. And she's seeing you now. Give her a glance over my shoulder. Let her know you see her."

Bella dared a look at the limo again. Knowing now

that there might be a vampire woman sitting inside, staring at her, lifted her anxiety level to a new high.

"Good girl," Severo cooed. "Now, we'll give the mistress of the night reason to believe you've no interest in that pasty human who spins discs in the club."

"How—"

He kissed her. And he manhandled her. Severo's hand slid up her thigh, raising her skirt. He pulled her against his body as he'd done last night. But this kiss wasn't as violent, only insistent and claiming.

Did he want to show the vampire woman across the street that Bella was his? This wasn't what she wanted. No matter who watched.

"Wait a second." She pushed against his chest—it was firm, solid—but he wouldn't be dissuaded.

"One more, sweet. Give the curious vampire bitch a show, or you'll have vamps on your tail for longer than you wish."

"But I don't—" *Want to kiss you* didn't come out. Because the protest didn't feel right. Did she want him to kiss her? "This isn't going to work."

"Worth a try. This time open your mouth for me, Bella. I want to taste that cosmo again. I think I may develop a liking for them."

"You're a jerk," she said on a gasp.

"A jerk who's trying to protect your pretty little ass."

With a protest stuck in her throat, he snuck his tongue into her mouth. Before she could weigh the possibilities of biting it, Bella found herself reacting to the powerful and disturbing intrusion by pulling him closer and matching his tongue dance with her own.

God, this was so wrong. He was a stranger. He could be dangerous. He wasn't even *human*.

But he could kiss.

He held her possessively, one arm behind her back, his strong fingers splayed down to cup her hip. Another hand caressed her torso, right up under her breast. He wasn't about to allow her to lead, and that should bother her, but it didn't.

"So sweet," he muttered into her mouth. "My Bella."

Okay, wait. The kiss was acceptable. But claiming her as his own?

"Let's go." He ended the kiss so abruptly, Bella thought he might have heard her crazy thoughts. He tugged her along, leading the way.

"You think Elvira got the hint?" she wondered breathlessly.

"Doubt it. Vamps are stupid, blood-hungry animals."

"And you're not?"

He swung her to an abrupt stop at the intersection, though the light was green. "I am not an animal."

"But you confirmed that you're a werewolf."

"Three days a month I howl at the moon, and yes, then I become an animal. But the other twenty-seven or twenty-eight days, I am a man. Got that?"

"Yep." She was not going to argue with anything that could howl at the moon and change into an animal, no matter how few days a month. "You don't like vampires much, do you?"

"I despise them."

Bella followed his swift pace across the street in time to beat the light. "I can walk by myself. I mean, I know where I'm going. You don't need to pull me."

He let go of her arm, and Bella walked faster, ahead of him. Normally she loved the sound of her heels marking her steps, but now they only reminded her how desperate this situation could become. Because if she thought she would be safe once she arrived home—accompanied by a werewolf—she must be ten kinds of crazy.

He whistled lowly, a satisfied sound. A comment on her back view, likely. She slowed to walk side by side. He did not meet her eyes, but she swore he wore a smirk.

So the man did have a soul. Maybe.

She flat-out asked him. "Do you have a soul?"

"That's an odd question."

"No more odd than your being a werewolf."

"Perhaps it is you, a human, who is the odd one. Yes, I do have a soul."

"Good. I mean, whatever. Do vampires have souls?"

"Yes. But they don't see their reflections."

They arrived at the door to her building, a three-story walk-up. Bella owned the upper loft. It was set into a hill, so her third level led out to the patio and the pool in her backyard.

"Here we are," he offered.

"Yes, I suppose you know that. I suppose every vampire in the city now knows, too."

"Exactly." He opened the door and strode into the foyer. "Which is why I'm seeing you right up to your door."

He knew she lived on the third floor? Dread curdled her saliva.

"I, uh, I don't think so. I'm fine now. I can lock this outer door after you leave. Just go, please?"

Stoic and determined, he stood on the bottom step. He was a head taller than her—and she was wearing four-inch heels. Broad shoulders squared the bruised leather jacket and caught his long, mussed brown hair, which looked clean but not combed. His dark beard was trimmed close and a mustache framed his mouth.

Bella didn't want to look at his mouth too long. She knew the feel of it. And it wasn't something she should be thinking about if she wanted to make the guy leave.

He splayed out his hands, but it wasn't a surrendering move. The man wasn't going anywhere.

"Fine." Bella marched past him, up the first few stairs, but stopped. "You go first."

"I prefer to bring up the tail. Easier to keep an eye out for intruders that way."

"But they could be lurking up ahead."

"I don't smell any," he answered plainly.

Bella sighed heavily, turned and marched up the stairs. So he was staring at her backside. She should appreciate the attention, but despite the wonderful kiss, it made her crawly.

Her mother had drilled the whole stranger-danger routine into her brain when she was a child.

So why had she taken a new route last night? It was as though she'd been looking for danger.

And she had found it. Rather, it had found her.

Now to get rid of it.

Sticking the key in her door lock, she decided too late that she should have waited. The man pushed the door open and prowled inside.

"I didn't invite you in. Now you're going beyond a protective walk home, and entering without permission. I thought you sorts needed permission to cross a threshold."

"'You sorts'?" He smirked and strode to the center of her living room, his limp more apparent now with the lights on. "Just the vamps, sweet. I can cross any threshold I like. Nice place. If a bit junglelike."

The loft had an open floor plan, the living room, kitchen and bedroom all open to share one huge room. Admittedly Bella had gone overboard with the plants, but she liked that they kept the air clean.

Severo's gaze followed the long white chiffon drape that hung from the cathedral ceiling to the floor, separating the living room from the bedroom at the far end.

Observing the wide planter with the massive blooming cactus, he strode to the patio doors and tapped the glass. "A pool, too?"

"Yep, living the high life. So, if you'll leave, I'll lock the door behind you and get out my garlic. I have a cross on the wall there that I can use in a pinch. So you see? I'm sure I'll be fine."

Bella kicked off her shoes and leaned against the kitchen counter. She wiggled her pinched toes, but her focus was not on comfort. The drawer with a butcher knife inside was a leap away.

"You won't be fine." He approached her so swiftly, the fear rose in her body and Bella felt it flush her cheeks. "They'll watch you all night."

"You don't know that."

"If my suspicions are correct, Elvira won't rest until she's satisfied."

"Meaning?"

"She must want you dead, or at the least, injured, if she believes you a threat to her latest snack."

"Seth is not a snack."

He backed her against the granite kitchen counter with an arm to either side of her. She should be getting used to his urgent obsession for uncomfortable closeness, but it still made her nervous. The plastic clicks of her skirt spangles made the situation slightly strange. His size made her feel small.

But she couldn't deny her interest in this overwhelming, in-your-face man who wouldn't take no for an answer.

"No human can ever be anything more than a snack to a vampire. Unless she turns him."

"Turns? You mean makes him a vampire? Oh, my God, can she do that? Will he know?"

"He'll know. But he'll be too infatuated to protest." He dipped his head and ran his nose along her neck.

"Stop it. I want you to leave."

"Make me."

Bella swung her arm up and slapped the man hard across the cheek. The sound of flesh to flesh echoed sharply. He reared back, shook his head and delivered her a leering grin.

"Try it again," he challenged coolly. "Come, Bella, raise my ire. Stir my blood."

This time he caught her hand before it connected with his cheek. Gripping her wrist, he licked her palm from fleshy base to quivering fingertips. And behind the lascivious act, he grinned again.

"By now you should know your fear excites me, sweet."

"Don't call me that. I don't want you here. Can't you understand that?" Bella's glance to the phone, which was too far away, by the couch, stoked him to action.

He pressed a palm over her throat. Bella feared he might become violent. Finally he would do what he wanted to do last night. Why had she allowed him inside the building?

Because she really was worried about the vampires.

His eyes were so intense, they stilled her. She could only gasp as he slid his hand to the red spangled neckline. His thumb slipped behind the fabric and over the top of her breast.

The sound he made was sexy and wanting, a moan for something he desired but wouldn't take. Clinging to the counter, Bella reacted to the illicit touch with a whimper of her own.

"Bella," he whispered as he moved nose to nose with her. "You want my touch?"

She shook her head. A squeeze of his fingers rocketed a delicious twinge of pleasure from her breast to her belly and down to her loins.

"Then remove my hand. Push it away."

She grabbed his wrist with both hands but didn't move it. And in her pause, he bent to kiss the top of her breast while he massaged the nipple with his fingers.

She craved the way he made her feel. The dangerous aura of his presence. The uncertainty of what he would say or do to her next. The erratic pace of her heart was caused by fear and a discomfiting desire.

"Please," she whispered. What had he said his name was? "S-Severo. It's…not right."

"What? A man you just met touching you like this? I told you to take my hand away. And then I'll leave."

"No, you…" *You're a werewolf!* Why did that bother her more than being touched so intimately? "Please just go. I can't do this. I'm too freaked right now."

"I understand." His hand slid up to her neck again, and Bella regretted the lost touch at her breast. "I'll leave, but I won't go far. I'm keeping watch tonight."

"Fine," she said, not because she approved, but because she wanted him gone so she could be alone with her crazy self.

He opened the door and turned to her, but he didn't say anything. Dark, glittering eyes held her in his grasp. Right there, still under his thumb.

"Thank you," she said. "For looking out for me."

"You've fixed yourself to my senses, Bella. I can't get you out of my head. And I don't wish to. Sleep well."

He closed the door and Bella collapsed over the counter, her arms stretched out and her cheek smushed against the cool granite.

"Vampires and werewolves? Oh, my."

Chapter 5

Following a long shower, Bella padded through the loft and switched off all the lights. The streetlights out front always cast a yellow streak across the floor. Tonight it comforted her.

After her encounter at Silver and her unnecessary escort home, she couldn't hit the bed fast enough. But on the way, she stopped before the window and tugged aside the blue chiffon sheer.

The connection of gazes startled her, but she didn't turn away. Severo sat across the street on a bus-stop bench, staring up at her. Her own personal security guard.

Or her own personal stalker.

Who was a werewolf.

She should be horrified, but to be honest, all she could feel was relief.

She looked but didn't find any vampires lurking

in the trees in the park across the street. Not that she would know what they were, anyway. Nevertheless, if they were out there, she was glad to have a protector on the beat.

Bella woke to sunshine. Because it was the weekend, she had all day to wonder over her strange new world.

"I have to call Seth."

She started for the phone but paused by the window to look across the street. The bench was empty. Vampires didn't do daylight, so her protector had left.

How could she be so accepting and calm? she wondered as she picked up the receiver and hit speed dial. Because she had proof.

Sunnyside Belladonna, Seth often called her when he wasn't addressing her as Bellybean. Always willing to see the good, even when standing amidst a muck of bad. And if shown the truth? She believed it. It was a waste of time to deny what she'd witnessed.

"Seth, how are you?"

"It's freakin' ten o'clock, Bella. How do you think I'm doing?"

"You're usually up by eight. Oh, no, are you no longer a morning person because of your girlfriend?"

"Can we have this discussion later?"

"Fine, but we do need to have it. Severo said something last night that makes me wonder about your girlfriend. I'm scared for you, Seth."

"Severo? Who in hell— Is that your werewolf?"

"He's not *my* werewolf."

"Yeah? Well, don't start sucking face with the guy. I've always imagined you walking down the aisle someday with a *mortal* man. And you know how scared you are of dogs."

"Tell me about it."

She had mapped out her jogging routes specifically to avoid any houses with dogs behind fences. Big dogs, little dogs, didn't matter. She didn't like any of them. Rather, it wasn't a question of dislike, but a real fear.

"Listen, Bella, let's meet at the Moonstone at six, okay?"

It was their favorite restaurant and was a few miles down the strip. "Deal. I'll see you later. Last one there picks up the check."

A brisk swim was in order. Releasing the latch on the patio door, she slid it open to the gorgeous summer day. Birds chirped and the grass was so green, it belonged in a cartoon. Everything seemed right. Truly, she must have dreamed the world doing an upside-down flip.

Padding outside in her undies and T-shirt, Bella never worried that anyone would see. The six-foot-high fence, and the fact that she lived at the top of a hill, guaranteed privacy. And the first-and second-floor owners had but a view of the street on the other side of the building.

Tugging up her shirt, she stopped halfway over her ribs when something jumped the fence.

He landed deftly, one hand to the ground in a predatory pose. With a smirk, he noted Bella's jumpy reaction. Severo rose, stretching back his shoulders. He utterly dominated the small backyard.

Her protector had returned.

Bella tugged her shirt down to her thighs to cover her spare pink underwear. She could make a run for it, but he'd probably beat her to the door. Then he'd crush her barely clad body against his and kiss her and—

"Good morning, sweet." Severo strolled to the padded lounge chair angled by the pool and sat. Stretching out his legs, he twined his fingers behind his head, though the leather jacket and biker boots were hardly pool wear. "Nice day for a swim. Don't let me interrupt. You were set on skinny-dipping?"

"Why are you here?"

"Still on the beat."

"But the vampires don't come out during the day."

"You're right. Truth is, I wanted one last look at you before leaving."

"Well, you've seen me. Now you can go."

"Your tits look great in that thin shirt. Makes me want to suck them."

She crossed her arms high over her chest. As crude as the comment had been, she lifted her chin and looked down through her lashes at him. He liked her breasts?

Stupid, Bella. You're playing with fire. This one is different than most men, who can tease without promising anything more.

His eyes strayed lower. It was either hug her arms across her breasts or hold the shirt down.

Bella decided to walk down the three steps and sit at the pool's edge. The water crept through her underwear and wet the hem of her shirt. The man's intent gaze hardened her nipples.

She plunged in. There. Now he couldn't see anything.

"I'm not going to perform for you," she said, frogstroking through the water, "so you may as well leave. Go home and get some sleep."

"You are insistent that I leave you. And after I've done you two favors."

"Two?"

"Saving your life and keeping said life safe. So I think you owe me at least a chat. Aren't you at all interested in learning more about me?"

Treading where the water dipped to eight feet, she eyed him curiously. Yes, she did want to know more. Like how he was able to track her merely by scent. Like why he felt that he had some kind of God-given right to intrude on her life.

Also, why it was that she couldn't simply call the cops and have him arrested.

And why was it that she found him more attractive today, in full daylight, than she had last night in the dark? He was still scruffy and unkempt. The beard and long hair framed his dark gaze and bold features. The look didn't so much say "Protector" as it screamed "Dangerous."

Ignoring her erratic thoughts, she dove forward and did an underwater somersault. Surfacing, she spewed water and slicked back her hair. The water refreshed her. Now, if she didn't have an audience, she would get naked.

"All I want to know is why you keep coming back."

"Like I said, you've stuck yourself to my senses. I can't shake you. So if I can't ignore the pretty woman, then I may as well enjoy her."

She flipped him off and did another deep dive. Touching bottom, she wished for the magical ability to breathe underwater. Not that it would make him leave. He'd probably dive in and try to rescue her.

Coming up, Bella found him squatting near the pool's edge. Why did that not surprise her? Had flipping him the bird angered him? She'd like to see him jump in, leather jacket, big, clunky leather boots and all, and try to wrestle her into submission now.

After abandoning dancing in high school, she'd joined the swim team to fill that need for movement and to physically challenge her muscles. She'd won a few medals for her back crawl and high dives. She could so take the guy if he were in the pool.

But thank God he was not.

Swimming backward, Bella landed at the opposite side. She stretched her arms along the tiled edge. If he was going to stare at her, she could do the same.

A trim brown beard traced his jaw, and stubble darkened the front and sides of his neck. Dark chest hair peeked out at the top of his shirt. Long brown hair topped off the deviant look. Talk about hairy. Made sense if he was a werewolf.

She'd never dated a man with chest hair or a beard. The look didn't attract her. And she had no intention of changing her preference now.

"Ask me," he prompted.

"Ask you what?"

"The question that burns in your bewitching green eyes. I'm not going anywhere, so you might as well make the best of it. There's nothing threatening about conversation."

Her legs floated to the surface, and Bella flicked her big toes, scattering droplets across the water's surface. "All right. If vampires suck blood from humans, what is it a werewolf does?"

"With humans?"

"Yes."

He clasped his strong, wide hands together between his bent legs, focusing across the horizon above and behind her. "We avoid them mostly. The less contact we have with the mortal race, the better. If humans haven't got proof of our existence, then you understand how much easier it is to survive?"

"I'll buy that. So why the continued contact with me? I'm a human. I have proof of your existence."

"I've already explained that."

"Right. You have my scent bouncing about inside your nose and can't shake it off. Peachy. So what about those three days around the full moon you mentioned?"

"In this human form I am called a were. *Were* means 'man,' you know? Then there is the wolf form, which is the caninelike animal most humans associate with wolves. The werewolf is the man and wolf combined. Understand?"

She nodded. The creature lesson was fascinating, in a stomach-curdling way. Shape-shifting and blood and fangs were not her idea of a good time, unless they were up on the big screen.

"During the full moon, the werewolf takes over as the moon peaks in the sky. All it can think to do is mate."

"Mate?"

"Have sex."

"With another werewolf?"

"If one is available. The female of our breed is rare. Which makes for a lot of frustrated males."

"They don't...try to mate with humans?"

"In werewolf form I should scare the shit out of you. Of course, during the day, when I take were form, as you see me now, I'm also horny as hell for those three days. That's when humans come in handy."

"I see." Seth's theory on the sex-freak thing was true. "So you basically live to have sex?"

"I live. And I have sex. They are two different functions, not dependent upon one another. But yes, I do like to have sex."

Yeah, she did, too. With humans. And at *her* pleasure, not on demand or forced because the moon was full.

"Would you have raped me the other night?"

"Never." A strong, sure answer. He tilted his chin up and met her gaze. "But I cannot deny I wanted you."

Bella peered into her reflection on the water's surface. "I know that."

She had sensed his want. Discussing it now, in a simple poolside chat, was strange, but that didn't dissuade her from seeking answers. "You don't have a girlfriend? I mean a werewolf girlfriend?"

"I've never had a mate."

"So you've not ever…"

"Not in complete werewolf form, no. And if we continue to discuss my sex life, I may have to strip down and swim over there. Being near you arouses me, Bella."

"I'd say that's good reason for you to leave."

"Make me."

Again with the bold challenge. She considered swishing a wave of water at him. Like that would deter the big, bad wolf. "What keeps back werewolves?"

He removed his jacket and tossed it on the lounge

chair behind him. The black cotton shirt he wore stretched across his chest and shoulders, revealing powerful biceps.

"Silver. It must penetrate and enter the bloodstream, though. You can't simply press a silver spoon against my head and expect me to sizzle and burst into bits."

"So you don't eat people?"

"You must have watched *An American Werewolf in London*."

"I saw an old video when I was a teenager. I'll never forget that scene with the dead girl and her throat ripped out."

"That's not going to happen. Unless you've tormented my kind, or are deserving of just punishment. Vampires are more likely to maul and kill humans than my breed will."

"That's weird, because I'd think the one closer to an animal would be more likely to do the mauling stuff."

"It hurts me when you label me an animal."

His confession stunned her. Men didn't reveal their feelings. Not most.

Sure, he looked like a man now. But he wasn't. Not really. And he'd explained he could be a *real* wolf. That was about as animal as a guy could get.

"May I join you?"

"Do dogs swim?"

"I am not a dog. I'm a wolf. And get that straight."

He began to unlace his heavy boots.

Dare she invite him in? That damned piercing gaze of his would not relent. Something about the challenge he pressed upon her excited her. And if she were the one to do the inviting, then she would still be in control.

"You're not going to leave until you've touched me, are you?"

"So quickly you learn my manner. I like that about you, Bella. Even as your heart races with fear, you aren't afraid to meet the next challenge. And no, I don't intend to leave until I've at least been allowed to stroke your soft skin."

Mmm, a stroke sounded nice. Romantic.

Bella's elbows slipped from the pool's edge, and she kicked to stay above water.

This was wrong. So wrong. And yet, part of her thrummed with anticipation. The man was growing on her. He wasn't shockingly handsome or charming, but something about his aggressively gentle approach intrigued her.

"Come on, then, but keep your distance."

He tugged the T-shirt over his head, revealing an abdomen that would have made an abs instructor whimper. He kicked off his boots, and he unzipped and tugged down his black jeans.

"Keep your skivvies on," she said when he stood before her in nothing but black boxer briefs.

"Fair enough."

Damn, he was a sight. Powerful thighs and legs pulsed with his movement. The cut muscles on his abdomen emphasized square hips. The dark boxer briefs did little to disguise his erection. Bella had never seen someone so appealing, so utterly powerful and intriguing.

He jumped in, splashing her with his grand entrance. Coming up in the center of the pool, he treaded water and shook his head, spattering water across her face. "This is heated. Nice."

"Really nice on a cool evening."

"In the nude?"

"Only when I'm alone. So wolves can swim?"

"Faster than you, so don't get any ideas."

Right. Not safe, Bella. Don't forget that.

"You're all about the he-man stuff, aren't you? Me Tarzan, you Jane. You know that's not attractive to most women."

"You like it," he said with confidence.

"I do not."

"You're aroused right now, sweet."

"Don't call me that. You have no right to give me a pet name. And if you think I'm aroused because my nipples are hard, it's only because the water—"

"Is warm." His prideful grin told her he'd scored the point on that one.

Okay, so she was a little turned on. His incredible body, rippling with muscle, went a long way in making him more human and real. And while she wasn't attracted to the hairy look, she couldn't deny a hunger for some washboard abs.

He swam closer and Bella held her position at the edge. She'd let him approach and see what he had in mind this time around. If he kissed her, she would accept it, but she was asking for more than a mere kiss, and she knew it.

"So you haven't called the police?" He treaded water a couple feet from her but did not drift closer.

"Like they'd believe me. Hey, three vampires chased

me, and now I've got a werewolf stalker. Send help right away!"

"You make light of it, but I know you're frightened, Bella. You needn't be scared of me."

"You insist on manhandling me every chance you get without asking my permission. What about that treatment should make me unafraid?"

"Again, you want it more than you know. I don't smell fear on you now. And though curiosity has no scent, I'd wager that is what you're feeling. You're curious about me. About us."

She was about to say "There is no us," but that was too easy. Instead, Bella lifted her leg and toed his chest, pushing him back about a foot. "Stay. Good boy."

The water rushed up around her face and into her mouth with his swift approach. He put her up against the tiled wall. Bella choked on swallowed water.

"Stop with the dog comments," he said. A low, throaty growl followed.

"All right, I'm sorry. Let me go. You're so damned sensitive."

"I want you to know the way of things." He positioned his body along the length of hers and dipped his head over hers, forcing her to look up at his face. "I will strike out against cruelty and wrongs, no matter who is responsible. But I can be kind to those I consider friends."

"You strike out…? What does that mean? Are you some kind of werewolf avenger?"

He chuffed a breath beside her cheek. "You think me an animal simply because I react to the way I am drawn to you?"

"I'm not trying to draw you. Hell, I just want you to leave."

"You don't want that, or else you wouldn't have invited me into the pool. Oh, Bella." He nuzzled aside her cheek and kissed her water-slicked hairline. A shiver tickled her neck. "Why did you come into my life?"

"As I recall, I wasn't looking for a friend the other night. I was running for my life."

"You run often. Your body is sleek and gorgeously muscled."

"I'm a dancer."

"Yes, you looked right at home last night in the club."

His closeness warmed the blood in her veins. Had someone lit a fire beneath the cauldron?

"I—I prefer ballroom and flamenco, but any kind will get me moving."

"Being tailed by vampires gets you moving, as well. Will you let me kiss you?"

"Now you have the consideration to ask first?"

He lifted her chin so she could not look away from him. A tenderness she did not expect to find softened his gaze. He was a real man. A man who could be hurt with inconsiderate words and be tempted to rescue her at the first scent of danger.

A man she wanted to kiss.

Bella leaned forward. Water slopped around her shoulders and his chest. Their lips, wet and soft, pressed, then parted with the wavery ripples. The hairs on his chest slicked to dark silk under her exploring fingers. A sinus-clearing bite of chlorine entered her mouth as she parted her lips to push her tongue into his.

Yes, she moved in first. It was inevitable. The exotic being who held her invited the dangerous exploration.

She wrapped her legs about his hips. Severo moaned appreciatively and coaxed her to fit herself against the landscape of muscles ridging his torso.

They bobbed backward in the water, folded in an embrace. He steered them toward the steps until Bella's feet touched bottom and she was able to balance.

Kissing this man was like drawing air. It was a need, a natural act, something she required more and more of. The rough beard, wet under her fingers, teased, and she slid her palms down his neck and gripped hanks of his hair to keep his mouth on hers.

Severo's fingers glided up her thigh and over her behind, clutching, squeezing. The thin undies were but soaked tissue over her flesh. Every move he made was possessive, inciting. Bella fed his want with murmurs and small movements until she lay on top of his body, stretched out across the half-submerged steps.

Struck by what she was doing—lying on top of this man—she lifted her body but didn't move aside. "Oh, mercy, this is going too far."

"It's going exactly where we want it to."

"We?"

"This is not a one-sided embrace." He grabbed her hand and pressed it over his groin. Through the wet cotton, his hard shaft felt immense, wicked. Bella stopped herself before giving it a squeeze. "I need you, sweet."

"Why? Is the moon full tonight?"

"No, fool woman. You think you can touch me like this and not expect me to react?"

"But *you* put my hand on your—"

"You've brought me to some kind of pinnacle, and I don't want it to stop."

"It has to. This is happening too fast, Severo. Please?"

He released her hand and she grabbed the steel hand-rail.

"Very well. I promise not to push this any further. But just stay."

Bella knew herself well enough to know that if she stayed, she would want to go further. And she wasn't cool with that. Not yet.

"Sorry." She stepped from the pool. At that moment the phone rang. "I've got to get that."

Severo groaned as he sat up on the middle step and flipped back his head in a spray of water. He made a noise that was half growl, half agreement.

Bella scuttled into the kitchen, dripping wet. It was Seth. He had to change the time for tonight.

"Is it your vampire woman?"

"Bella, don't be like that," he complained. "I'll meet you around nine at the restaurant, 'kay?"

"Fine. I'll see you later."

She clicked off but held the phone to her chest and glanced out the patio door. Severo sat alone at pool's edge. His broad shoulders flexed as he pressed his palms to the patio floor and leaned back.

"Marvelous," she murmured. "Poor guy. Left him high and dry. I did play the tease."

Her soaked T-shirt clung to her breasts, hard nipples jutting. "Better change before I go out there."

The human woman had some kind of grip on him. But he wouldn't force himself on her. He'd never do that to a woman. Besides, she had just met him and discovered the world was populated with paranormal creatures.

She was taking things well, as far as he was concerned.

He'd put himself in this situation; he should have known better. But when he was near Bella, his brain softened to mush. And that was not his style.

Was she the one who could be his lifelong mate? Only time would tell. And, more important, the were-wolf

Right now he knew only that he wanted to be close to her. So close that their flesh slicked with sweat when they were against one another, their lips melded, their bodies joined.

He groaned and eased a hand over his wet boxer briefs. A glance to his dry clothes lying on the bench decided it for him. He pulled off the boxer briefs and wrung them out over the pool. He'd have to go commando.

Using the towel on the lounge chair, he dried off. Ignoring a hard-on took monumental willpower. Dressing and tying up his boots, he stalked inside Bella's home after finding the patio door unlocked.

So she wasn't keeping him out? Good girl.

He scanned the room, dodging the jungle of plants hanging from the ceiling and sprouting up from pots on the floor. She wasn't on the phone; the cordless sat on the counter.

The vast room was like a big studio, divided down the center by the flimsy white fabric. A big couch and a plasma TV designated the living room on one side, and on the other, against the wall, sat a low bed and a nightstand.

Bella appeared from what must be the bathroom, wearing a loose white top and pants. Some kind of yoga wear. It appealed to Severo because her nipples pointed through the thin fabric, and she did not wear a bra.

"What's that?" she asked.

He dangled his underwear in his hand. "Can I hang these in your bathroom to dry?"

"Uh, sure." She pointed over her shoulder and he took direction. "Will you leave, then?"

"I will if you want me to," he called.

Her pause gave him hope, but with a shake of her head, she confirmed, "I do want you to."

"Fine, but I'll return when the sun sets."

"Do you think that's necessary?"

He strode out from the bathroom and met her at the couch. "Yes, I scented vamps all night. They were prowling. Looking for something."

"Really?" Now the nervousness he recognized warbled her voice. A twinge of fear filled Severo's nostrils, acrid and hot.

"It'll be fine. Just keep that stake and cross close at hand. Holy water would be great."

"Oh sure, I keep a liter in the fridge for such occasions."

"Sweet."

"Don't *sweet* me. In what alternate universe do you get to boss me around and expect I'll tolerate another of your kisses?"

"Another?" He lifted a brow. "You like my kisses."

"They're fine." She surprised herself with that answer.

"You wish to have one more before I leave? Be decisive, no maybes."

"Yes."

He did love this woman's daring.

Severo swept her into his arms and kissed her soundly. She accepted his command and answered with an eager reply. Plunging in deeply, he explored her, noting the texture of her tongue, the soft insides of her mouth. Her sweet breath. Every moan she murmured only made him all the more determined to possess her. To win her.

To get the hell out of here before he couldn't resist the desire to rip away those loose clothes and lave his tongue all over her flesh.

"Tonight." Severo kissed her on the forehead and walked out the patio door.

Chapter 6

Severo arrived home to find a turkey sandwich on the kitchen counter. Actually, it was like a Thanksgiving feast stuffed between two innocent slices of French bread. Stuffing, cranberries, gravy and loads of meat.

Heloise, the cook/housekeeper, had worked for him for twenty years, and he dreaded the day she considered retirement.

Not only was she a great cook, but Heloise also understood his foibles and knew what he was. She knew when not to press and when a defiant tone would be tolerated. She worked Monday through Thursday, noon to whenever, and would never move in, despite his frequent suggestion she do so. She had a family; he understood.

Demolishing the sandwich, he then tipped back a couple glasses of water. His appetite never waned. He loved meat. He ran off the calories nightly, so he needed not fear a gut. Besides, he was still young.

At ninety-some years, Severo was only about a third through the usual werewolf's life expectancy. Three centuries were more than enough. He wasn't immortal, and he was thankful for that.

He'd endured much in his near century of life. He'd seen unspeakable horrors, and he'd participated in the horror himself. He'd loved but once—an unrequited love. And that had taught him to be wary of future love.

Until he'd caught the lovely Belladonna Reynolds in his arms. He'd only intended to keep her safe from the vamps, then release her, never to see her again.

Setting the empty plate in the sink, he headed for the office.

Funny how life never follows the plans a man makes, he thought. He didn't need the distraction of a sexy human woman. He lived a simple life, yet he was always busy with real estate purchases. He systematically purchased forested land in the upper northern areas of the state. Much was state forest release.

If Severo had his way, he'd buy it all. But there were the Indian reservations, and he would not deny them their bid to reclaim some of the land. He was getting close to beginning construction on the wolf preserve. At this moment an architect in Minneapolis was designing the project to Severo's specifications.

A lifelong dream, the preserve would protect those he considered his closest relatives in the animal kingdom. The wolf packs were few in Minnesota, thanks to frightened farmers shooting wildly at wolves that strayed from the pack, and hunters seeking a prize to mount and display for friends.

If only there was a way to protect his kind from the vampires. Beyond their banding together in multiple packs and standing strong against the longtooths, or allying themselves with the bloody bastards, it was better that a werewolf kept to himself.

There were some packs who participated in the blood sport—a vicious retaliation against the vampires—but Severo did not condone senseless violence.

Though a member, Severo had not attended the Council for years. It was a conglomeration of representatives from the various paranormal nations. Vampires, witches, werewolves, faeries, elementals and others. They tried for peace among the nations but accepted tolerance.

No humans served on the Council. Humans were but distractions to the paranormals. To be avoided by the werewolves. Few considered them a necessity, save the vamps.

And yet, Severo would not fight his body's attraction to the human female. He hadn't experienced such a powerful pull since, well, not even since Aby.

Aby had been different. Theirs had been a close, friendly bond, like family. Yet not. He'd been more sexually attracted to her than she had been to him. But she had felt it. He knew it.

Picking up the picture frame from the shelf behind the document-littered mahogany desk, he tilted it to erase the reflection from the window. Bold red hair spiked about a pixie face with a smile so bright, it hurt him to know she was no longer a big part of his life.

He tapped the glass over her face. "Miss you."

Aby was but a phone call away. Ten numbers. Three states.

And one wedding ring.

He set the picture down and heaved out a sigh.

Had he not walked this earth long enough that love should finally be his? He did desire it. He craved the connection and emotional bond that accompanied what he believed love to be.

But most of all, he wanted to hold another in his arms and know he was loved in return. That he was not merely a friend.

Could Bella be the mate this tired werewolf had dreamed to find?

For a human, she impressed him with her acceptance, her teasing foray into discovering him. It was as if she dared herself to step over the cliff, to take the plunge into the unknown. He suspected she lived a neat, orderly life within her jungle of a loft. Yet she fed on adrenaline more than she realized.

He liked that about her. Any woman who got involved with him would need to be comfortable with the adrenaline rush. Introducing chaos into her life would please him immensely.

But it worried him that Elvira and her mindless sycophants might be after Bella. If her friend Seth was involved with Elvira, it made sense that the female vampire would seek to remove all human connections the idiot boyfriend had. That's how the longtooth worked.

Severo growled in disgust. He punched a fist into his open palm with a smack. He cared little for the man. But no one would harm a hair on Bella's head.

It mattered little what she thought about him. All that mattered was that he had to follow this feeling of desire. If she was the one for him, he would not relent until she was his.

An hour before she intended to meet Seth, teacup in hand, Bella peeked out the window. Like clockwork, he again was sitting on the bus-stop bench. Silently stalwart. Clothed in leather and looking like something no fool would want to mess with. A force not to be overlooked.

A force whose black boxer briefs had hung like a blatant you've-been-naughty flag in her bathroom. She'd plucked them down and folded them neatly. How did she return such a thing to someone she hardly knew? Discreetly slip them from her purse and mutter, "You forgot these"?

Bella rolled her eyes. Wasn't it usually the woman who slipped her underwear into the man's things? She bet Mr. Big Bad Werewolf would love to find her panties among his things. But not when he was dutifully guarding her from the other Big Bads.

She wondered about the relationship between vampires and werewolves. Severo had made it clear he didn't like vampires. But was that just him, or did they all battle and clash?

Either way, with vampires after her, she was glad to have a vampire hater on her side.

Although when he was around, no real sides existed. He had no respect for her personal space. He got close enough to breathe her air, and she his.

Initially it had disturbed her. Now it felt…nice.

Had she really gotten close to naked with him in the pool?

She didn't think she'd ever touched hard muscles like his before. And his kisses…

There weren't words for the way his kiss made her feel. Instead, a sensual shiver whispered over her shoulders, reminding her of his power.

Clinking her spoon against the porcelain teacup, she wandered across the room. It was the perfect evening to sit outside on the lounge chair and watch the sun disappear on the horizon. Glamorous light glittered across the pool. But she wondered if her protector would have her back if she was out of view.

Surely he'd smell them coming a mile away, she realized, and decided outside it was.

Three minutes passed before her fence jumper appeared. Bella didn't even startle. She merely glanced over the rim of her teacup at the imposing hunk of male.

"You shouldn't be outside at night," he told her.

"It's *evening*. The sun hasn't set."

"Do you always correct people, Bella?"

"I—" She did. It was a bad habit. "You can't keep away from me, can you?"

"I'm going to take that comment as an invitation. Mind if I join you?"

She slid her knees up on the lounge chair so he could sit on the other end. Naturally, he chose the middle, stretching his legs before him. A deft slide of his arm put her legs over his lap. He stroked her skin above the anklebone and grinned at her.

"Chai?" he asked.

"Good guess."

"I could smell the cardamom, cinnamon and honey from the bench out front. Anise, too, I think. Or is that your clove perfume?"

"Okay, you've impressed me with your olfactory superpowers. Tell me something I don't know. You tracked me to my home? So you can pick out anyone and find them if you have their scent?"

"Usually. Within a range. The suburbs are spread out, so the range is not so difficult. But in the city proper so many people are wedged into every nook, cranny, car and house that it takes a while to detect some."

"But you followed me like a bloodhound to the bone, eh?"

"Something like that."

He bent and kissed her ankle. The ends of his hair tickled the top of her foot. Bella curled her toes. Had she been thinking that long hair didn't attract her?

"You're more comfortable with my presence now." It wasn't a question.

"Apparently. I may even invite you in to watch a movie."

"I enjoy movies. But let me guess. A werewolf flick?"

"No, it's a romance I picked up the other day. Probably a tearjerker."

"And you want *me* to watch it with you? I'll take a rain check."

"Ah, I've uncovered a weakness. The man doesn't do emotional scenes."

"This man prefers action, gun fights and explosions. Besides, I don't need a movie. I'm plenty entertained sitting right here, watching you sip tea. Your lips purse and look like candy treats when you sip. I'd love to nibble on that thick upper lip right now."

"You'll spill my tea."

"Set it down."

"You're bossing me again."

"And you're going to listen."

He held his hand out for the teacup.

With but a two-second pause to consider her options, Bella set the cup on his palm. He set it on the patio.

The man's body glided along hers. His fingers raked through her hair and his mouth met hers in a soft collision. The throaty sound of his pleasure rumbled against her senses, bruising them, opening them to every soft breath, touch and sound. The air changed, as it usually did when Severo kissed her. It became light and heady and so unnecessary.

A dash of his tongue to the underside of her upper lip stirred up a pleasure-drenched moan from Bella.

"Angry you succumbed?" he asked against her mouth.

"When do I get to boss you around?"

"Whenever you wish, I shall do as you command. Except leave or stop watching out for you."

"*Anything* I ask?"

"Within the realm of the possible. I'll not humiliate myself for you, so don't ask me to do something silly." The brush of his beard across her collarbone drew a sigh from her. "And just so you know, I prefer anything having to do with touching you and making you feel good."

She did, too. But what could she ask of him? What *dare* she ask of him? This was a fantasy come true. Only, she'd never fantasized about a paranormal lover.

Just a commanding one. A man sure of himself and what he could do for her.

And wasn't that the opposite of how she envisioned herself? Bella Reynolds, strong, capable, not about to take shit from anyone.

Unless he asked with that mischievous glint to his eyes.

He still leaned over her. She touched the base of his neck where the fine hairs flowed down and across his chest. She twirled her fingertip among them, liking the silky play of them across the whorls of her skin. He stretched his neck, as if he were a cat coaxing her to stroke him.

"You like that?" she asked.

"I should not admit this, but your touch… It gentles me."

She liked the sound of that. Of taming a wild and wicked stranger. Because she still considered him a stranger.

Heck, she didn't know his full name. By now she should have looked him up on Google. Was Severo even a name? It was probably his last name. She couldn't decide if she wanted to know his whole name. Might spoil the adventure, which, he'd correctly guessed, she loved so much.

"Take off your shirt," she decided. Bella grinned, savoring the empowerment she hadn't thought he would allow her.

The small black buttons slid from their slots faster than she thought possible. Shirt abandoned on the ground before the lounge chair, her wicked stranger smiled in anticipation and waited for direction.

This was too easy. This wasn't empowerment. The man was just plain horny. He'd strip naked for her if she asked.

However, nothing was wrong with a better view of this guy's ripped body.

She ran her fingers across his chest, raking her nails over his tiny rigid nipples. He clenched his jaw and gave her quick kisses to her chin and at her earlobe.

"I've never touched a man with chest hair before. I like it. It's so masculine."

"Your touch renders me hungry for more, sweet. What is your next command?"

"Hmm, take off my shirt," she said, sliding up a knee to hug his hip. "And that's it for tonight. Deal? Shirts off, nothing else."

"Second base. I can live with that."

"You'd better not make me regret it."

"Never."

She lifted her arms as he tugged off her T-shirt. The air swirled across her bare breasts, only to be quickly replaced by his hot mouth on her nipple.

Arching her back lifted her breast up against his mouth, and he answered her plea with insistent suckling and a gentle tweak to the other one with his thumb.

"Your breasts are gorgeous. I could feast upon them all day and night and never wish for more."

"Sweet talker, you. Oh, mercy, that's good. That tongue of yours makes me tingle all over."

"Tingles are for amateurs. I'm going to make you come, sweet."

"But we agreed second base was it."

"I don't need to go further." He lashed his tongue

across her nipple and dipped his head to the left to pay the other breast its due. "Mmm, your breasts fit my hands as if they were made for them. I like them this size. Small yet so round."

With a hand behind her back, he lifted her and pressed her groin against his. The intense tugging and laving at her nipples sent exotic shivers scurrying through her body in all directions. He alternated between quick laps with the pointed tip of his tongue and long, sweeping tastes all about her rigid flesh.

Her breasts were so sensitive to a man's touch, but more so at Severo's attentions. Bella felt his tongue all the way through her body as the delicious sensations traveled up, down and everywhere in between.

He dizzied her with his talent. And he was making her so wet that she clenched her thighs to capture the feeling, to increase the intensity that hummed there.

"Yes, squeeze your thighs together to make it happen, sweet. Come for me."

No man had ever talked to her like that. But the words sounded so sexy coming out in his husky voice and in a wanting, deep tone that hummed against her flesh.

Pushing her fingers through his hair, she dug in and tugged.

He laved across her nipple slowly. "Hot and… receptive. God, you are so sensitive, Bella. Do you feel this in your—?"

He used a word that startled her yet at the same time made her gasp with desire. Because he was right on target. The man knew what his touch was capable of. He could make her come merely by—

Could he? She might have an orgasm if he slicked his tongue a little to the right.

A soft nip at the outer edge of her areola was what did it.

Bella cried out as an orgasm utterly blindsided her and swept her up. Her body shook beneath his powerful torso. His hands glided across her breasts. He kissed them slowly, dragging his tongue around them and then up to her mouth, where he caught her surrendering sigh in his mouth.

Bella clung to him, gripping his hard muscles, as if letting go would make her fall endlessly.

He let out a smirking chuff next to her ear. "You've never come that way before, have you?"

"Are you kidding? That was amazing. How'd you do that?"

"You're very sensitive to my touch."

"No shit. Oops."

He smiled against her breast. "You don't use language like that, do you?"

"Never."

"Do the things I say offend you?"

"A little. No. I mean, they sound good the way *you* say them. Oh." She moaned again, catching a lingering wave of orgasm. Muscles languid, she melted in his strong embrace.

"I like the sound of your pleasure. You cry out to the heavens. Feel how hard you've made me?"

Despite her resolve to stay planted on second base, she reached down and stroked his hardness through the snug leather pants.

Bella wanted to feel him. To stroke him. To give him return pleasure.

She unzipped his pants, but he caught her hand in a clutch. "What happened to second base?"

"I think I slid over the plate. I want to touch, to feel you."

"You can't *just* touch, sweet. You know how things work. You're a big girl."

"And you're a big boy."

He growled and gave her a bite on the neck, softened with his lips stretched over his teeth. "Very well, but you were the one to break the rules. I want that one to go on the record. Aaah."

She gripped his erection and tugged it out from the tight confines of his pants. He shifted his hips and pushed down his pants to offer her easier access.

He was big and Bella delighted at the feel of the soft velvet skin. It was like suede covering steel. The smooth head snuggled against her palm as she stroked over it lightly, gauging the funny little bobs and jerks it made with her every touch.

"You'd better mean business," he hissed at her ear. He nipped the lobe and sucked it hard. He pinched her nipple.

Bella gripped her prize firmly and stroked up and down. Flesh shrugged along the hard column. He breathed heavily against her neck, loving her work, which she knew from his lack of commands or comments.

Severo pressed both hands to the chair arm over her head. The flimsy wicker creaked. She didn't stop.

And he met her eyes, branding her with his deep,

dark intensity, which still managed to frighten her, yet also gave her confidence. She stroked the beast, taming him to her command. He loved it. He touched her with his eyes. Pleading. Thanking. Promising. Daring.

Shudders racked his immense shoulders, and as he came, he maintained eye contact. His seed warmed her belly, over and over.

When he was finished, he reached for a towel and wiped off her stomach, then tossed it aside and collapsed on top of her.

"I like third base the best," he said on a satisfied huff. "Your turn?"

"I've already had a turn. That was…"

"Worth doing again?"

And again. The weight of him upon her made her giddy. This powerful man was so relaxed and comfortable with her. A man who was more than human.

"I hate to be a spoilsport, but I'm meeting Seth tonight. I probably should get ready."

"You have a date?"

"It's not a date. It's a 'what the hell are you doing dating a vampire?' kind of meeting with my friend."

"And what if he asks about your werewolf?"

"I'm not dating you. You are not mine."

"No, but we're involved in something here, Bella." He stroked her neck like a cat. The sticky head of his penis nudged her belly. "*This* is not two people being casual."

"You're my protector."

"And you—" he bent to kiss each breast and smoothed his hand down her stomach and adjusted his new erection so that it lay straight along her belly "—are my destroyer."

"I don't want to hurt you."

"It's a good destruction, trust me. I want it over and over, if you'll give it. But I'm not sure about you going anywhere alone. It's night. Will you allow me to escort you?"

"Do I have an option?"

Seth expected only her. But if Severo's guess about Seth's girlfriend siccing vampire slaves on her was anywhere near correct, then she'd like to have him along for support.

You want the werewolf to go along because you're not ready to say goodbye to him.

How could she after what they'd just shared?

Chapter 7

She'd dressed sexy to meet her friend Seth. A body-hugging black top and skirt with white polka dots decorating the double layer of ruffles at the hem. Bella claimed it was her dance-practice skirt. Whatever it was, it showed every curve!

She'd tugged her hair into a sleek ponytail that emphasized her sharp cheekbones and narrow face. And her eyes were all dark and smoky with makeup.

Severo wanted to eat her alive, suck her until she moaned for him to stop. He wanted to feel those short, glossy fingernails dig into his muscles again and to capture her climaxing cry in his mouth.

God, he loved holding her body when it shuddered beneath him.

But she gave him the excuse that she had to dance at the club this evening, after she met with Seth. Part of her dance-class requirements.

They strolled along the boulevard, heading toward the Moonstone. He knew it was a family diner that served well past midnight. Steaks, fries and lots of grease. Heart attack on a plate. His kind of watering hole.

"So I'm not invited to watch you dance?" he asked.

"You can come along if you like."

"But you'd rather I not."

"I didn't say that. Do you want to sit and watch me beat the floor with my feet? Or would you rather play security outside the back door?"

"Now you're taking advantage of me. Did you consider I might have something to do after your little meeting?"

"Like watching me?"

She had him there.

He didn't like being a third wheel. Just who was this Seth, and how had the mortal attracted attention from the likes of the insufferable Elvira? She normally didn't do mortals. Not for long.

"He's already inside. I can see him." Bella waved and then touched Severo's chest.

Severo knew what was coming. "I can stay outside if you prefer to keep your dog tied up on the leash."

"Now look who's getting snarky." She toyed with the collar of his leather jacket. The dark shadowing around her eyes made the green irises so bold, like sweets to be devoured. "I was going to invite you in."

"I'd like that. But?"

"But let me do the talking, okay? This is weird enough introducing you to Seth."

"Weirder than him confessing to you that he's dating the mistress of the night?"

"I suppose not. *Are* we dating?"

"I consider you the only woman in my life. But if we must do some sort of ritual involving movies and dinner and roses, I confess I've fallen short."

Her shy smile made him want to kiss her, to show the world how she had captured him. But they were in the parking lot of a family restaurant. He had a sense of decorum. Unlike vampires, he could control his animal instincts. Most of the time.

The hostess directed Bella and Severo to a table at the back of the restaurant that was lit by a flickering plastic Tiffany reject hanging overhead.

Already standing in wait, Seth hugged Bella and kissed her on the mouth. A quick kiss, but a kiss all the same. *Some friend.* Severo's hackles prickled, but he played the cool one, waiting until the jerk noticed him.

"This is Severo," said Bella, introducing them.

Severo offered his hand, but the twerp stumbled backward and landed in the booth.

"You didn't tell me you were bringing him along. Bella, what the hell? Three days ago you learn about paranormals, and now you're dating one?"

"We're not dating," Severo said as he slid onto the vinyl booth behind Bella. He made a point of leaning over to kiss her cheek, then tilted her jaw so he could kiss her fully on the mouth. He glanced to Seth. "We're just exploring mating possibilities."

The man's stunned gape served Severo a satisfying victory. "Christ, Bella, you said this guy almost raped you."

"I would never. Did you say that to him?" asked Severo.

"He's cool, Seth. And no, I didn't say you raped me. But I wasn't sure what you were capable of that night." She patted his hand. Severo didn't like the condescending move, so he pulled back his hand and slipped it, fisted, inside his jacket pocket. "Seth, Severo has been keeping an eye on me in case the vampires come back."

"What? Why would they? Like, come back for *you?*" Seth quizzed.

Severo did not like the tone in the man's voice. Hell, he was hardly a man. Lanky and pale, he looked like a teenager. Why did young men think that wearing their hair in their eyes was attractive?

"Has he been filling your mind with stupid fairy tales to get you to forgive his callous treatment?" Seth asked. "What's your deal, man?"

"You're a testy one, aren't you? Elvira's lovers are usually more subdued. Drained, actually," Severo replied.

Seth blinked. "Elvira?"

"He calls your girlfriend that," Bella offered.

"Her name is Evie," Seth snapped. "And how do you know her?"

"Oh, we go back a long way, me and the mistress of the night," said Severo.

"The mistress…"

Seth's sputtering affront did not impress Severo. The idiot mortal was caught up in the vampire's allure. Actually, he was probably heavily under vampire persuasion and unable to resist the longtooth bitch.

"Just listen, will you?" Bella pleaded with her friend.

"Tell him what you suspect, Severo. Why the vampires are after me."

He did not owe this mortal a thing, but Bella asked so nicely that he wanted to please her. "I believe Evie is jealous of you and Bella. That's why she sicced her sycophants on her the other night."

"Jealous? Of what?" asked Seth.

"Of your relationship with Bella," Severo said calmly. He scented the man's growing rage. It wasn't a normal reaction. The vampire bitch had been drinking from him; he could smell the vile longtooth oozing from his pores. "She's seen the two of you together, I'm sure."

"We're just friends," Seth hissed.

Severo nodded. "But you love Bella, yes?"

"Of course I do."

"Vampires are pernicious creatures. While they toy with love as if it were meant to be batted about like a volleyball, they will also smash it to oblivion if it serves their pleasure," Severo explained.

"Yeah? What about werewolves? I thought you guys were the ones who were so protective of your mates?" Seth challenged.

"We are." Severo slid a hand around Bella's shoulder and pulled her against him. "You want to try me?"

"Jeez, Bella." Seth shoved his glass of ice water to the center of the table and slammed his arms across his chest. "I don't want to talk to this creep." He sneered at Severo. "What made you think you could invite yourself along?"

"Because you don't have Bella's best interests in mind," Severo stated calmly.

"That's it, man. I'm out of here," Seth thundered.

"Back to your vampire mistress?" Severo asked as the guy slid out from the booth. He was but a kid. Couldn't be a day over twenty. Which made him wonder how Bella had ever hooked up with him in the first place. "She's seen you interact with Bella. My guess is she doesn't want the competition."

"Bella means nothing to me," Seth spat. He shrugged his fingers through his hair. "Well, you know, Bella. We're not like *that*. We don't 'explore mating possibilities.' Christ, now I'll never get the image out of my head of you and wolf boy here—"

In less than a breath Severo held the man by the shirt lapels. He didn't lift him so high that his feet left the ground. Didn't want to cause a scene. "You tell your mistress to back off."

"Severo." Bella's quiet plea calmed the elevating rage that threatened to obliterate Severo's patience.

Seth nodded agreeably, and Severo set him down.

"Call me, Bella," Seth said. "You're dancing tonight? I'm sorry, I didn't know. I've got plans."

"I forgot to tell you, Seth. You can catch me next time," replied Bella.

Seth nodded and vacated the restaurant quickly.

"Why did you have to do that?" she said as Severo slid into the booth seat next to her. "Always playing he-man. Gotta be the alpha dog."

Instead of berating her for her uncouth word choice, Severo leaned in and kissed her silent. The high booth granted them privacy. The kiss did the trick, and he enjoyed it much more than chastising her. Her fingers slipped between the buttons of his silk shirt and he felt her nails dig into his chest. *Yes, hurt me. Mark me.* Mmm, she was exquisite.

"Still feel the need for dancing?" he asked.

"I have to. It's part of dance class."

"Would you entertain the idea of returning to your home and allowing me to undress you, starting with those wicked shoes, and lick my way all the way up to your mouth?"

"I think I've lost the mood. I'm still angry with you for being so mean to Seth."

"Very well."

With a resolute sigh, Severo toyed with the flatware that had been placed squarely before him. His thigh touched Bella's thigh, and his shoulder hugged hers.

Her presence did not cease to still him like a muzzle on a raging beast. He would have liked to shove the idiot Seth through the window, but Bella had gentled him again. What a wonder.

Tilting his head, he laid it upon her shoulder. A smirking breath escaped her. She slid a palm along his cheek. It didn't matter if she was angry with him. This quiet moment meant the world to him. Just him and Bella together.

Must he wait for her to dance before taking her home and having his way with her?

He asked, "How about now? Change your mind about being angry with me?"

"Yes, werewolf." She laughed softly. "You win. Let's head to the club and get this dance over with."

Severo was familiar with the flamenco style of music. He enjoyed the intricate guitar rhythm and understood some Spanish words the cantor sang. But he'd never watched a flamenco dance performance before. Bella hypnotized him.

She danced with a female partner, each mirroring the other and then at times breaking off to do their own thing upon the small wooden dance floor. The intensity between the two blazed through the small room.

He sat in the back of the club, which was no more than twenty feet from the makeshift dance floor.

The craggy-faced man next to Severo reeked strongly of menthol. He clapped his veiny, long-fingered hands in rhythm, matching the others in the crowd, who encouraged the dancers with their clapping and occasional shouts of olé.

Settling against the wall, he observed through narrowed eyes as his woman seduced the crowd. *His woman.* Dating wasn't necessary. Claiming her was, though. He'd already learned her climax. But he wouldn't truly claim her until he'd made love to her completely.

And then there was the werewolf. That part of him would provide the final test of whether or not Bella could be his true mate.

A rapid *rasgueado* by the guitarist brought the women together in a floor-pounding explosion of stomps and hand claps. The crowd's enthusiasm increased.

The man next to him voiced his approval, and Severo found the beat with all the rest.

Bella strode ahead, leaving Severo to close the door behind him. She opened the patio door. A soft night breeze drifted through the screen, tickling the chiffon that hung from the ceiling down the center of her loft. A flowery aroma steeped the air, but she couldn't guess what it was. Mrs. Jones had a wild and abundant garden on the other side of the fence. Wolf boy might know.

She chided herself for thinking of him that way. He was a man, as he'd explained. But she was curious about the wolf part. Yet curiosity led to dread. Vampires with sharp, shiny fangs were bad enough. What would a fully wolfed-out werewolf be like?

Maybe she wasn't so curious, after all.

"Want something to drink?" she offered when he wandered back and forth before the couch. "I have vodka and Sprite."

"No beer?"

"I'm not into the icky stuff."

He grinned. "I'll take a swig of vodka, neat. But don't slip any of that fruity stuff in there."

"Gotcha. One anti-cosmo coming right up."

Tossing his jacket on the couch, he dodged the bamboo plant and stretched his broad shoulders and flexed his arms. He didn't stop moving, striding across the floor as if he were measuring for a marriage bed.

Oh, stop, Bella. That's the wrong image. A caged animal was more appropriate and intriguing.

Was he nervous now that they were alone and sex might be the next step? Full-on sex, that is. Wasn't like he hadn't already rocked her world.

If he could bring her to climax merely by licking her nipples, Bella could not guess how wondrous getting naked with him would be. On the other hand, she could imagine such a scenario. But why imagine when all the elements to the fantasy were at hand?

Severo had told Seth that they were "exploring mating possibilities." But it hadn't sounded as disgusting to her as she thought it should. Mating? With the virile man who filled the room with his presence?

Bring it on.

Vodka straight had never appealed to her, but she took a sip before handing the tumbler to Severo. He downed it in one swallow, set the tumbler on the birch coffee table and tugged her into his embrace.

"I needed that," he said.

"I have difficulty believing you require a drink to loosen up."

"Oh, I'm loose."

"I know that. I saw you doing *palmas* while I was dancing."

"The what? I wasn't doing anything untoward, sweet."

She smiled at his teasing allusion. "*Palmas* is the clapping of hands, which are as much a musical instrument to flamencos as their feet."

"Ah. Yes, I think I picked it up." He tapped a rapid rhythm with three fingers against her collarbone. "Yes?"

"Very good for a newbie."

"You dance often?"

"Couple times a week at the studio. Then I try to pick up at least one performance a week at the club. Next week I have an important audition at the studio. If I can pass, I'll become an apprentice. After a few years of intense study, perhaps they'll allow me to start teaching."

"Impressive. You are a marvelous dancer." He

swayed, prompting her to move with him. "But I thought that wasn't your job?"

"It isn't. I do web design to pay the bills. But teaching a couple days a week would be awesome." She shifted her hips into a sway and the ruffled hem of her skirt swung out. "You dance, Severo?"

"Nope."

"Never?"

Without a word, he tugged her to him and traced a finger along the low-cut V-neck of her top.

"Not in all your... How old are you, exactly? Are you immortal?" With the slightest push from him, Bella spun out and did a half twirl.

"Close to one hundred years," he said. "But not immortal."

"A hundred? I'm dating an older man."

"So we are dating?"

"I think so." She did a double *golpe* foot stomp to punctuate her decision.

"Works for me."

She stepped out and twirled up to him. Her skirts spun wide and crushed against his legs. His fingers glided through her hair and he drew the veil of soft brown tresses across his face.

"I want to dance with you," she said.

"Oh, we'll dance."

The skim of his fingers down her midriff stirred a rhythm in her blood similar to the insistent beat of flamenco. Bella palmed his hands and guided his movements up, over her breasts. He glided his palms across the sensitive swells, cupping them and thumbing the nipples.

"I don't like it when you wear a bra. Harder to get to the sweets." He nipped her breasts through the fabric.

"I have to when I'm dancing. Don't want to be jiggling all over."

"Mmm, no. Only for me."

Bella's appreciative purr drew him closer.

At her neck he kissed the heat of her pulse. Once, twice. A dash of his tongue sent shivers across her flesh.

A tilt and twist of her hips spun her about, so that the pulse of his heart beat against her shoulder blade. Bella pressed her derriere into his groin. His wanting moan gave her a smile.

He caressed her breast, cupping it, squeezing. His low sigh vibrated against her back. The sound of a man's pleasure proved a delicious aphrodisiac. Alone, in a room lit only by the low bulb over the kitchen stove, Bella danced with the only man she desired.

Spinning, she placed her hands on his shoulders. The dancing shoes only put her eye level with his mouth, so she lifted *en pointe* to claim a kiss. Vodka tainted his breath. Desire quickened his motions.

He lifted her with ease and turned her around to set her upon the back of the couch.

It felt right, the two of them coming together in this strange dance that was not quite human and not quite sane.

That thought put her off.

Bella slid from the couch and walked a few steps, the nails pounded into her shoe heels clicking precisely. Severo caught her hand and spun her to face him. The aggressive alpha that she'd experienced most often was not present in his eyes. Instead she saw a gentle pleading and knew that he silently wondered why she was so reluctant.

She knew the answer. It pounded in her heart.

"I'm afraid," she replied, "that I could fall in love with you."

"What's so wrong with love?"

"Nothing. Only, I'm not sure I'm looking at this rationally."

"And the rational viewpoint would be?"

"One mortal human fooling around with one non-mortal werewolf. How far off the sanity scale is that one?"

"Are you disgusted by me, Bella?"

"Not at all. Well, you initially put me off. I mean, I was freaked that night the vampires were chasing me, and you did come on strong and a little creepy—but not anymore. Now? I find you the most attractive man I've ever known."

"You mean that?"

She nodded. "You're so sexy. Every time you're close to me, it's like my body responds before my brain can process the information. I hunger for a glance from you. I ache for a touch. I want you, Severo. And that scares me."

"The werewolf isn't going to intrude upon our liaisons, Bella, if that is what concerns you."

It did. And it didn't. Honestly, she was unsure about how quickly their relationship was moving. Sure, she'd had a couple of one-night stands before. Sometimes two people came together to have sex, nothing more.

But her and Severo? It was much more than one night of sex to serve a need. It had to be.

"You're thinking too much, sweet. I won't hurt you."

"I know you won't." It wasn't physical hurt she worried about, but the emotional pain he might cause. Could she, a mortal woman, do this?

"Take off your clothes," he said.

Yes. Just surrender. Let it happen, Bella. You want him.

Bella bent to pick up his tumbler, saying over her shoulder, "You want them off? Come and get me."

She wasn't sure how he made it to the kitchen counter before she did, but Severo met her there, took the tumbler and placed it in the sink, then lifted her into his arms. "Your wish is my command."

When she thought he might carry her to the bed, he stopped at the couch and set her on the arm. Okay, this was good. Not as much pressure as she would have endured if he had gone to the bed. They were easing into things slowly.

A stroke of his hand slipped the sleeve from one of her shoulders and then the other. His hot breath skimmed her skin from the top of her arm to the base of her neck, burning into her, marking her.

Grasping for an anchor against the dizzying pull of his command, Belle grabbed his shirt in her fists.

He remained focused on her, kissing the bodice of her top and tugging the stretchy rayon lower with his mouth. His hand glided down and slid her skirt high up her thigh.

She began to slip off her shoes, but he said, "No, leave them on. I like them. They're so powerful."

He pulled the top to her waist. Her bra clasped in front, and with but a flick from Severo's fingers, it snapped open and the straps slipped to her elbows. He took her nipples with hungry precision, and Bella arched backward. Mercy, she loved his mastery of her body.

With one strong hand across her back, he lifted her and wrapped her legs about his waist. The wide flamenco skirts splayed along his legs. He ripped off his shirt and then unzipped his pants, and she tugged them down his hips.

Once she saw the prize, her inhibitions fled. It was thick and heavy in her palm. Bella gripped it firmly.

"You're in a hurry." Not so much a question as an agreement. "I still haven't landed on third base." He reached down and struggled with the many yards of skirt fabric. A toss spilled ruffles over her stomach and breasts. "Let me get your panties off."

Elastic ripped as his urgency ignored caution. He mumbled, "Sorry," but there was little care in the word.

Bella wrapped her legs tight about him, hugging his hard, hot shaft against her stomach. As she moaned, he pumped against her, sliding his erection over her bare flesh.

He kissed her across her collarbone, the base of her neck, the rise of her breasts. She put her hands on the couch and took his bruising kisses with abandon.

She ground her mons against his erection. The head of it poked against her stomach, insistent, the proverbial sword ready to slay her.

"Do you have condoms?" he blurted.

"I'm on the Pill."

"Good. I can't wait any longer. Say it's all right, sweet. Let me come inside you."

He wanted permission? The man was a dream. "Yes, please."

He hooked one of her legs with his arm and stretched it over his shoulder. Not awkward for a dancer. Bella trusted he wouldn't let her fall backward. Supporting herself with her hands to the couch, she cried out as he entered her. Hard and heavy and thick, a perfect fit. Every slide tugged at her; the friction brought her to a frenzy.

"You were made for me," he growled, echoing her thoughts. Always he held her with his eyes. And she wasn't about to look away. He looked into her as he slid into her. He filled her, mind, body and soul. "So right, sweet. It's never—" he tensed, his jaw clenching, and she knew he neared the verge "—been like this before."

Remarkably they climaxed together. The world fell away and the two of them remained, locked together in a bond that defied anything either had known.

Later they lay on the rumpled bedsheets in the gray shadows of early morning. Severo's lover traced his chest from nipple to nipple in a lazy dance. She smelled like sex and vodka.

"So, earlier," she said in a sex-softened voice, "you said it had never been like this. You mean the sex?"

"God, yes, Bella. I've had great sex over the years, but the first time I put myself inside you it was like I'd found my place. You are the only one. You are my mate."

"Your mate? Is that like calling me your girlfriend?"

"Yes, I suppose so." He chuckled and pulled her on

top of him. He had a raging erection again. "Fit yourself where you belong, sweet. Mmm, right there."

He was too relaxed to move. Didn't matter. Feeling her wrapped about him, her fingers dancing across his flesh and the tips of her long hair dusting his wrists was enough to make a man come. And he did.

Her laughter alerted him, and he dodged through the overgrown thicket of field grass, his paws beating the ground to find the source of mirth. The day was new after he'd spent the night wandering the countryside.

The world was different when he was not standing on two legs. Better this way.

Rounding the trimmed hedge, he bounded onto the tiled patio area, tracking her summertime scent to one of the lounge chairs.

"Oh, Sev! Your nose is wet and cold. Stop licking me! You're always so playful in the mornings. Go inside and shift, and put some clothes on. I have work to do today, and I want you to meet the witch who'll be invoking the demon."

"Aby!"

Severo sprang up in bed. It wasn't his home. And Aby was far from his arms.

Bella woke to find Severo sitting alert. He'd called out something. A name? He didn't seem aware that she was awake, and for a moment she merely observed him as he sniffed the air. He got off the bed and reached for his clothes.

"What is it?" she whispered.

He shushed her and pulled up his leather pants.

"You're scaring me, Severo." She sat up and tugged the sheet over her breasts. The patio door was still open and the room had cooled.

The door was open? But there was a screen.

Before she could curse her stupidity, the screen flew inside and two dark figures crashed through. The patio door cracked, and glass shattered.

Chapter 8

"Stay right there," Severo called to Bella as he dashed into the fray.

The first vampire swung out at Severo and missed. Severo, while dodging, tilted his torso and snagged a glass shard from the floor. He swung his arm up, slashing the glass across the vampire's neck. Blood beaded the air in a long chain and splattered the white chiffon drape hanging nearby.

"I thought you said the wolf wasn't here?" the other vampire shouted and ran for Severo's back.

The first vampire didn't answer. He fell to his knees, clutching his spurting throat.

Bella gripped the sheets and found herself crawling to the end of the bed to kneel there. Huddling in fear was the furthest thing from her mind. This was exciting.

Her lover stretched out an arm and delivered a fist to the second vampire's skull. The hit only made the vamp blink. He cracked a bloody grin and charged Severo. The two landed on the floor in a crush of flesh and bone. They rolled across the hardwood, exchanging punches to vulnerable body parts.

A wolflike growl preceded a masterful kick. The vamp flew backward, shoulders hitting the wall with a crunch—but he wasn't down.

Severo stood and shook out his shoulders. He growled, vicious and violent, his fingers curving to angry claws. Every muscle across his back bulged and tensed. The tendons in his forearms pulsed with movement. He was marvelous. A beast of power and strength. Bella couldn't be afraid for him, because somehow she knew he would defeat the opponents.

Meanwhile, the bleeding vampire collapsed on the floor, arms out and facedown.

Severo slid across the floor, colliding with the glass shards. He gripped a long piece of glass and lunged for the fallen vamp. The glass pierced the vamp's back, blood gushing up from the heart.

And then something remarkable happened. The fallen vamp shuddered, his entire body reacting to the injury. Within seconds, he was reduced to ash, piled upon the bloody pool.

Scuffling with the remaining vampire, Severo shoved him against the wall. His powerful thighs flexed. He forced the vamp's shoulders into the wall. The Sheetrock cracked. A cloud of chalky dust flew about their heads.

His eyes fell upon the cross on the wall. A gift from Bella's grandmother, who had passed a decade earlier. He grabbed the foot-long cross and slammed it against the vampire's face. Smoke hissed and the vampire yowled. The cross burned through to his jawbone.

Severo dropped the vamp at his feet. He flicked away the cross, sending it clattering across the floor.

"Damn, that was real silver." He shook his hand and stalked about, surveying the bloody mess.

With intense focus, he marched up to the bed.

Now Bella did cringe. His eyes held the same intensity she'd seen when he'd made love to her, yet it had darkened and grown deeper, if that were possible. Was he in a rage? Some werewolf state that made him violent toward anyone?

He gripped the bedpost and yanked it off. "Mind if I use this?" He wielded the serrated wood stake. "Holy wounds take forever to kill," he commented as he strode back to the suffering vampire. Plunging the stake into the vamp's heart brought his struggles to an end. Another ash reduction and the room fell silent.

And Bella let out a breath she must have been holding since the vampires charged through the patio door.

Severo wiped his bloody hands on the white chiffon drape. He looked over the destruction and winced. When he glanced to her, Bella rushed to him.

His bare chest rose and fell roughly. It was spattered with blood, which she didn't want to touch. She took his hand, which he displayed palm up. A deep burn from the cross reddened his flesh.

"Will it kill you?" she asked.

"No. But it'll hurt like a mother for a while. Get back on the bed, sweet. There's glass everywhere."

Realizing the danger, Bella complied, backing carefully away until she climbed onto the bed.

Though barefoot, her lover stood still, surveying his destruction. He must have taken cuts to his feet, yet he appeared only angry about the intrusion, and not at all concerned about his wounds.

"Sorry. I'll have someone come clean this up." He dug a cell phone from his pocket and made a quick, mysterious call. When he hung up, he said, "Stay right there. I'm going outside to check the periphery. You okay?"

Okay? In what sense? A glance to the piles of vampire ash made her wonder if she was safe. Nothing could come back from the ashes, right? "No problem," she managed.

As soon as he marched outside, Bella ducked her head and muffled a scream against the pillow. She didn't want to look at what lay on the floor. It smelled so strongly of blood and ash, she didn't need to look.

The sight of the vampire's slashed throat had been seared into her eyes forever. The blood-spattered chiffon. The ash piles that had once been living men.

But he'd saved her. Again.

Now she wanted him back. Holding her. Protecting her. Sheltering her.

"Severo," she whispered. "Please hurry."

He'd woken from a dead sleep to the scent of those nasty longtooths. Not soon enough to prevent Bella from witnessing the bloody killing. He hated himself for that. But that he'd kept her from harm meant he'd accomplished his goal—to protect Bella.

Protect his mate. The one woman he connected with

on a visceral level. Even Aby he hadn't connected with like this.

You woke from a dream, calling her name, he thought.

Why had he been dreaming of Aby while lying next to Bella? And after they'd made love. That disturbed him. He and Aby had never had a sexual relationship, though they'd been close on other levels.

But he wouldn't think of that. He must not. Bella had captured him by the tail, and he liked that just fine.

I'm afraid that I could fall in love with you. He remembered her words.

How could he erase her fear of him? He knew it was because he wasn't human. Did she fear his werewolf?

He'd been careful not to change when the vampires had attacked. Had he shifted, he could have taken both out with one swipe of a taloned paw. Vampires were no match in physical combat with werewolves. Yet Severo's strength was not to be disregarded while in mere were form.

With one last scan across the horizon from the roof of Bella's loft, he satisfied himself that no others were in the neighborhood. He scented vampires at a distance— probably five miles to the north—but their presence didn't agitate him.

Had the bitch Elvira sent the vamps to kill Bella? That was going too far for jealousy. He owed the mistress of the night a visit.

But first, he had to get Bella safe. She would probably balk at such an idea, but he wouldn't take no for an answer.

Jumping to land before the pool, Severo surveyed the

damage as he strode inside the home. The patio door would need to be boarded up, which the cleanup crew would do. As well, they'd sweep up the vamp ash and clean the blood. The flimsy drape was a loss.

During the height of the war between the vampires and witches, which had ended only a few years earlier, the need for discretion had grown paramount. As a result, most paranormals carried the number to a reliable cleanup team. No smart wolf left evidence for mortals to peruse and wonder over.

Bella waited on the bed, as if afraid to leave the safe island amid the blood and destruction. She plunged into his arms and he held her tight, the sheet wrapped about her and her limbs shivering against his body.

"Sorry," he whispered. "I heard them coming, just not fast enough. You shouldn't have had to see that."

"You were so brave," she said. "I love you, Severo."

That confession knocked him over, so he had to lean against the wall as he held her. She loved him? It was a wondrous confession that he'd never hoped to hear from a woman—let alone a *mortal* woman—in his lifetime.

He'd given up on love after Aby.

"You weren't frightened?" he asked.

"Yes, but watching you took away the fear. How is it that you are so much stronger than vampires? Are werewolves on top of the heap?"

"Not always. When I am in were form, I'm a match in strength to a vampire. As a werewolf...well, look out. But they were idiots. And I did have the cross."

He splayed open his hand. The burn was now a red

indentation, as if he'd gripped the thing tightly for a long time.

"It's already fading," she observed.

"The silver didn't enter my veins. I'm fine. Just a burn. You're still clinging like a koala, sweet. Sure you're not afraid? It's okay."

"Of course I'm afraid. But I think it's that I want to be sure you're solid and real, and that I didn't just lose you. Kiss me."

Her lips quivered at his mouth as they connected gently. He wanted to indulge that tremor of her fear; it was what had first attracted him to her.

He wasn't human, and he was different from her. He fed upon the different, the unusual. And Bella's fear fed him.

"Your skin is goose bumpy," he whispered as he slid a hand up her back. That induced a real shudder from her, but he sensed it was a sensual reaction to his touch.

"I want to make love again," she said. "Right now."

So the adrenaline rush had the same effect on her as it had on him? Unfortunately, they couldn't indulge right now.

"I called for cleanup. They're usually very prompt. And I don't think you should stay here any longer than it takes to pack. You're not safe here, Bella." He tucked her hair behind an ear and kissed her eyelid where it tasted like soft woman. The flutter of her lashes tickled his mouth. "Come stay with me."

"At your house? Where do you live?"

"About twenty miles north of the city. You'll be safe there. I have protection wards against vampires, demons and others. No one messes with me out there."

"Leave my home? I'm not sure."

She glanced about the havoc, still clinging to the sheet wrapped about her. She was still frightened, he knew, but too proud to admit it. She impressed him with such bravery.

"I have my work, and tomorrow I practice at the studio. This is all happening so fast," she said. "I've only known you a few days."

"It doesn't take a lifetime to fall in love, Bella."

"Love. Yes. I said that, didn't I?"

Maybe he had been too quick to grasp for the untouchable. "It's the adrenaline talking."

"No, I…I think I meant it." She stroked his beard and kissed him again. "But is it because I've fallen down the rabbit hole?"

He quirked a brow. "The rabbit hole?"

"Alice's tumble into the wild and weird. First there's you—and believe me, that's all good. But now vampires want to kill me and my best friend?"

"And they will if you don't take action. You cannot beat them here, unprotected and vulnerable. You need my protection to stand against them. Will you take it?"

She stared at his outstretched hand. Once before she'd accepted that offer.

Could he win her? She'd confessed love, and that felt splendid. But she hadn't fully entered his world yet. And indeed, it would be a tumble down some kind of rabbit hole.

"You can do your work from any computer, yes?"

She nodded.

"Come with me, sweet."

Bella slid her fingers over his. "Yes."

* * *

The cleaners arrived as Severo toted Bella's suitcase out the front door. He paid them in advance and shuffled Bella out before she could see their equipment. They were not overly respectful of the dead. A Hoover vacuum picked up vampire ash "real swell," as one of the cleaners commented. Severo was cool with that, yet he didn't want to push Bella over the precipice she'd been forced to toe this morning.

There was yet a good amount of tumbling down the proverbial rabbit hole to be done.

The sun dashed a thin line of orange across the horizon as they stepped out onto the sidewalk.

"Where's your car?" she asked, yawning. They'd had about an hour of sleep after a night of making love.

"I don't normally use it. We can hail a cab." With a suitcase in each hand, he headed a few blocks up, closer to the businesses.

She followed, clicking along beside him in the high heels she'd tugged from her closet. He loved that she was a practical woman who did unpractical things, like slipping into spike heels at dawn.

"You don't drive? But how do you get from your house to town?"

"I drive on occasion. Gotta take the Mercedes out for a spin once in a while. But usually I walk or run."

"As a wolf?"

He chuckled. "No. When I change shapes from wolf to man, I'm naked. The clothing doesn't change with the rest of me."

"So what if you wolf out during a fight with some vampires? Does that leave you...?"

"Naked, but successful. I tend to carry extra clothes with me in my backpack." He looked up the street. "There's a cab. You can sleep as soon as we get to my house. You need it after the night we've had."

Chapter 9

Bella woke to find herself eye level to a tray with orange juice and breakfast sitting next to the bed. Warm, buttery toast, and fresh-picked strawberries sat atop the ramekin of sweet jam.

She didn't remember much after arriving at Severo's mansion in the country. Exhausted after a long night, Bella hadn't taken the time to look around. Her lover had carried her to his bedroom, like some kind of knight delivering a princess to her slumber.

The last thing she recalled was him kissing her on the forehead, her chin, her breasts, and he must have navigated lower, but she had nodded off by then.

Long dark velvet curtains, half-closed, allowed but a narrow strip of bright afternoon sun down the center of the room and across the bottom of the bed.

The bedsheets were soft white and the comforter was

a deep navy satin. Piles of pillows supported her as she sat up and reached for the orange juice.

Cold and freshly squeezed, it hit the spot.

She took her first opportunity to look around.

The simple room was huge, as big as her whole loft. The walls stretched to a barrel-vaulted ceiling painted with pastoral scenes. All the overstuffed, overlarge furniture was upholstered in the same navy velvet as the curtains.

A painting on the wall opposite the bed attracted her interest. Looked like birch trees. The face of a wolf was cleverly hidden among the birches, so a glance might have never picked it out.

At the end of the room were two doors—the closet and the bathroom. Bella went to shower.

After the shower, with a towel wrapped around her, she found Severo waiting at the end of the bed. He wore boxer briefs and no shirt. Daylight surfed across his broad chest, glinting on the dark hairs.

"Waiting for the shower?" Bella asked.

She boldly stepped between his legs and he eased his hands about her hips. His hopeful gaze pleased her.

"I would have liked to join you, but I just got in. Will this work, then? You staying with me?"

"I think it will," she said. "You're unsure?"

"Only because I don't want you to feel forced into anything. I would never do that."

"Oh, really, Mr. I Like To Tell Bella What To Do?" She smiled and kissed him. "I'm here of my free will."

"Good. If you should ever change your mind—"

"I'll be gone before you can argue otherwise. So!

After that nap, I'm starving. I don't think a piece of toast is going to cut it."

"Heloise is making something savory right now. She's my cook and housekeeper."

"Does she know what you are?"

"Yes, and she's a faerie, so she's cool with that."

"A faerie?" Bella chirped in an entirely too wondrous tone. "Does she have wings?"

"No, she's more of the brownie persuasion. You'll meet her. She's great. Been with me for years. If you need anything, just ask Heloise. You don't mind staying in my room? There are other bedrooms, but I'd prefer if you slept with me."

"Of course you do. You like to be the one in control. The man on top."

"Is there any other position?" He clasped her wrists before him and squeezed.

"I think you'd like it rough, wouldn't you?"

"Mmm, Bella, you would be pretty tied up." His eyes glittered with desire.

The suggestion startled her, but only because she didn't react offensively to it. Tied up and at his mercy? Warmth spread up her neck and hardened her nipples. "I won't rule anything out with you. But let's take things slow, lover."

"You undo me with your acceptance, sweet. Why are you so accepting?"

"I'm not sure. I just… I said I love you earlier."

"You made me feel like I'd been given the greatest gift."

"And I mean it, even if it still feels a little crazy to

fall in love so quickly and with a man who isn't even the same species as me."

"There's a lot you still don't know about me. Things you haven't seen."

"Like the werewolf?"

"Yes. Your tumble down the rabbit hole has only begun. The full moon is in three days. I'll want to get myself far away from you before then."

"Why? I want to see you as you are. Is it the wolf? Would you, or he, or whatever you call it, be violent toward me?"

"I don't suspect so. When I am the wolf, I am in canine form, but I, this man, am in there, as well. But I don't ever remember what the werewolf has done after I've shifted."

"Really? So the werewolf can go out and do something and you wouldn't know?"

She straddled his legs and ran her fingers through his chest hair. "It's interesting that you talk about this other part of you as another entity."

"I do and I don't. I have a subtle influence over the werewolf. I mean, part of my were mind is present in that form, but it's mostly instinctual. Bella, listen to me."

Again he gripped her wrists, but gently, and kissed her knuckles.

"When the full moon is out, the werewolf comes out, too. You wanted to know what werewolves do if they don't drink blood? We seek to mate. Unfortunately, there aren't many female wolves to satisfy my werewolf. Let's say the werewolf has been going through a dry spell—an exceedingly long one—and is very frustrated. I sense it lashes out and does other things that I wouldn't be proud of."

"Like killing?"

"Not humans. Rabbits and such."

"So…it needs a mate?"

"Yes, and…" Kissing her knuckles, he held them to his lips. "I've found one."

"And that means the werewolf…?" Bella swallowed. She didn't want to think what she was thinking.

"Yes. It would expect as much."

"Ah."

So if she was Severo's girlfriend, that also made her the werewolf's girlfriend. Which disturbed her on a new level. Because if the were part of Severo enjoyed mating with her, well then, it was likely the werewolf would, too.

"Don't worry. I'll keep it from you. I promise. If I can be away from you the day preceding and following the full moon, we'll have beaten it for the month."

She nodded, not having words to say anything hopeful or promising. *For the month?* So that meant this would become a monthly thing.

"Though there are ways to keep the werewolf at bay entirely," he said, his tone becoming less serious and more playful.

"Such as?"

"Sex until I'm sated."

She delivered him a tight but wicked grin.

"It's true. If I have copious sex on the day preceding the full moon, then the werewolf will be kept at bay. I've never tried it before. It would require a lot, from any woman, to sate me."

"You don't think I'm up for the challenge?"

"I'm sure you are. But there's always the risk of what would occur if we were not successful."

The werewolf would come out to play.

Bella could deal with the man. She didn't want to deal with the animal.

"So, what's to eat?" she asked.

He leaned in and nipped her earlobe. "Besides you? I think Heloise has stew simmering. Let's go check."

With his bare feet propped on the black granite coffee table, Severo settled in the overstuffed easy chair and nursed a plate of beef stew. He never sat at the kitchen table. Too formal. Even the bar stools before the counter held no interest for him. Heloise could huff about his messy eating habits all she liked.

Bella did sit at the counter and had the neatest manners. It was fascinating to watch her interact with the elder servant.

Heloise was short, dark-skinned and jolly. Cleanliness was a vocation to her kind, and she cooked as if she were a four-star chef. But she didn't approve of profuse thanks. That would result in his white shirts being laundered with a red towel in punishment. House brownies were hard workers with little pride. A simple thank-you went a long way.

After a taste of the delicious stew, Bella wanted to know what the brownie had put in it. She didn't fawn but seemed genuinely curious, which, instead of bothering Heloise, brightened her disposition even more.

The brownie was currently showing Bella the fridge full of beef cuts she'd picked up at market the other day.

"Filet mignon!" Bella called to him and displayed the plastic-wrapped meat cut. "I'm in heaven."

And he was, too.

Suddenly life seemed bearable. Beyond bearable. He could venture to label it *right*. It hadn't felt this way for a long time. Since Aby.

He glanced to the wall beside the plasma television. Photographs hung in gold frames, put there by Aby. The one of him and Aby still hung there. He wouldn't dream of taking it down. He hadn't spoken to her for months, and he…missed her.

Friends were not easy to come by, especially for a man who'd been born and raised in a pack. The pack mentality did not allow for companionship, only constant competition and attempts to become the alpha. He'd been the principal alpha in the Northern pack for decades. And while they'd had their scuffles with the vampires over the years, Severo was proud his leadership had seen the wolves protected from humans.

After finding Aby, he had left the Northern pack. He'd found what had been missing from his life. Compassion. Companionship. And infatuation.

He had been more than willing to make Aby his mate. She had not.

Bella's giggle redirected his thoughts. She sat before the counter, soaking up the stew gravy with a slice of freshly baked oat bread.

To think, he had Elvira to thank for sending her thugs after Bella—and pushing her into his arms.

That was as far as his gratitude reached toward the vampiress. Today he would locate the mistress of the night and determine exactly what her intentions were toward Bella. And if Bella cared about the milquetoast Seth, he'd see about him, too.

"You have a pool, too," Bella said as she settled into the oversize chair alongside him. He set his plate on the floor and pulled her onto his lap. She wiped some gravy off his beard and stuck that finger into his mouth. He licked it clean. "Want to go for a swim tonight?"

Perhaps Elvira could wait.

Severo had told Bella that Heloise spent her evenings in the basement, laundering clothes, and usually left in time to get home for the late news. Still, Bella had been reluctant to strip naked and dive into the pool. Until her lover had done the stripping for her. With his teeth and tongue.

Now she surfaced in his arms and received a long, wet kiss. The weight of his embrace begged for entrance, so she wrapped her legs about him. His shaft slid into her, filling her. Severo was strong; he could tread water in the middle of the pool, allowing them to keep their heads above the water, while he pumped inside her. It was like floating and drowning at the same time.

They came together. Bella stretched her arms out across the water's surface, releasing her climax in a shivery cry.

"Severo," she murmured and then repeated his name.

He nipped at her chin. "Yes, love?"

"Is that your real name? It's so interesting."

"Strange, you mean?"

She gave him a nodding smile. "Is it your first name or last?"

"My surname, but I've never used my first. You don't think it suits me?"

"It does. Is it Italian?"

"It is. My parents immigrated at the turn of the twentieth century."

"What's your first name? I promise I won't tell if it's Percival or Eugene."

"It's Stephan," he offered. "But I don't use it, because it reminds me of my father. That was his name, as well."

"Your father? You have parents? Well, of course you do. Were you born a werewolf?"

"Yes. Both my mother and father were of the breed."

"Are they still alive?"

"No." He released her and swam backward.

The water temperature fell at the loss of contact with his warm flesh. She'd said something wrong. His parents must be a sore spot with him.

"I'd prefer you didn't use my first name," he said and heaved his body up to sit on the edge of the pool. Reaching back, he snagged a towel and sopped at his hair and chest. "Unless it's important to you."

What memories could he have of his father that made him want to renounce his name? She wanted to ask but sensed he'd put up a wall. "Severo works for me."

Bella dove deep, leaving him alone. The water muffled her senses, and the depths, which glowed aquamarine before her eyes, blocked out the world.

Here she swam, deep within the rabbit's adventure. Would he see her as a mere rabbit if the werewolf managed to find her?

Severo drove Bella to town for dance practice and promised to return for her in two hours. He shifted the Mercedes into Drive and rolled slowly down the street toward Minneapolis proper.

He wasn't sure where to find Elvira. She moved about the country but made her home in Minneapolis. Probably because she'd be laughed out of vampiredom in any other metropolitan area. He couldn't figure out if the chick knew she was copying the television personality, or if she genuinely believed the mistress-of-the-night look worked for her.

Vamps. He'd never figure them out, nor did he want to.

It had felt great ripping those two vampires apart in Bella's home last night. They'd had it coming, and he hadn't felt his energy like that for a while. The werewolf took a lot out of him during the three nights a month it reigned.

That was probably why he was so forceful with Bella. He needed an outlet for all that aggression. Sure, sex helped some, but he'd never lie to himself that romping the countryside as the wolf wasn't the ultimate.

With the full moon so close now, the dilemma arose of leaving Bella for three days, or remaining and seeing if he could sate the werewolf into submission. But he'd want to do that only for two days, the ones preceding and following the night of the full moon. The werewolf did need to roam at least once a month, and he wouldn't deny it.

That meant endangering Bella. Because Severo sensed that should the werewolf be anywhere within a sixty-mile radius of Bella, it would recognize her scent and seek her out—and then attempt to claim her as its mate.

And wouldn't that be grand? Finding a mate for the werewolf was all he could hope for. The culmination to a quest most males never achieved. Females of the breed were rare, and mortal females, well, they were too fragile. And to be approached by a werewolf for sex? Mortal women would run screaming.

Would Bella?

She'd wanted to quickly change the conversation about that. She might not think it, but much as she liked to believe she could accept him in his werewolf form, she never could.

He'd leave her this month. He must if he wanted to keep her.

Parking, because he preferred to walk outside and scent the surroundings, Severo got out and locked the car. Walking along Washington Avenue, he perused the bar offerings. A couple of strip joints flashed sexy pink neon. He could only feel pity for the women who danced inside.

Vampires were about this evening, both male and female, indulging in blood and lust. Their scent was nasty, like regurgitated blood.

Spying the black limo, he congratulated himself on an easy job. He wondered if Seth was inside the nearest bar, spinning discs. Probably. Which meant a confrontation was now or never.

An erratic techno beat filtered outside and must have disguised Severo's near-silent approach, because the two thug vamps in dark sunglasses standing outside the limo didn't turn until he was upon them.

The click of a semiautomatic alerted him, and Severo raised his hands in compliance but didn't stand down. "I promise I can break your wrist before you can pull the trigger," he offered slyly.

The thug glanced toward the back passenger window, blacked out with dark film.

"I want to talk to your mistress." Severo held up his hands in placation. "No funny stuff, promise."

The vamp snarled, revealing a yellow fang.

The back window rolled down and the scent of cheap perfume assaulted Severo's olfactories. "What does he want?" snapped the female.

"To chat," Severo said. He put down his arms and leaned over the window. "Mind if I join you?"

Her pale breasts, stuffed with silicone and barely concealed by the tight black sheath dress, rose and fell with a huffy sigh. Long black fingernails waved him around to the other side. The door unlocked and Severo gave the other thug a sneer before sliding inside.

Christ, but he wouldn't last long in this boudoir of perfume and vampire reek. Rolling down his window, Severo kept his distance from the vampiress, not because he suspected she'd slash him with those nails, but because he required the fresh air to keep his senses clear.

"Severo," she drawled with a classic night-mistress burr. "Long time. Thought I'd seen the last of you after that bloody debacle in the seventies."

He'd thought the same, but the woman was far from subtle. He caught wind of her whenever she blew into town, though he had to give her credit for keeping her messes to a minimum and being quick to clean up those that were not.

"Guess why I'm here?" he prompted.

"I saw you groping the mortal female the other night.

Since when does one of the most powerful werewolves in the country stoop so low?"

He'd relinquished that "most powerful" title years ago to Amandus Masterson, after he'd left the Northern pack. No longer did he get off on conflict and pack politics. Nor could he conceive of indulging in the blood sport the wolves participated in. He was a lone wolf, and happy for it.

"She's mine, not the boy's—Seth, your plaything. The mortal woman poses no threat to you."

"They have a certain relationship that disturbs me."

"Leave her alone. Or next time I smell vamps around her, I'm coming after you."

She pursed her glossy black lips. "You're such a bully, Severo. Sexual frustration tends to do that to a man. Makes him rigid and aggressive." Fanning a black-nailed finger down her cleavage, she cooed, "You sure you don't want to try some luscious vampire flesh?"

He eyed the white breasts, which seemed to glow in the darkness. "Not if my life depended on it. Your kind is vile, Elvira."

"Don't call me that. It's Evie."

He sighed. "So will you comply? The woman is his friend. That is all."

"Make them stop being friends, and I'll consider it."

What a pouty, insolent vamp. "Just get over it, long-tooth. You don't want the hurt I can promise you, so be smart and suffer your new toy his mortal friends. You know he won't last much longer. The thing is so drained, you can read by his flesh."

"I'm turning him."

Hell. Not good news for Bella or for the guy. "Haven't you enough sycophants?" he asked.

"I like this one. He's humorous. You know our sort can be so dreadfully dreary."

Like the chick next to him, clad in black and looking the queen of the Goths?

"I've said what I have to say. Whether or not you choose to take my words to heart will determine your fate. Nice talking to you, Elvira."

He swung out of the car and gasped in the night air to clear his senses. Striding away, Severo fisted his hands and growled. This was not over. It was just beginning. And much as he savored the fight, he did not favor waging war with one to whom he owed a debt.

Evie leaned over and plucked a long hair from the leather seat. She studied it, sniffed it. "So nasty."

And yet… There could be a use for this remnant from the werewolf.

She curled the hair about a forefinger until the pale flesh grew deep purple. "I will never bow before a dog."

Chapter 10

Severo had left the mansion last evening. He wouldn't tell her where he intended to stay for two nights. While Bella appreciated that he was only trying to protect her, after only twenty-four hours she missed him desperately.

Was this how it would be if their relationship continued? Him disappearing for three days every month? Certainly she could manage the distance. It was only three days. And what relationship wouldn't grow deeper with that time apart?

But her love for him was so new. Bella felt raw and uneasy as she lay alone in the king-size bed, her fingers gliding across the sheets on his side. Where was he? And in what form?

Tonight the full moon would shine brightly in the August sky. A harvest moon, which the weatherman had been encouraging everyone to go out and look at.

Bella flipped off the television and padded out to the patio. She slipped off her silk robe and dove into the pool naked. She'd gotten used to Heloise's schedule, and she tried to not strip when she knew she might run into her. The brownie was doing laundry and she usually left in the evening without a goodbye.

The pool was heated, which was a necessity in Minnesota. Floating on her back, she giggled as a falling red maple leaf landed on her belly. She let it lie there. Like a leaf floating in a pond, she was carried around the pool by the gentle current.

This could be the life. Living in a mansion with a housekeeper, gourmet meals and an attentive lover. What lottery had she won?

Okay, so the lover was not completely human. And though Severo had intimated that he'd like to support her, Bella could never allow that to happen. She liked work. It exercised her brain when her dancing was not moving her body.

Miss All About Control needed the independence of supporting herself. But that didn't mean she couldn't work from her own office here at the mansion. She had a choice of plenty of extra rooms.

One of the patio deck lights flickered. Bella's heart did a sudden dive. She treaded water in the center of the pool.

Severo had given her explicit instructions to go inside and lock all the doors after 10:00 p.m. The werewolf knew where home was, and while it rarely ventured close, it might come sniffing about.

He did say that early morning usually found his beastly form reduced to a regular wolf, and if she wanted to look outside on the third day for that, she could.

"My lover, the wolf," she said. Her heartbeat resuming normal pace, she continued floating. "And Seth loves a vampire."

Severo had not said what had gone on between him and Evie, but he did say he'd given her an ultimatum.

Evie. *Evil,* spelled wrong. Which was what she sounded like. A self-obsessed vampire whom Severo laughingly referred to as Elvira.

Bella wondered if Evie truly resembled the tall, beehive-coiffed mistress of the dark. She wasn't sure she'd be able to keep a straight face if she ever met her. How far off Seth's scale was she? He normally went in for flirty, stupid and shallow.

A tap on the patio door alerted her. Heloise gestured. Bella dropped her legs and sank into the water to conceal her nudity. The housekeeper opened the door and made a dismissive gesture, as if she'd seen it all before.

"It's almost ten, mistress," Heloise called. "Best be getting inside."

"Already?" She hadn't thought it was that late when she'd come out here. "Yes, fine. I'll be right in. Are you turning in for the night, Heloise?"

"I go home. I have nice little house, given to me by Severo. Good night, mistress. You stay inside, yes?" She left the patio door open.

"Night." Bella swam over for a towel and slid up onto the ledge of the pool.

The open door taunted her. *Come quick, before it's too late.*

The housekeeper didn't stick around during the full

moon? And she was a faerie. She should be more comfortable with the whole paranormal realm and all its dark shenanigans than any mortal.

Did that mean Bella should be treating this night as more ominous than she had last night?

Skittering across the flagstone tiles, she hastened inside and locked the door behind her, dropping the Charley bar, as Severo had taught her. The sky was dark and there, above the treetops, the fat harvest moon sat low and proud.

A canine howl sounded in the distance.

Bella's heart fluttered.

"I'd better check all the doors and windows."

Doors locked? Check. Windows locked, all fitted with special security bars that locked into a steel casement? Check. If the high security didn't give her the willies, then nothing else should.

It was nearing 1:00 a.m., and Bella sat in the middle of the bed, the soft shirt she'd picked up from the floor clutched to her chest. It was Severo's and it smelled like him, so she'd pulled it on after a quick shower to wash away the chlorine.

And here she sat, as she had last night, staring out the window. Severo's house sat at the bottom of a valley. The countryside rose in the distance. Hundreds of acres of forested land, he'd explained, all belonged to him. The moon had tucked itself out of view, but the sky was luminous against the black tree silhouettes.

An owl hooted. A dog howled. The wind picked up. And now branches scraping the windows kept her alert.

Any little noise set her heart to a jackrabbit kick against her chest.

In the horror movies, it wasn't the gross creature or the blood that got to her; it was the anticipation of evil.

"He's not evil," she whispered.

Their romance had been fast and more than furious. He'd captured her from day one, literally, and Bella appreciated now that he had not relented his pursuit of her. Never had she been with such a man. Virile, strong, attentive and, yes, commanding.

And much as she'd never wanted to be controlled, she didn't feel controlled by Severo. But an edge of domination existed, which she willingly surrendered to.

Because with Severo's control, she also received safety and a feeling of contentment.

Even sitting here, listening to the night spooks, she had to admit she was safe. The windows were secure, as were the doors. Surely the wolf wouldn't attempt to break through?

Part of her wanted to see the werewolf, to know her lover in all his forms. Another part thought it fine and dandy that she sat inside and it was outside.

Eyelids flickering, Bella yawned.

A squabble between worm-seeking robins outside the window woke her hours later. She'd made it through the second night, which, as Severo had pointed out, was the most perilous of nights, because during the full moon the werewolf most felt the call to mate.

The werewolf howled a long, lonely cry to the moon.
Bring her to me. Give me what I have wanted for so long.

It sensed something had changed. It had no notion that when it was not stalking the countryside, it could be in any other form than this man/beast shape. It knew only that humans were to be fiercely avoided.

And yet, a new scent clung to its form, the taut muscles that stretched its legs and forearms and twined within its flesh. It smelled human, and like a sweet plant it had once scented so many years ago.

Where did it come from? And how to find the source?

The werewolf wanted to know it, to feel it. To lick it and taste the sweetness that the lingering scent promised.

Yet the strange inner caution that often kept it from wandering onto private mortal land again held it back. Made it cower, for fear of revealing itself to the world.

It would not seek the scent. Not yet.

Night three. A glance to the clock revealed it was 2:00 a.m. Severo had said it would be safe after three on the final night. Anticipation kept her vigilant.

Bella had never been a dog lover. She didn't hate them, but she did fear them, for rational reasons. A dog had once bitten her. Another time, when she was a teenager, a huge rottweiler had chased her down an alley.

A wolf must be ten times more dangerous than a dog.

Bella smirked and tugged up the loose shirt for the countless time to draw in Severo's scent. Now she understood how he could take pleasure in scents. Scents reassured and excited her.

She slid the shirt across her bare stomach and glided her fingers lower to press upon the rise of her mons. There was where he mastered her with his tongue, flicking and pressing and teasing her to a climax that always made her see stars.

She'd never had make-me-see-stars sex with other men. And she couldn't get enough of the constellation Severo.

A loud noise outside, in the patio area, stiffened her shoulders. Bella waited, her neck straight and ears perked. A hot streak of fear stretched along her collarbone. She didn't know what to expect. A shadow crossing outside the window? A monstrous shape creeping before the shrubs?

Time passed slowly.

The next time she looked, the clock flicked to three forty-five.

Exhausted from sitting alert all night, Bella longed to fall asleep. But a niggling curiosity pushed her from the bed.

She scampered down the hall and across the vast marble foyer in the shirt, her legs bare. The house was still and illuminated with moonlight shining in through the sunroof three stories overhead.

Heloise took joy in revving up the floor polisher and going at this marble expanse. Bella wished she could get the housekeeper to come to her loft once in a while.

Severo had reported that the glass in the patio door at her place had been replaced and the floor and curtains cleaned. What he'd not said was that he wanted her to move back to town. Until he asked, she was content here. As long as she didn't miss practice or the audition in a few days.

Approaching the patio door, she scanned outside. The maple trees about the pool filtered out the moonlight. If a beast lurked in the shadows, she wouldn't be able to see it. And she'd never pick up its scent, as Severo did so well.

Still, she released the door latch and stepped outside. Burned peat sweetened the air. She had seen the fires that afternoon and had guessed that they were about two miles to the west. Farmers burning brush in the ditches, no doubt.

The flagstones were cool underfoot. Clutching the shirt at her breasts, she scanned the circumference. Nothing.

Sitting carefully at the pool's edge, she decided not to dip her feet in.

A breeze flirted with her hair, blowing a few strands across her cheek. The soft touch reminded her of Severo's kisses when he was being lazy after they'd made love for hours.

Because normally everything about him was aggressive—go, go, go, and don't stop until you've gone beyond. She liked that about him. It made her strive to keep up, to release some control and let chaos reign.

She smirked at the notion that she'd relinquished control to a man. An incredibly assertive man who would not allow her to forget he was in charge of her pleasure. A charge he fulfilled beyond her dreams.

A click sounded to her side. Animal claws on stone.

Bella swallowed down her fear, and bravely turned to find a dark-furred wolf staring at her. Her heart seemed to stop beating. Her stomach loosened, while her neck muscles tightened.

It stood six feet from her. Black markings on its face made it blend it into the murky, predawn surroundings.

Only the paler belly fur made it stand out. It was a big wolf, perhaps the size of a monster German shepherd.

Don't think about monsters. It's just a nice puppy. It's not going to hurt you.

To turn and dash inside might startle it. The wolf might think she was being aggressive and attack.

Don't be silly. He said his were mind is also present when he is the wolf.

Inhaling, Bella drew up courage. She could do this. She wanted to do this.

She held out her hand, not sure if she was offering friendship or her scent for it to smell. Probably both. Just so long as it didn't find her tasty.

It? No, this was her lover. That same piercing dark stare took her measure now. At the corner of its jaw, one canine tooth peeked out. It wasn't snarling at her, though. She hoped.

And then it bowed its head and lifted a paw to its jaw.

She didn't know what it was trying to convey.

"Severo?" She leaned forward on her elbows and the wolf padded closer. "Come to me."

The wolf whined lowly and padded up to her. It sniffed at her hands, then at her hair. When its nose grazed her ear, she flinched and cautioned herself not to make any quick moves.

Closing her eyes, she wished it gone. Why had she thought this a smart idea? It was smelling her. Probably wondering how easily it could rip her up for dinner.

No, don't think it. He is Severo. There must be some part of the wolf that recognized her and wanted not to harm her.

A nudge of its nose to her wrist made her wonder if it wanted her to…touch it?

Bella lifted a hand, and carefully, slowly, she reached to smooth her palm over the short fur between its ears. The wolf nudged her wrist again in an encouraging manner.

It didn't seem to be hungry or to have a carnivorous intent in mind. Bella released her breath and relaxed.

She ruffled her palms through its soft fur. It was thick and silken, unlike that of any dog she'd ever accidentally touched. And it didn't threaten her at all.

"You're gorgeous, lover."

Chapter 11

He awoke with a start. The air breezed across his back with a cool kiss of oncoming autumn. The night had died and he lay on the patio tiles, naked, scratched on the forearms and legs. And hungry, as usual.

A soft murmur made him turn over. Bella smiled, coming up from a sleep of the angels. "Morning, lover."

She'd come out to meet the wolf? *Brave woman.*

But not the bravery that meeting his werewolf would require. And he did want that to happen. The urge had struck last night. The werewolf had *known.* A potential mate was close by. It had taken all Severo's influence to keep it away from the house.

"I love the wolf," she said on a sleepy smile.

And he bowed his head against her breast and held her tight.

* * *

"How's it coming along?" Evie strode into the brightly lit laboratory and traced a finger along the stainless-steel counter. "Was the hair sufficient?"

Ian Grim glanced up from a grimoire he'd been poring over. His dark hair hung over one pale eye and he licked dry lips. "Excellent actually. I've almost figured out how to deactivate the protection wards."

"And the binding spell?"

"I'll need another week for that. Patience, my lady. You've been dreaming of this revenge for decades. Another few weeks will only make the reward much sweeter. I don't understand your goal, though. Why not kill her?"

"Think about it, Grim. Of all the paranormals in this realm, what two species most clash and hate one another?"

"Used to be we witches and the vampires."

"Yes, but now that the protection spell has been lifted, I've no fear of your blood. So you know what that leaves."

"It is an interesting prospect. I wish you the best."

"I don't need your wishes. I need your spells. Back to work, Grim."

The studio was small, lined from a mirrored wall to a cement wall with raised hardwood flooring. Off in the corner, a guitarist strummed as a female dancer breezed through a routine of stomping feet and twisting arms and hips.

Tonight was the audition session Bella had told him

about. It was important to her, so he'd wanted to be here for her.

Severo wasn't interested in any of the women waiting for their chance to dance. He grew alert only as Bella took the floor, her arms moving out gracefully and twisting above her head to assume a beginning pose.

The black skirt hugged her legs and the heavy white ruffles fell above her ankles. A fitted black leotard put her breasts on display and made him jealous that two other men stood in the room.

He lowered his head and observed through his lashes as the music began.

Bella's body, sinuous and sleek, captured the music and spoke to his most feral desires. Below the waist she was forceful and loud. Above, she wove a sorrowful story with her arms and dramatic twists.

And then a man approached her, cocky and stiff, as if he were a bull approaching the cape. Which, Severo guessed, was the purpose of the dance.

He didn't like this man. The dark hair that slicked over his ears and the focus he gave to Bella raised Severo's hackles. He stomped out a rapid array of footwork, which stirred the other dancers to a cheering rhythmic clap.

Bella bent backward, one hand clutching her skirt up high, so a half arc of ruffles swirled from wrist to ankle. Fiercely determined, she snapped her wrist to a hip and spun about to mirror the male dancer as he tormented the floor with his heels.

The man charged her with the dominating steps of a bull. Shoulders thrust back and body sleek and straight, the man focused his attention on Bella's face. His feet tortured the wood floor as he stomped about her, claiming, defying. Owning.

Severo exhaled. Hell, he was jealous of the man wearing dance shoes and a gold-spangled bolero jacket.

But he checked his anger. If he was jealous, that could only be a good thing. That meant he wasn't obsessing about Aby. The realization made him momentarily sad, but he chased the feeling away with a try at the *palmas,* or hand clapping.

It didn't work. His focus remained on the mere inches of space between the male dancer and Bella.

The air was charged with pheromones, and the scent of their dance disturbed Severo. And then the man reached up to stroke the side of Bella's face—

"Enough!" With two strides, Severo insinuated himself between the two.

The guitarist stopped. The male dancer swore in Spanish and stomped off. Bella's look cut Severo sharply, but the small pain did not squelch his anger.

"You're leaving now," he barked.

He tugged Bella from the room and slammed the door behind them.

In the hallway she wrestled her wrist from his grip, then shoved him in the chest.

"You ass! What do you think you just did?"

"I didn't like the way he was touching you."

"Touching? *Touching?*"

"He was marking you with his scent."

"His scent?" She let out a frustrated groan and, grabbing her duffel from the assortment of bags on the floor, marched away. "You've embarrassed the hell out of me and made damn well sure I never dance at this studio again. Marking? Get a clue, wolf boy. We were danc-ing!"

He rushed after her, but she eluded his grip. "Don't touch me."

"Bella, he was being aggressive with you. You may not be able to perceive such subtle cues, but I can. He had more in mind than dancing."

She spun and swung up a palm. The slap to his face cracked loudly. Severo retaliated with a growl and he clasped her throat with one hand.

"You are an animal," she said. He dropped his hand then and, turning, she stomped off, the metal on her heels clicking angrily.

"I'm not an animal." He swallowed. His hand was still clenched and ready to choke anyone, anything. "Oh hell. Am I?"

Chapter 12

Bella stomped inside her loft and barely took time to unbuckle her dance shoes before kicking them across the rug.

The violet suede shoes were her lucky shoes. "Lot of good they did. That idiot wolf!"

Heading directly for the shower, she squeezed past the overzealous bamboo plant, shedding her skirt and top on the way. "He thought Tony was putting his scent on me? What kind of freak is he? Oh right, a werewolf freak."

It was good to be home. It had been nice at Severo's estate, but after tonight, she wasn't in the mood for his raging alpha hormones.

At least he had taken a hint and had not followed her home.

A shower and scrub with lots of lemon bath gel refreshed her, but Bella stayed under the water stream for half an hour, till the water got cold. Lost in the patter of water, she allowed her thoughts to flee and she found a tolerable medium between anger and peace.

That the man could so easily toy with her emotions troubled her. And then she knew it was because he meant so much to her. If she meant half as much to him, shouldn't he have known his actions would destroy her?

The sun had set by the time she exited the steamy paradise. Tugging on a silk robe, she padded into the kitchen to browse the fridge. A few nonperishable items remained, though none appealed to her. Not even the half tub of milk-chocolate frosting.

"I miss Heloise's cooking. Oh! What is it with that man? He's always so…macho. So controlling."

She'd thought she liked that about him. But how could she after what he'd done tonight? He'd ruined any chance of her getting the apprenticeship.

She didn't know how to deal with his possessiveness. How did a girl date a wolf and make it work? "Mom never had any advice for that one," she told herself aloud.

Diana Reynolds, who had headed off to Tunisia a month ago to work with a charity organization, would have told her daughter to face the challenge head-on. *Don't let it upset you. Look at the reason why it's in your life. To teach you something.*

Teach her? But what?

To be less controlling? But in exchange for being controlled?

That didn't jibe.

To be more accepting of those unlike her? She'd always been open-minded. *Prejudice* was not a word in the Reynolds household.

To love? She loved. Many. But Bella had never loved deeply like this before.

Was romantic love supposed to ache as well as feel good?

Scratching her head, she surveyed the room. She didn't feel in the mood for a swim. The computer sat silently mocking her lack of attention.

"I should check my email." It had been over a week, and though her current clients didn't require immediate attention, she never knew when a new client would contact her.

Booting up the Mac, she waited while the Entourage program downloaded 220 emails. That would take a while to sort through. And she was still too frustrated to sit quietly and do work.

Instead, Bella went to the internet and searched Google for *werewolf.*

Wikipedia called them lycanthropes, humans with the ability to shape-shift into a wolf or a wolflike creature.

The *loup-garou* in eighteenth-century France was a feared and hunted creature, blamed for killing dozens of men, women and children.

Their weaknesses were silver and wolfsbane. And the idea of a werewolf bite transforming a mortal into a werewolf was purely a fictional creation.

Weren't werewolves themselves supposed to be fictional?

And yet, knowing they were real wasn't so awful. Just...

"Pissed," she muttered sharply. "So pissed at him."

She clicked to another site and another. They all rehashed the lore and legend and featured artists' renditions of the creature. But none of the sites told her about the man she was dealing with. She searched Google for *wolf.*

According to the internet they usually ran in packs of six to eight. Yet, she thought, Severo had never mentioned other werewolves. The site also said a wolf could be an alpha, but to do so, it must find an unoccupied territory and a female to mate with.

Bella clutched her throat.

She read more. The wolf's sense of smell was about one hundred times greater than a human's. She knew that. They also marked their territory. So it was an ingrained thing with Severo, she realized. Was he worried Tony was marking his territory?

That still didn't explain his reaction at the studio.

She read more. "A wolf may growl to indicate warning or dominance."

Severo growled a lot. And it always turned her on if they were making out. He was dominating her.

A shiver traced her shoulders and arms. A good shiver.

A rap on the patio door made Bella sit up, alert. It was getting late. Who could that be? A vampire? In her anger, she'd forgotten the danger, the reason Severo had coaxed her away from her home in the first place.

Would a murderous vampire knock first? she reasoned as she walked over to the door. Through the long white sheers she saw the shadow outside—a big male shadow who wore a leather jacket.

"Go away!" she called through the glass door.

"I'm sorry," Severo said, his voice calm and low. "Please, can we talk?"

"I'm not in the mood." She peeked through the curtain, found he stood with his back to the door, and then dropped the curtain and paced around the living room.

This seemed to be his M.O. Stalk her when she hated him. Overwhelm her with his caveman aggression and awkward charm to win her over.

"It's not going to work tonight," she muttered, with a glance to her abandoned dancing shoes.

He could have no idea how much earning an apprenticeship with Tony meant to her. Web design was fun, and it paid the bills, but it required one's butt in the chair all day. Dancing? Well, Bella couldn't get enough of the motion, the freedom, the utter abandon.

"Bella, please."

"Don't say my name," she whispered. She clutched her arms across her chest in a less than reassuring hug. "Just go away."

He couldn't hear her soft, trembling plea. But if he was so keen on picking up her scent, why couldn't he also hear through walls and windows? Shouldn't paranormal sorts be able to do all kinds of fabulous things with their senses?

And yet, his sense of propriety was off the scale.

"Wolves are protective of their mates. They mate for life," she said, repeating the information she'd read online. "And werewolves are creatures, not humans."

With a shudder, she paused before the patio door. His shadow was not there, but she could see a figure now standing before the pool's edge.

"He's not going to leave."

Resigned to make the best of it, at least to try convincing him to leave, Bella pulled the door open and slipped outside. He remained before the pool, looking down.

At an amazing sight.

Bella joined Severo at his side. Dozens of white water lilies floated on the surface of the water. The streetlight across the alley shone over the water and glinted in the droplets dewed on the pale petals. Gorgeous. And fantastical.

Bella swallowed and looked up at Severo.

"Roses are so common," he offered. "I figure you've received dozens from previous suitors. These caught my eye. They're a pitiful apology, but they're a start."

Her anger dissipated. The tenderness in his voice struck her. He knew he'd done wrong. She wished it hadn't been such a devastating wrong.

"The pool man is going to have a fit," she said, and bent to sit and dangle her legs in the pool. Lifting her toe, she caught a bloom on top of her foot and balanced it there. The bright yellow center winked at her as it bobbled. "This doesn't begin to make up for what you did earlier."

He knelt, one leg stretched out to the side, hands clasped between his thighs. He hadn't yet met her gaze, so she knew he was feeling remorseful. *Good.* Mr. Big Bad needed to be knocked down a few pegs.

"I should not have accompanied you to the audition. I'm sorry. I just… You can't understand what it's like for me to stand by and watch my mate interact with another man."

"It's called dancing. People do it all the time without falling down and having sex."

He swiped a hand over his face and gritted out, "But you're mine."

"I don't belong to you. I don't want to be owned by you."

"You're my mate, Bella."

"Is that how it's supposed to be for a werewolf's mate? Secluded away from the rest of the world, never allowed to hold a conversation with another man for fear he may look at her the wrong way or, heaven forbid, shake her hand?"

"Please, Bella." He clenched his hands into fists, fighting aggression. "This is new for me. I'm trying not to be the he-man, as you call it, and to make this relationship work."

"New?" She tipped the flower off her foot and cast her toe about in search of another. "You've never had a mate before?"

"No."

"But you've had sex with women."

"Doesn't make them my mate. I explained this. You are the only one for me. You've met the wolf, and it accepted you. No other woman has met the wolf."

He was trying, she could tell. It must be killing him not to simply grab her, kiss her and drag her home by her hair.

Home. She'd just considered Severo's mansion to be home. She'd known him but a short while, and already she felt as if he was a part of her life. And some parts of life weren't always fun and joyous, but occasionally sticky and downright meddlesome.

"Severo." She breathed out and closed her eyes, drawing in the lilies' scent. "Despite the fact that this is the strangest relationship ever…and that you are not a gentle or compassionate person…and that you insist that everything goes your way…*and* that when you find someone you want, you take them, no matter their concerns… Despite all that, a part of me is in for the ride. I mean…"

She sighed. Was she going to admit this after only moments ago reveling in her anger?

It was futile to resist.

"This feels right. And I do love you."

Smiling a careful smile, he reached in to the pool and plucked a blossom. He tucked it over her ear, and a few droplets of water ran down her cheek. He traced one droplet down to her jaw.

"And yet, I don't want to sacrifice my life to be a part of yours," she added.

"You needn't."

"But dancing means a lot to me. I had hopes of getting that apprenticeship. It would have advanced my studies and allowed me to teach part-time."

"I'll call the studio tomorrow. No, I'll go there and apologize in person."

"No, don't. It's over. I'm sure Tony has already selected an apprentice. I don't want you going anywhere near the studio."

"I will not, then. Good thing for Tony."

She smirked. "He's gay, big boy."

"Really? But he moved so sensually with you. Ah, I don't have that… What is it they call it?"

"Gaydar?"

"Yes, that. I'm sorry, Bella." He removed his hand from her cheek, but she took his palm in hers.

"Apology accepted. But I have a life, which you need to accept if you want me in yours. And I have a job."

"You needn't work, Bella. I will take care of you."

"But I like my job, and I like to work. It gives me a sense of purpose. Heck, it's a means of communicating with others."

"I have an office at the estate. It is yours to use when you wish."

"I know." She sighed again.

She would get nowhere arguing about her need to keep hold of the real world. Not the weird, marvelous world at the bottom of the rabbit hole that Severo occupied. That world was interesting, and she liked being a part of it. But rationally, she knew she had to cling to her world as long as possible.

His presence, so immense and overpowering, was softened by the flowers' perfume. At once she hated him, and she did not. He was a lost soul, roaming the earth in search of another soul who could fulfill him, make him happy, erase his pain.

She hadn't thought she needed a relationship, but feeling needed did something to her idea of remaining single. It obliterated the idea.

And if that didn't do it, Severo's kiss did.

He tilted up her chin and leaned in to kiss her. So gentle, lingering, not a hint of the intensity his kisses usually wielded. *I'm sorry,* the kiss said.

And then it was gone, and he sat next to her, stretching his legs out to the side so they wouldn't dangle in the pool. Bella snuggled her cheek against his chest. "I want to make this work," she whispered.

He stroked her hair and simply held her. His silence was the best thing he could have given her.

Bella hung up the phone and rubbed her palms along her bare arms.

"Something wrong, sweet?"

She turned to hug up to her lover on the bed. They'd retreated to the bedroom. Last night she had agreed her loft in the city wasn't safe and had gone home with him after they'd made love beside the flower-filled pool.

They spent most nights making love. It was as if they couldn't get enough of each other. He was her air, and she his. The man was insatiable.

"That was Seth." She rested her head against his shoulder and stared up at the ceiling. "He wants to talk."

"And he couldn't do it over the phone? Bella, how did he sound?"

"What do you mean?"

"It's been over a month. There's no way he could have survived as Elvira's blood slave. She must have turned him."

"He would have told me."

"Maybe he intends to tell you when you meet. You can't go see him. I won't allow it."

"I'm not asking your permission." She slid out of bed, thinking it was time to get dressed. A woman could not survive on sex alone. Breakfast was in order, even if it was two in the afternoon. "I'm going to see him."

She tugged a loose sundress over her body and took off.

"Then I'm coming with you."

Heloise was not in the kitchen, and Bella was glad for that. She wanted an apple, and a few minutes to think about her friend without the wolf bellowing at her.

Peace was not to be had.

Her lover padded in, wearing jeans and a frown. His limp was always more noticeable when his mood was foul.

"Last time you came along, Seth clammed up." She bit into a juicy green apple.

Don't look at the half-dressed werewolf's muscles. You can't stay angry at the man's ripped abs, and you know it.

"You're staying home, if I have to find a leash," she said.

He snarled. So she'd used one of the bad words. Get over it.

"And if I lock you in the bedroom?" he challenged.

"You wouldn't dare."

"I will if it means keeping you safe."

"He's a friend, Severo. Seriously, I'm adjusting to the possessive stuff, but you take it too far sometimes."

"You have no idea what his mind-set is. And if he is a vampire, he is not the same friend you used to know. Don't be stupid about this, Bella. You know better."

She did know better.

Setting the apple on the counter, Bella stretched her arms along it and laid her head on an elbow. "I don't want to believe it." She stared at the framed picture tucked behind the toaster. "Don't you have friends you worry about? Family?"

"I have no family. And friends are few and far between."

"So who is this?" She tugged out the picture and displayed it to him.

His intake of breath made Bella stand up straight. In the picture, a pretty red-haired woman snuggled up to Severo, beaming, as was he. Which had startled her the first time she'd seen it. Severo was not a smiley fellow.

He seemed ready to grab the photo away but wasn't sure how to do it.

"She means something to you. What's her name? And why haven't I met her? Is she an old girlfriend?"

"Enough!" He snatched the photo and studied it for long seconds before tucking it into a drawer. "She's someone I used to know."

"Really? Her picture is everywhere. Over by the TV, in the hallway. Down in the laundry room."

"When have you been to the laundry room?"

"I like to chat with Heloise. Which has nothing to do with the question you're trying to avoid. If she was a lover, I'd understand. We both had lives before meeting one another. I want to know who is important to you, Severo. Is she to you as Seth is to me? Talk to me."

He drew a hand over his mouth and jaw, delaying a reply. Looking about, he paced. Always he became antsy when he was riled or scented something wrong.

"She was a lover," Bella decided and took another bite of apple.

"She was not," he hissed. The ferocity in his stare made her choke on the apple. "And this conversation is over."

Chapter 13

Bella sorted through her few dresses in the large closet, which, surprisingly, held only a few items of Severo's clothing. The man did like his dark jeans and shirts. She guessed that made less work for Heloise. But if he'd lived for so long, surely by now he should have collected a wardrobe.

Or maybe not. Though the house was grand, the man lived a simple life, which she admired.

Yet she still wasn't sure what he did. Something related to buying forested real estate to create a wolf preserve. But how did he make his money in order to do that?

Feeling only a little guilty about leaving for town tonight, she decided she had every right to go out by herself. And it was to meet a friend. He couldn't begrudge her that.

Though she knew he meant well, wanting to protect

her. But she needed to keep her life, as she'd hoped she'd made clear to him. It wasn't as though he didn't have a whole life she wasn't a part of.

That woman in the pictures. She had to have been a lover. Bella could feel it, no matter how much he denied it. And he had called out a woman's name that night the vampires had attacked in her loft.

Did she have a rival for Severo's heart?

Jealousy flushed her chest. And then she realized she was behaving like him, getting angry over something that likely wasn't a problem.

Though she had to admit, Severo's jealousy did make her feel special. No man had ever been so fiercely protective of her. There he went again, making a girl feel like a princess.

The bedroom door opened, and Bella didn't bother to turn around. She wore spike heels, panties and a bra. Let him ogle.

"Her name is Aby," he said.

Bella lowered the red dress she held and turned to him.

Severo, head down, limped a few paces. "She lived with me for ten years before moving out last year. She was…everything to me."

Ten years? And they *hadn't* been lovers? Now this was interesting. But his edgy tone cautioned her. *Don't rile the beast, Bella. Leave him to simmer.*

"Sorry. It seems a sore spot with you. I shouldn't have asked."

"You need to know. I shouldn't hold things back from you, Bella. Know that I try to be as forthright as I'm able."

"I know you do. I trust that you'll tell me what you think I need to know when the time is right. So thanks for giving me that part of you."

He nodded. "I'm going out to look at the car before you leave."

And with that, he was gone.

Bella stared at the open doorway. She had grown accustomed to her lover's constant presence, and so his swift absence pricked at her heart.

She stepped around the bed and pulled open a dresser drawer by the bed where she knew he kept a photo of the woman.

Ten years.

She traced the woman's face and Severo's beaming smile.

"Will you ever smile so big for me? Or is she always in your heart? What did she mean to you if you weren't lovers?"

A child? A friend? A relative?

"Maybe Heloise would know?"

He held the Mercedes' keys and waited for Bella. She had insisted on going into town to meet Seth without him. He knew she'd meet trouble.

After their argument this afternoon about Aby, he did owe Bella further explanation.

It hadn't been an argument. More like him clamming up and not knowing how to face the feelings he'd kept buried for more than a year.

For ten years he had shared his life with her. Now Aby was gone. Stolen by another man.

He'd given Bella what information he could about

his and Aby's relationship. It wasn't much. Perhaps he could give her more. But how did he release the feelings that sat in his chest like a black mass unwilling to be pried out?

It was generous of her to say she would accept what he could give her when he felt right about it. "Bella. My Bella."

"You're not coming along?"

Surprised he'd not caught her scent, Severo hardened his frown. She wore red, and that angered him. Seth was just a friend, he reminded himself. Just as he and Aby had been friends?

He attempted to remain stoic. "No. I promised I would not."

"You won't follow me?"

Well, he hadn't promised that.

"At least stay out of sight, if you do. I know you will follow me."

"I loved her," he said and clutched the keys tightly. "Aby. I loved her. I could have made her my mate, but she didn't want that. I respected her for that."

Bella dropped her purse on the front seat and gave him an expectant look. "You don't have to talk about this."

"I need you to know me."

"Thought we were taking it slow now. I won't meet the werewolf until the next full moon. I don't need to meet the old girlfriend. Ever."

"She wasn't my girlfriend. She was my…" Even after all these years, he still didn't know how to describe their relationship. "Aby is a familiar. Do you know what familiars are?"

She shook her head.

"They are bridges for demons from their realm to this one. She is a tool. And she's a shape-shifter like me. But familiars shift to cats."

"Really?"

He could read her thoughts and answered them. "Cats and wolves do not get along, nor should werewolves and familiars. But I found Aby when she was a kitten—rather, the wolf did—and led her home. She had just begun a new life. Familiars have nine of them. They forget their experiences, though, from one life to the next.

"Aby grew up here, and we were like friends and relatives and lovers. Though we never made love, I wanted to have that relationship. And there were times I could sense the same desire in her, but mostly, she thought of me as a brother figure."

Bella didn't speak, which made the confession easier. Or maybe not.

"She fell in love last year. With a good man. A demon hunter. Someone I did not initially care for, but now I'm glad she loves him."

"Someone you didn't care for? The poor man. I can imagine the rough time you must have given him." Bella's smile soothed Severo's anxiety. "It must have been hard for you."

"It still is. I miss her. She doesn't call often enough. It's been months since I've spoken to her."

"Maybe you should call her."

"No, she's on the road all the time. She and her highwayman."

"Highwayman?"

"He's a demon hunter. Bit of a celebrity in the paranormal realm. I didn't like his cocksureness when I first met him. I felt threatened. But we've come to an understanding."

"Sounds like you've decided to accept him, if only because he means so much to Aby."

"That's about it."

He bowed his head, and Bella stroked his cheek. He loved her touch. The warmth of her, standing so close, yet not threatening, felt exquisite. She accepted him.

"Aby is who the wolf thinks about when he howls to the moon, I am sure. They used to get along, the wolf and the cat. It's bizarre to imagine, but we were happy."

She kissed him, barely touching his mouth. "Is it all right, then, with me? I don't want to step on her memory."

"You never could. I try to keep the two of you in different places in my heart. You are my mate, Bella."

"But will I ever be as close to you as you were to her?"

"I hope so."

She understood what he could not put into words. Bless her for that. And it gave him all the more reason to try his damnedest never to allow Aby into that place in his heart that Bella now occupied.

"I suppose you should be going?"

She eyed the keys he held out. *Please change your mind. Stay away from the vampires, and make love with me tonight.*

She took the keys. "Remember what I said about staying out of sight."

"I bow to your command, sweet. But know, if all hell breaks loose, I'm going to be there, loud and proud."

"Deal."

Scarlet was a local bar that catered to Goths and, now that Bella thought about it, probably paranormals, as well. She'd been here only once previously, with Seth. The entire place was lit in red: the booths were red vinyl, the dance floor was lit underneath by red bulbs, the windows had red stained glass and even the toilets were red.

An appropriate place to meet vampires, she supposed. If one wanted to meet a vampire. Which she did not.

"Please don't let him be a vampire."

Thankful they were meeting in public, she parked the Mercedes in the lot and hopped out. Wearing red might be overkill, but she never failed to dress the part when clubbing.

Though consciously aware of her surroundings, she didn't spot a werewolf lurking in the shadows. Of course, Severo would be discreet. She smiled to think he was out there somewhere, keeping an eye on her. And it didn't feel like she was being stalked, only that she was loved.

Her black velvet stilettos clicked on the sidewalk, and she had merely to flash the bouncer a smile for admission.

It took a while to adjust to the atmosphere. The red tricked her eyes and painted the faces around her.

Dirgelike music surprised her. Seth liked the funky techno stuff. He'd call this stuff a snoozer.

"Where are you, Seth?" She sipped her drink and scanned the crowd and the upper level. Seth waved and lifted his drink.

With a glance to the door—would Severo make good on his promise to follow her?—Bella headed upstairs.

Seth rose and kissed both her cheeks and mouth. Lemon, cologne and beer—the scent worked on him. His hair seemed darker, the long fringy bangs hanging over his eyes. A couple of silver rings flashed on his fingers. Seth had never worn jewelry; bling, he said, was for posers.

Bella slid into the booth next to him. He held her hand, so she had no choice but to sit close. That was usual. He seemed to be the same old Seth, except for the rings. But a turtleneck in this weather?

"I've missed you," he said close to her ear so she could hear over the music. "You look great, Bellybean."

"You don't look so bad yourself. You dump Elvira?"

"No bitchy stuff tonight, Bella. Please. She's my lover, and you're going to have to accept that."

"I can, but does that mean you're a vampire?"

"Why do you ask?"

"Severo said you couldn't have survived this long without her turning you."

"You still hanging around that bastard werewolf? Is that why you're never home?"

"I had to move out to his place after vampires tried to kill me. Did you hear that, Seth?" She leaned close to his ear. "Vampires tried to *kill* me. She's doing this, you know. She's jealous."

"I don't want to get into this argument again. You're being brainwashed by that dog."

"Don't call him a dog. He's a wolf."

"Yeah, and I'm Renfield." He slugged back the beer.

Bella stroked the stem of her cosmo goblet. She had no appetite for alcohol right now. Or for snotty friends.

"Hey," he said in a calmer voice, "we started on the wrong foot. Let's just chill and catch up, okay?"

"Is that why you wanted to see me?"

"It's been so long, and I know I've been ignoring you. So you've moved? Permanently?"

"No, I still have the loft. I'm not sure about moving to town right now."

"Fair enough. What about the audition? Wasn't that a few nights ago?"

He'd remembered. Good old Seth.

"I didn't get the apprenticeship." She shrugged. "I'll give it another go next time."

"Bella, I'm sorry." He hugged her and kissed her jaw. Beyond his usual scent, he smelled like something darker. Blood? She didn't want to think about it. "Want to come to a party next weekend?"

"At your woman's house?"

"My house. But she'll be there. I'd like to introduce you. Sans wolf, of course."

Next weekend was the full moon. Bella didn't want to go anywhere. Nor did an invite to meet Elvira sound particularly intriguing.

"Can I take a rain check? Severo's got some things going on."

Seth laughed and a jerk of his arm spilled the cosmo across the table. "Ah, shit. Sorry. Just push it all to the other side. That's cool." He pressed his nose against Bella's hair and kissed her hard on the neck, lingering too long. "Let me guess. Full moon coming soon? He's going out on the prowl. Does the werewolf fuck you, Bella?"

She hauled off to slap him, but the small booth wouldn't allow her to get her arm around. Seth caught her fist and kissed it. His wicked smile disturbed her.

"You're crude, Seth."

"Yeah, but you know what they say about werewolves, don't you?"

"What?"

"They aren't happy unless the werewolf has a mate. That it's the monster, not the man, who needs to get boned every full moon. I can't see you screwing a hairy beast, Bella. It's so not you."

"Like letting some Elvira wannabe suck out your blood is any more sane? God, Seth, just…sit back. You've changed."

"So have you, Bella. You're uptight now. More so than usual. Bet if I asked you to dance, you'd make an excuse not to."

"My shoes are wet with cosmopolitan."

"See?" He grabbed her wrist when she stood and roughly tugged her back to sit by him. "Don't go yet, please? Or is your master here, lurking in the shadows?"

"Is yours?"

His drunken smile cut into her heart. "Touché. As a matter of fact she isn't. I wanted it to be just us tonight. Let's go to my place and watch a movie and make like old times again. Would you like that?"

His eyes were bloodshot; she could tell that even with the red lighting. And he was so pale. He was a vampire. He had to be.

Severo had said he could scent vampires. Bella wished he'd taught her to pick up that distinctive odor.

"Tell me one thing before I decide. And it has to be the truth, Seth. You know I can tell when you're lying."

"Very well, Miss Uptight. What truth do you need?"

"Are you a vampire?"

He smirked and mumbled a lackluster, "No."

Seth always mumbled his lies. God, what had happened to him?

"I've got to go. Bye, Seth." She leaned in and kissed his forehead. This time he let her go and tilted his head toward the dance floor, not even watching her leave.

Bella's feet raced as fast as her heart as she shoved through the club.

Severo was sitting on the passenger side of the Mercedes when she arrived. Bella got in, and before she could sniff away the tear, he reached for her cheek and wiped it away.

"I'm sorry," he said. "It was inevitable."

"At least he won't die now," she murmured. Forced optimism didn't work this time. Gripping the steering wheel, she closed her eyes and tilted her head against the seat. "Is there any way he can change back?"

"Impossible."

What she'd suspected.

"Will you drive home?" she asked.

"Climb over me, sweet, and I'll take you away from this nightmare."

The drive home was quiet. He didn't ask her what she was feeling. Bella sensed he knew her thoughts. She could understand Severo hating vampires now.

Halfway home he took her hand in his and pulled it

onto his thigh. His silent reassurance made her cry. A gift he couldn't realize meant so much to her.

God, she loved this man. She ached for him. She loved him for the compassion he would never admit to possessing. For the domineering spirit that always erred toward protection over humiliation.

And she loved him for his humanity, for the fact that he loved and lived as she did, and was the same as her, except for the one small thing about his ability to shift shapes.

They pulled into the garage, and the radio shut off with the engine. Severo reached to open the door, but she told him to stop.

Bella climbed onto his lap, straddling him, and he inched over to the middle of the seat. She was grateful it was an old car, the kind without a floor shift and with a full front seat.

He found her mouth with a fierce kiss. She moaned into him, releasing the last remnants of sadness and surrendering to the desire that had built during the drive home.

Shucking off her sleeves, she tugged down the front of her dress and lifted her breasts to his mouth. He sucked at each one, again and again, drawing up the intense coil of climax with expert precision. It took no longer than a few minutes before she came, long and loud and crying out in the confines of the car.

"You're mine," he growled.

Bella eyed his fly and he tilted up his hips so she could unzip him. "And you are mine, wolf. I need you now."

"Tell me you want me, then. Where do you want me?"

"Inside me." Yes, she could use his rough language, because she trusted him. "I'm so wet for you."

He sucked in a hissing breath as she fitted herself onto his hardness. They clung together, moving little, for she squeezed him with her muscles, milking him to a fierce and triumphant climax.

This wolf was hers. And though he might think he controlled her, Bella knew otherwise. He was hers to command. And tonight she wanted him to serve her.

Sliding from his lap and lying across the seat, she put her heels on his thigh, pushing him away.

"I want your mouth on me, lover," she said.

Severo opened the door and stretched out his legs. He pulled her hips up and entered her with his tongue.

With her shoulders deep into the seat and her heels on his broad, muscled back, it didn't take Bella long to find the stars a second time.

Chapter 14

Bella's shoulders hit the wall, her arms stretched above her head. Her lover clasped her wrists, pinning her roughly. His greedy smile thrilled her. Every part of her was hot and wet for him.

He dove for her jaw, nipping along it up to her ear, where he sucked in the lobe. His erection ground against her bare thigh. He was naked, too, and had been since that afternoon, when they'd started making love.

Tomorrow night the moon would be full. Which meant tonight it was waxing and the werewolf would come out if it was not kept at bay with sex. This was a challenge Bella met eagerly.

"I've said it before," she murmured as his kiss found her mouth. "You like it rough."

"You do, too, sweet."

"Your strength is an aphrodisiac."

She tried to wriggle her wrists from his hold. It was

loose, but she didn't want to be set free. The faux containment only made her more eager to satisfy his insatiable desires.

"Someday, sweet," he whispered in the harsh growl that accompanied his frenzied quest for sex, "I will bind you with ribbons and fall on my knees to worship you."

"I'd like that."

"Bella, my sweet, you own me. Know that."

He lifted her by the thighs and fitted her onto him. It was a slow, sure glide as he found a familiar position deep inside her. He pounded into her, with one hand at her hip, the other holding her hands against the wall. His determination was fierce, the fire in his dark eyes intent.

With a growl, he bent his head to suck in one of her nipples. He tugged at it, not biting hard—he never would—but his technique matched the force of his need for climax. He'd already come half a dozen times, as had she. Wrapped in each other's arms, they vacillated between urgency and a sweet, lazy lingering.

The clock struck midnight. So long as he kept making love to her, the werewolf would not show.

By now, sated and achy, Bella could no longer sense when orgasm neared. Instead it attacked without volition, ripping through her core and forcing out her pleasure in an unabashed cry. She dug her fingernails into his shoulders, which were already raw from her fantastic struggles.

"Yes," he hissed.

She dug in deep, sure she would draw blood, but knowing the wolf could take it.

Swinging his arms, he laid her on the bed and

pounced upon her as she floated down from the climax. He was randy and frisky, like a puppy eager to play all day long. The more sex they had, the more alive and vigorous he grew. Bella sensed she would collapse from exhaustion soon. But what a delicious collapse.

Severo reached for the water pitcher Bella had placed near the bed hours earlier and drank right from it. Water glistened down his chest and splattered Bella's stomach.

"It's still cold," she said in surprise. "Share some of that with me, lover."

He dove in to kiss her, his mouth filled with cool water. It trickled out the sides of her mouth, and some she swallowed. Drinking from him, she giggled. He slashed his tongue across hers, performing a dance they both knew well.

Every touch stirred her. Every look devastated her. Every time he withdrew from her, she died a little, only to be resurrected when he entered her.

He nuzzled his bearded chin under her jaw, tickling her roughly. "Getting tired?"

"Not if the werewolf has in mind to make an appearance."

"I think you're close to putting it off," he replied.

"Really? I don't believe that. You're not near being sated. You could do this all week, couldn't you?"

"With you, sweet, I could. Once more?" he said with such enthusiasm, Bella laughed and tugged him down on top of her.

She didn't get to sleep until six in the morning.

Tonight was the night. He'd known Bella two months. He loved her. She loved him. When he'd asked her to have sex with him to keep away the werewolf, she'd gladly done so. Even when he'd known she was exhausted last night, she'd kept at it, stroking him, teasing him to another and yet another orgasm. The woman was a marvel.

But now the true test of both his and her love would be put to them.

Could Bella love the werewolf?

Rather—and more important—could the werewolf accept a human mate?

Dropping his shirt on the flagstone patio, Severo hissed in a breath as Bella embraced him from behind. Kisses down the back of his neck and spine ignited his libido. Not that it needed jump-starting. He'd been frenzied with her in bed this morning. It was as if the werewolf sensed that tonight would be its turn.

All his life he'd had to deny the werewolf's instinctual needs. He'd become accustomed to riding out that ache for what was missing, content to serve his werewolf's needs in other ways, through hunting and racing the moon through the night.

Was it really about to happen tonight?

The idea humbled him. Maybe he asked too much of Bella? She could be agreeing just to please him. Not that Bella did anything simply to please him.

"Are you sure about this?" he asked over his shoulder.

"I want to meet the werewolf." She slid a hand around his waist and stroked him over his pants, toying with the zipper.

"The werewolf will want to do more than meet." His

erection pulsed for attention, but he would not have her now. Not yet.

"I know. You've prepared me."

"But *are* you prepared? I don't wish to harm you, Bella, and I will not. As I've said, I'm not completely myself when I'm the werewolf."

"The werewolf wouldn't harm a potential mate, would it?"

"No, but I can't imagine…"

How the beastly part of him perceived a human woman. It was the most dreadful thought, and yet it focused him and made him more eager to call down the moon.

He knew that some of his breed took humans as mates, and had sex with them. When in werewolf form he was mostly shaped like a man, with arms, legs, torso, rib cage and a penis—but with a wolfish head and shoulders. And fur, lots of fur. But he'd never spoken to a single werewolf who had had a successful long-term relationship with a human.

They were a lonely breed, forced to find satisfaction with human females, which was never the ultimate mating.

"I'll be fine," she offered from behind him.

Bella's delicate embrace would never fit around the werewolf's torso; he knew that much. God, he didn't want to scare her away from him forever.

"Maybe we should wait until next month."

"Who's more afraid?"

"I am." He hugged her, pressing her head to the base of his neck. Her skin smelled of cloves, along with wine and the strawberries Heloise had left in the fridge for them. "I admit it, Bella. I'm terrified about the shifting tonight."

"Does it hurt?"

"No." He kissed her hair. "The werewolf instinctively knows it'll be allowed to come up to the house. I can't do this."

"You can and you must. I want to know all of you, Severo. Isn't this what you want? Besides, if the wolf could romp around with a cat, then I think I'll survive."

He knew she meant Aby. "That was different." The werewolf hadn't had sex with the cat, nor would it have considered such a vile act. In fact, his werewolf had rarely gone near Aby. "Bella, it burns in my heart to worry about you."

"Then don't." She kissed his chest, gliding her fingers through the fine hairs. When she snuck her fingers under his waistband to toy with him, the swollen head of his erection bulged, desiring release.

The worst part of it all? He wouldn't recall what went on tonight between the werewolf and Bella.

Could he be jealous of himself?

"The sun's almost set," she said. "Are you going to… stick around here?"

"No, I'm off. I'll return. If you get frightened or change your mind, don't hesitate to lock yourself in the house."

He clutched her arms, lifting her to her tiptoes. "Promise me you'll not put up a brave front?"

Her mouth tasted like strawberries. Never would he tire of her kisses. He would die fighting an army of vampires for another of Bella's kisses.

"Promise," she whispered, and he swallowed her

sweet strawberry breath. He'd take that part of her into the wilds tonight.

And pray the werewolf did not steal her breath forever.

As the clock struck twelve, Bella sighed. She sat on a wicker chair, dangling her bare feet over the grass where it met the patio flagstone. Her white silk nightgown did little to protect her from the chill in the air. It was late September, a cool night, instead of the Indian summer she'd wished for. A sweater sounded great, but she hadn't yet brought her winter clothes over from the loft.

She tugged the terry-cloth towel from the chair and wrapped it around her shoulders.

The canine howls in the distance soared across the horizon, as if the animal paced, unsure which way to go. She couldn't know if it was her lover, but her heart sensed that it was.

Was the wolf unsure? Or was Severo so focused on maintaining control that even in wolf form he exerted enough influence to intimidate that part of himself that he referred to as the werewolf? What form was he in right now? Was he the caninelike wolf or the man-wolf creature?

Anticipation kept her awake. She wasn't fearful in the least. Okay, maybe a little.

More than a little.

She'd met the wolf. Despite her fear of dogs, she'd handled it remarkably.

But tonight? This was like an introduction to the last part of a man she loved, the one part of him he kept hidden from others. The core of him.

He wanted to share this part with her, to have her know him completely. She understood how difficult it was for Severo to do this. He couldn't know what his werewolf would do to her.

And how would she react? Would it be as that night when she'd first been chased by vampires? She'd fled out of fear of what she'd seen. And that had merely been fangs.

"Be brave," she coached. "He is your lover."

She would look at Severo, no matter how beastly he appeared. He'd explained to her that all the important parts were still like those of a man, though his head and shoulders sort of wolfed out. She'd not watched many werewolf movies to know what to expect. But then, coming to this with an open mind and no expectations was best.

If he wanted her, she would give herself freely, no matter what it entailed. She trusted him that much.

Standing and pressing her feet into the cool grass, she closed her eyes. The night surrounded her with clean, heady air and a hint of sap from the maple trees. The last lingering hedge roses released a surprisingly sweet aroma. She spread out her arms, and a breeze tickled her beneath the thin silk, sending shivers across her flesh and raising goose bumps.

And then the world changed.

An animal noise pierced the darkness. Not quite a growl. More a throaty murmur.

Bella stepped out a few paces. The house loomed twenty feet to her left, and the hedgerow six feet behind. Lush grass blades speared her toes.

Eyes closed, she could feel a presence. Not human. Feral, perhaps. Predatory, yet cautious.

Brisk air cut her cheek. She started but knew better than to make a sudden movement.

She heard the sound of a great weight crushing the grass, limbs bending, stretching out, sharp and clear. Were they feet or…paws?

Breath spilled hotly over her shoulder. Bella turned abruptly.

The dark shadow cringed but did not flee. She couldn't immediately make it out in the shadow of the maple tree, but it was big. It breathed heavily, panting like an animal.

It had to be four heads higher than her, and its shoulders, silhouetted against the pale brick house, were wide. It was not a man, though it stood on its hind legs and long, muscular hands hung near its muscled thighs. The chest was wide yet deep.

It was too dark to make out details and the fur was black, so while she knew it wore no clothes, she couldn't see anything below the waist.

A glint of talon caught her eye as the werewolf approached. It bared its teeth and shook its head, which ruffled the thick dark mane from head to neck. Not like a man there. The face of a wolf peered at her.

When she thought a scream imminent, Bella realized it smelled her. It read her as Severo so often did, trying to figure her out.

Drawing back her shoulders, she closed her eyes and allowed the curiosity. She understood its world was navigated by scent.

Severo had said the werewolf had on only a few occasions encountered humans. He sensed his werewolf had feared them and hadn't gotten too close.

But it seemed at ease now, if that was what she could call the sniffing. Perhaps it simply knew it was at the top of this short food chain.

If it smelled her fear, would that excite it as that did her lover? Or make it aggressive and her position perilous?

She trembled as she stood before the werewolf. And yet, her fear did not prevail. Rather, the atmosphere felt…provocative. And, dare she say, safe?

Maybe. She dared to believe it.

The werewolf came closer.

Bella exhaled and her heartbeats slowed. Sudden calm lifted her courage.

Curious, she put out her hand, as she had to the smaller version, to allow it to sniff. Which it did.

Thick black fur covered its head, shoulders and chest. Though the rest of the body was dark, almost black, its torso was lighter. It was colored like the fully furred wolf.

"Severo?" she said softly.

The werewolf opened its jaws to expose teeth. Longer than vampires' teeth, and so many more of them, all sharp.

Severo had said nothing about it biting her. Would it bite?

A reedy moan escaped her, and Bella pressed her fingers to her mouth, holding it back.

She could do this. This was *her lover.* A man who loved her. This werewolf, this creature, if it had wanted to harm her, would have done so by now.

Suddenly it stretched out its massive bulk and howled. The night air echoed with the coarse, low-range howl. In the distance a few short yips answered. Was it a real wolf fearing the cry of what it knew was something larger and stronger than itself?

And when it lowered its head to look at her, Bella stared into a fierce gaze. *His* clear brown eyes. Looking into her. Seeing her.

"I love you," she said firmly. "I'm not afraid of you."

She put out a hand to touch its muzzle, but it jerked away from the shaky touch. "Sorry. I'm new to this. Not sure what to do."

Another howl silenced her. It must want her to be quiet. She could do that.

Her legs shook, threatening to bring her down. Bella focused on inhaling deeply and exhaling slowly. The scent of roses was so heady, she thought she might be drunk.

Wobbling, Bella did fall backward, catching herself with her elbows on the soft grass. It was like a half faint. She wasn't so much embarrassed as relieved to not have to stand on her weak legs any longer.

The werewolf reached down with a clawed hand yet did not touch, only lingered above her stomach. It was more a hand than a paw. Longer than anything human, yet finely boned and articulated, with a tuft of fur on the knuckles.

It studied her so intensely, she felt sure it must be struggling with Severo's interior warnings while it wanted to meet its own purposes.

Mating.

A talon slashed before her so quickly, Bella hadn't realized what the werewolf had done. Until the front of her nightgown fell open, exposing her breasts and stomach.

The werewolf growled lowly. She understood it as a gentle growl, perhaps approving. As Severo did so often while they made love and after he'd climaxed. The werewolf pressed a hand to her shoulder and she winced.

I'm not ready for this.

Then again, how could anyone be ready for this?

"So what's next?" she said, forcing a casual tone. "First dates are always so awkward, aren't they?"

The werewolf sniffed her face. Its fur brushed her chin as it moved lower, lingering over her breasts and down her stomach, till it sniffed at her sex.

Claws pricked her hip, but briefly. At the werewolf's touch, she turned over onto her stomach. She understood what it wanted.

Rising onto all fours, she flinched as a heavy hand hit the grass next to her and its torso touched her back.

The claiming had been quick, frantic. Once satisfied, the werewolf had loped off across the valley. The silhouette of her masterful beast had crested the hill and transformed itself into its smaller wolf size. It returned, loping up like a playful puppy and lowering its head to nuzzle her open palms.

Now she curled against the wolf's soft fur and snuggled up to it in the thicket of grass. The night had grown quiet. No longer did the ferocious huffs and grunts from the beastly werewolf echo in the air. Nor did she feel it inside her, moving so quickly she couldn't keep track of how many times she'd orgasmed along with the werewolf.

Initially, it had been frightening.

The first time it entered her, her body had ached.

And then, everything had changed. The werewolf had not spoken or looked into her eyes, for she'd remained in the doggy-style position. Yet, as it had taken her, Bella had forgotten it was the werewolf and had known only that Severo, the man she loved, was inside her.

Severo woke in the grass and jerked abruptly to a stand. Bella lay on the matted grass in a torn nightgown, her dark hair strewn across the grass blades. Sunshine toyed with her toes. Dirt and grass streaks marked the tattered white silk and her palms and knees.

"The werewolf did it," he said, not sure what exactly he felt.

Horrified? A little. And shocked. But surprised? No, the werewolf had been waiting for decades.

He was also worried for Bella's well-being. What the hell had she been put through last night? Would she be mentally scarred from this?

He reached out to touch her, but his nakedness suddenly felt so overt. He called her name, but she didn't rouse.

Forgoing running inside for clothes, he lifted her into his arms. She slept soundly as he carried her inside to the bedroom and as he laid her on the rumpled white sheets, she woke and smiled at him.

She grasped his hand and pulled him to sit beside

her. When he wanted to ask her if she was all right, she put her fingers over his mouth.

"I love the werewolf," she said, and closed her eyes and fell to sleep.

Must be something about having sex with a werewolf that'll put a shine to a girl's smile. Bella posed before the floor-length mirror, turning from side to side to check the brown jersey dress that hugged her curves.

She had showered and hadn't yet seen Severo. She figured he might feel strange about approaching her today. He shouldn't.

Stepping into her low-heeled mules, she sought breakfast.

Heloise was off for the three days, so she scavenged a kiwi and a banana and cut them on a plate. An English muffin would hit the spot, but she couldn't find any. Oat toast it was. The guy was into fiber and meat.

From around the corner Severo appeared. Rather, he lingered, like he was unsure about approaching her. He was clad in dark running pants and no shirt, and his tight six-pack drew Bella's eye. Head bowed and thumb to his lip, he looked up through his lashes at her.

"Come here, lover," she urged him.

"I…" He remained in the doorway, the sunlight upon his shoulders. He rubbed the heels of his palms together. "I didn't harm you, did I?" He winced as he said it.

"You did not. Besides being well and thoroughly sexed. But that never harmed a girl before."

"The werewolf had sex with you?"

"Yes. You don't remember?"

"You know I can't." He slid onto a bar stool across the counter from her.

All she wanted to do was hug and kiss him and show him how much he meant to her, but she sensed his apprehension and would allow him this slow approach. He had to struggle with the right and wrong of it. He was that kind of man.

"Do you want details?"

He winced again. "Not sure. Was it…terrible?"

"Not at all. You're magnificent as the werewolf, Severo. All muscles and growl."

"You weren't horrified?"

"Honestly? A little scared at the beginning. Okay, a lot scared. But the werewolf was gentle."

"Really?" He let out a breath.

"As gentle as it could be. I don't have any scratches or bruises. I checked. I want to do it again," she said.

"Y-you do? Should I be jealous?"

She slid around the counter and climbed onto his lap. Spreading her palms across his chest, she nipped his lower lip. "It's the same guy. One's a lot more intense than the other, and not as handsome."

"You think the werewolf's hideous, don't you?"

"Not at all. Just not as cute as you. There's no competition over whom I'd pick from looks alone. Besides, the werewolf has back hair."

"You make light of everything."

"Severo, it's fine. The werewolf and I got along, and we had sex like bunnies."

"Like bunnies? I don't want to know. Yes, I do. Did you…enjoy it?"

She nodded. "Might be achy today, but that's nothing given all the orgasms."

"Christ, how many?"

"Maybe you're better off not knowing some things."

"Tell me, Bella."

"I stopped counting after six."

He huffed out a breath. Then he laughed and kissed her. "You're cool with it, really?"

"I think you've got yourself a mate, lover."

Chapter 15

She did need a rest from sex after three days and nights of endless passion.

Heck, a girl could only take so much pleasure. Seriously. So tonight Severo ran Bella a hot bath and sprinkled rose petals from the hedges out back in the water. He lit candles and left her to soak.

He spoiled her. Was it guilt at subjecting her to the werewolf's overwhelming sexual needs? Bella hoped he'd get over that. She could handle it. On the other hand, being spoiled was nothing to complain about.

Blowing a handful of bubbles through the air, she settled into the water and closed her eyes.

Life had a way of tossing you the good stuff, then pulling the rug out from under your feet when you least expected.

It was after Severo overheard Bella talking to Seth

that he fisted his hand and put it right through the Sheetrock.

Bella hurried out from the bedroom, eyed the hole and his fist. "I know he's up to something this time. I'm not stupid. He wants me to come to a party."

"Elvira will be there, as well as other vampires."

"I know. I told him I couldn't come." Her cell phone rang again, and Bella stared at the screen. "Seth's number. I thought I'd made myself clear."

"Let me talk to him."

"No." She hit the answer button. "Seth, I said I didn't want to come."

Severo heard the female voice over the phone and tore it from Bella's grip. "Elvira, what the hell are you up to?"

The vampiress laughed.

"I warned you about starting this with me," he said. "If you want a war, you got it."

"Then let the games begin," she snarled. "You can start by retrieving the head of your bitch's dead friend. I've already put the body out in the sun, but you know the new ones take so long to ash."

Severo sucked in a breath. Bella stood beside him, intently watching his face.

"It's not about them anymore, is it?"

"It never was," the vampiress said. "It's been so long since we've dallied, Severo. I look forward to the match this time. Oh, I've such plans!"

The phone clicked off and Bella took it from him. Severo swung around and punched the wall again. And again.

"What did she say? Would you stop tearing the house apart? Is Seth okay? What's going on?"

"Stay back, sweet." He rubbed his knuckles. "This isn't the time."

"It is if it's about my friend. Where is he?"

"It's between me and Elvira now."

"What does that mean?"

"He's dead," he snapped. He should not be so cruel, but he had never been one to couch the truth in euphemisms. "She killed him out of spite. It's me she's been after this whole time. She wants to twist the knife as deeply as it will go."

"Seth is dead? B-but I just talked to him."

Bella's body wavered. Severo caught her as she collapsed against his chest.

"Bella, I'm sorry." His world had finally caught up to hers. It wasn't fair.

"Why is it you?" she asked. Her wide green eyes sought the truth from his. "What did you do to her?"

She deserved the truth, and she'd get it.

"Seventy years ago, I killed her family. She owes me this."

"You've killed? You said you'd never…"

Yes, he'd told her he'd not harmed humans. Unless it was necessary. And those deaths had been necessary. It had been too long since he'd thought of that time in his life. The memory filled his nose with an acrid odor.

"But Seth means nothing to you. Why would she go after him?"

"In war one always kills off friends, family and loved ones first. That's how it works."

"What? But that means—"

"She'll come after you next."

Bella's shoulders shook. She rubbed her arms, attempting to fight off the shivers. He had frightened her and her fear scent filled him with shame. He shouldn't have said anything. But not telling her would have blemished the trust he had earned so far.

She settled at the edge of the couch. Severo touched her hair tentatively. He wanted to take her in his arms and make the world go away. To make it all better.

He fisted his fingers. That power was not in his hands.

"So," she said softly, so faint he had to lean in to hear, "you killed her family?"

"Her brother and father."

Sitting on the couch, he pulled her lithe body onto his. She tucked her head into his neck and cuddled as he wrapped his arms about her. He wanted to be a safe harbor for her, but he feared her trip down the rabbit hole was only just beginning.

"Before Elvira—Evie—had blooded her teeth, her family used to hunt werewolves. At one time, in the nineteen fifties, the United States had a bounty on all wolves. Paid something like a dollar a pelt. The nation went into a hunting frenzy."

"Mortals hunted you?"

"No, they hunted the real wolves. Mortals were—and are, for the most part—unaware of our breed. But noting the hunting frenzy, the vampires took it upon themselves to hunt werewolves. They didn't get paid for the pelts, but it didn't matter. It was for the thrill of the hunt. They captured my parents."

He had to swallow, to digest this cruel memory,

which he'd thought to press back, far from reach. It hurt in his heart to recall it, as if the steel trap crushed his muscles all over again.

Bella's fingers played across his chest. So fragile. And yet she was far stronger than him, for she had stood boldly before his werewolf.

"Do you know what happens when a werewolf is skinned?"

"You don't have to tell me if it hurts."

It would wound him far worse to keep his secrets from the woman he loved.

"I stood at the edge of the vampire encampment after following my parents' scents for miles. They were dead, strung up by their heels alongside a wood cabin with half a dozen other werewolf pelts. It takes only a few hours, though, before a werewolf transforms itself into a were."

Bella's gasp heated his chest. He clutched her, clinging, stopping his own tears only through force of will.

"I fled at the sight. I knew I had to protect myself. And yet I ran right into a trap. A bear trap clamped about my left ankle."

"That's why you limp."

"Yes, the bone never did heal right. They took me into captivity. I vowed that if I ever escaped, I would kill the men who had done this to my family."

"And Evie? Was it her family who did this to you?"

"Yes. Yet Evie's father was a mortal. The father took vampires for lovers and there were a few witches who served the family. They used their ability to tame us wolves as a power magnet for vampires. There would be days they'd set the vampires on us for fun. To torture us."

"Oh my God."

"It was Evie who asked that my life be spared when her father wanted to force me to shift and skin me alive. She begged for a plaything. I…knew she favored me, but she also couldn't understand that freedom was what I most wanted. I played along, bending to her desires, allowing her to think she was seducing me, preparing me to be the one who blooded her fangs."

"She bit you?"

"No. She didn't get the chance."

He cupped Bella's chin and held her as a most precious thing. He'd been given one more chance to have goodness in his life after Aby. He didn't want to lose it. But she needed to know everything.

"Weres come into their werewolf at puberty. The young ones are always the most difficult to control as the new skills of shifting are honed. Because of my uncontrollable rages, I was able to escape. I killed both the father and his vampire son, and left Evie crying on the porch of their home.

"I ran into her years later. Still she professed a pining love for me. I had never had anything but disgust for her and her family, yet, though I did not admit it to her, I was grateful to her for sparing my life. Still, I spurned her. She vowed revenge, which I deserved." He exhaled, tracking the swift beats of his heart in his throat. "So, yes, Bella, I have killed."

"You were only avenging your family. I can't imagine seeing your parents being tortured like that. You poor man."

He snarled. "It's been over seven decades. I take care of myself. Those who think to threaten my peace, or my former pack, have only to answer to the werewolf. Evie has every right to pursue a vengeance she holds to be just—but Seth was a cruel blow."

"He had no idea what he'd gotten into. Oh, Severo, what will happen now?"

"She's not coming after me directly. And that means she's playing a very dangerous game. I will protect you with my life, Bella. But I'd feel better if we spent some time teaching you how to handle a few weapons."

"I think that would be good."

Her desire to learn defense surprised him. Truly, she was as strong a mate as a wolf could wish to have.

The man actually had an arsenal in the storage room behind the garage. She was surprised only because it was so huge, not because he had one.

Bella lingered in the open doorway as Severo strode before the shelves and counters, selecting a few throwing stars and tucking them in the pocket of his leather jacket, hooking what looked like a medieval mace over his arm. He paused before a wall of pistols and rifles.

Over his shoulder, he grinned at her. A boy with his toys.

Last night had been sweet. She hugged herself at the memory of the quiet darkness and his soft breaths as they'd lain in bed. No sex, just tender kisses, strokes. Mostly they'd spooned into one another. They hadn't needed words.

After hearing how Severo had witnessed his parents' cruel deaths, Bella believed any vengeance he had taken had been just.

Now, more than ever, she wanted to meet Elvira.

"Bitch," Bella muttered.

"What's that?" He approached her with an armload of interesting weapons.

"Just thinking about what I'm going to say to the mistress of the night when I finally meet her."

He nodded as they exited, and pulled the door locked behind them. They headed outside. Crisp fall air necessitated that Bella wear a jacket, and she'd pulled her hair behind her head in a ponytail. All business. She wanted to learn.

"If all goes well," Severo said, "you'll never see Elvira. I want that bitch's head on a platter with as little collateral damage as possible. My grievance is only with her. Though, if any of those vampires who chased you are still alive, I'll take their heads, too."

They strode across the backyard and through a rusted iron gate that led them through the ten-foot-wide hedgerow and out to the valley. The hill was clean of trees and cut a sharp line against the overcast sky.

Though it was the beginning of October, Bella guessed it would probably snow soon. She liked winter. But it would be colder this year without Seth to share a fall hayride or pumpkin carving.

She sniffed at a tear. Severo noticed, but he didn't say anything. She loved him for his ability to let her feel, to let her have a good crying jag if that was what she needed.

And that he'd softened and let himself feel last night, during his confession, meant the world to her. He hadn't cried, but Bella figured that letting down his defenses was probably the closest he'd get to an emotional breakdown.

He laid the weapons on the ground and picked up a huge pistol and showed it to Bella. "It's a big one, but it's your best protection against a longtooth."

"You've not talked at all about your breed." She made herself use his terminology. "Are all vampires and werewolves enemies?"

"Most. The vamps have difficulty stepping down from their self-imposed pedestals. They don't play well with others. Just ask the witches."

"Why? What did they do to the witches?"

"Enslaved them. Drained them of their magic. So much so that centuries ago witches created a master spell that made their blood poisonous to the vampires."

"Clever."

"Indeed. The spell was broken a few years back. The vampires and witches have come to an agreement. The one vampire I can tolerate is actually married to a witch."

"How does that work? If her blood was once poisonous?"

"Very careful sex? He's a phoenix, actually. If a vampire survives a witch's blood attack, he becomes indestructible. Anyway, the wolves get along with the witches for the most part. Here."

With both hands she took the pistol by the handle, and it still dropped heavily. "This must weigh ten pounds. I've never seen a gun with such a big spinning thingy before."

He cast her an incredulous look, wincing against the

sunlight. "You've never touched a weapon in your life, have you, sweet?"

"Nope. But I'm willing to learn. What are those?"

He displayed a bulletlike object before him. "Bullets made of Brazilian ironwood, one of the hardest woods available. Shoot one of these directly at the vamp's heart. It won't take the longtooth out, but it will set it back and give you time to reload or use something more powerful, like a thick, heart-exploding stake."

She examined the wooden bullet. A cross had been burned into the flat, round end of it. "And I'm supposed to be able to aim this thing long and sure enough to hit the target, which is likely coming at me at Mach speed, with fangs bared?"

"Exactly."

Severo placed a few wooden bullets in the chamber and spun it into place for her. Demonstrating a good grip, he helped her to hold the pistol properly with both hands.

"Longtooths, eh?" she said. "A nasty word for vamps?"

"You bet."

"What do they call you?"

"If they're smart, they run. If they have a death wish, they call me dog."

"Oh." Wincing, she offered him an apology, remembering how she'd jokingly called him dog and other derogatory terms when they'd first gotten together. "Sorry."

He kissed her cheek. "Call me what you wish, sweet. Just don't stop calling me. Now hold it up and aim."

"At what? The tree?"

"That's too far. You've only about fifty feet with

one of these things. Hmm, what could you shoot at? We need to see if you can hit something, and it should be moving.... How about me?"

"No!"

"Oh, yes." He stepped back, his arms held out in challenge. "Wood isn't going to kill me. It will just smart a little. Aim for my shoulder or a leg. Not the face. I may be a dog, but I don't need any more scars."

"Severo, there's no way I'm going to shoot you. You said you aren't immortal!"

"That's right."

She lowered the pistol. "Then why can't you be killed?"

"I've explained. Silver is the only thing that does it."

He splayed out his hands and walked backward. His dark brown eyes twinkled menacingly.

Bella dangled the pistol with both hands. It knocked her knees. "Come back here, please, Severo. I'll try for a bird that flies overhead or something."

He shed the leather jacket as he swiftly increased the distance between them. When he was hundreds of yards away, he turned and charged her.

"I'm not doing it. I'll miss and hit you in the eye! What if I hit you in the brain? You'll be a brain damaged wolf who can't die and is crazed for sex!"

"Do it, bitch!"

He was trying to rile her. She wouldn't fall for it.

A toothy snarl and suddenly the man racing toward her became something clsc. Bigger, hairier, more monstrous.

The werewolf.

Which she thought she loved. But she'd never seen it in daylight and—

Bella squeezed the trigger. The pistol didn't make a noise. The wooden bullet exited with a forceful kick that tugged at her shoulder sockets. She dropped both hands down, following the bullet's trajectory.

The werewolf took the bullet without flinching. Yet it stopped charging her, digging its feet into the ground and spinning about with a leap and a running dart up the hill, away from her.

"I hit him. Oh, no, I didn't mean it. Severo!"

When it had crested the hill, the silhouette shifted and took on the were shape. It happened so quickly, and he didn't shed any skin, or anything creepy like that.

Clothing lay abandoned on the ground forty feet away. He'd shed his shirt and pants as he'd changed, which meant he was now naked.

And likely wounded.

He ran down the hill, gaining on Bella with supernatural speed.

"There you go, sweet." He pressed the flesh on his shoulder and popped out the short wooden bullet. Blood oozed down his pale flesh.

"Oh my God, you're bleeding. I really hit you. I could have taken out an eye!" Bella wailed.

"Or rendered me brain damaged."

"You bastard!" She shoved the pistol against his chest and stomped away. "Don't ever do that to me again. You know I love the werewolf!"

"Yes, but you were frightened of it just now."

"Because I've never seen it during the day. I didn't

know you could change like that. I thought it was only during the full moon."

"Surprised?"

She rounded on him, but the boldness of him standing there, bleeding and naked and strangely apologetic, messed with her need to remain angry.

"Come look, Bella. Please, it's fine."

She'd done it. She'd fired a weapon at another being. And if she could fire it at someone she loved, then she could sure as hell fire it at some bitch of a vampire who wanted her dead.

The creep had done this for her own good, and damn it, she was thankful for it.

"Let me see." She stalked up to her lover, but by the time she touched his shoulder, the wound had already closed. She wiped away a streak of blood. "That's cool."

"I promise that'll be the only time I ask you to hurt me."

"Did it hurt?"

"'Course it did." He kissed her. "About as much as this might hurt you."

He pinched her nipple and she jumped, slapping at him playfully. "Stop it, or I'll try the throwing stars on you next."

He caught her and swung her over one arm, dipping her into a dramatic kiss that would have made a silverscreen rogue jealous. "You make it so difficult to be serious sometimes, sweet. I like that about you. You allow me to remember what it's like to just be."

"Have you ever laughed for the heck of it?"

"Yes, many times."

"With Aby." He nodded, and she decided that someday she was going to have to meet that enigma of a woman. "Okay, what's next, naked werewolf dude?"

"Another kiss right—" he tugged up her shirt and bent to her stomach "—here."

And with more and more kisses, and the quick removal of her clothes, the weaponry lesson was postponed for a few hours.

Chapter 16

They strode at Severo's quick pace through the marble hallway, checking windows and verifying security codes. Bella knew the routine, but she sensed it gave him greater peace of mind to do this than it did her. She trusted she would be safe, no matter what occurred, so long as Severo was here to protect her.

Not for a moment did she honestly believe she could wield that monster of a pistol, especially with a snarling vampire approaching.

If it came to that.

It was hard to imagine the war Severo sensed was brewing. One person had died. And while Seth was a sad loss, Bella couldn't see the matter escalating to gangs of vampires versus werewolves.

Not that she'd seen other werewolves. Severo was a loner who had left his pack years earlier. He'd said the packs were slimming down and seeking shelter in the northern areas of Canada and Europe. The werewolves were not particularly social creatures, which didn't surprise Bella, considering what she knew of Severo.

"And the security code is four-nine-zero-eight-five-two," she repeated by rote when he looked to her.

The code increased by twelve with each door, starting with the front door, then the garage doors, the side doors, the patio door and various other exits. The windows were all on one central control, activated with a push of a button in the bedroom or kitchen.

"But you said the protection wards would be the first line of defense, anyway, right? What are protection wards, anyway?"

"They're magical shields, so to speak, against demons, vampires and other sorts. Designed by a witch for me when I moved in. I can't be too cautious. One never knows what those longtooth bastards have up their sleeves."

"I'm hungry," she grumbled. "I think I've got it. Let's see what Heloise has cooking."

He grabbed her about the wrist with his usual forceful squeeze, but a second later he let up. "Bella, you're not taking this seriously."

"I shot you and you don't think I'm taking this seriously? Severo, this *is* a lot to take in."

"You accepted vampires and weres easily enough. Why is it so difficult to want to survive?"

"I want to survive," she said on a surprised gasp. "I love you. I want to spend more time with you. As long as I can. Forever, or for the rest of your three-hundred-some years. I don't want to die, but… Just let me handle this my way, okay?"

"Yes. Sorry." Occupied with security, he wouldn't come down from the command mode for a bit.

He strode off toward the kitchen.

She followed, loving his no-nonsense gait, fierce and solid despite the slight hitch in the left leg—due to being caught in a trap. A tear pooled in her eye when she imagined her lover suffering.

It was a good reason to hold a grudge against the longtooths.

"So tell me," Bella said as Heloise motioned for them to sit and wait for the dinner she was plating, "if you're not immortal, then do you just drop dead at the big three hundred?"

Now more relaxed, he dragged her onto his lap in what had become their favorite chair to sit in and snuggle and make out. Bella pushed a thick hank of his hair over his shoulder and laid her head at his collar, where the heat of his blood brewed a delicious man scent.

"I'm guessing at the three hundred number." He skated a palm along her bare leg, inching up her skirt, but not so high that it was inappropriate in front of Heloise. "Weres can live hundreds of years. I think the oldest was around three hundred twenty-five."

"I can't imagine a life so long. It would be amazing."

"I was born in 1935. I'm still but a pup, I guess. Though there are days I feel I've lived these nine decades and died a thousand times over."

She palmed his abdomen under the brown sweater, which matched his eyes, and snuggled closer. "What's going to happen with us? I'm not getting any younger. And you certainly don't want to be dating an old woman in another five decades."

"You can't imagine how good that makes me feel when you speak of us in terms of decades, sweet. Doesn't matter how old or wrinkled you become. I'll always love you."

"Oh, please. When I'm eighty, and you're still looking like a sexy thing, you can't tell me I'll appeal to you. And when I die...?"

"I will wish to go with you."

"Don't say that, Severo. Maybe we should just concentrate on the now."

"You will always have my heart, Bella. Never forget that. It is yours. You stole it from me months ago, and I shouldn't wish it back."

The clink of a plate clued them in that Heloise had served the meal. She was respectful of the two of them and left the room to tend to household chores.

"Smells delicious," Bella said.

"Salmon, I think."

"I mean you." She licked under his chin, where his trimmed beard was sensitive to the slick touch of her tongue. "She won't come back in now. How about a quickie before we eat?"

"And you call me insatiable." His hand drove up her thigh and cupped her derriere. "Unzip me, sweet, and hop on for a ride."

Three weeks later...as the full moon mastered the sky, the werewolf sought its mate three nights in a row. Bella had learned to wear nothing but a robe, because otherwise the visits always entailed shredded silk and sometimes tangled limbs.

If she thought about what she was doing—with a

werewolf—all sorts of moral and rational arguments could be conjured.

But she didn't think. She acted with her heart. She made love to Severo, and no matter what his form, at his core, he was a man who loved her and put her above all others.

She'd driven into town earlier that day and found a Realtor to sell her loft. While there, she drove by Seth's place. The small house had already been resold. She knew his parents lived in Florida, and that they had been distant the past three years. They knew her from when she and Seth had danced together in competitions in middle school. She didn't feel the need to contact them. Let them grieve, and hopefully their son's death had been explained to them in terms they could accept, like a car accident.

Not that she expected the coroner's report would list vampire bite as the cause of death.

She wondered now if the death had been reported. The cleaners Severo had called had made efficient work of mopping up the vampires he'd slain in her loft. It was likely that Seth had been erased from this world without a trace.

That thought had reduced her to tears as she'd driven the gravel road out to Severo's mansion.

Sniffing tears and whispering a blessing for her friend, Bella strolled through the marble foyer, calling out for Severo. He usually called to her or appeared at her side to sweep her into a kiss.

"Hmm, must be outside. Heloise?"

The sun was already a glow of red on the horizon. It glinted over the white plastic covering the yard crew had placed over the pool a few weeks ago. A scatter of leaves dotted the taut tarp. They'd had a light dusting of snow a few days ago, but it had melted.

Bella opened the patio door but didn't step outside. The breeze snuck into her pores on a shiver. Wind rushed through the trees, tugging the branches to a rocking-chair creak.

"Maybe he's in the arsenal."

He'd been spending an inordinate amount of time in that storage room to ready the weapons then place them all over the house. He was a one-man gang preparing for a war that Bella still didn't believe would happen.

It disturbed her, but not enough to frighten her.

Had she become complacent with him always close by to protect her? Had she forfeited the control she'd once so staunchly wielded?

"A bit," she said as her heels clicked down the hallway. "But it's worth the sacrifice."

She punched in the security code but found the arsenal dark. Walking inside, she traced her fingers over the monstrous pistol's cold metal barrel.

With a glance she took in the assorted weaponry. Wooden bullets and holy water and gold crosses. A mace, a few swords and dozens of pistols and rifles.

She wondered what weapons the vampires would use against a werewolf. Silver, surely. Probably a silver dagger to pierce the organs and poison the blood.

Another tear dropped onto her thumb and slid cleanly over the pistol's barrel. "Please let us be safe," she whispered.

Something clanked against the steel door.

Bella gripped the handle of the pistol.

* * *

He strode across the hilltop that paralleled his land and plunged into the valley. Land was at a premium here in northern Minnesota, but he wouldn't give his estate up for a sweet little apartment in Paris or a penthouse in New York. He belonged to the land and didn't believe he could survive in a big city for long.

He had been born into this world the minority and was of a species forced to hide and protect itself from discovery. He accepted that. He'd learned to walk amid the shadows and keep to himself. The wilderness, freedom—and Bella—meant happiness.

And now his happiness had been threatened. If Elvira targeted Bella, that would be akin to ripping out his heart and slamming it against a wall.

He would protect his own.

Thinking about shifting to wolf form, he decided against it. He'd been out long enough. Bella was due from the city, and he missed her when he could not scent her nearby.

The air had changed as he'd tracked the boundaries of his property. The world was not right.

Standing upon the pinnacle that looked over his land, Severo stretched out his arms and tilted back his head. Sniffing, he took it all in.

The air touched his fingertips, cheeks and nose, imbuing his senses with a catalog of the now. Nearby a jackrabbit darted for an underground burrow thick with her younglings. Tree roots that stretched dozens of feet underground stirred minutely beneath his boots.

The acrid odor of gasoline, which he rarely sensed so far from the city, now made him turn toward the house. All was quiet. The sun had just set, so he could make out a few lights, one in the kitchen, the other illuminating the recessed window high on the basement-laundry-room wall.

Perhaps Bella hadn't yet returned.

He clasped a hand over his heart and smiled. That he had been given this gift of love did not cease to humble him. When he'd thought he could make a go of it with Aby, he had always known that that was not the direction their relationship was meant to take. Still hurt like hell.

And yet, someone new had laid a bandage over that hurt, and he'd peeled it away to find the wound almost gone. He was ready to forget what might have been and to accept what he already had.

"Love," he murmured and smirked. It was grand.

Starting down the hill, he used the incline to hasten his steps into a run. Halfway across the valley, a force hit Severo on the back of his left shoulder.

He spun. There in the shadows emerged half a dozen vampires.

She pulled the trigger and the heavy pistol kicked, forcing Bella backward against the steel counter. She grunted at the impact. The steel edge dug into her hip.

The hulk of a vampire who filled the arsenal doorway took the wooden bullet in the heart. He clawed at it, but the bullet had penetrated deeply, as intended, and could not be drawn out. One hand ripped the front of his dark shirt. Clawing at his exposed, bleeding flesh, he staggered.

Her thoughts honing, Bella remembered what Severo

had said about the bullets. They'd slow a vampire down but would not kill him.

She eyed the wooden stakes, which hung in militant rows; each stake was twelve inches long and as thick as a chair leg. She reached for one, then another and another. The titanium syringe filled with holy water lay on the table, but her hands were full.

Racing forward, she didn't care that she was a dancer whose greatest achievement was the double *golpe* with spin, or that the first time she'd touched a weapon, she'd almost cried.

Somehow a vampire had breached Severo's protection wards.

"And the freaking security codes," she barked out. How had anyone managed to decipher those?

The vampire struggled with the bullet in his chest and didn't expect a skinny mortal woman to leap at him with a stake held at the ready.

Gripping the one stake firmly while she clutched the other two in her left hand, Bella planted the thick piece of wood in the vampire's chest. It slid in easily. She didn't have to push hard to make it go in up to her curled fist.

The vampire spasmed. Hissing steam escaped from around the stake. The awful smell of burning blood entered her nostrils. Bella scrambled backward, into the open doorway, securing a stake in both fists.

The creature's agonizing yowl filled her ears. She bit her lip and almost called out, "I'm sorry." Jelly legs quivering, she sunk to her knees.

"Please," she begged. The thing staggered and spouted

smoke. It clawed the air, growling. "Just die. Don't come back to life. Where is he? Severo!"

A burst of ash dust filled the air. The vampire disintegrated into a human-shaped heap of gray ash. The stake rolled from the ash over to her knee, blood staining her white slacks.

"I did it," she said, amazed. Was she supposed to be horrified? The dread feeling didn't emerge. Instead, adrenaline pushed her to stand and pump her fist in triumph. "Yes!"

"Think you're quite the slayer, eh, pretty?"

Stake held at the ready for another attack, Bella let out a throaty squeak as she spied the three vampires who blocked off the hallway and any chance of escape.

Chapter 17

Six unarmed vampires? No challenge to him. They'd been going at it for a bit. One vampire would charge, and Severo would strike at his shoulder or deliver a roundhouse and thrust him off him.

He was rolling on the ground now with a snarling beast of a longtooth, its long fangs bared. A bite from a vampire would piss Severo off, but it couldn't change him.

On the other hand, he'd never experienced a vampire bite. It would leave a permanent mark. And that was the last thing Severo wanted on his body. A vamp bite was a stigma he'd never bear.

The longtooth twisted Severo's arm around behind his back and yanked sharply, tearing the muscles. Severo could endure it. He needed a moment to flip and...yes. On his back, he struck his opponent in the chest with his heels and sent him flying.

Darkness had fallen, and the trees were silhouetted against the gray sky. Now two vamps charged him.

"Have at me," Severo muttered.

He could take them. For now. But the werewolf was beginning to rage. Then the stupid bastards had better run.

Surprisingly, none *had* tried to bite him yet. Odd. It was the vampires' best defense, weakening their opponent through blood loss.

What kind of idiots had Elvira sent after him?

And only six? Perhaps she wanted to toy with him. Give him a preview of the war yet to come.

Or maybe she needed to wear him down. The obvious reason was she wanted him alive for something.

He caught a charging vamp about the neck with a vertebra-crunching swing of his own. The vamp yowled, but his partner knocked Severo off balance by kicking his ankles. He hit the ground with a growl. Spitting blood from his mouth, he rolled to all fours and decided the werewolf had been kept at bay long enough.

Three more vampires had been destroyed in the arsenal. Bella couldn't think clearly about how she'd done it. But she now knew that holy water to the eyes was no way to go. The vamp's face had peeled away.

Kicking off her high heels, she ran out as fast as she could, though she had no idea what to do, where to go. Adrenaline sharpened her senses. In the garage, the odor of gasoline seemed to hang in the air. In the house, the smell of the wax Heloise used on the floor rose in invisible waves. And her perfume seemed far too strong.

As she checked the front door, her hands shook and

she dropped the stakes twice. It was locked, completely secure. She stepped back and scanned the three-story foyer. The huge skylight windows lining the upper story were unbroken.

Where had the vampires gotten in? If not through the front door or the garage...

"Heloise." Bella hadn't heard the housekeeper, and surely the commotion would have alerted her. Heloise insisted on using the servants' entrance near the laundry room, much as Severo wished she'd come through the front door. "Heloise!"

She ran for the laundry room, praying the housekeeper had had the sense to hightail it to safety at the first sniff of vampire. Or at least hide.

Bella had no idea if faeries could defeat a vampire, but if they possessed any skill against the threat, she doubted that squat and kind Heloise had the ability to keep back anything larger than a dragonfly.

Hugging the pistol, which was loaded with three wooden bullets, to her chest, she skidded up to the laundry room doorway. And fell to her knees in horror.

A clear, thick substance pooled about Heloise's head. Her throat had been torn out, and it leaked more clear liquid. An unfolded bedsheet, still clenched in her hand, soaked up the stuff.

Reaching out and squelching the need to scream, Bella bent over and gripped her gut. "Don't do this. Be strong."

She examined the brownie's neck. The clear liquid must be faerie blood, because it sparkled. Had to be. "Those bastards. She was an innocent."

Standing, her back skidding across the wall, she

hugged the pistol to her chest and checked both ways down the hallway. It was clear.

"I have to get to Severo."

Nodding, because nothing else made sense at the moment, Bella ran upstairs to the living room.

Where three vampires waited.

"She's mine," growled the tallest, sporting a black Mohawk. A fang glinted brightly at the corner of his mouth. "Secure her!"

Bella fired, but the wooden bullet went astray, missing the vampires and ricocheting against the wall. The picture of Severo and Aby cracked and dropped to the floor.

Two vampires charged, and before she could again squeeze the trigger, the pistol was pulled from her hand. Her shoulders stretched painfully as, one to each side of her, they wrenched her arms behind her back.

"Nice," the Mohawked leader said as he approached. "And brave."

Bella spat at the vampire. In punishment she took a knee to her spine. Pain shot through her skeleton and she yowled.

"Gentle, boys," said the leader. The dark vampire's eyes were pale blue, and the pupils large.

Bella thought, for an odd moment, that his eyes appealed to her. She stopped struggling as he reached out and stroked her hair.

"Severo's mate," he drawled. "She smells like dog, doesn't she?"

The two vampires grunted.

"Let me go, and I won't sic my dog on you," she warned.

"I'm not at all frightened, green eyes," replied the leader.

The vampire loomed over her, his face close to hers, as if to sniff her, as Severo often did. And yet he maintained the stare that Bella could not look away from. Something in his eyes…provocative. Sensual.

"That's right. Look all you like. What do you see in my eyes? Freedom? Pleasure?"

Her mouth dropping open, Bella felt her eyelids flicker. Part of her wanted to kick the vampire in the nuts. He was in the right position. But a bigger part of her wanted to melt, to succumb.

"No, no, don't look away. It's only going to get better, pretty one."

Brilliant white fangs descended over the vampire's lower lip. So pretty. And long. They would sink deeply into her flesh.

And she wanted it.

As he began to shift, and his shoulder bones stretched and his flesh thickened and grew, the whip's icy lash of cold steel wrapped about Severo's biceps. The rigid yet flexible steel locked tightly, scraping the leather jacket. A jerk of the whip brought him to his knees, stopping the shift to werewolf before his human features began to fade.

He gripped the steel lash. It burned, eating through his palm. With a hiss, Severo dropped it. Not steel, but silver. In a flexible whip?

He struggled, but the silver drained his energy. Heaving himself forward, he was thankful for the leather jacket. It kept the silver from touching his flesh, but the whip was sharply edged, so he knew soon it would cut through the jacket.

If he didn't struggle, he could survive this.

The air darkened. Vampires crowded about him. He could not see who held the whip, holding him captive. There were more than a dozen now. All men. Their scents made him want to retch, and he was fast losing strength. Longtooths wielded daggers and pistols, but they weren't pointed at him.

Bella's gorgeous smile flickered in his thoughts. He jerked a look toward the house. More lights were on. She was home? He must hold back these vampires and keep them from her.

Unless they had already gotten to her?

"Severo." The gang of vamps parted and Evie strode through the grass. A feat, surely, considering the open-toed spike heels peeking out at the bottom of her black gown. "We meet again."

"You think this will hold me back?" he growled.

"Appears to be doing the trick. Ian Grim stole it from the Highwayman for me. Nice, isn't it?"

The Highwayman? Christ, that was Aby's husband. Had they harmed him? What of Aby?

He fought against the powerful silver. The bladed edge of the whip cut leather. He'd once trusted Ian Grim. Until he'd learned the man was a nasty witch who should be labeled a warlock for his crimes against the faith he claimed.

"Careful, dear. Wouldn't want to bring on your death as you kneel, humbled, before a crew of vampires," the vampiress hissed.

A few longtooth assholes chuckled.

Humbled, yes. But never defeated.

"I thank you for the show," she said. Ruby blood glinted at Elvira's throat, a thick droplet that seemed suspended there without a chain. "I could have watched my boys go at you all night. You can't be put back, can you?"

"So you came to watch me perform, is that it? A carnival freak show for the biggest freak of them all? Bring out your weapons. I'll match them all."

"Oh, so brave and proud, my bruised little puppy dog."

He snarled and snapped at her. A seam of his jacket tore but the silver did not touch his skin.

With the silver containing him, he could not complete the transformation. Instead, he was suspended in midshift. His shoulders and neck had thickened, as had his legs and torso, but the bones had not yet changed. Nor had he the weaponlike talons, which could cut the whip as if it were made of ribbon.

She leaned forward, coming face-to-face with him. The foul scent of her tweaked at Severo's senses. And yet he'd once remembered her scent as the perfume of his savior when he'd been held captive by her parents.

"I could remove you from this earth right now." She glanced aside to one of the vampires who'd eagerly stepped forward. "Back, all of you. He's mine."

"He's mine." Severo chuckled lowly and shook his head. "It's been so long since I've heard that from you, Evie."

"Yes." She stroked his brow, and he nudged her away, but she persisted, placing her fingers to his cheek. The edges of her nails were as sharp as a blade. His flesh opened and blood trickled down to his beard. "You know I was the only reason you were never bitten while my family owned you."

Yes, he knew that. Evie had been the one to plead with her father to save the young werewolf for her. She had wanted him. And her father had given him that lecherous sneer and had bent to his daughter's whim.

"So will you finally have that bite you've been dying for?" he asked.

For a werewolf, the stigma of a vampire bite was great. For while the bite would not turn the werewolf into some sort of vamp/wolf hybrid, it would increase the werewolf's blood hunger immeasurably. He would crave blood, which usually resulted in hunting humans to satisfy the need for a fix. Other werewolves could smell the taint on the inflicted wolf and would sooner kill the bastard than suffer his pitiful disgrace.

"Go ahead," Severo said in defiance. "I will wear your bite with pride, knowing I have made your family pay for the travesties visited upon my own."

She crossed her arms under her breasts and sighed. Taking in the surroundings, she twisted her head about and then said, "I understand what you did was just."

"Do you? Then why this war now?"

"Because you know revenge never ends." Splaying her fingers before her, Evie observed the blood on her nails. "One man takes revenge for the sins against his family, which then breeds new revenge, to be enacted upon his own. It continues on endlessly, Severo." With the tip of her tongue, she licked the blood from her nails. She had a discerning look on her face. Obviously it wasn't enough blood to serve any need. "You're not so foolish that you believe this can ever be finished?"

"It will end when one of us dies," he said briskly.

"Just so. You want to kill me now?"

He swallowed and jutted his chin. Were the silver whip not about him, he could swipe her with a taloned paw and take her head from her body. But it didn't feel right.

Truly, revenge only spawned further violence.

"Do it, then," he said, tilting his head aside to expose his neck. "Mark me, and take leave knowing you have the satisfaction of this gauntlet."

"Brave werewolf."

She leaned into his neck. The warmth of her nose slid down his tense muscles. The pass of her finger along the jugular tickled. Would she murder him?

"Over the years you've walked a wide path around me when you could have easily slain me," she whispered, so others would not hear. "I offer you the same regard."

Her eyes glinted with unnatural light, a silvery shard of hunger. "I wish you no harm physically. My mark would mean little for one so proud and one who walks alone. Were you in a pack, it would be different. I'd drink you until you moaned for me to satisfy you."

She spoke truths. A vampire mark would mean little to him now—unless he ever wished to start a new pack. Should she bite him, he would feel it as a human would. As an intense orgasmic draw at the core of his being, one that commanded he submit.

The idea of succumbing to this bitch's persuasion brought bile to his throat.

"Besides——" Elvira tilted up his chin "——there's another who'll wish to take a bite out of you soon enough."

She propped her hands at her hips. The pale globes of her breasts were the only discernible shape on her black-cloaked figure. "Come on, boys. Our work here is finished."

Turning, she marched off, her sycophants in tow.

The whip dragged across his shoulders, slicing his jacket and jerking him forward to the ground. He landed, digging his fingers into the pummeled grass and clutching dirt.

Severo could only repeat the words she'd said over and over until he understood them.

...another who'll wish to take a bite out of you...

"Bella!"

Rage twisted Severo as he made a quick shift. Within moments, the werewolf howled out its anger. Vampires had hurt it. Yet though it could sense that they were close, it did not seek to track them.

A stronger scent drew it into a loping race across the field, toward the house.

The patio door was smashed in. The granite coffee table lay on the patio flagstones, on top of the shattered glass.

The werewolf charged across the debris. Glass shards pierced its paws, yet it did not slow down. Barking at the fierce cuts to its flesh, it trotted into the living room.

A thin streak of crimson ran across one couch cushion. The werewolf knew that scent. It was tainted with cloves. The scent briefly calmed it. Her. Its mate. Where was she? Was she harmed?

Calm turned to rage.

Rushing through the kitchen, it followed a trail of broken dishes and a crack in the wall where a force must have punched through.

Moving quickly, it took the steps downstairs, scenting blood so strongly, it growled and punched the walls as it made it to the laundry room.

Not a wolf or vampire, but not a human, either.

Not your mate.

It loped upstairs. Closing its eyes, it twisted its neck, scenting the air. Longtooths. Three of them dead. Others, no longer in the house, had left a scent trail that led toward the front door, which hung on one hinge.

Another scent grabbed at it. Mate.

Down the hall.

Inside the room with a bed the werewolf found her. The limp, bloodied body of its mate lay across the tousled white sheets.

A howl birthed from its core and vibrated through its entire being.

Severo shook off the sharp tingles of the shift and became instantly alert on the floor before the bed.

He clutched his foot and gripped the glass shard that had penetrated all the way through the top of his foot. Growling as he pulled it out, he tossed it aside. Blood spilled from his foot, but he gave it no mind.

He spied a body on the bed—and let out a cry.

Clenching a fist, he wondered if Elvira's minions had finally done what they'd set out to do that night of the chase. Please, they must not have raped her. He would tear those vampires limb from limb, and then...

But no, she'd been *placed* on the bed. Perhaps she had not been violated, after all.

She moaned, and he lunged to the bed and leaned over her. "Bella, I'm here."

"I did it. Killed…vampires." Her voice cracked and her head fell back as he lifted her by the shoulders.

A pile of ash on the other side of the bed startled him.

"Good girl. You got them. I'm sorry. I don't know how they made it through the wards. I was outside. There were so many of them. Bella, you're bleeding."

He reached to flick on the lamp. Just leaning over her, filling his senses with her blood, sickened him. He should have been inside to protect her. What hell had she gone through while he was out batting around vampires?

What he'd thought a head injury was quickly revealed to be neck wounds when the light gleamed across her side. Thick, viscous blood glittered. It had begun to coagulate, but there was so much, he couldn't tell if she'd been slashed or stabbed.

His heart knew it hadn't been a weapon of steel that had harmed her.

Fingers shaking, Severo touched the blood. He winced when the nature of the two wounds was revealed. Teeth marks.

Gathering her into his arms, he rushed into the bathroom and deposited her in the tub. As water filled the tub, he tore her clothing from her and tossed it behind him. He tugged down a towel from the bar and plunged it into the water.

Scrubbing the towel over the wounds on her neck, he wasn't sure what he could accomplish. He only knew he had to wash away the blood.

Chapter 18

Emerging from a groggy dream of ash-filled air and snarling fangs, Bella blinked and groaned. Was she underwater? Her skin was wet, yet the pressure of the water did not pull her down. The steamy scent of lemons made her wonder if she was in the bathroom.

Opening her eyes, she saw her lover sitting there, his shoulders bowed, his hands hanging between his bent knees. There was such intensity in his eyes. They were what had held her since day one. A promise of truth, trust and honor lived there in Severo's eyes.

Beyond him, she saw a strange disaster. The doorway had a big bite out of it. A force had punched the wall and taken out part of the door frame and Sheetrock. Bloody footprints led from the bedroom to the bathroom tiles.

Every part of her ached and her muscles had been stretched beyond their capacity. But of course, after battling a houseful of crazed vampires, what did one expect?

"Oh my God, the vampires." When she tried to move, her hand slipped on the edge of the porcelain tub and she fell back into the water. "What the hell?"

Now she realized Severo sat on the toilet lid, not reacting to her distress, but waiting patiently. He wore only jeans. Watery blood pooled at his bare feet. His face was dirty and his shoulder had blood on it.

"Why am I in here?" she asked. "Why am I all wet?"

She followed his gaze over the floor. A pile of bloody towels sat heaped before the vanity.

"I had to clean the wound," he offered in a raw, quiet voice. "It's still bleeding. It was left unsealed. I...couldn't take it away. I'm sorry."

She shoved herself up but the slick tub kept her sliding to a reclined position. "Wound? Your shoulder?"

"No, sweet. You."

"Was I cut? None of them had weapons. I ran from them. Took a few out with those wooden bullets and a stake. They got Heloise. Oh, Severo, Heloise."

She slapped a palm to her forehead, and when she thought the tears would come, she realized she had gone beyond them. Her chest heaved. Sorrow for the fallen housekeeper prodded her sympathy, but she had abandoned tears sometime after that first vampire had been staked.

Among her thoughts she remembered what Severo had said.

"What do you mean, 'left unsealed'?" she asked him.

Why didn't he just hug her? More than anything she wanted him to hold her and make her know everything was all right. That the vamps were all gone. They were alive. That meant they had won, right?

"Saliva is necessary to seal the wound and prevent the vampire taint from rushing into the bloodstream," he explained. "You don't remember?"

Standing, he loomed over her. He had blood all over him—at the corner of his eye, on his shoulder and at his abdomen. Blood had dripped onto his jeans. Not from fresh wounds. Streaks of dried blood from earlier wounds that had rapidly healed.

"Bella..."

He sucked in a breath. His eyes shifted up and along the shower curtain rod, searching for something. The pulse of his jaw, which she had once thought so sexy, now disturbed her.

"You've been bitten. And there's nothing I can do to reverse the imminent change," he blurted.

She gripped her neck and flinched at the pain. Slippery blood coated her fingers. "A vampire *bit* me?"

She met her lover's tired gaze and he nodded. "I'm going to tend to Heloise. She should not be left as she is. You'll be fine until I return?"

Fine? What was fine? She'd been bitten by a vampire. Was she going to change? Would she die? Would she want to drink blood?

Severo awaited her reply. Why wasn't he holding her?

If she closed her eyes and opened them again, would this crazy nightmare go away?

"Bella?"

She nodded, though she couldn't meet his tired eyes. "Sure. Fine."

And he walked from the room without bowing to kiss her or offering to help her out of the tub.

Was he horrified by her?

"He hates vampires," she murmured. Sliding a finger along her neck to feel at the gaping tooth marks, she now found tears. "Will he hate me?"

Severo jogged downstairs. A sense that he had been here recently—as the werewolf—put up his hackles.

As suspected, he did not find Heloise's body in the laundry room. The ichor pool glittered brilliantly, and he knew that, by some strange and magical means, her body had returned to Faerie, whence it had come.

He knelt before the devastation.

Sheets were shredded, some spattered with red. It could only be vampire blood. So Heloise had put up a fight? *Good girl.*

Closing his eyes and bringing his joined palms up to his face, he wondered what he could say, then knew it would be better to say nothing. Thanks for all she had done for him would be inappropriate. It was a bittersweet moment.

He slammed the laundry room door closed behind him and made a hasty retreat to the kitchen. Piles of vamp ash sat among the debris of broken furniture, of his life.

How many vampires had gone after Bella? There must have been as many inside the house as outside.

How had they breached the wards? And the locks?

Looking around, he realized he did not know where to begin. How did one make things right when they were so wrong?

She is wrong now.

Catching his balance against the kitchen counter, he gasped in a breath. Wrong? No, not his Bella.

"Please, let her be right."

He placed a call to the cleaners, who promised they'd arrive within the hour.

Well and fine. He should probably tend his own wounds. Not that it mattered. They'd all healed—save the gaping gash through his heart.

"Bella," he whispered. "Bella."

Not wrong. Never wrong.

The wards and locks would have to wait before he could figure out why they had failed. He wouldn't need them now. He sensed Elvira had gotten exactly what she'd wanted, and would not return.

And what had she won from this round of battle? She would turn the one thing Severo most loved into the one thing he most hated.

"Masterful revenge," he muttered, then kicked aside a bloodied couch cushion.

The patio-door glass clinked beneath his boot toe. Sunshine tickled across the shards of safety glass as if they were large pieces of faerie dust. Poor Heloise. She was an innocent.

As was Bella.

He snapped a finger against a shard stuck in the door frame. Soaring through the air, it landed and slid across the pool tarp.

"I should go to her."

She would want him to hold her, to reassure and kiss her, to give her proof of his love.

For a long time he'd sat in the bathroom after scrubbing furiously at the wound on her neck. If only he could have washed away any trace of damage, taken the bite from her with the cleansing water.

What now would he feel when he again looked upon her?

"I love her," he growled at his insensitive thoughts.

Could he love a vampire?

A minute possibility remained that she would not change. To do that, she had to survive till the next full moon. Elvira had planned this so well. The moon had been waning but a day. There were four long weeks till the next full moon.

"She'll never survive without going mad."

Exhausted, and knowing that Severo was busy with the cleaning and security crews, Bella slept through the day. After she'd showered, the wound had stopped bleeding. She crawled naked into bed and fell instantly asleep.

A fitful sleep. She'd been aware when the water in the shower again beat against the tiles, and then when Severo had carefully tiptoed about the bedroom, selecting clean clothes and leaving her alone.

All she craved was spooning against his body and knowing that everything was going to be all right. But the dread that their relationship would never be the same kept her in bed, even when her stomach growled for food.

When the noise from the cleaners ceased and the sun had again set, she decided to sneak out for a morsel. At least now she wouldn't have to see piles of ash or signs of the struggle she'd been through.

Pulling on a black silk robe, Bella combed her hair and leaned toward the mirror. The bite mark was swollen and red. She couldn't conceal it with makeup. It didn't hurt, only ached.

"How did you do it, Seth? This is not my idea of a good time."

Of course, when the wound healed, she could get on with her life. She suspected Severo was avoiding her for the very reason that she bore the mark of the vampire on her neck. It couldn't heal fast enough.

Answering her hunger pangs, she headed to the kitchen. It was spotless, with no sign of broken dishes or the wooden stool she'd thrown at a vampire and had broken across his shoulder. She opened the fridge and grabbed the plastic bottle of pomegranate juice.

When she closed the door, she dropped the juice. Tall and strong, Severo posed as if ready for a challenge, head lowered and fingers coiled, ready to fist. She thought she could smell the fury on him, and his eyes appeared even darker.

The vampire's eyes had been so beguiling. Blue, deep and seductive. She couldn't remember anything after looking into them.

"I'm sorry. I was hungry." She picked up the plastic bottle. To run into his arms felt wrong but she so desired it.

"How are you feeling?"

"Better. Much. I think this stupid bite mark will heal in a few days. I know how it must make you feel. I understand you haven't had time for me. You've been busy all day, I'm sure. Can I make you something to eat?"

His inhale stabbed her in the heart. Bella closed her eyes. *Please, touch me. Hold me.*

"We need to talk, Bella."

Call me sweet. I am yours. You won't abandon me after you realize this bite means nothing.

"Sure." She screwed off the bottle cap and took a slug. She didn't realize how achy her jaw was until she swallowed. "Let's sit over there."

Drawn to their favorite chair, she waited for him to sit and pull her onto his lap. "Severo?"

He nodded as if jerking himself out of busy thoughts. "Yes."

He sat, and when she wanted to climb onto his lap, he allowed it, but he didn't cradle her as he usually did, only sat stiffly, as if he wouldn't push her away but would like to if he could.

"Are you angry with me?" she asked.

"Never. No. I'm sorry, Bella."

"It's the bite, isn't it? It reminds you of them. It'll soon be gone—"

"It's going to change everything, Bella."

"No, it won't. When it's healed, you'll forget all about this stupid incident."

"It will heal. But you will not. You will be transformed."

She pushed against his chest and leaned back to study his face. He couldn't meet her eyes. How dare he not look at her, to make her feel as if she were contagious. Now she wished she would have found a scarf to tie around her neck.

"Transformed? You mean…? But Seth didn't change when he was dating Elvira. Not until she wanted him to."

"Because a vampire usually licks the wound after it takes blood from a mortal. The infusion of vamp saliva seals the wound and keeps back the vampire taint. A bite that isn't sealed introduces the taint to the mortal's system. It will stir up the blood hunger in you, Bella, and you will change with your first taste of human blood."

"No." She shoved off from his lap and paced toward the opposite wall.

The now glassless picture of Aby and Severo had been rehung there. In the ten years they'd been together, why hadn't Elvira gone after Aby? Was it because he'd never made love to her?

"I don't want to be a vampire. I don't want—" To be the one thing her lover despised. The thing that would always remind him of his family's tragic suffering. "There must be some way to stop it."

"There is."

The warm weight of his hand on her shoulder made her flinch. Bella did not turn to him. Aby's bright smile taunted her. She had had Severo for an entire decade. Would Bella lose him after but a few months?

"You can wait for the full moon." His voice hurt her heart. So calm. Yet not affectionate, as it had been. More removed, clinical. "If you don't drink human blood before then, you'll be in the clear. But you'll be mad from resisting the intense hunger. Damn it, Elvira planned this well. It'll be another month before the full moon comes again."

"But you said if I drink *human* blood. Maybe I could…drink yours?" She winced at the thought of doing something so reprehensible.

"Bella, listen. There are three options for a mortal bitten by a vampire when the wound has not been sealed. You can answer the blood hunger—which should emerge within days—and complete the transformation, thus becoming a vamp."

"What are the other two?"

"You could kill yourself."

She gasped.

Severo punched a fist into his palm.

"Door number three, please?" she asked softly.

"You could try to wait out the full moon. If the victim can go without drinking blood until the next full moon is over and the moon begins to wane, then the vampire taint will pass from their system, leaving them completely mortal."

"Well, that's my pick. See, this won't be so bad."

"One problem."

"There's always a but."

"Bella, I don't know of anyone who has been able to resist the insistent blood hunger. If they did resist the insatiable need, madness would generally take hold before they made it to the full moon.

"There is a legend of one man who survived until the full moon—at the expense of his mind. His family, after committing him, decided to attempt to have him bitten again, in hopes of curing the madness. He'd changed to a vampire and yet remained mad.

"Bella, what's been done to you is irreversible. You are destined to become a bloody long—" He stopped.

"Longtooth," she whispered. Then she spun about and insisted boldly, "Say it. I know you hate them. And now you will hate me."

"No, I love you." But she heard so little conviction in his tired tone. "I could never…"

"Never look me in the eyes again? You won't. You can't. My God, that bitch really did know what she was doing."

She paced the floor. Wanting him to wrap her in his arms wouldn't earn her the reprieve from the horror she could never shake.

The patio door had been boarded up, and the smell of fresh paint made her wonder which wall she had seen her own blood splattered on last night, as the vampire had bent to bite into her neck.

A bite she recalled wanting.

She shivered as she recalled a memory. "It was the same ones who originally chased me." Severo had been there that night to rescue her. Why hadn't he been there for her last night? "Where were you?"

He leaned forward, hanging his head.

"Severo?"

"I was out back. Elvira and a dozen vampires detained me with some kind of silver whip. I had no idea they had infiltrated the house, or that you were even home, until it was too late."

"A silver whip? Are you hurt?"

"No more than my pride."

His pride. And while he'd been suffering a pride-busting tête-à-tête with the mistress of the night, Bella had been getting her throat chewed on.

"I'm sorry, Bella. This would have never happened if I had not pursued you after that night in the warehouse. If I had not kept you in my life."

"Don't say that. Seth was already dating Elvira then.

It would have happened much sooner, is all. I'm glad you followed me home and seduced me into loving you, Severo. Do you…"

She wanted to ask.

She could not.

He could not love her now. It would be cruel to ask it of him after all she had learned of his past.

"So what are we going to do?" she asked instead. "Do you want me to pack my bags?"

He narrowed his gaze but still did not meet hers. Did he look at Aby's picture?

"That's ridiculous. This is your home. I swore you would be my mate—" He fisted his fingers and the air in the room shifted as if a ghost had just breezed through. Bella felt the chill. "We'll get through this."

"I want that. But I'd feel much better if you'd hold me and…and kiss me." She waited for his eyes to find hers. They did not.

"The security crew is still outside working at the terminal. I need to go out and check on their progress. I'll return soon, I promise."

"You don't want to touch me now, do you?" Tears slid down her cheeks. Bella resisted the shivers that threatened to shake her body uncontrollably. "Will you touch me when the bite has healed?"

"It's not like that, Bella."

"Yes, it is! Don't lie to me. Everything has changed between us now, hasn't it?"

He didn't answer. And that was answer enough.

Chapter 19

He was being a bastard. Two days had passed since the attack and Severo had used the excuses of installing new windows and rechecking the grounds and restocking the arsenal as means to limit his time with Bella.

Hell, he wanted to go to her. To hold and kiss her, to make love to her, and find his place inside her again.

But the vampire's scent lingered on her, and he didn't want Bella to know that. To sense that he was repulsed by her. He was, and he wasn't. Yet he was stupid to think she didn't already sense his reluctance.

Rationally, he knew nothing had changed between them. She was the same woman he had fallen in love with and had wanted to mate with for as long as their days would allow.

Illogically, his brain found her offensive. He cringed every time the fading red bite mark on her neck was revealed as her hair swept over a shoulder.

Vampires had viciously murdered his parents and enslaved him. They had gone to war with the witches with little respect for human life. Vampires were filthy, nasty creatures.

And soon Bella would become one.

He couldn't push her away. And yet he knew ignoring her was far worse. She needed him as much as he wanted her. She wasn't yet a vampire.

If he could not accept her now, how could he possibly do so after she changed?

Because it was starting. Last night she had moaned in her sleep, a deep, wanting whine that wasn't sexual. The blood hunger had begun to infiltrate her system.

Each night, after she drowsed off to sleep, he'd sleep on the chair in the bedroom, or rather, sit there with one eye open. He hadn't slept for days, and though exhausted, he would continue to keep watch on her. For any changes. For her needs.

Kiss me.

She said it every night before slipping between the sheets. But she wouldn't look at him, as if she knew he could not meet her gaze.

"Idiot!"

He would not fall victim to mere thoughts. Mind games. His brain had convinced him of something irrational. He would make the best of this. He must. The longer he separated himself from her, the further they would disconnect.

"I want her. I will go to her."

Yes, he'd kiss her. And it would be as it always had been.

Or he would sooner die.

* * *

Bella sorted through the negligee drawer. She normally slept in the buff, but she'd been wearing pajamas lately because it was cold in bed at night.

Severo had been sleeping in the chair so he wouldn't accidentally rub up against her. He probably believed she didn't know, but she was aware in the middle of the night, when her sleep grew light, that he watched her. From afar.

She shivered and swallowed a desperate need to cry.

"You're stronger than this, Bellybean." Using Seth's nickname for her, she released a teardrop, which slid down her cheek. "Suck it up. You have far worse things to deal with than a confused boyfriend." Like how to deal with what she was becoming. She could feel it.

She traced her throat and then her chest. There, at the base of her lungs, was where the pining had first surfaced. It was a burning, like heartburn, but not. It wanted. Craved. And it needed to be slaked.

"The blood hunger," she whispered, her lower lip wobbling. "I don't want to do this. I can't drink blood. It would be so much easier…" If she had support.

"Bella?"

Tugging the pink silk nightgown from the drawer and clutching it to her naked body, she turned to find Severo on the other side of the bed. Leather pants, chest bare, looking so handsome. So fine.

Yet no longer yours.

"Is something wrong?"

"Yes, everything," he replied heavily. A sigh lifted his shoulders. He prowled around the bed to her side. He hadn't stood so close to her in days. Tentatively, he lifted a hand and traced a finger down her arm. The heat of him, his musky male scent cloyed. Her skin tensed in anticipation. "I've been cruel to you."

The confession stirred her hope. But Bella was not quick to clutch it. "With good reason."

"No." He touched the silk fabric hanging over her forearm. "I've succumbed to an ingrained belief. I should not look to the past. I must move beyond. My world, my beliefs and prejudices, are formed, but I need to think about what I am willing to accept. What I think I should believe. I need to change my thinking. You should not go through this alone."

"You really feel that way?" The heat of his body poured over her like a desert sun, warm and rich. Could she melt against him without fear of him stiffening and pushing her away? "I just need you…to hold me."

"I can do that."

He embraced her, drawing her against his chest. The thin silk garment slid to the floor, and they stood flesh to flesh. But Bella did not fool herself into thinking he did not flinch. He did. And the embrace was noticeably stiff.

But it was a start.

"You've been feeling the hunger," he whispered. "I can see it torment you at night."

He smoothed her hair, and she remembered how she'd felt so safe in his arms. She wanted to know that feeling again.

"The hunger will only increase," he said. "I've no means to understand or deal with what is going on inside you. I think I need to contact a friend."

"Someone who knows about the transformation?"

"A vampire."

"But you called him a friend?"

"That may be too generous a term. I've mentioned him before. He is the one vampire in this world I respect. He was once a brain surgeon, and though he heads tribe Kila now, he has fought for peace between the vampire and witch nations. I admire him for his values."

"So you can accept a vampire."

He tilted up her chin. "I *will* accept a vampire. And I love you, so don't think I could ever stop."

"I think you've already stopped." She lifted her quavering chin bravely. "You just don't realize it yet."

"That's cruel, Bella. I love you."

Hearing the words forced her to swallow back tears. She nodded. "But it will be hard."

"I won't lie and tell you it's going to be easy."

"And I won't push. I'm just happy to stand in your arms. Will you hold me until I fall asleep?"

"Yes."

"I'll talk to Bella and get back to you. Thank you, Ivan."

Severo clicked the cell phone off and swiped a hand over his face.

So he was going through with this. He'd given Nikolaus Drake a call, the vampire he knew he could trust with the situation, but he'd been away in Africa. Instead, his son Ivan had taken the call. He was in Minneapolis for another few weeks.

After Severo explained the situation, Ivan agreed to help.

Not that it was his deal to go through with. It was all about Bella. Or it should be. He'd put on a good face the past few days. He'd even slept beside her last night, holding her, kissing her. But not on the mouth.

How desperately he wanted to make love to her, but she'd told him it was all right. She'd read his reluctance.

Why could he not get past this?

If he didn't master his feelings now, they would not climb up from this chasm and when she did turn, he would never be able to accept her.

"What's up?" Bella asked as she strode through the kitchen, a book in hand. She wore loose-fitting white yoga pants and a tank top that showed her peaked nipples beneath the fabric, and her hair was swept up in a neat ponytail.

"I spoke to Drake," Severo said. "He's out of the country, but his son Ivan is in Minneapolis."

"Oh. And?"

"I trust the Drakes, Bella. You would be in good hands with either father or son. But with the son you have the added factor that his father is a vampire and his mother a witch. And that vampire father is a phoenix."

"Is that a good thing?"

"A phoenix vampire has survived a witch's blood attack and has an immunity to the sun. If you chose to accept the transformation, you will have that blood running through your veins."

"This is my choice?"

"Can't be anyone else's."

"But I thought there was no other option. I mean, madness doesn't ring any of my bells, nor does suicide. I don't want to do anything that's going to see you hating me."

He gripped the back of her head. "I love you." Teeth bared, he snarled out the words, "I will always love you."

"You can speak the words," she said, "but I don't see the truth in your eyes."

That made him rear back and slam a fist against the kitchen counter. "Bella, I'm trying!"

"It's okay. If you won't have me as a bloodsucker, then I'll have to learn to accept that."

"You won't do any such thing. How can I make you understand how I feel about you?"

"By being truthful." She set down the book and crossed her arms over her chest. "Severo, you're as scared as I am. Admit it. You're losing the woman you fell in love with. I'm not the same, and I'm never going to be the same. And every time you look at me, you will see the horrors of your past."

"It won't be like that."

"Just, please, look me in the eye."

It was such a simple request, and yet he struggled to hold her liquid green gaze for longer than a second. In her eyes he saw so much. Their shared love. The good times, when they'd spent days making love until they were both too exhausted to rise for breakfast. And the teasing play. And the jealousy he felt whenever another man got close enough to breathe her air.

She is yours. Look at her.

Bringing up his chin, Severo found Bella's pleading stare.

"You love me?" she asked.

He nodded.

"And you're afraid?"

"I am. I...want it to be as it's been, but it never will be. And what scares me the most is the werewolf will kill you first chance it gets."

"It will not. I love the werewolf, and it loves me."

"The werewolf takes off vampire heads with one swipe of a paw."

"You can control it." She hugged him and kissed his neck. "If you want to."

If he wanted to? So easy as that, she thought.

Yet *would* he want to?

Bella kept a firm grip on the passenger-side door handle as Severo navigated the potholes on Highway 35W, which stretched to Minneapolis. He seemed unsure and frequently slowed to read the signs.

"You've not driven this road before, have you?"

He cast her a knowing smile.

"You've run here," she decided.

"Saves on gas, and the wolf needs the exercise. I can make this distance in half the time it takes a car."

"Well, aren't you speedy on four legs."

"Don't worry. I've a driver's license. I drive into town on occasion to stay in practice."

"You navigated our small town pretty well." She twisted on the seat and curled a knee up to her chest. "So, you've told me about Ivan. How does this all work? How long do you think it'll take?"

"Ivan suggested a few days. The initial bite can take place right away, but you'll then need to drink human blood. He intends to show you the ropes, which is generous of him. You'll be in good hands, Bella. You could have just ventured out on your own, attacked a mortal and found your own way."

"You'd never allow that."

He smirked. "Only because I want what's best for you."

"You are what's best for me, lover. Are you going to be there when we…do it?"

"I will not watch another man hold you in his arms and sink his teeth into you, Bella. I don't think it would be comfortable for either of us, do you?"

The man did have a ferocious jealous streak. "Yes and no. I mean, I want you there for support, but it would be kind of squicky for you, I'm sure."

"Squicky?"

"Yeah, squirm icky."

He turned onto a highway off-ramp. "I'll stay at a motel and pick you up when you call. Might be safer for Drake that way, too. I know if I get anywhere near him after the fact, I'll want to rip his head off."

Ivan Drake lived in a forty-second-floor penthouse in downtown Minneapolis. Bella swallowed during the elevator ride, because fast elevators made her ears pop.

As they waited before the door, she slid her hand into Severo's. He leaned in and kissed her on the mouth—slowly, like he meant it—and she didn't sense any disgust or repulsion. In a way, it was a goodbye kiss. Goodbye to the woman he knew, the woman *she* knew.

"It's going to be fine," he said and pressed his forehead to hers.

What she wouldn't give to have back the randy,

charming Severo who had once seduced her with suggestive moves and aggressive will. That charm was still inside him, but she would never be able to touch that part of him again.

"Just tell me what you think of me."

"I love you, sweet."

The endearment went a long way in reassuring her. Superficially. "I love you, too."

Ivan opened the door to the vast penthouse. The foyer was stark white and modern, as was the living room beyond it. The man had to be rich, because, Bella thought, from what she could see, the place deserved to be in a magazine.

Ivan stood as high as Severo and was equally as built. What was with all these paranormals? They were all muscled and so sexy. He had dark hair that feathered about his ears and neck, a regal nose and piercing eyes, not to mention a friendly disposition.

Cripes, her lover was delivering her to a male model so she could suck on his neck and exchange bodily fluids. The rabbit hole kept getting weirder and weirder.

"You must be Belladonna Reynolds," Ivan offered when Severo forgot the introductions. "Come in, the two of you, and sit down."

Severo put his hands on her shoulders, pulling her to him. "I won't be staying."

"Oh, of course. I could have a car take Belladonna home," Ivan offered to Severo.

"No, I'll pick her up when..." Severo let the end fizzle.

When? she thought. When she had become what he most hated?

"I trust your father," Severo said to Ivan, his hold still firm upon her shoulders. He wasn't ready to hand her over, and that reduced Bella's anxiety. "He's promised me that the same trust should not be lost on you."

"I know your struggles with the vampires, Severo, and believe me, I appreciate the work you've done with the Council. If my father could have been here, he would have helped you. But I promise to be a complete gentleman, or my wife will come after me with some wicked magic."

"You have a wife?" Bella hadn't been aware of that. The squick quotient suddenly rose exponentially.

"Yes, she's in Venice right now with her friend Lucy Morgan. Truvin's wife," Ivan said to Severo. At the mention of the name, Bella felt Severo's body tense. "Truvin," Ivan said to Bella, "is not one of Severo's favorite vampires. But his wife is a charm. She's involved in a sort of paranormal debunking venture right now. Dez, my wife, has been helping her with it. They keep the myth a myth, so to speak. It is a project that is invaluable to the safety of all paranormal nations. And Truvin—" Ivan cast a wink at Severo "—has mellowed greatly since the protection was dropped."

"The protection?" she asked.

"The spell that made witch's blood poisonous to vampires," Severo said. "So do you intend to take her out and show her the ways of your kind...after?"

"If Belladonna wants to stay an extra day or two, I would be glad to," replied Ivan. "If one can have a mentor, then it can make a difference for one's entire future."

"I agree." Severo hugged Bella. "So I guess I should leave. Do you feel all right about this, sweet?"

Who could feel right about being left alone with a stranger whose only intent was to make you a vampire? The one creature her lover could not stand. A creature who lived on human blood. A *creature*.

Was madness such a better option?

"Yes, I'm good about this."

She wished he would stay longer. Truthfully this didn't feel anywhere near right. But what, since she had met Severo, *had* felt right?

Only him holding her in his arms, making love to her.

Would they ever make love again?

She slid around in Severo's arms. Sensing that Ivan had stepped away to give them a moment alone, she bracketed her lover's face with her hands, sliding her palms over his rough beard.

Remember this, the roughness of him, she told herself. *His earthy scent. His whiskey eyes. The mouth she could get lost in.*

"I haven't been away from you since the day we met," she said.

"That first full moon I was gone three days, sweet."

"I'm going to miss you."

"I will stay close by. Perhaps a few blocks away."

"Thanks, but don't worry too much. I'm a big girl."

She kissed him and it didn't matter who watched; she just needed to fall into him. One last time. Once more as a mortal woman who had crazily fallen in love with a werewolf.

Once more, and then forever.

Chapter 20

After a walk-through tour of the immense pent-house—there was even a lap pool—Ivan led Bella to the main room.

The living room had floor-to-ceiling windows that looked out over the city. It might be a nice view, but Bella avoided walking too close to the windows. She got a woozy feeling even when walking too close to the guardrails on the fourth floor at the Mall of America.

"Would you like something to drink?" Ivan asked.

"Maybe."

His smile was warm and not at all creepy. Not a hint of fangs, either. "Wine? Or I have Evian."

"I'm not sure."

He crossed the room so quickly, she didn't realize he'd moved until his presence loomed behind her. Bella didn't see any drinks in his hands, which made her frown.

"Let's get everything out in the open, shall we?" he offered. "I'm sure we're both feeling awkward about this situation, yes?"

She nodded but avoided looking directly into his eyes. Last time that had happened... She refused to recall it.

"We don't have to be comfortable with it, but know I do genuinely want to help you. My father reveres Severo and would do anything for him. You have nothing to fear from me. And if at any time you do start to experience fear or get uncomfortable, just say so. We'll take this at your pace."

"But I just have to drink your blood to make the change, right?"

"Right."

"So we should just do it and get it done with."

"I'm going to pour us some wine first."

Ivan padded toward the kitchen and Bella followed, to sit on a bar stool across from the counter. He opened a glass-fronted wine cupboard.

"I don't want it to feel like some kind of pseudo-seduction," he said. "Trust me, I love my wife, and I would never betray her. But we're going to be about as intimate as a couple can be without removing their clothes."

"Oh good." She blew out a breath. "I can keep my clothes on."

Ivan smiled and set two goblets before her. "I would insist you stay clothed. Do you know about vampires and their bites?"

"Just that it is what they must do to survive. And that it hurts like a mother."

"Yes, blood is the life."

She nodded, recalling how Seth had waxed lyrical over Elvira's bite. She didn't recall her own bite. Everything from that night was a blur, save those blue eyes.

"Do vampires hypnotize people? Make them *want* to be bitten?"

"Ah, the persuasion. It's not hypnosis, but an actual persuasion of the mind. Some call it the thrall. If you gaze into a vampire's eyes, you will be caught."

"Yep, I know how that one works."

"And when a vampire bites someone, the victim is not in pain for long. They experience the swoon, which is…orgasmic." He slid a half-full goblet toward her. "And when you bite me, well…I, in turn…"

"I see." He'd experience the same orgasmic swoon. She looked toward the door.

"We can call him back and have him present, if you wish."

"No, that would be too weird. I want it this way. I just…"

"Need to relax and get comfortable with the place, surely. Why don't you step out on the terrace for a while. The view is gorgeous, and I have a heater out there so you can enjoy the view. Take your time and get your bearings. Come back when you're ready for this."

"Thanks, Ivan. I think I will."

Severo rented a gallery suite at the Chambers, a luxury hotel down the street from Ivan's penthouse, but he had to take care of something back home first. He made the hour-long drive to the northern suburb where Bella used to live and parked under a willow tree. He strolled along the boulevard, taking in the nightlife.

His cell phone rang. It was Bella.

"What's wrong?"

"Nothing. So you going to hang out for a day or two? Listen to some Skynyrd?"

"I have something to take care of tonight, but then I'll be sitting around thinking of you. Are you okay? Why the call? Is it Ivan? I left too quickly, didn't I? I should have lingered, but it felt awkward."

"Ivan's letting me get my bearings. And don't worry about it. We're both doing things we never in a million years thought we'd do. I just needed to hear your voice." She paused, then added, "It's never going to be the same, is it?"

"Bella, don't cry. Please, sweet, be strong. You can do this. And when it's done, you'll come home to me and everything will be fine."

He heard a heavy gasp, as if she fought to catch her breath. "You're lying."

He sighed. A quick and reassuring rebuttal wasn't so easy for him.

"Goodbye, Severo," she said and hung up.

He clicked off the phone and stopped in the dark shadow that crept out from an alleyway. He didn't want to lie to her. He didn't want to be the man who needed to lie because he couldn't overcome this one small issue.

It could be good between the two of them.

He hoped.

The night was cold, and the wine lushly warm. Bella inhaled the crisp October air. It was supposed to snow tonight. She hoped she wouldn't miss the first flakes.

Resolute, she turned to face a future that she would likely manage on her own. She didn't want to do it alone, but she was a big girl.

Ivan sat in the living room, on a white sofa, an empty goblet on the coffee table. Soft jazz music played in the background. His bare feet tapped, his head was tilted back and his eyes were closed.

She approached cautiously but knew he was aware of her entrance. "What is it with all you immortals and the white furniture?" she said. "Do you have a great cleaner, or what? I mean…blood spots, anyone?"

Ivan smirked and nodded toward the black leather chaise opposite the sofa. "I don't usually hunt on my sofa. But believe me, the wife has tried to get me to change the furniture here dozens of times."

"Smart girl. We women look at furniture and wonder how it can be kept clean, not how aesthetic it is. So, will you tell me about your wife?"

Well-worn and riddled with scratches, the leather chaise was soft and Bella found it more welcoming than her and Severo's chair had been lately.

"Dez is a witch who is twelve hundred years older than me," Ivan offered. "She swept me off my feet a few years ago and succeeded in releasing me from a pact with the devil Himself."

"Wow. Sounds like an incredible woman."

"Amazing. But I suspect you may rank alongside her. Severo speaks highly of you."

"I think I'm the first relationship he's had since Aby."

"I don't know about her, but if the werewolf is willing to allow his mate to transform into a vampire, then you know you've got yourself a keeper."

"Willing or simply has no other option? I'm not much for madness. Oh." Bella doubled over, clutching her ribs. Stronger than it had been previously, the ache eroded her insides.

"It's the blood hunger. It will only increase. You've done well so far."

"It's not in my gut. It's right here." She tapped her chest, just below her diaphragm. "Will it always be like this?"

"Not so strong. It'll become instinctual."

Instinctual sounded animal. Animal sounded like her lover. *Oh, Severo, don't stop loving me.*

"Let's do this, please. Before I change my mind," she said.

Ivan stood and knelt before her, touching her knees comfortingly. His wide hands, traced with thick veins, were beautiful. "You can change your mind."

"Have you seen someone who went mad?"

"I have."

"Not pretty?"

"Not particularly." He clasped one of her hands. "This life, Bella, is wondrous. You should not fear it. The idea of drinking blood may repulse you now, but trust that it will quickly become second nature. You will be gifted with immortality, so you may live with your mate as long as he lives."

"But he has only a few centuries left."

"And don't you want to spend that time with him?"

"I do. If he'll have me."

"Give him a chance to adjust. Severo has been wounded."

She nodded. Vampires had stolen his family. That was a wound she doubted anyone—even mortal—could get over. "Do you have enemies? What about werewolves?"

"I grew up during the height of the war between the vampires and witches. My mother actually killed my father once. But he rose from the ashes as a phoenix and then managed to fall in love with her."

"That sounds weird, yet wickedly romantic."

"I imagine it was. So no, I've never been prejudiced or hated any particular species or breed. I have the blood of both witches and vampires in my veins. And you will have that gift, as well. You will be a rarity among vampires, Bella. Very strong."

"I like the idea of being strong. And I don't ever want to call another species my enemy, either. Hell, a species? You can't imagine how my life has changed these past few months."

"I can't, actually." He smiled. "I was born this way, so humanity is a curiosity to me."

"But you're humane."

"We all are, so long as we don't succumb to the darkness that threatens us with every sip of blood we take. We vampires are called the Dark, but it's only a label. It's nothing we have to embrace. Witches are the Light. Though I have my doubts about that one at those times when my wife is angry with me."

His smile shied from his lips as he looked aside.

"So what do we do?"

"You need to drink my blood." He tugged his sweater

off and held up his wrist. But Bella didn't notice his wrist, because the hard pecs and washboard abs distracted her.

"I thought you said we didn't have to get naked?"

"Oh, sorry. I didn't want to ruin the sweater. I can put it back on."

"No. It's fine. Just show me what to do."

"I'll bite into my wrist and then you drink. Simple as that. But don't pause, because I heal quickly."

"H-how much?"

"You'll know. Ready?"

"Wait." She gripped his wrist, holding it over her lap.

This is your last chance to run away from it all, Bella, she told herself. *You can end it. Not have to face drinking blood for a freaking eternity.*

No.

She wanted to live. With Severo. And she'd be damned if she was going to allow him to use the longtooth defense to weaken their love. She was in it for the long haul. The werewolf was going to have to accept her.

"I'm ready."

Crimson blood bubbled on Ivan's wrist like candy beads. It didn't smell awful; in fact, it smelled delicious. Bella didn't pause. She took his arm and pressed her lips over his bloodied flesh.

The vampire moaned, but not out of pain. It stirred Bella from her intent sucking. God, this tasted good. It filled the aching hunger that had been clawing at her for days.

"More," she murmured.

He'd told her the swoon would affect the victim, but it took hold of her, as well. Bella dropped Ivan's wrist. Thrusting her head back, she smiled and drew up her knees as she twisted on the leather chaise.

She was sated.

"Rest," Ivan whispered near her ear. He put a blanket over her. "Your teeth should come in quickly. We'll take the next step then."

Bella closed her eyes to dreams of Severo taking her in the pool, his strong arms holding her against the cement wall, his hips bumping hers as he thrust deeply into her.

She slept, or maybe it was a reverie of sorts. Either way, Bella came to clarity with a prick at her lip. She touched her mouth. The spot of liquid wasn't saliva.

"Oh, hell."

From around the corner Ivan popped his head. "Ah, your fangs have descended. How do you feel?"

Like she had a bad toothache. "Not sure."

"Come look in the mirror," he suggested. "It'll help you to acclimate."

Bella followed Ivan down the hallway. The bathroom was another all-white, blinding splendor of modern-day privilege.

He hung back at the door as she approached the mirror. Dark circles had formed beneath her eyes. Her skin looked faded, in need of a tan. *What a wreck,* she thought. But there, glinting in her mouth, were sharp fangs.

"How am I going to do this?" she said with an open mouth, not wanting to bite herself.

"You can will them down when you need them. Most often when the hunger strikes, they will descend automatically. You might cut yourself a time or two until you become accustomed to them. They're pretty."

She shot him a look over her shoulder. "Pretty? You think?"

She bent toward the mirror and touched the fangs. They were small, about twice as long as a normal tooth. And pinpoint sharp.

Severo would not like this.

And yet he sported fangs that were much the same in his werewolf form.

Bella sighed and leaned against the counter to face Ivan. "I'm losing him, you know. You and he both say he can accept me, but he's fooling himself."

"I wouldn't be too sure about that, Belladonna. Sure, Severo's hatred for the vampire goes back many decades. But it is a focused hatred, which he has allowed to expand for reasons that have no tie to the original hate. There is no reason he cannot love you exactly as he has."

"You talk a good game, Ivan. Your wife is a lucky lady."

"I'm the lucky one. So how do you feel?"

"The same. Still have that strange ache below my lungs."

"You need to drink more. Then the change will be complete, and you can learn to stalk a human victim."

"Peachy. So I'm no longer human?"

"You, Belladonna, are now a vampire."

He pronounced it with such grandeur, as if bestowing an honor.

Oh hell, what would Seth think of her now? Or her mother? Probably she could keep this secret from her mother. They were distant at best.

"So let's get on with it," Bella said. "Shall I do the other wrist?"

He rubbed his neck and raised his brows.

"Ah. The neck. Suppose I need to learn the routine, eh?"

He nodded. "It would be best. You know the difference between the carotid and the jugular?"

"Nope."

"Then let's get you up to pace, because I don't want you biting into any arteries."

"On the bed?" Bella gripped her throat.

The fangs already felt natural. And after a quick lesson on discerning veins from arteries, she was ready for this. But Ivan stood before his king-size bed, covered with rich emerald damask, as if it was the most natural thing to expect her to climb on with him.

"Do you prefer the chaise?" The narrow chaise longue in front of the window was covered with pillows. "The bed's going to be more comfortable."

She climbed on the bed, needing a lift from Ivan because it was so high.

Not wanting to wait awkwardly for the right moment or signal, she pushed him against the pillows and dove toward his neck.

Canines to skin. The act felt natural. Her sharp teeth easily penetrated his flesh. Blood pooled in her mouth.

Ivan didn't flinch, and she thought to ask him if it was all right, but then put that worry aside. Of course it was all right.

Then again, nothing would ever again be right.

Dashing her tongue over the bite mark, she licked up his slowly flowing blood. She would need to suck to make it come out easily. The first bite was more delicious than the one in the living room.

The more blood she drew from him, the headier the taste. Bella lifted his shoulder and head to bring him closer to her.

He made a noise of satisfaction. His hand palmed her back—not stroking, nothing overt—but she took it as a sign to continue. Closing her eyes, she drank until she thought she could drink no more.

And when Ivan let out a moan and tilted his head, his body shuddered against hers. The swoon. An orgasm.

What he must feel, knowing his wife was off in another country while a stranger was literally getting him off. Bella realized Ivan had sacrificed much to help Severo and her.

Drawing away from her, he pushed up to sitting position. "Did you lick the wound?"

"Yes. But I don't need to for you, do I?"

"No, but you should get used to it. How did that feel?"

"Great. You, uh…"

"It felt awesome." He slid off the bed and offered her a hand. "Let's go talk semantics."

Good. He was keeping this businesslike. And while she'd much prefer to loll in bed and slip into a heady reverie now that her soul had been fed with blood, she followed him out to the living room.

He stood in the entry to a mansion east of the city. Elvira's limo had driven here an hour earlier. Severo had hung back under an elm tree, watching as a crew of vampires followed her inside. Four of them. He recognized one who had chased Bella that fateful night of their first encounter. He hadn't seen his face, but the longtooth's foul scent lived in his brain.

He snarled. His teeth descended as the wolf fought for release. There was no need to completely release the werewolf. He didn't need that strength. But he'd go halfway. Enough to ensure swift and final death.

The foyer was empty, and the front door had been left unlocked. Careless vampires. Loud rock music blared from somewhere beyond the doors at the end of the vast foyer. One vampiress and four slobbering minions? He could imagine what sort of debauched play went on in there.

Something stirred in his periphery. As soon as the vampire sighted the werewolf standing in the entry— stripped to the waist and half shifted, with long, muscular arms and taloned claws—he charged Severo.

Severo swiped the air. His talons cut through the flesh and bone at the neck, removing the vampire's skull in one leathery tear. Severo tossed the head. The vampire ashed, all except the head.

The music stopped, and two male vampires sped toward him. He made quick work of them, not moving from his position.

Letting out a howl that had been birthed deep in

his chest, Severo stomped forward, scenting the final longtooth. This one cowered behind a marble column. Severo grabbed him by the head and swung him across the floor. The vampire slid through two piles of bloody ash and landed at the front door with a crack of bone.

Severo pounced, landing with his forepaws upon the vampire's chest. He beat down once, forcefully with fisted talons, penetrating the vampire's rib cage and slicing through pulsing heart muscle. He ripped out the beating organ and tossed it behind him.

The vampire gnashed his fangs before Severo ripped off his head and threw it to the wall, not a foot from another staring head.

Huffing and heaving, Severo stretched tall, shedding the werewolf and resuming were form. Since he'd only half shifted, he still wore his leather pants. He shook off the blood from his hands.

The scent of another vampire made him bring his head upright, his ears pricking.

Stilettos crossed the marble floor, one heel slightly worn and creating a louder tone upon landing. Severo swung to face her, arms arced out at his sides. He breathed with triumph. A bittersweet win.

Elvira regarded her fallen comrades with a bored sigh. The still-pulsing heart elicited a small sneer from the vampiress. "Does this mean we're even?"

Severo snorted and punched his fist loudly into his opposite palm. "As even as the two of us will ever be."

"I can accept that."

As could he. He had no intention of harming the one individual who had been responsible for his remaining unmarked while in captivity. But he would never forgive Evie her indiscretions toward Bella.

"My bags are packed." She pouted. She couldn't shift her dark-shadowed eyes away from the heart, not five feet to her left. "I think Berlin will be lovely for a time."

"Good riddance." Severo turned and marched out.

Chapter 21

"I don't need to kill? Whew."

Ivan drove a black BMW around the city. Bella sat on the passenger side. Though it was midnight, she hunted a human victim because the blood hunger had not relented.

"Vampires don't need the kill. A small sip often or a larger drink less often. You choose," he explained. "But to kill takes the nightmares of your victims into your soul. You will relive those nightmares in what we call the *danse macabre*. It's not pretty. And those vampires who kill indiscriminately usually go mad from the nightmares."

"There seems to be a lot of madness associated with vampirism. So do we have a connection now? I took your blood, so do I know things about you?"

He cast her a smile. "Do you?"

"I don't think so."

"And you won't. I am considered your blood father, but our only connection is that my blood runs through your veins now. There is a theory that vampires exchange pieces of their soul when the transformation is made. I'm not so sure about that, but I wouldn't rule it out."

"Huh. And you'll show me how to enthrall a victim?"

"It's easy once you accept that your mind is a powerful tool."

"I see." She looked out the window when he was about to turn. "No, not that alley. It's too dark and creepy."

"We want dark and creepy, Belladonna." Ivan pulled the car into the alley.

"Yeah, but I don't think I can do dirty homeless guys or drunks."

"For tonight, you will take what we can find." He scanned the street as the car rolled smoothly over the tarmac. There weren't any flesh-and-blood humans out and about.

"What, besides being a vampire, do you do, Ivan?"

"I serve on the Council."

"Severo said that is some kind of council of vampires, witches and werewolves that oversees the paranormal nations."

"In a nutshell, yes. We have members from all species on the Council, but when there is an issue, it's usually only the representative nations that show."

"So are they discussing the divide between the werewolves and vampires now?"

"There have been suggestions of ways to bring the two nations to terms. Perhaps arranged marriages between principle players in each nation. Nothing's come of it yet. Of course, if Severo openly takes a vampire as a mate, that can only be a good thing."

"So we're to be an example?"

"Only if Severo chooses to allow it. He's very private."

"He is. Says his kind has to hide from humans. But you seem outgoing. What do you do beyond serving on the Council?"

"I'm a philanthropist."

"Are all immortals rich?"

"Depends on how you manage your money. If you're going to live forever, you'd better learn, because I can't imagine doing the homeless thing for long. What is your profession, Belladonna?"

She liked that he used her complete name. The man was too charming for a creature. *Nix that,* she thought. He was no creature. He was a kind man who happened to be a vampire.

"I work from home designing web sites. It's enough to get by. And I also dance flamenco."

"A dancer? I figured you for some kind of athlete. You have a gorgeous body."

"Thanks." And she accepted the compliment for what it was. Not a flirtation. She did feel a connection to Ivan, but nothing sexual, despite their intimacies.

"So tell me how you and Severo met. I bet he didn't find you dancing in a club. Don't think the guy does the scene all that much."

"A gang of vampires was chasing me, and Severo pulled me into hiding while they searched for me. He intended to do exactly as the vampires wanted once they found me. But he didn't."

"The werewolf is an interesting breed. But fiercely devoted to their mates."

"You say that, but how can they remain devoted to those not their breed?"

"Give him a chance, Bella. What do you say about stopping by a dance club before we find your next donor? There's an underground tapas bar close by. If you like flamenco, it'd be your kind of place."

"You want to dance instead of hunt?"

"Might take the edge off your nerves."

She clasped her shaky fingers together. "You noticed?"

He smiled. "Let's stop in and see what's up."

She was dressed for the club. A knee-length black velvet skirt with ruffles down the back that spilled to her ankles. And a leotard top, also in black. It was the only stuff Bella had taken to Ivan's, and it had felt right to go all black for her first hunt.

The club was underground, very small and dark like a cave. Ivan led her in, but Bella eagerly followed the music, which already had her snapping her fingers and rotating her wrists with the urge to dance.

"The atmosphere here reminds me of the Caveau de la Huchette," he said to her. "A little underground club in the Latin Quarter of Paris. Tourist trap, but they play some great jazz and swing. I'll get us some wine."

"I'll have water, please."

She didn't need the wine to loosen up. Just walking into the room relaxed her. Here were her kind of people.

Besides, Bella wasn't so sure wine wouldn't make her sick. She'd not eaten for days—except for the blood. And that suited her fine.

Ivan returned and pressed a cool glass into her hand. "They're all vamps," he said. "Save the faerie over in the corner."

She spied the grizzled old man, his front teeth missing, enthusiastically doing *palmas*. A faerie? She would never look at people the same again.

It was a comfortable crowd and they all took turns on the small dance floor. Right now a couple danced *sevillanas* to a quick beat. Castanets trilled and the singer encouraged *palmas*.

She tilted back the water and licked the cool liquid from her lips. "Do they know I'm a vampire?" It felt surprisingly empowering to say the word.

Ivan's soft chuckle carried over the Spanish rhythm. "Vampires don't know one another unless they touch."

"Then how do you know they're all vamps?"

"Because I've been here before, and the faces are familiar."

He touched her arm, clasping his fingers around the flesh. A thrilling shiver traveled her veins. Not a sexual shiver, but one of…knowing. "Feel that?"

"Yes. What is that?"

"We call it the shimmer."

"Appropriate. So unless I see fangs or touch another vampire, I have no way of knowing? Nor does the other vamp?"

"Exactly. Comes in handy once in a while."

"Good to know. So do you dance at all?"

"Not this stuff. I'm more a waltz kind of guy."

"Romantic. I'm going to have to meet your wife someday."

"I know she'd like meeting you."

The rhythm wasn't about to release Bella from its hold. She twisted her free hand before her and stomped her feet to the beat. The guitarist strummed a *bulería*. Bella loved this fast, demanding rhythm.

"Hold this," she said to Ivan. He took her glass, and she headed out to the dance floor.

The air in the cavelike club expanded and caressed at the same time. Bella did a *golpe* across the stone floor in her high heels. Not the best shoes to perform flamenco in, but they would serve in a pinch. Raising her arms, she rotated her wrists and played the sensual music through her body.

For a while she danced by herself, beating out the rhythm with a tilt of her hip or an exact heel-toe. One man joined her. He was older, probably sixty, but fit and tanned. He approached, stiff and cocky, a bullfighter striding up to challenge the bull. And she was his cape.

Bella loved the game of the dance. She circled him, fingers lifting her skirt only slightly, because it was already so short in front. Elbows high, she spun her back to him and clicked out a few beats before they both spun to face one another.

He smiled and winked. She tried to keep a solemn face, but she was enjoying this too much and let out laughter as the two of them spun and repeated the move the opposite way.

Dancing with a fellow vampire. How surreal had life become?

A glimpse of Ivan found him doing *palmas* with half a dozen other men who stood by the walls. Vampires, all of them? Yes, the room hummed with a presence she felt a part of.

As an introduction to her new life, this night rated high on the scale. How wise of Ivan to bring her here, to a place where she would feel comfortable and safe.

She didn't understand Spanish but knew from her dance studies that the singer spoke of love, loss, struggle and renewal. It was how all the flamenco songs were. Tragic, sorrowful, but always expressing a lively connection to life.

Bella fancied she could feel the blood rushing through the veins of each and every person in the room. It invigorated her. It made her feel alive.

She wanted more of it in her mouth. The pulse of hot blood danced a beat upon her tongue, at the back of her throat. In her body.

Suddenly she was tugged from the dance floor. A firm hand about her upper arm took her captive. She butted up against a hard body but did not feel the shimmer.

The male dancer stomped up to whoever held her, his arms held defiantly back so his chest puffed up in a challenging pose.

"She's mine," growled the one who held her.

"Severo?" He was supposed to be in a motel, waiting for her. "What are you doing?"

His breath hot near her ear, Severo whispered harshly, "You never dance for me, sweet."

He pulled her from the dance floor, past Ivan, who did not make a move to intervene, and up the stairs outside. Nondescript brick walls sandwiched them in darkness. Snowflakes fluttered softly.

"How did you know where to find me?" She tugged from his grip and walked away a few paces. The air was cold tonight. She could see her breath, yet she was flushed with warmth and the adrenaline soaring through her system. "That was rude!"

"I scented you."

"Tell me something I don't know. Am I forever destined to unfinished dances with men?"

He bowed his head and ran fingers through his hair. "Sorry. I… He was so close to you."

"Here's a reminder for you. We were dancing. You *know* that. You've seen those same moves before. Jeez, jealous much?"

"I am." He stepped in front of her, without touching. Dark eyes held hers, searching; then he looked down and stepped away. "I thought you'd call to come home this evening. When you did not, I wanted to find you. Quite a surprise to discover you dancing when you are supposed to be learning a life skill."

"Ivan thought it would relax me."

"And did it?"

"Severo, don't do this. Hey, Ivan. Sorry about that little scene."

The vampire stopped in the doorway and leaned a shoulder against the frame. He didn't say anything. Wine tainted his breath. But nothing could overwhelm the scent of Severo's rage.

Suffering humiliation was no way to end the evening.

"I'll be in the car," Bella said and stalked down the alleyway.

* * *

Both men listened, heads bowed, as the click of Bella's heels took her to the end of the alleyway. Severo breathed in heavily through his nose and shook his head.

He owed Ivan an apology. He owed Bella one, too. But he'd been taken off guard. He'd expected her to tag along behind this vampire, learning how to drink blood. Then to find her dancing so suggestively with a stranger?

Okay, so it was not suggestive in Bella's mind. But to him, any closeness she experienced with another male disturbed him. Would he never learn?

And yet she had never danced for him. Would she ever give him a private concert? He'd love that. It was a part of her that still belonged to the mortal realm, a part he wanted to preserve as much as she probably did.

"I need to apologize," he started.

Ivan stepped into the street. "It's fine. It's not going to be easy."

"You were supposed to teach her."

"After she mentioned she was a dancer, I thought this little aside would relax her. She was very nervous."

"Yeah, well, I'll take her home now."

"She hasn't taken human blood yet. I'll want to supervise. Why don't you come along. We'll find a donor and she can get over her hesitation."

"I can't do that. I can't..."

"Watch? You don't have to. But having you close by may mean more to her than you can imagine."

* * *

Ivan pointed to a lone man walking down the alley. He looked young, in his twenties—perhaps he was a college guy—and clean. Bella's only requirement.

She glanced to Severo. He approved with a barely perceptible nod.

The threesome loitered at the alley entrance, Bella between Severo and Ivan. She hadn't spoken to Severo since he'd dragged her out of the club. Now, though, she looked to him and gave him a not-quite smile.

"You're not going to watch?"

Severo shook his head. But he was glad to sense that she was as uncomfortable with this as he was. And then he admonished himself for such thinking. Of course she was uncomfortable. She was new at this.

And here he stood, participating in something so far from his comfort zone. It opened the doors of memory to another vampiress, dressed all in black, looking pale and hungry.

But Evie had once saved him.

He knew Bella would never harm him or his kind. He had to look beyond the past. Give her his presence and be strong for her.

"I'm ready," she said to Ivan and stepped down the alley.

Though his arms reached out to pull her back, Severo did not call out. He would simply be here, in case she should need him. A witness. A supporter.

"I can do this," he murmured.

The skirt swung from her hips and about her knees. Long legs in spike heels put Severo in instant lust mode. Those legs should be wrapped about his hips right now.

Yes, even as he fought the repulsion, he craved the woman he had fallen in love with. She was sashaying so sexily toward another man. A human she would put her hands on and talk to sweetly. She would take a part of the mortal stranger inside her. So deeply. The act of drinking blood was wickedly sexual.

Severo shifted his shoulder around the corner and pressed his back to the wall so he could not watch. He knew Ivan would step in if Bella needed assistance.

"She takes to this so easily," he said hoarsely.

"The hunger overwhelms the most rigid inhibitions," Ivan told him. "I know you don't want to be here, Severo, but you need to watch. It'll show you what she is."

He knew what she was. Severo had seen vampires drink blood from victims time and time again. And he'd seen them murder and maim for no reason other than for the macabre joy of it.

What of the blood on your *hands?*

Those vampires he'd killed tonight had deserved to die.

"She's not like those you hate," Ivan whispered. "She never will be. I'm going closer. She needs guidance."

His back against the wall and his eyes closed, Severo listened, trying to hear beyond his own pounding heartbeats.

Bella cooed to the man, who said things like, "You're hot" and "My place is close."

Jerk, Severo scoffed.

It was a strange departure from that first night he'd rescued her, while the vampires had searched the warehouse. Her heart had pattered like a bird's. Then she'd been so frightened. Now she was so eager.

Releasing his clenched fists, Severo reminded himself that this was part of the deal. She had to come in close contact with humans, unlike him, who put as much distance between them and himself as possible.

And now he had a vampire in his life. A *longtooth*.

The taint of blood carried to him. Beer and fast food littered the human's scent. Unappetizing. He wondered if Bella liked the taste. It would kill him if she did.

Turning, he crept around the building. Bella was silhouetted before the man, whose legs buckled. Ivan stood on the other side, his hand to Bella's shoulder.

It was like some kind of twisted sex scene. A ménage à trois Severo had no desire to join. And yet…

When she tilted her head back in pleasure and the moon glinted on her pale neck, he wanted to know that pleasure. *Her* pleasure. To touch the luscious rise of her breasts. And perhaps to be the one to kick the other man aside.

As it was, the man slid down the wall and collapsed. Bella began to topple as one of his legs twisted between hers, but Ivan caught her. She tugged free and swung about to walk away.

As she approached Severo, the drunken grin on her face bemused him. A trace of her forefinger wiped away a drop of blood from the corner of her mouth. She thrust the finger between her red lips and sucked, smiling as she came upon him.

A strong blood scent forced Severo backward. Yet arousal had widened her pupils. God, she was gorgeous.

Bella grinned a sloppy smile. "I'd kiss you," she said, "but you wouldn't like it."

She wandered off, swaying but sure-footed, toward his Mercedes.

"She's drunk," Severo hissed as Ivan joined his side.

"It'll be that way the first few times she takes human blood," the vampire said. "It's overwhelming in so many ways. She is not used to it and needs to be cautioned not to take too much, or she might accidentally kill."

"Christ."

"If you love her, you'll go with her the next few times."

"I can't do that."

"Then she will kill." Ivan strode off.

And Severo beat a fist against the brick wall.

Chapter 22

For the first time in ninety years he was prepared to welcome a longtooth into his home.

Not exactly prepared. How *did* one prepare for such a thing? Since his hatred against them was so ingrained, he wasn't sure it could ever be truly siphoned from his blood.

Severo drove the Mercedes toward home. On the passenger seat, Bella lolled in a blissful state as the blood swoon lingered. Her skirt was hiked high on her thighs—another inch and she'd reveal things only he should see. He liked those long, slender gams. Better, he liked imagining what lay beneath the flirty ruffles.

And that image gave him hope that it was all going to be all right. He still desired her. *Nothing has changed,* he repeated silently.

"Ivan said you should drink once more before going home tonight. That it would sate you for at least a week."

"Sounds good to me," she offered sweetly.

She was no longer silly drunk, but relaxed and in a strangely heightened state, what he'd normally call arousal.

"This may be cruel, but I have to ask," he said. "Do you get off on it?"

She sighed. So much pleasure in that sigh. "You know vampires swoon from the blood."

Yes. He also knew the swoon was orgasmic. And surely she and Ivan must have shared some swoons. His grip tightened on the steering wheel.

"But get off?" she said. "No. That would imply I get some kind of thrill from a stranger. It merely serves a need. Though I had wished you were standing beside me instead of Ivan."

For a moment, he had wished the same thing. Because standing at the end of the alleyway, listening to his lover's sweet coaxing and the human's moans, Severo had gotten hard. From the temptation Bella offered with her sighs and touches. From the kiss he'd struggled to label sweet when he knew it was now dangerous.

"Let's go down Poplar." She pointed out the street. "It's not far from where I used to live. It's quiet, but we may find a college kid walking around this late."

In the quiet neighborhood, they found a new development. Bella approached an acceptable candidate with the same sensual daring she'd exhibited downtown.

Severo parked and followed, but by the time he gained on them, Bella was holding the man close in front of a green Dumpster in an alleyway. Blood scent filled the air. Both her hands on the rim of the Dumpster, she sucked at his neck. The guy initially stroked his hands over her hips, but quickly his hands dropped to his sides and he let out a long, appreciative moan.

His jaw tensing, Severo forced himself not to interfere. The guy was giving blood, so he deserved the swoon. And he wouldn't get far with Bella if he did try to put the moves on her.

Was this what his life had become? He must accompany his lover each time she sought blood in order to ensure no one touched her overtly?

Hell, he'd have to get used to it. He couldn't go along every time. It would kill him. And it wouldn't be fair to her.

Bella needed this. And he grew hard as he imagined stroking the hair away from his lover's face to reveal her blissed-out expression.

Yet he could not touch her. He didn't want to disturb her. He didn't want to touch what he could not approve of.

Christ, but he breathed as heavily as she did. When the unconscious victim slipped from her and settled onto the ground, Bella remained, leaning against the Dumpster, hands fitted to the rim, her legs spread.

She smirked and licked her lips. There was no blood. She was surprisingly neat.

"Ivan taught me the persuasion," she said. "Makes them forget I was ever here."

Looking over her arm at him, she sent him an air kiss.

"Don't look at me all judgmental like that," she said.

"I'm not judging you, sweet." It wasn't worth the

wasted thought. Besides, he'd gone beyond that. Her bold and sexy position had made him consider taking her from behind. "I'm admiring you. A gorgeous vixen of the night."

"You're turned on?"

"Yes."

Before she could react, he stepped up close behind her, bumping her, and placed his hands over hers on the Dumpster. He fit his erection against her derriere, pressing, making her know what watching her had done to him. Kissing down the back of her neck, he bit at the thin fabric covering her torso and licked along her shoulder.

Sliding a hand up her thigh, he swept his fingers across her silken skin and found her panties. The lace, crisp and barely there, gave easily at his tug. She wasn't wet—which pleased him; the act of taking blood was not so sexual, after all—but with but a few flicks of his fingers, she was there.

Stroking her and rubbing his erection against her, he brought her to a swift orgasm. Her quiet murmurs entered his ears as music. Her shudders he drew into his body. He hadn't come, but he didn't need to. Experiencing her bliss did it for him.

"I'll take you home now," he said, and lifted her into his arms and carried her away.

A light dusting of snow whitened the brown grass behind the mansion. Bella had headed right for the shower, mumbling something about brushing her teeth.

He'd done it. Watched his lover take blood from another man.

And it had turned him on. How sick was that?

Or was it sick? He'd shared an intimate new part of Bella. Something she would keep private from the world, except for him. He could only love her for allowing him to witness her new ritual.

And he did love her. That would never change. But right now it felt tenuous. Yes, he was unsure. Would she want to bite him? And how could he refuse her when he knew the one thing vampires required to become close to their mates was sharing blood?

The notion of being bitten or sharing blood did not appeal to him. The werewolf did enough of that for his taste.

So she had become the animal he already was, and *he* was having trouble dealing with it?

Lifting his head, he sniffed the air through the open patio door in their bedroom. The snow cleaned the fall rot from his senses and his focus immediately found her. She was behind him, sweet with lemon shampoo and minty toothpaste.

Yet he wasn't confident he truly wanted to be here.

Yes, he was.

Probably.

"Hell, pull it together, man," he muttered.

She smelled like the Bella he remembered. But there was something else. Some undertone he didn't want to translate into thought. Yet his mind processed the scent and reacted to it before he could argue. His body stiffened, his fingers arching into claws. A defensive tickle ran up his neck.

Vampire.

"Severo?"

Shaking out his hands at his thighs, he cursed his instincts and put on a smile as he turned to her.

The white silk robe clung to her nipples. Like a bride marching down the aisle for her groom, Bella stepped up to him. Winter's blossom—with a taint of blood.

He hated that he could not make this perfect for her. For himself.

You can. Just put off all doubt. See her for the woman you first fell in love with. Remember you savored her fear?

He could scent that same fear now. And he hated himself for making her feel that way.

"You look great, sweet. Two days away and I'd almost forgotten how bright your eyes were. Come here."

Yes, he could do this. He wanted to do this. He needed to make the effort of stepping into the usual, with the hope that it would erase his rising doubts for the future.

Her body fit against his. The scent of lemon in her hair and the silk threads briefly overwhelmed her clean smell. And yet she was no longer clean or human.

Her chest melded with his. He buried his nose in the crown of her hair. She might be tainted, but she was his mate.

"I missed you," she said. "I didn't know if you'd welcome me into your arms. I know this is hard for you."

"Nonsense," he murmured and stroked her hair down her back.

The feel of her made his body react as it always did. He hardened and the lust surfaced. Good, then. He hadn't lost the desire. The quick interlude out in the alley had simply been a reaction to something so intense. This was different. They were alone now. No secrets. No lies.

"You're mine, Bella. My mate. Forever. Did you learn what you needed from Ivan?"

"He was a perfect gentleman and showed me the ropes. I've blooded my fangs, as Ivan called it." She smirked. "I like that. Sounds so decadent."

She was different. Not so uptight, easier with him. Accepting of what, he imagined, was an incredible change in her life.

A stroke of her finger along his beard, accompanied by sad eyes, made him look aside. "It made me feel good that you took me in the alleyway, after watching," she said.

"I needed you. It was an instinctual thing."

"It felt great. Like it always feels when I'm with you. You controlled me. I belong to you."

"As I am yours."

"Will you kiss me now?"

A kiss?

Why the hell had this been done to him and Bella? They had been so perfect. His future had been designed with her at his side. Even the werewolf loved her.

All that had changed now. The werewolf would never accept a vampire. Never.

"I won't bite," she whispered, a touch of hope lifting her voice.

A nudge of her nose along his jaw sweetened the lust, which predominated over the all the emotions he'd rather not deal with right now. Maybe she had the right idea.

Just let go. Concentrate on the now.

Severo kissed the corner of her mouth. She tasted like Bella. Soft, salty, clean.

Things would be fine. This kiss bonded two souls. It drew the two together, wanting and needing and giving.

They hit the bed stripped of their clothes. Bella couldn't have dreamed of a better welcome home than this. He had accepted her. The werewolf had welcomed a vampire into his home.

He'd once said to her that she would always have his heart. And she did still.

Severo's hand glided up her back as he pulled her on top of him. She bent to lick his nipple, a small, hard jewel. His satisfied groan heartened her. A familiar tune, yet one she could listen to over and over.

His fingers massaged her breasts. Her loins tingled, aching for his entrance. He flipped her on the bed so she lay on her stomach. He trailed kisses down her spine as he slipped a finger inside her.

"So ready," he growled. "So hot. I've missed this, Bella."

"Quickly, please," she cried.

Gripping the pillow, she spread her knees as he lifted her under her hips and brought the backs of her thighs against his. His favorite position.

He pushed inside her and she gasped as his length filled her. Fast and frenzied, he worked them both up to a spectacular climax. Bella gasped and reached for the headboard. He drew her up against his chest. She wanted to wrap her arms around him. This position gave her an incredible orgasm, but it always left her aching for face-to-face contact.

It was the wolf in him that liked to take her this way, and she loved it for that reason. When his body relaxed, he dropped onto the sheets by her side.

Bella kissed him along his torso, licking the sweaty moisture and reaching to grip his semihard shaft. A lick to his biceps, and she trailed her tongue upward and kissed his neck. Opening her mouth wide, she leaned in—

"Bloody hell!" Severo shoved her off him and scrambled away. The palm of his hand, held before him to keep her back, hurt worse than a slap. "No fangs, Bella."

"What?" She ran her tongue along her teeth and a sharp canine pricked it. "Oh hell, I didn't realize. I would have never—"

He stood. The back of him, naked and muscled, flexed as he gripped his fists.

"I wasn't thinking," Bella offered. "I didn't feel them come down. I don't know why—"

"Because your kind have sex and they want to take blood. And vice versa." He spun on her. "Didn't Drake teach you that?"

"Well, yes, but like I said, he was a gentleman. We didn't do anything…sexual."

Though the swoon *had* been sexual. She couldn't deny that. Ivan had explained about the blood and sex desires being intertwined, though at the time, she'd thought it incredible. Every time she had sex, she'd want blood?

That wouldn't be good for this relationship.

"I must need more time to get a handle on things. I'm so sorry, Severo. I didn't mean to freak you out."

"Well, you did." A heavy sigh lifted his chest. "I don't want your bite."

His confession hurt. Deeply. He was denying her. Denying her very nature.

He approached the bed to sit at the edge. "I mean, I love you, Bella. And I know you can bite me, and nothing untoward will come of it, save an increase in blood craving, but…there is a stigma attached to wearing a vampire's bite."

"You were never bitten, and if you were now, it would mean you'd succumbed to the captivity once again."

He winced.

"I won't do that to you, lover. I don't need to bite you. I think. I may need to give Ivan a call." She rubbed a palm down her leg and shivered. Sex was over. But was the relationship? "Can we make this work?"

The ferocity of his gaze chilled her. Once she had admired that look, so intense and ever focused only on her. Now it made her scared for what he might never share with her. He put up a good front, but the truth was Severo might never be able to accept her.

"It's not what you think," he said carefully, so gentle. "Bella, I can accept you as you are now. And those fangs, which fit so prettily over your bottom lip? They're kind of sexy."

He reached to touch her mouth, and only then did Bella realize her fangs were still down. She willed them back up.

"Mine are bigger," he said with a smirk.

"What about the werewolf?"

"The werewolf." He pulled her so she sat with her back against his chest. The touch of his hair on her shoulder tickled her. "That is what is keeping me from surrendering to you, sweet. I know the werewolf, and it doesn't like vampires."

"It loves me."

"Bella, the werewolf takes off vampire heads for entertainment. Why do you think it would be any different with you?"

"Because it does love me. Aren't you willing to find out? If the werewolf could accept me, could you?"

"Of course I would, but I'm not willing to set you out as bait for a vampire-hating beast. I won't do that. I can't."

"The full moon is in two weeks. You can't stop me from trying to seek out the werewolf. No matter how far away you go."

He hugged her tightly. Bella wanted him to break her, to fit her into his soul and keep her there forever.

"Don't ask me to sacrifice you," he whispered. "Please, sweet. Just accept what we have now."

Accept him as a lover, but never as a soul mate?

"It's my sacrifice, as well. Don't you think I make a sacrifice when I'm out in the yard with the werewolf? A facsimile of you takes me quickly, and to fill a need, and then later, when you are a man, you have no recall!"

"It hurts to hear you say that. I never asked you to make such a sacrifice."

"You wanted the werewolf to accept me so I could be your mate. Well, I'm asking a sacrifice of you now. Let the werewolf come to me. Give it the opportunity to decide if I truly am the mate it desires. I know it will harm me only if *you* allow it to."

"Bella, you know I have little control over it."

"But you can influence it."

"Yes, in small ways. But what if something goes wrong? What if..."

"It tears me apart? That's a chance I'm willing to take."

Severo stood abruptly. "Vampirism has made you bold, Bella. Perhaps stupidly so."

"It's freed me, lover. It's made me not care about the past. Not care what others think. Give me this one small gift, please?"

He grimaced but nodded. "I'll think about it."

It was all he could offer, and Bella accepted that. But she fully intended to go out wandering when the moon was round and high in the sky.

Two weeks later, when the moon was full, Severo did what he had to do.

He'd hated to do it. To lure her into the arsenal on the pretense that he wanted to lock away the weapons he used against vampires—as a sign of acceptance. But while Bella had collected the wooden bullets he'd purposely dropped on the floor, Severo had locked her inside.

She'd pounded on the steel door, pleading for release. It had cut into his heart to hear her tearful pleas. She would be safe from the werewolf for the night.

Now he tore away his shirt and stepped out of his pants. The air was cold and fat snowflakes fell like down from the heavens. He shivered and shifted into the furred wolf.

Taking off through the backyard, the wolf loped into the valley, intent on tracking that rabbit Severo had sighted earlier in the day.

Chapter 23

"Bastard!" Bella kicked the steel door for the third time to no avail.

She paced.

Here she'd thought Severo had resolved to make this work. And the only way she could possibly foresee that happening? *Let the werewolf decide.*

If it accepted her, Severo could banish his apprehensions and worries that she'd never be safe around it. And if the werewolf tore out her throat... Well, there wasn't much of a way to argue if that happened, was there?

Rationally, she understood his fear. So much had happened to them since coming together. He could have never anticipated that his girlfriend would be transformed into a vampire. And then to face losing her should the werewolf protest?

This might be the safest place for her during the full

moon, but having blooded her teeth, Bella had lost all trace of fear. And she was hungry.

She gave the door one more good kick but succeeded in only denting the steel.

Shouldn't she have superpowers by now? she thought. The other vampires were so strong, they'd rip this door from the hinges.

Though she had noticed many changes since the transformation, Ivan had said it would take until the next full moon before she was completely a vampire. Whatever that meant.

Right now her senses increased. She could smell the gunpowder in the plastic containers at the back of the arsenal. And though night had fallen and she hadn't switched the light on yet, she could see very well.

Stalking to the table's edge, she grabbed hold of the stainless steel. The corner of the table bent. "So I am stronger." She glanced to the door. "But not strong enough for that mother."

Maybe if she pried out the hinges?

Searching for a tool, she grabbed a crowbar and hammer and went to work.

A ghostly howl outside made her stop pounding. Another howl sounded closer to the house.

"He must not have gone far away. Is he coming for me?"

Bella leaped onto the counter and peered out the ten-inch-high glass-block window. It was impossible to see through the distorted blocks.

She jumped down and resumed pounding at the door. One hinge pin popped out and clanged onto the cement floor.

She positioned the crowbar beneath the next hinge pin but paused. "Do I really want to do this? Do I think I'm some kind of big bad vampire now who can take on anything in my path? I don't think I can win against a werewolf."

But she didn't have to win; she just had to seduce.

Glass crashed to the ground. Bella guessed it was the patio door that Severo had only just reinstalled a week earlier. The werewolf had entered the house.

She worked at the second of three hinges, but it wouldn't budge no matter how hard she hit it with the hammer. Instead of creating more noise, she set down the tools and bent before the door to listen.

Snorts and huffing breaths sounded. Far away. The werewolf was probably walking through the kitchen. Talons scratched across marble. The thunder of each footstep—it was not running, but was slowly taking the foyer's measure rocketed her heartbeat to her throat.

He was looking for her. He must smell her. Hell, the werewolf could smell her from miles away. Now his head must be filled with her scent.

Her vampire scent.

"There must be deodorant for hiding vampire pheromones," she muttered. "Just…let him be calm, to see *me* before he rages."

And she closed her eyes and pressed her fingertips to the steel door. *See me,* she repeated over and over. *Know me.*

The wolf stalked the hallway toward the arsenal. A bang outside the room shook the wall. It seemed angry, impatient to find the creature it scented. It was on the hunt.

On bent legs, Bella twisted to eye the arsenal. What kind of weapon would work against a werewolf? Not a lethal weapon, one that contained silver, but something to hold it back if it intended to take off her head. Something to pin it to the ground while she ran for the garage and hopped in the car to speed off to China.

She didn't want to die. And to be ripped apart by her lover was not on her top-ten list of adventures.

But she did want it to recognize her—if only for a moment—and know that she had not changed. Sure, she now needed blood to survive. But her heart had not altered. Her soul needed Severo…and the werewolf.

A bang against the door pushed in the steel in the shape of wide knuckles. A chilling scrape of talons down metal sent a shiver up the back of Bella's neck.

The werewolf howled. Bella did not recognize it as that "I see you and want to mate with you" kind of howl with which he usually greeted her. This one was low and menacing.

A prick to her lower lip made her jump. "Now is no time for the fangs." Try as she might, she could not will them back up.

The vampire she had become was prepared to fight for survival.

Two more fist marks bulged in the door. The middle hinge, partly released, cracked in half. A kick brought the door down inside the room.

The bullets and guns and knives sitting on the counter behind Bella clattered to the floor as she backed into it. Her hip bone hit the steel, and she winced but did not take her eyes from the approaching threat.

The werewolf seethed, its fangs descending along its extended jaw and glistening with saliva. It howled at the sight of her and stalked up in two long strides, forcing her to jump onto the counter and crouch defensively.

"It's me," she cried. "Severo, see me!"

It snarled and tossed back its head. The muscles strapping its shoulders pulsed as it did a caveman chest pound. Powerful thighs flexed. It stomped. One paw swept across the counter, to Bella's right, tearing the steel in four jagged lines.

Blood drooled down her chin. She'd bit her lip. *The blood scent must enrage the wolf beyond measure,* she thought. "Hell, I can't sit here and take it," she said aloud.

She dropped to the floor and thought to crawl away, but a hand connected with her side. One blow swept her across the room and out the door. She skidded along the waxed marble floor and slammed into a wall with a groan.

Blood seeping from her thigh, Bella scrambled along the floor. Behind her the werewolf stalked at a distance, as if it planned to play with her, exhaust her before the killing.

"You're not playing fair!" she shouted and scrambled to her feet.

Dashing toward the front door, she reasoned that outside the werewolf would have her at an advantage. The garage door was behind her, behind the werewolf, so reaching the car was out of the question.

Veering right, Bella headed toward the bedrooms.

Perhaps the smaller rooms and the furniture would impede the werewolf. For a few seconds.

"Severo, I love you!" she called back. Gripping the door frame, she swung herself into a bedroom.

She slammed the door and locked it, knowing the gesture was futile.

In proof, talons ripped through the wood as if it were fashioned from mere leather. Bella stumbled backward, her spine colliding with the bed. She scrambled across it to the other side. The werewolf pushed the door into the room. On all fours, it lifted its head and sniffed.

With one leap it soared across the bed and knocked her on the floor, its deadly taloned fingers on her shoulders and its knees pinning her feet.

Bella screamed.

She was beyond caring about hurting Severo's feelings. Obviously she'd been wrong. The werewolf did hate vampires. It didn't matter if its alter ego was screwing one and claimed to love her. All that mattered was instinct.

"Please," she said, her voice reedy and shivering with fear. "Please."

Just...please.

The werewolf sniffed her body. The graze of its teeth over her breast shocked her. Its canines didn't break the skin, but it wasn't a sexual touch by any means. Panting and emitting a low growl, it sniffed along her neck. Its tongue swept out to lick under her jaw.

Tasting her? Why not get it done with? And please, if she were to die right now, she much preferred losing her head to being...munched.

Oh, Bella, don't even think it.

Turning her head, she winced as the fingers curled and talons dug into her shoulders. Not deeply, but it wasn't aware, obviously, how easily it could damage her tender flesh.

Feeling her heart finish the race, she whined miserably and shook her head. The scent of her own fear was like bad cologne wafting in the room.

But the werewolf's earthy scent was sweet to her. Her lover.

Don't forget it is your lover. The man who claimed you as his mate.

"No!" She bashed her elbow across the werewolf's snout and scrambled away. The werewolf snarled and leaped for her. It gnashed its teeth but halted abruptly, short of biting her on the cheek. "You know me. Remember me? I'm the same Bella. The same one."

She dragged herself up over the edge of the bed, kneeling, and stepped off the other side. Slowly, she backed away. The werewolf would not kill her before she could give it her all. This vampire was willing to fight to win her lover.

"You once said you loved the smell of fear on me. Recognize it now, Severo. And know I am yours."

Something clicked in her brain. Bold courage. A willingness to die to achieve her greatest desire. *Trust.*

She trusted this man would make the right choice, no matter his form.

Bella drew her shoulders straight and lifted her chest. Drawing in a breath through her nose, she found a strange calm amid the chaos.

"Very well, wolf boy." She bowed her head and looked up through her lashes. "You like it rough?"

The werewolf slashed the bed, taking out some cotton stuffing.

"You think you're such a beast? All he-man and stalking me?" Tracing her tongue over her fangs, she smiled widely. "Come to me, werewolf. Take me if you can."

Unzipping her pants, she slid them down and tore open her shirt. The werewolf licked its maw.

Slowly, she slinked around to the end of the bed. Tilting her head, she put back her shoulders. The shirt slid off, leaving her naked. Her breasts sat high and her nipples hardened.

A throaty growl signaled her lover's desire. She loved that growl.

Turning, Bella bent over the bed, placing her palms flat on the sheets. "Take me. I am your mate. It's death or mating. Your choice."

A heavy hand slapped the back of her neck, shoving her face against the bed. A sharp talon cut into her skin. And then it entered her and gratified its instinct.

Bella cried out at the pleasure of the intense friction. If this was to be her last breath, she would breathe it gladly.

The wolf howled its familiar boon of triumph, and then it was gone, leaping over the bed and dashing out through the patio door.

Bella collapsed on the bed. She breathed heavily. Her heart still had not started. And her lips were slick with her own blood.

But she had won back her lover.

Severo shivered and came fully awake with a start. He was naked, lying on the icy flagstones by the pool.

As he moved something slashed his ankle. It was glass, scattered everywhere.

The werewolf had broken into the house last night. He'd tried to hold it back but not even he could stop his beast.

"Bella."

Rushing inside, he didn't want to think of what he might find. Blood put a metallic taste in his mouth, and the scratches on his arms and palms indicated a struggle.

"Please be alive. I'm so sorry, Bella!"

He jackknifed as he rounded the corner to the bedrooms and ran right into a white towel, stretched out to receive him.

"Thought you'd need this," she said. A sweetly wicked smile curved her red lips. "Cold out there last night?"

"You're…" He eyed her up and down as he wrapped the oversize towel about his waist. She was dressed in a sheer pink negligee that revealed the tawny areolae on her breasts and the thatch of dark hair at the apex of her thighs. "Okay?"

"Peachy." She strode past him into the kitchen and straightened a stack of mail he'd been avoiding for days. "And you?"

"Besides being frozen, I'm… The werewolf didn't get to you? You were safe in the arsenal?"

She pointed over his shoulder. Hard to miss the havoc in the foyer. The front door had slashes through it. The walls had been clawed and Sheetrock was busted everywhere. He couldn't see the arsenal door, but a memory of last night flashed before his eyes.

The steel door clattering to the floor…Bella's eyes flashing wide with fear… The werewolf approaching…

"Tell me," he said, fighting against the horrid vision.

She leaned in and kissed his jaw, then tapped his chin. "The werewolf loves me."

"It…didn't harm you?"

"I got a nasty slash down my thigh, but I don't think it was intentional. The werewolf was initially out for blood. But then it calmed down. I dared it to take me. Then I offered myself to it."

"Offered yourself?" he said, his voice falling.

"We had sex. Just like old times." She kissed him again, this time pulling his head in for a long, deep, hard connection, mouth to mouth. "Mmm, you taste good the morning after, you know that?"

"So the werewolf…"

"Could care less that I'm a vamp."

Severo shook his head, taking it all in. It was wondrous. It was astounding. The werewolf had accepted Bella. Which meant he need not fear for her. Not ever.

"You're so brave. I'm sorry I didn't trust the werewolf. Sorry I locked you away."

"I think that might have been a good thing. It made it difficult to get to me. Might have given it a chance to think. Anyway, I look forward to tonight. What about you?"

"Tonight?" He lifted her in his arms. "We've some catching up to do, sweet. No time like the present."

"What happens if the fangs come out to play?"

"One rule. No biting."

"Severo, I've sacrificed everything for you. Is a little bite too much to ask of you?"

This time he did not stiffen in her embrace, as expected. Instead, he hugged her tighter and buried his face in her hair. "It isn't."

"I want to taste you, lover."

"Feeling your teeth enter my flesh may just turn me on. But I honestly need some time. Please, Bella, can you love a man who is willing but wary?"

"I already love you. Nothing changes that. And I can wait until you're ready, until you ask me for the one thing that will bond us completely."

"It won't be long. Promise."

Epilogue

"Soon," was Severo's rote answer every time Bella asked when she could bite him. She would never stop asking. One of these days his answer would be "Now."

It had been a few months since she'd become a vampire. The world was amazing as viewed with her heightened senses and newfound confidence. She'd always been confident, but now she was strong. And standing beside her werewolf lover made her feel powerful.

She enjoyed walking by humans on dark streets, drawing in the scent of their blood. There were as many scents and flavors of blood as people, and she loved to indulge. Severo waited in the car sometimes for her return to him. She would be woozy from the swoon and eager to make love.

Life was good. And it only promised to get better.

Now Severo parked and gestured to her to grab the whip from the backseat. They both got out.

A couple held hands near the hood of a black Mustang. Bella didn't know a thing about cars, only that this one was cool. The man was tall, lithe, and wore his hair tousled about his handsome face. He had movie-star good looks.

The woman holding his hand was petite and red-haired, and when she saw Bella and Severo approach, she bounced on her heels and stretched out her arms.

Severo let go of Bella's hand and rushed up to meet the woman. He pulled her into a hug that lifted her feet from the ground.

A prick on her lip alerted Bella. She willed her teeth—and her jealousy—back to the shadows. This woman was no threat to her. She had a man. And Bella was now willing to fight any woman who thought to lay hands on *her* man. Unless it was a friendly hug.

"Bella." Severo set the woman on the ground and held out his hand to her. Bella took it and kissed him on the cheek. "This is Aby Fitzroy. Aby, my mate, Bella. I love her. We're going to marry in the spring."

"It's such a pleasure to meet you." Aby's green eyes twinkled as she pumped Bella's hand. "This is my husband, Max."

The man leaned in to shake Bella's hand and offered a wink to Severo. "Nice to meet you, Bella. Marriage? Congratulations. I wish the two of you as much happiness as Aby and I have."

The man, after releasing Bella's hand, stared at it, and then brushed his own off, as if he'd touched dirt. He winced.

"Wondering what she is?" Severo asked the Highwayman. "He has a sixth sense for paranormals, though the man is mortal himself," Severo said to Bella. "My future wife is a vampire."

Bella did not miss Aby's gasp.

"And I love her." Severo wrapped Bella in an embrace. "Do you have the whip, sweet?"

Bella held out the coiled silver whip and handed it to Max.

"I happened upon this a few days ago," Severo said. "I believe it's yours."

"Thanks. I thought I'd lost it. Ian Grim stole it."

"That bastard needs to be taken down," Severo growled.

"I agree," Max said.

Aby rolled her eyes and reached for Bella's hand. "Let's go inside the restaurant and get a table. We'll leave the menfolk to growl and plot to take over the world. I love your shoes. Manolos?"

"Louboutins." Bella clasped Aby's hand and they wandered away from the guys.

"So you can walk in the daylight?" Aby asked.

"Yes, I have phoenix and witch blood in me."

"Interesting that Severo chose you."

"I wasn't a vampire when we met." Bella opened the restaurant door. "He's accepted me."

Aby halted at the threshold. "I know he has. I've never seen that man smile so big." She turned to Bella, her green eyes sparkling. "You're the one, Bella. I know it. I'm so happy for both of you."

* * * * *

REQUEST YOUR FREE BOOKS!

2 FREE NOVELS FROM THE PARANORMAL ROMANCE COLLECTION PLUS 2 FREE GIFTS!

YES! Please send me 2 FREE novels from the Paranormal Romance Collection and my 2 FREE gifts (gifts are worth about $10). After receiving them, if I don't wish to receive any more books, I can return the shipping statement marked "cancel." If I don't cancel, I will receive 4 brand-new novels every month and be billed just $21.42 in the U.S. or $23.46 in Canada. That's a saving of at least 21% off the cover price of all 4 books. It's quite a bargain! Shipping and handling is just 50¢ per book in the U.S. and 75¢ per book in Canada.* I understand that accepting the 2 free books and gifts places me under no obligation to buy anything. I can always return a shipment and cancel at any time. Even if I never buy another book, the two free books and gifts are mine to keep forever.

237/337 HDN FEL2

Name _____ (PLEASE PRINT) _____

Address _____ Apt. # _____

City _____ State/Prov. _____ Zip/Postal Code _____

Signature (if under 18, a parent or guardian must sign)

Mail to the **Reader Service:**
IN U.S.A.: P.O. Box 1867, Buffalo, NY 14240-1867
IN CANADA: P.O. Box 609, Fort Erie, Ontario L2A 5X3

Not valid for current subscribers to the Paranormal Romance Collection or Harlequin® Nocturne™ books.

Want to try two free books from another line?
Call 1-800-873-8635 or visit www.ReaderService.com.

* Terms and prices subject to change without notice. Prices do not include applicable taxes. Sales tax applicable in N.Y. Canadian residents will be charged applicable taxes. Offer not valid in Quebec. This offer is limited to one order per household. All orders subject to credit approval. Credit or debit balances in a customer's account(s) may be offset by any other outstanding balance owed by or to the customer. Please allow 4 to 6 weeks for delivery. Offer available while quantities last.

Your Privacy—The Reader Service is committed to protecting your privacy. Our Privacy Policy is available online at www.ReaderService.com or upon request from the Reader Service.

We make a portion of our mailing list available to reputable third parties that offer products we believe may interest you. If you prefer that we not exchange your name with third parties, or if you wish to clarify or modify your communication preferences, please visit us at www.ReaderService.com/consumerschoice or write to us at Reader Service Preference Service, P.O. Box 9062, Buffalo, NY 14269. Include your complete name and address.

PARA11

*Something's going on in Conard County's high school...
and Cassie Greaves has just landed in the middle of it.*

Take a sneak peek at RANCHER'S DEADLY RISK
by New York Times *bestselling author Rachel Lee, coming
in November 2012 from Harlequin® Romantic Suspense.*

"There comes a point, Cassie, when you've got to realize that stuff you got away with as a child is no longer acceptable or even legal."

Linc paused, realizing he must seem to be going around in circles. Well, he probably was, between her damned scent and his own uncertainty about what was happening.

"I'll be honest with you," he said slowly. "I'm wondering what's been bubbling beneath the surface at the school that I'm not aware of. That makes me uneasy. On the one hand, I'm trying to paint it in the best light because I know these kids. Or thought I did. I don't want to think the worst of any of them. On the other hand, I guess I shouldn't make too light of it. There have been three transgressions we know about with you. Four, if we add James. I'm not going to dismiss it, but I'm not going to be Chicken Little yet, either. The mind of a teenage male is impenetrable."

She surprised him by losing her haunted look and actually laughing. "You're right, it is. And girls aren't much better at that age."

Girls weren't much better at any age, he thought a little while later as he drove her home. He'd certainly never figured them out.

"Thanks for a wonderful time," she said as he walked her to her door. "I really enjoyed it."

"So did I," he answered more truthfully than he would have liked. He had to bite his tongue to keep from suggesting they do it again.

She was still smiling as she said good-night and closed the door.

He walked back to his truck, keys jingling in his hand, and thought about it all, from the bullying to the rat to the evening just past. The thoughts were still rumbling around when he got home.

Something wasn't right. Something. He'd grown up here, gone to school here, been away only during his college years, and now had been teaching for a decade.

His nose was telling him something was wrong. Very wrong. The question was what. And who.

Find out more in RANCHER'S DEADLY RISK
by Rachel Lee, available November 2012
from Harlequin® Romantic Suspense.

HARLEQUIN® Blaze™
red-hot reads

Double your reading pleasure with Harlequin® Blaze™!

2 GREAT NOVELS SAME GREAT PRICE

As a special treat to you, all Harlequin Blaze books in November will include a new story, plus a classic story by the same author including...

Kate Hoffmann

When Ronan Quinn arrives in Sibleyville, Maine, all he's looking for is a decent job. What he finds instead is a centuries-old curse connected to his family and hostility from all the townsfolk. Only sexy oysterwoman Charlotte Sibley is willing to hire Ronan...and she's about to turn his life upside down.

The Mighty Quinns: Ronan

Look for this new installment of The Mighty Quinns, plus *The Mighty Quinns: Marcus,* the first ever Mighty Quinns book in the same volume!

Available this November wherever books are sold!